D0983196

THE PILLOW FRIEND

BY LISA TUTTLE

Because of the mature themes presented within,
reader discretion is advised.

White Wolf is committed to reducing waste in publishing.
For this reason, we do not permit our covers to be "stripped" for returns, but instead require that the whole book be returned, allowing us to resell it.

ISBN 1-56504-938-1

Cover and interior photos by Pamela Dawn
Cover and interior design by Michelle Prahler

Borealis is an imprint of White Wolf Publishing.

White Wolf Publishing
780 Park North Boulevard, Suite 100
Clarkston, GA 30021

World Wide Web Page: www.white-wolf.com

CONTENTS

To Colin

PROLOGUE:

THE DREAM

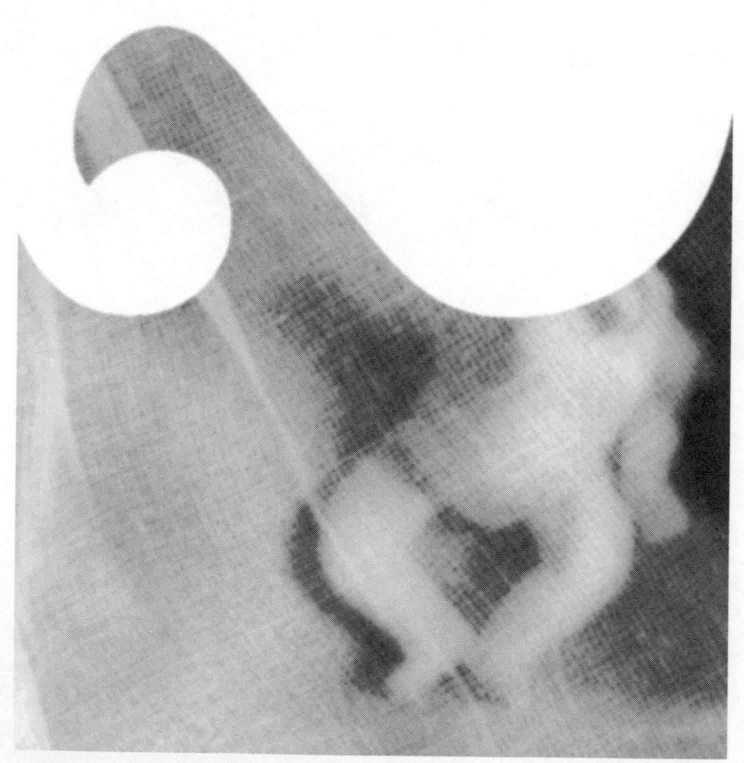

Whenever the pain let up for a few seconds she fell back into the dream. It was always there, reliable, sustaining, her best friend, the deepest truth she knew. The dream had shaped her life, defining who she was by what she wanted.

The pain began again and she struggled for breath, for control. She had no drugs or technological aids to cushion her against the agony; her only resource was her own mind. She focused all her concentration, all her willpower, on recalling the dream, and how happy it had made her.

PART ONE:

THE DOLL AND THE BOOK

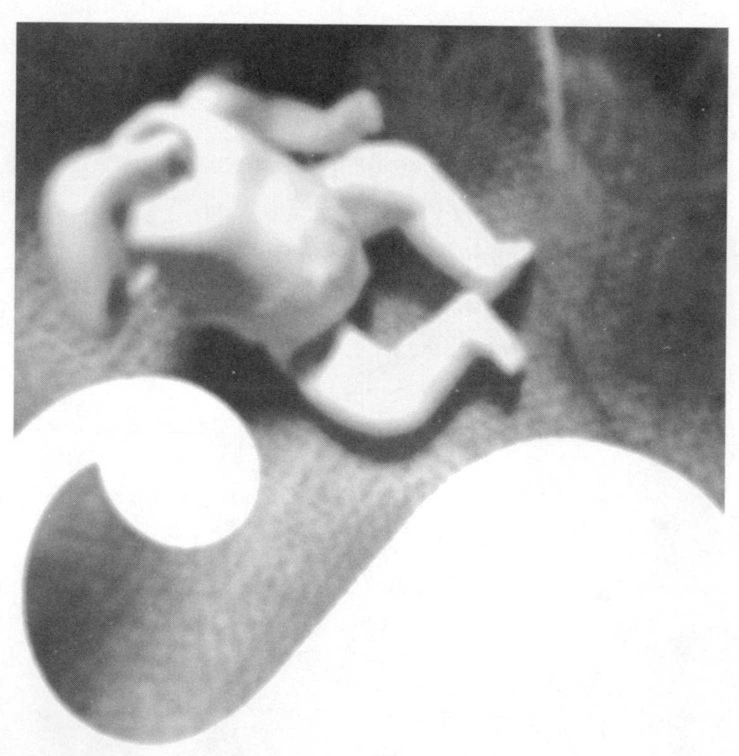

Loneliness drove her to create an imaginary object of worship. This sublimation of her need of love she named Corambé, and for many years this glorified being was her constant companion. When she began to write, it was Corambé who composed her stories—she merely heard and recorded the words he spoke.

—Marie Jenney Howe on George Sand

Agnes Grey had a new doll, a present from her mother. It was what she had always wanted. Nothing had ever made her so happy.

The doll was almost as big as a real baby, and it was warm, and soft, and cuddly. It had the sweetest face she had ever seen. As she gazed lovingly into its big blue eyes she suddenly realized, with a warm thrill of excitement, that the doll was looking back at her. The eyes were real. The doll was real. And then it spoke.

Agnes woke, the sound of the doll's words still ringing in the quiet air of her bedroom. Wanting to reenter the dream, she kept her eyes closed and concentrated on the warm, golden glow of happiness she had felt while holding the doll. In a moment, she would feel its welcome weight in her arms and understand what it was saying to her. But reality was too strong. Instead of the doll's voice she heard the central heating blowing warm dry air through the ceiling vent, and felt the sunlight which sifted through the Venetian blinds onto her arms and eyelids. She was sweating beneath the covers, so she kicked her legs until the quilt slipped off the bed like a sulky cat. Then she sat up and looked around, hoping that the dream was true, a memory instead of a fantasy, and everything would be changed.

But as she looked around her familiar, cluttered room, none of the toys on the shelves looked back at her.

Everything was the same as when she had gone to bed the night before: the same furniture, the brightly painted pictures taped to pale blue walls, the string of valentines. She had missed Valentine's Day, home with bronchitis all week, but her best friend Leslie had brought her valentines by yesterday, and her sisters had stapled them all to a length of red ribbon and hung them from the ceiling above her bed. She counted them again, and found there were still twenty-two: one from everyone in her class, plus the big one at the bottom which her grandparents had sent.

She coughed experimentally, wondering if she was well enough to go back to school yet. She couldn't remember what day it was, but the silence of the house and the heat of the sun made her think it must be late. She got up.

The twins' room was empty, their beds unmade, clothes strewn on the floor. She walked in, lured by the forbidden, and went straight to the record player. She picked the top record off the stack of paper-cased singles beside it and read the title, her lips moving: "The Lion Sleeps Tonight." The Tokens. She could almost hear Rozzy screaming at her to put it down. She wished Leslie was with her, to give her the courage to play it, but Leslie was at school. She replaced the record carefully on the stack, exactly as before, and then, to erase her presence, walked backward out of the room.

She felt suddenly tearful with boredom. The day stretched ahead of her, long, dull, predictable and slow.

Her mother was usually very good for the first day or two of one of her daughters' illness, willing to play games and create small treats, but she'd been totally fed up yesterday—she'd retired to her bed with a sick headache as soon as her husband came home—so Agnes knew she couldn't expect any special attention from her today. She'd be on her own with coloring books and a daytime television diet of game shows and soap operas. A lump rose in her throat at the idea of her own loneliness. She shut her eyes, crossed her fingers, and wished with all her might that something *different* would happen today. Then she went downstairs.

The radio was playing in the kitchen; she could hear "Moon River" as she came down the stairs. Last year's most popular record, more like an atmosphere than a song. Leslie's mother would put it on the hi-fi sometimes when Leslie's dad got home, a signal that it was time for cocktails and grown-up conversations and children to disappear. The music made her think of a smell, something sweetish and unpleasant, like when the grown-ups had been drinking. It made her feel stifled and bored. The idea of growing up into someone who would listen to "Moon River" on purpose felt vaguely threatening. She could not imagine herself changing so much, no matter how large she grew.

"Moon River" was abruptly cut off, replaced by the flickering blurred sounds of other stations, and then by Sam Cooke singing "Twistin' the Night Away."

Agnes was filled with a mysterious, half-fearful joy. Who had changed the station? Her mother would never choose rock 'n' roll over Henry Mancini; she could be scathing about the twins' taste in music. And drifting through the air with the music was the smell of burning cigarette—something her mother had given up four years ago. She remembered her wish, and crossed her fingers again before she walked into the kitchen.

Sitting at the table, reading a paperback book, with the radio, a pack of cigarettes and a cup of coffee within easy reach, was Aunt Marjorie.

Marjorie's visits were never announced and never for long. Although nothing was ever said—indeed, her parents rarely ever mentioned Marjorie's name in her presence—Agnes knew her father didn't like his wife's twin sister, and she wasn't sure her mother did, either. The air of something forbidden clung to Marjorie like a personal scent. She was wildly unpredictable and deeply mysterious in her comings and goings. She was artistic, unmarried, without a job or fixed address. Her origins were in rural East Texas, but she preferred to stay in London, New York, San Francisco or Paris. Exotic words and places peppered her conversation. Often Agnes didn't know what she was talking about, but she rarely asked, too appreciative of being spoken to as an adult to risk spoiling the moment. She relished the sound of Marjorie's voice, clipped and rapid, with an accent that sounded almost English. It was very different from her sister's drawling Texas twang.

Now Agnes shrieked with delight and rushed to hug and kiss her aunt, greedily inhaling her smell, a combination of Joy perfume, cigarettes and coffee.

"Mind my cigarette! That's enough now, you little rascal—you'll crush me."

She let go at once, although reluctantly. Her aunt never hugged her, didn't like being touched, disapproved even more than her more maternal sister of "clinging" children.

"How long are you here for?"

"What sort of question is that? I've just arrived, and you want rid of me?"

"Nooo! I want you to stay forever!"

"Nothing lasts forever. I'm here now; can't you enjoy that without asking for more?"

Agnes wanted to please her aunt by agreeing, but she couldn't. Already, her pleasure was souring, turning desperate. It was always that way. She didn't understand why it happened, why she couldn't be happy with what she was given, but Marjorie's presence always made her greedy for more. Showing her need made Marjorie withdraw, which made Agnes feel even more needy, and she couldn't seem to learn to hide what she felt. "Why don't you ever spend the night? Why do you always go? You could sleep on the rollaway bed in my room with me. Please."

Marjorie regarded her steadily out of blue eyes so much like her mother's, so unmistakably not. "Don't think I don't appreciate the invitation, but... Your father wouldn't like it. Or your mother."

This was so unarguably true that Agnes couldn't say a word. She must have looked miserable, though, because Marjorie gave her an unexpectedly gentle smile. "I'm here now, sweetie. Enjoy. Don't look a gift horse in the mouth."

"What does that mean?"

"There's a saying in Spanish which roughly translates to, 'I give you a hug, and you ask for a squeeze!' It means to be grateful for what you've got. If you keep pushing and questioning and asking for more you're just setting yourself up for unhappiness. Which is silly, because it's so unnecessary. It's very easy to be happy. You can have whatever you wish for—as long as you accept the consequences." She turned her head slightly to exhale a plume of smoke, and then stubbed out her cigarette.

"What would you wish for?"

"Oh, I've already had my wish."

"Do you only get one?"

Her aunt considered. "Not necessarily. You can have as many as you like, as long as they aren't contradictory."

"What's that?"

"Mutually exclusive. Two things that are so different they can't both exist at the same time. Like your mother. She wanted a family, wanted it more than anything. And she got it. She met your father, married him, had the twins, had you—but instead of being content with that she's gone on wishing she'd taken the other path she used to dream about. I suppose if she really was an actress now she'd be regretting the children she never had, and drinking too much or popping pills to soothe the loneliness. She got what she wished for but instead of being happy she keeps on looking that gift horse in the mouth, and dreaming about a career she is simply never going to have. She only makes a fool of herself, trailing around to every open call at The Alley."

Agnes felt the slow, poisonous seep of guilt that came with any mention of her mother's thwarted career. She could have been, should have been, an actress, and would have been if she hadn't met and fallen head-over-heels in love with Mike Grey. Her children had heard that story often enough from their mother. And it wasn't the twins who had truly settled their mother's fate—she had been so young when they were born, only nineteen, she would still have been young enough to embark on a stage career after they'd started school. Except that by the time the twins were at school all day, baby Agnes was on the way, putting an end to her mother's career plans. But the dream had not died, and every now and then Mary Grey would vanish to attend an audition, sometimes at the Alley Theatre, sometimes for a movie being shot in the area. There weren't that many opportunities in Houston for an actress, particularly an inexperienced hopeful now past thirty, but Mary Grey built her hopes up around every single one. Her husband seemed indifferent, resigned to Mary's little hobby, the twins were sarcastic and embarrassed by their mother's fantasies of an acting career, but for Agnes each attempt and each failure felt like her own fault. She wanted her mother to be happy, she wanted to be absolved from the blame of ruining her mother's life, yet she was terrified of the great changes that would follow if Mary ever got a job. It would be bearable if she landed a role in a production at The Alley, but what if she became a movie star? What if she had to move to Hollywood? Would her father leave his job, would they leave their house and friends and life that they knew here, or would Mary abandon them? She suffered her fears in silence, there was no one she could confess them to; only Leslie, her best friend, knew, and Leslie thought it would be "neat" to have a mother who was a star like Doris Day or I Love Lucy or Beaver Cleaver's mother—"Of course your mom won't leave you. You'd all move to Hollywood and meet all those famous people. Maybe the Beaver would be your next-door neighbor!"

"Did my mom go to an audition today? Is that where she is now?" asked Agnes.

Marjorie gave a loose shoulder-roll of a shrug and picked a pill of wool off her black sweater. Although physically identical to Mary, she inhabited her body in a different way. All her gestures were easier, more relaxed; she didn't sit or stand as straight. Mary was a fastidious, fashionable dresser concerned with every detail and matching accessory, but Marjorie's wardrobe appeared to be limited to black sweaters, mannish white shirts, plain black skirts or chinos. She always wore flat-heeled shoes which made her seem shorter than her elegantly turned-out sister.

"There's a Hollywood scout visiting Houston this week. Mary read about it in Maxine Messenger's column and there was no stopping her. Your mother doesn't seem to realize that it's not about acting talent—we're talking about a Hollywood talent scout, not Lee Strasberg, and to those guys talent equates with sex appeal. Pardon my French."

"What?"

"He's not looking for actresses, he's looking for starlets. Pretty, sexy young things. Your mother might have qualified back in 1949, but she's thirty-two now, and that's way too old for the meat market. Sure she's kept her figure and she looks really good for what she is, but what she is ain't a starlet. But try to tell her that. Easier just to let her go, say, sure, I'll look after Nessie for you."

She felt a tingle when her aunt smiled and called her Nessie, she felt like someone different. Agnes didn't like her name, and "Aggie," which was the name Leslie and the other kids at school used for her, was no better. It sounded like someone gagging. Her father sometimes called her Nes or Nessie, but her mother didn't like nicknames and said that Agnes was a lovely name. It meant "pure."

"I wish," she began impulsively, but her aunt cut her off.

"Be careful what you wish for. You might get it."

Her tone was so sharp, as if Agnes was in real danger. She felt a thrill, and everything was bright and clear around her. Maybe this was it, at last, the moment like those in the stories she loved, when the fairy appears and wishes are granted. Maybe Marjorie was a fairy, or a good witch, able to work magic. It would explain so much that was mysterious about her.

"Will I really get what I wish for?"

"That's what I said."

"I mean right now, if I wish."

"If you really want it."

"I do." She thought of her dream, the way it had made her feel, how happy she had been. "I'd wish for my dream to come true."

Marjorie smiled. "Of course you would. What is it?"

"I had a doll that was really alive. I was so happy, I felt so good, just looking at it. It was looking back at me, and it was just about to talk—it said something, I can't remember what, but it could really talk!" She stopped, frustrated by her inability to describe what was so important about the dream. It wasn't just the doll, or what it could do—in fact, she found it hard to remember what the doll had looked like, exactly. The special thing was the way the doll had made her feel. It was the feeling she wanted to describe to her aunt, the feeling she wanted to recapture. The important thing about the dream—she realized it now more clearly than before—was that moment when she and the doll had looked at each other, the closeness that had linked them just by looking, even before the doll spoke.

Despite her feeling of frustration, she saw that Marjorie was nodding, as if she understood exactly. She had a serious, intent expression on her face. "I had a doll just like that when I was little."

Magic charged the air like electricity. "You did? Really? Exactly like in my dream?" Agnes stared in awe at her aunt, but Marjorie seemed to be looking inward, and did not meet her gaze.

"Mmmm. I called him my pillow friend, because I kept him beside me on my pillow, and that was when he talked to me, at night in bed. He told me the most wonderful stories." She smiled to herself and turned aside to light another cigarette.

Agnes felt as if her heart would break with longing. "I wish—I wish I had a pillow friend!"

Marjorie took a long drag on her cigarette and said nothing. They were both silent, listening to the sound of Agnes' wish rising to wherever wishes were granted.

"Aunt Marjorie?"

"Yes?"

"Did you get what you wished for?"

"Of course."

"What was it?"

"The only thing that matters. A life of my own."

"But—everybody has a life."

"Ah, but not everybody has their own life. How many people do you know who can actually live as they want to, do what they want to do when they want to do it?"

"Grown-ups do."

"It looks like that to you. Do you really think your daddy likes his job so much that he goes into the office every day because he wants to? Don't you think he might rather spend more of his time traveling and reading; haven't you heard him say how much he'd like to live near the water and have a boat?"

Agnes felt a little wobbly. She knew her mother was unhappy, but her dad, too? Despite her fear that her mother might run off to Hollywood, given half a chance, she had never imagined the possibility that her father might leave them....

"Hey, don't look like that! Your dad's happy enough—he made his choice, he got what he wished for, and he doesn't complain. Everybody has some regrets, including me.... Christ, me and my big mouth! I keep forgetting you're just a kid. Which reminds me. You haven't had your breakfast. Your mother would shoot me, letting you starve. What do you want? Eggs? French toast? My special pancakes?"

"What about my wish?"

"Hmmm?"

"When do I get it? When does it come true?"

"Oh." Marjorie pursed her lips. "Well, when do wishes most often come true? You have a birthday coming up soon, don't you?"

"Not until May. I'll be seven in May."

Her aunt smiled her mysterious smile. "Well, May sounds like a very good month for wishes to come true."

The Greys lived in a two-story wood-and-brick house on a corner lot on Rosemary Street, in a subdivision of Houston called Oak Shadows. When it was built, in the early 1950s, Oak Shadows was on the edge of the city, but Houston was booming, and by the time Agnes started school her neighborhood was considered a very desirable, central location. It was a quiet, residential enclave, the homes in their green, tree-shaded yards set well back from the street, with sidewalks for roller-skating, and little traffic to threaten the bicycle-riding children. The adults were all agreed that it was a good place to live, the ideal setting for a happy childhood.

For Agnes' seventh birthday on May twenty-third the weather was clear, hot and humid, as it had been all week. She went to school in the morning wearing her new red and white birthday dress with the flounced petticoat underneath. It was too heavy for the weather, but it would have been unthinkable to wear anything other than her birthday dress on her birthday. It was looking a little limp and bedraggled by the late afternoon, but she was still buzzing with excitement.

Her mother had tied red balloons and paper streamers to the branches of the big pecan tree behind the house and pushed the picnic table, covered with a festive cloth, beneath it. A pile of presents waited for her at one end of the table, and her mother was in the kitchen putting the finishing touches to her birthday dinner as Agnes ran between the front and back yard, watching for the rest of the guests to arrive, despite pleas from her father to sit still.

It wasn't a large party, just the family, her father's parents who had come up for the day from Beaumont, and Leslie and her parents. When Leslie's family arrived, Mary Grey emerged from the kitchen with a pitcher of drinks and began directing the others to carry trays of food outside. "We might as well start with the cake, before our little birthday girl explodes."

"Mom," said Agnes urgently. "Mom, not yet. Marjorie's not here!"

Her mother's beautiful, made-up face tightened. "We can't wait on her, I told you, she probably won't come."

"Did you send her an invitation?" Agnes had nagged her mother on this subject for weeks.

"Of course I did. But I haven't heard back. It might not have reached her. She could be anywhere. You know what she's like. She turns up when she feels like it. Family birthday parties aren't really her scene. If we have to wait on her, we could all starve."

Agnes hadn't seen Marjorie since February, and not a day had passed without thoughts of her, the wish, the dream, the doll. She was certain she would get the doll for her birthday, and had imagined that Marjorie would bring it. But Marjorie had never said so, and there were other ways for wishes to come true. She did want to open her presents, so she shrugged and nodded at her mother, and let Leslie link arms with her and pull her away.

After the singing of "Happy Birthday," as the flash-bulb in her grandfather's camera popped, she blew out all seven candles with a single breath. Now she *had* to get her wish. She looked at the pile of presents and wondered which one held the doll.

Leslie pinched her. "Go on."

"Which one should I open first?"

"Mine, of course. I'm your best friend." She pushed forward a tiny, pink-wrapped box which turned out to contain a round locket on a golden chain, just like the one Leslie wore, which was in turn just like the one Hayley Mills wore in "Pollyanna," their favorite movie.

"Oh, boy! It's just what I wanted!"

"I know. I was afraid you were going to steal mine, that's why I got you one. Ha ha just kidding."

Her sisters both gave her books: *Charlotte's Web* from Rosamund, and A *Child's Garden of Verses* from Clarissa. The other gifts included a piano for the dollhouse, a Snoopy beach bag and towel, a jigsaw puzzle, a box of pencils, and bubble bath. Finally there was only one package left, the one she had been saving. It was obviously "the big one," but it looked too big for her heart's desire.

"Well, what are you waiting for? There's still one left," said her mother. Her cheeks were flushed, her lipstick faded, and she was fanning herself with a Japanese paper fan.

"Maybe she's had enough presents for today," said her father. "You going to save that one for tomorrow? Or maybe you want to give it to somebody else?" He leaned across the table as if he would take it from her, and she tore the paper off in one jerky motion, and lifted the lid of a plain white box to see what was inside.

Dead blue eyes in a hard pink plastic face glared at her, the finger of one hand pointed accusingly. Her chest went tight with shock.

All around her the others were making noises of awe and delight. A flash-bulb popped.

"She talks," said her father, his face gone soft and round in a big grin. "Pick her up; let's hear what she has to say."

When she still didn't move, Leslie reached past her and picked the thing up out of its box, speaking self-importantly: "I know how it works; I saw it on TV. There's a ring at the back of her neck that you can pull. Look, want me to show you?"

There was a whirring sound and then an eerie, wavering voice declared, "I like you."

"What'd she say?" demanded one of the twins.

"'I wike you,'" replied the other, and they both hooted.

"Please brush my hair." The whirring sound of the ring-pull. "I like you." Whirring sound. "Will you be my friend?"

Agnes screamed.

Everyone went quiet. Leslie pushed the doll into her arms. The horrible closeness with the dead, plastic body, her recollection of that ghastly, robotic voice grinding on, was more than she could bear, and she hurled it savagely to the ground.

There was a reproving gasp from her grandmother. Leslie giggled. "Leslie," said Leslie's mother sharply.

"I'm sorry," Leslie muttered.

"Honey, what's wrong?"

It was her father who asked, but she looked at her mother when she replied, at her mother who stopped fanning and turned a disapproving face away from her awkward daughter.

"It's not real! That's not what I meant! I want a doll that really talks!"

"This doll talks," said her father. "At least, it does if you haven't broken it."

"It does not! It just says things, like a record. That's not talking. If I say something, it can't answer me back!"

"I'd call that an improvement," said her father. Then he sighed. "Look, Nessie, you're a big girl, you know dolls can't *really* talk. Maybe by the time you're grown up the scientists will give us walking, talking robots, but for now that's as good as it gets. It honestly is. I asked in the store, and although there are a couple of other, cheaper, talking dolls, this is the very best one."

"It's not, it's not, it's not!" Still her mother would not look at her, move, or reply, and she burst into howling tears. "I want the real one! I don't want that thing!"

And so her seventh birthday ended with Agnes in disgrace, banished to her bedroom without her dinner, without even a chance to taste her cake. She fell across her bed and wept until she fell asleep.

When she woke up it was dark outside, the lamp was on, and her mother was standing beside the bed with a tray. "Here, you'd better have something to eat and then get undressed and go to bed."

She sat up, feeling dazed and uncomfortable. She rubbed her arms where the elastic on the puffed sleeves had cut into the flesh, then pulled up her skirt to scratch her legs.

"Stop that."

"Huh? It itches."

"It's not meant to be slept in. You've probably ruined it, like you ruined your own party."

Tears sprang to her eyes but she kept her gaze down and went on stubbornly scratching at her thighs.

Her mother set the tray down on the little table with a jarring clatter and seized her wrist. "I said, stop it. Get your clothes off, go on."

"I can't help it if I itch."

"No, but you can help scratching. Now get that dress off before you completely destroy it, and get your pajamas on."

"Can't I have a bath first?"

"No you may not. Do you know what time it is? You just get into your p.j.s and eat your dinner and then go straight to bed. And if you don't hurry up you can forget about eating."

Sullenly, she did as she was told, and then sat down at the table and looked at the tray her mother had prepared. There was a ham sandwich surrounded by small mounds of coleslaw, potato salad and beans, a glass of milk and a slice of birthday cake, but what caught her attention was a package about the size of her new pencil box, wrapped in shiny green paper with a purple ribbon. "What's that?"

"That's your present from Marjorie."

"Oh! Is she here?"

"No. You missed her." Her mother sounded grimly pleased. "You were having a temper tantrum, and she didn't have time to stick around until you decided to behave. But she left you that present. If it'd been me, I'd've taken it back."

"Can I open it now?"

"You can do what you like. It's yours."

She could hardly breathe, she was so excited. Her earlier disappointment and fury were forgotten as she opened the last present.

Inside the paper, inside the box, something was swathed like a tiny mummy in strips of soft white tissue paper. Gently, patiently, she peeled away each layer until the doll was revealed.

Her first, instinctive, response, quickly suppressed, was disappointment. It wasn't anything like the doll in her dream. But because it came from Marjorie, because this must be the pillow friend, the answer to her wish, she could not be disappointed, only surprised by how far reality diverged from her fantasy.

It was neither a baby nor a girl like her other dolls, but a small, old-fashioned gentleman in a painted black suit. He was about five inches tall, bigger than the dolls in the dollhouse but much smaller than Barbie. He was made of something hard and breakable—porcelain, she thought, or china, like some of the ornaments on her grandparents' what-not shelves which she knew to handle with care. But this was different from an ornament, because the arms and legs moved. His face and hair, like his clothes, were painted on.

"I can't believe she gave you that."

Something in her mother's voice made her shoulders hunch and her hand close protectively around the doll.

"That's not a toy, it's an antique. It's valuable, too valuable for you to play with. Give it to me and—"

"No."

"What did I hear you say?"

"It's mine. She gave it to me."

"Of course it's yours. I know that. I want to put it somewhere safe for you, and look after it until you're old enough to appreciate it."

"I am old enough now. That's why she gave him to me."

"She gave it to you because she has no sense, she has no idea what children are like. She doesn't realize that you'll treat it like any other plaything. That's not an ordinary doll."

"I know." Excitement surged up in her. "Marjorie told me about him."

"Then you know he's not for you to play with. You'll thank me for this later, when you're older. Now, give him to me."

She shrank back from her mother's reaching hand. "No, no, I'll take really really good care of him. I know what to do. Marjorie told me. He's the pillow friend."

All at once the remote expression came over her mother's face, that deliberate blankness and distance she always dreaded.

"Well, if you know best, you know best, I guess. I'm only your mother. Don't come crying to me when you break it, or lose it, as I'm sure you will. Just don't come crying to me."

She watched, confused and dismayed, as her mother left the room, hating to see her go, hating the feeling of dread her words instilled, yearning to call her back, yet knowing that there was no point unless she was prepared to give up the pillow friend. And she couldn't do that. She had made a wish and it had been granted. Now she had to accept the consequences.

Agnes had been alone in her room often enough, sent there by her mother when she'd been bad, or because it was time for bed, but this time, for the first time, she was not really alone. A thrill of pleasure ran through her. She'd gotten her wish, she had a pillow friend, she would never have to be alone again.

For once in her life she felt no desire to delay bedtime. She ate her cake and drank the milk but nothing else. As she munched her way through the sweet cake she held the little doll in one hand and stared at the tiny, painted face, at the bright blue eyes and rose-bud mouth beneath a mustache as fine as an eyelash. When she had finished the cake she knew his name. Very carefully, aware of how monstrous her huge, wet lips must seem to someone so small and delicate, she kissed his cold, smooth face and said it out loud: "Myles."

She put him on her pillow with a handkerchief laid over him, and then she put out the light and climbed happily into bed. What a difference it made to have someone, her pillow friend, close beside her in the dark! Having to go to bed alone had always seemed so unfair. Her mother had her father, and the twins had each other, but she was always the odd one out. Now, finally, she had someone, too, and the pleasure of his presence was so calming and satisfying that she fell asleep before she ever heard him speak.

The next day she dumped all the pencils out of her new pencil case and lined it with a green silk scarf her mother had given her. Myles would be safe from accidents there, and with the pencil box fitted snugly into the bottom of her school bag, she could take him everywhere. When she showed him to Leslie, in the playground before the bell rang, she could see her friend was not impressed.

"Oh, neat," she said, unenthusiastically. Then, "Too bad he isn't big enough to be Barbie's boyfriend."

The idea made her bristle. "I couldn't play Barbies with *Myles*."

"Why not? What's so special about him?"

She was used to telling Leslie everything, but just then Mindy came along, making secret sharing impossible.

"That's a funny looking doll," said Mindy.

"It's not an ordinary doll," she said coolly. "It's a *valuable antique*."

"Oooh, neat-oh."

The bell rang then and, as she was settling Myles back into his box, Mindy linked arms with Leslie and walked with her into the building. She fussed over Myles longer than was necessary, forbidding herself to look after them, trying not to feel betrayed.

Agnes and Leslie had been best friends forever, paired off at the dawn of time by their mothers who had plonked them down in a playpen together when they were too young to do more than stare at each other. They lived only four houses apart, their parents belonged to the same country club, and there were no other girls their own age in the immediate area. From the time they were allowed to walk down the street alone they'd been in and out of each other's houses, almost as much together as if they'd been sisters. After they started school, friendship had become a major issue. All the little girls were obsessed with the hierarchies of likes and dislikes, and Leslie and Agnes slipped into the routine as if born to it. Degrees of closeness had to be defined, and the superiority of their own bond continually asserted and confirmed as they rated other girls as "second-best," "third-best" or "just" friends. Yet even though these conversations always came to the same triumphant conclusion, exalting their own relationship above all others, they left Agnes feeling dissatisfied. If they were really so important to each other, and understood each other so well, why did they have to keep talking about it? Rosamund and Clarissa never said anything about how close they were—why should they, when they communicated so well without words? And Agnes knew, even though her mother seldom mentioned Marjorie's name, that her mother and her aunt were as close as two people could possibly be. But she said nothing of this to Leslie. Her friend would only take it as a criticism of herself, and Agnes didn't mean it that way.

She couldn't help resenting Mindy, and feeling that Leslie really should have pulled away and waited for her, but the thought of the inevitable long discussion she'd have to have with her friend later, yet again dissecting and discussing both their friendship and Leslie's feelings for Mindy, made her tired. There ought to be a way of just knowing someone, of looking into their eyes and understanding, without words, the way it had been in her dream of the doll.

She stroked Myles with her forefinger, gazing at him wistfully for a long moment before she put him back into the pencil box and went into her classroom.

As she waited that night for Myles to speak to her she began to feel that maybe he was waiting for her to do something first. She wondered if there was a magic word which Marjorie had forgotten to tell her.

"I know you can talk," she said. "Marjorie told me so. She told me you used to tell her stories at night. It's okay, you can tell me stories now."

But he didn't. She knew that he could, if he would, because he wasn't like any other doll. She could feel his life, a dormant vitality, even though he never moved. Why was he refusing to speak? She wondered if she had done something wrong. When her mother refused to speak to her, it was because Agnes had offended her. But what wrong could she have done to Myles in the short time she had known him?

"Is it your name?" she asked. "Did I choose the wrong name for you? Marjorie didn't tell me. Myles seemed right, but—how'm I supposed to know what to call you if you won't tell me? Please talk to me—please, tell me your name. Tell me what's wrong!"

The thin strip of yellow light marking the boundary of her dark bedroom suddenly expanded as the door was opened. "Agnes? Did I hear you say something?"

She shut her eyes tight and kept very still. After a little while the door closed, but she kept quiet a little longer in case her mother was still listening.

Finally she picked the doll off her pillow and held him suspended just above her. The white blur of his face in the darkness was like a tiny, distant moon to her near-sighted eyes.

"Who are you?" she whispered. When he did not reply, she drew him down close enough to feel the hot breath of her words as she spoke. "You're Myles, and you're mine. Marjorie gave you to me so you're my pillow friend now and you have to talk to me, okay?" His silence continued. The small figure never moved as her hand closed more tightly around the fragile body, squeezing it harder and harder until abruptly, furious and ashamed, she opened her fingers and closed her eyes and felt him fall, bouncing off the side of her face, then slithering down the pillow to come to rest half on her neck, half off, still unspeaking. She closed her eyes on tears.

Eventually she fell asleep, but it was not the deep, easy sleep she was used to. Instead, it was as if she continued to listen for Myles even as she slept, as if her awareness of his presence in the bed was too strong, too vital to relax. She woke several times believing that she had felt him move, that he was about to creep away from her in the dark.

In the morning, for one heart-stopping moment she thought he had gone because he was no longer beside her head on the pillow. She jumped up and pulled the covers all the way back and found him about half-way down the bed. She stared at him for a little while before she picked him up, wondering if he had traveled that far on his own, or if she had pushed him away in her sleep.

Despite her mother's cautions and her own feelings about his difference from other dolls, she tried once to play with him, introducing him into the dollhouse one afternoon after school.

The dollhouse had been built by her father. He had also made one for the twins before she was born, but this was his masterpiece. It had a hinged front, and he had designed it to look like their own house. The resemblance was closest from the outside, when the front was closed—a shingled, gray, two-story wooden house with white shutters and a white front door—because although the floor plan was the same inside, with kitchen, utility room, hall, living room, and den downstairs, three bedrooms and two bathrooms upstairs, the furnishings were different. It was both familiar and strange.

Myles dwarfed the family who lived in the dollhouse, and looked awkward in conjunction with most of the furniture, although he was not actually too big for the space. She put him in the kitchen, her favorite room, thinking he would be better there because the wooden table and chairs, a recent acquisition to replace the pink plastic set she'd had at first, were actually too large for the dollhouse family. She'd been right about the new furniture being his size, and the feast which was spread out on the table-top—the loaf of bread, the bowl of fruit, the plate of pink meat—were all just about in proportion. But when she sat him on a chair he looked all wrong with his legs thrust out before him (they had not been made to bend). It was obvious that he did not belong, so horribly obvious that she was ashamed of herself for having put him there. In her haste to remove him she knocked some of the little dishes off the table and left them there, where the sight of them, the next time she played with the house, would recall her shame and the feeling of frustrated sadness she had carried away with Myles.

School ended and summer vacation began. She continued to sleep badly, and Myles continued to keep his silence, but still she hoped and waited for the night he would reveal himself to her for what he really was.

The days were bright and mercilessly hot. Agnes' mother, or Leslie's, took them swimming at the country club three or four mornings a week. Apart from those mornings in the pool, or the weekly visit to the library, she liked the evenings best. Her father was teaching her to ride a bicycle, and sometimes the twins would include her in running and hiding games, imaginative variants on hide-and-seek which they'd invented and taught to all the children in the neighborhood. The cooler evenings, in the couple of hours of light between dinner and bedtime, provided time for her best games with Leslie, when they became explorers, or pirates, or spies, riding their bicycles or climbing trees.

One long afternoon they worked at the table in her bedroom creating a wonderful map, with a coded rating system, of all the climbable trees in the four blocks that comprised their immediate neighborhood. The pecan tree in her backyard was pretty good, but they both agreed that the best tree of all was the huge old oak on the corner at the other end of the street, in Mr. and Mrs. Darwin's front yard. The Darwins were an elderly, childless couple, but they were the friendly natives who never objected to having their yard taken over and used as a playground. Rosamund and Clarissa had given up climbing trees as being too childish shortly before becoming, officially, teenagers. If that was the kind of deal you had to make to become a teenager, Agnes thought it was definitely not worth it. She was pretty sure that she and Leslie were the only children who played in that tree now. There was a hollow in a branch near the top which they called their "cubbyhole," and they left treasures and messages in it which no one else had ever found.

There were also things to do indoors, during the heat of the day. Often she played with Leslie, but, for the first time this summer, Agnes found herself wanting to spend more time on her own. Myles wasn't the only thing she couldn't share with her friend—there were also books. Agnes had fallen in love with reading, but Leslie couldn't understand why anyone would want to sit quietly with a book outside of school. It puzzled and hurt her that Agnes would rather read than play with her. One day that hurt came spilling out.

They had been at Leslie's house all morning, playing with dolls, and then outside in the inflated wading pool, with the hose and the Slip 'n' Slide, splashing and shrieking and scooting along on their stomachs through the wetness. Leslie's mother, Jane-Ann, had given them lunch, and after lunch they'd been sent off to Leslie's room with instructions to stay there and play quietly for at least an hour, so Jane-Ann could have a rest.

"Maybe I should go home?"

"No, you can't go home. Let's play games. We can play 'Candyland'."

So they had played 'Candyland' and Go Fish and Old Maid and Beetle, and all the time Agnes had been fretting, impatient to get away, her mind wandering off to the stack of library books waiting for her at home. She had read the first one last night, but the others called to her, tempting, tantalizing, each one different, exciting, new. The one she wanted to read next was called *My Favorite Age*. She had peeked at the first page that morning and was in a tingle of excitement trying to imagine what would happen next. She had expected to go home for lunch, after which it would have been easy to curl up in the big leather chair in her father's den, surrounded by his books, and lose herself in the undiscovered pleasures of a new library book.

"Aggie, will you just play *right*?" Leslie threw down her cards and Agnes stared at her in astonishment. She was crying.

"What's the matter?"

"I don't know! You don't want to play with me, I don't know why. Aren't we best friends anymore?"

"Of course we are!"

"Then why don't you tell me things like you used to? Why don't you tell me the truth about him? Why don't you ever let me hear him talk?" She gestured at Myles, on the floor, and Agnes reached down without thinking to cover him with her hand.

"What do you mean?"

"Do you think I'm stupid? You told me what your aunt said about her pillow friend, and then for your birthday she gives you that doll. It was her doll, wasn't it? Well, it's obvious. You carry it around with you all the time, it must be special, but you don't play with it. So what is it with that doll that you won't tell me?"

Although Leslie left pauses for her to speak, Agnes was unable to say anything. She had not told Leslie anything about Myles, because there was nothing to tell. It had been nearly two months now since her birthday, and Myles had still not spoken, or moved, or given her the slightest sign that he was the special, magic doll she still longed to believe in. She continued to hope, and always kept him near her, to be ready for the magical moment, but her faith was getting a little wobbly.

She had not meant to keep a secret from her best friend; she had only been waiting until there was something to tell, something to share. She couldn't share her doubts; she was afraid that as soon as she voiced them, they would become the truth, and Myles would become ordinary. Aunt Marjorie would be revealed as just another grown-up who told stories to credulous children—stories Leslie would have been too smart to swallow.

But now she had to say something. "He *is* special. It's just, it's hard to explain why, he just is. I know he is. I wasn't keeping that a secret from you. It's—it's just—well, there's not that much to tell."

"Does he talk to you?"

"Sometimes." The lie was out before she had time to think. "Sometimes, late at night, when we're in bed, just before I go to sleep, he'll tell me a story or something."

"Neat!" Leslie's blue eyes were round and shining; the faintly freckled skin of her face fairly glowed as she leaned forward, drinking in the story. "Like what, can you tell me one?"

"Maybe... not right now. It's hard to remember all the details, you know, after a few days."

"Next time he tells you a story will you tell me?"

Agnes nodded.

"Promise."

"Yes, I promise. Leslie, I wasn't trying to be mean, or anything, not saying anything before, I just didn't think you were interested."

"Well, of course I'm interested! Geeze, Louise! Honestly! Some people's children!" They laughed at the phrase which was their own adaptation of a frequent exclamation of Leslie's mother, and they were close again, closer than before, despite the guilt Agnes felt about her lie, a guilt that was worse for knowing she could never, ever confess it.

They played happily together for the rest of the afternoon, and when it was time to go home—her mother had called to say that dinner would be on the table in five minutes—Leslie walked her half-way. At the half-way point (which had been instituted at their mothers' insistence, to keep them from walking endlessly back and forth with each other) Leslie asked, "Could I keep him tonight?"

It was like something cold and hard sticking half-way down her throat, like swallowing a cube of ice. She looked at her friend's eager, pleading, loving face and knew she could not deny her. They had always shared everything. Even Leslie's most valuable possession, the square-cut emerald ring she'd inherited from her grandmother, too large to wear, had been in Agnes' pocket, and her jewelry box, for a day and a night despite the fact that Leslie was strictly forbidden to take it out of the house. Although Myles, too, was valuable, Agnes was under no such prohibition, as her friend knew perfectly well. Selfishness was her only reason for wanting to say no, and selfishness was not allowed between best friends.

"He probably won't talk to you. He doesn't always talk, and..."

"Oh, I know. That's okay. He's your pillow friend, I wouldn't expect him to talk to me, but can't I borrow him anyway? Just for tonight? Please?"

Silently, painfully, she handed the doll to her friend, who received him with reverent gentleness. "Oh, thank you. I'll be so, so careful. I'm sure he'll tell you that I was when you see him again tomorrow. Bye-eee!"

Agnes had thought she would lie awake for a long time that night, and she did. What she had not thought, had not even considered, was how comfortable she was, alone in her bed for the first time in over two months. For once she didn't have to strain to listen, didn't have to examine her own behavior for whatever she might be doing wrong, didn't have to struggle to go on hoping and feel her hopes dashed again. She fell asleep, surprisingly at peace.

"He talked to me!"

Agnes looked at the little doll which Leslie had thrust into her hand and the familiar painted face stared coldly back. They were in Leslie's room, and as soon as Agnes had come in, Leslie had bounced over to her and dropped her bomb. She looked from Myles' ungiving face to her friend's lively, excited eyes, searching desperately for a tease, not daring to display disbelief.

"Really?"

"It was so neat!"

"What did he say?"

"He told me a story. It was just like you said! I can't remember it exactly, but it was really exciting. It was about us, you and me, finding a treasure—jewels and everything, buried under a bush. We put them in the cubby so the grown-ups wouldn't take them away from us."

It numbed her, this betrayal. Unless, she thought, Leslie was pretending, or had dreamed it—but that was something she did not dare to hint at, or Leslie would suspect that she had lied. "Neat. Um, look, I can't stay, I have to go now, my mom's taking me to the library."

"I'll walk you half-way. Just wait for me to get dressed."

"No, I really have to go. I told my mom I'd run straight back."

"You going to come over later?"

"Probably."

"You're not mad at me?"

"For what?"

"I don't know. Maybe something about... Myles? I know he's yours, and it was really nice of you to let me borrow him."

"I'm not mad." She knew she had no right to feel so murderously hurt. She was jealous, of course, but who was she mad at? It wasn't Leslie's fault if Myles had spoken to her... "I'm just in a hurry. I'll see you later."

"Alligator."

"After while, crocodile."

Half-way home, clutching Myles in one sweaty hand, she stopped to have another look at him. He looked the same as ever, like a cold, dead, antique doll. But she knew that wasn't so; she could still feel the reality, the life buried beneath the surface. The question was no longer why wouldn't he talk; it was why wouldn't he talk to her. Or maybe the question was, why couldn't she hear him? Leslie had heard one of Myles' stories—and it didn't even really matter to her.

It's me, thought Agnes. There's something wrong with me. Myles had spoken not to Mary but to her sister Marjorie; he had spoken not to Agnes but to her best friend.

She began to walk again, blindly and fast, her sandaled feet slapping the hot pavement as the unwelcome truth pounded through her brain.

He'd talk to me if I were different. If I was someone else, I could hear him.

She didn't notice that she had passed her own house until she had turned the corner. When she did realize, she just kept going. She had lied to Leslie. Her mother wouldn't mind if Agnes stayed out all morning.

Agnes kept walking without a plan in mind. She soon left the familiar, four-block area that was her regular territory, driven by the desire—so powerful it seemed a need—to be somewhere new and different. It was strictly forbidden to venture beyond the boundaries of Oak Shadows without an adult, and she didn't feel brave enough to defy that rule. She was supposed to ask permission if she wanted to cross The Boulevard, but her sisters were allowed, and she knew it was a much smaller sin. She was careful to look both ways before crossing, although at this time of morning, after all the adults with jobs had gone to work, there was no sign of a car moving on any of the quiet streets.

The first two streets she came to on the other side of The Boulevard looked familiar. There was even one house which was practically identical to her own, only the wood trim was painted gray instead of green. The sight of it brought Agnes up short. She stood and stared, fascinated, until a woman, a stranger, appeared at one of the large front windows to stare back at her. Then, unsettled by the idea of complete strangers living in a house so much like her own, Agnes hurried away.

Gradually, as each successive block took her farther from Rosemary Street, the atmosphere began to change, and Agnes was aware of more differences than similarities to the houses that she knew. This was the more expensive side of Oak Shadows. The houses and the lots were larger, and some of them had swimming pools.

Something—some sound in the hot, quiet air—caught her attention, and made Agnes stop. She looked around, but nothing moved. She raised her hot, sweaty hand and unclenched her fingers. She looked at Myles, and he looked at her.

It was as if she had been struggling along in a high, buffeting wind which had suddenly stopped. Coolness flowed over and through her. The eyes of the little doll were shining and his face was sharply alive, intelligent, knowing. There could be no mistake about it. He had just spoken—the words had been muffled by her hand. She waited, holding her breath, for him to speak again.

She began to feel dizzy. She broke their eye contact and breathed again as she looked up at the nearest house. It was large, Southern plantation-style, with a second-story verandah supported by white pillars. Flowering magnolias and other glossy-leaved trees and bushes dotted the immaculate green lawn. There was a red-brick path which began a few inches from her feet and led up to the front porch.

She suspected—and then she *knew*—that the house was significant. It wasn't by accident Myles had broken his silence on this spot; there had been good reason for it. She looked at him again, sharply, to see if he would confirm her thoughts. He made no sign, but that didn't matter. She knew she was right, and she knew what he wanted her to do.

Slipping the little doll into the pocket of her shorts, she walked up to the front door. It was unlocked, as she expected, so she walked in.

The front hall was elegant and spacious, high-ceilinged and with a thick, beige carpet underfoot. Framed prints hung on the pale walls, progressing up the wide staircase. Agnes stepped forward, toward the staircase, and began to climb. She felt excited, tinglingly aware of her own disobedience even as the reason for it remained a mystery. Words, a jumble of broken sentence fragments, swirled in her mind, but none of them explained what she was doing. The house did not feel empty, but she made her way safely upstairs without encountering anyone.

The first room she looked into was a bedroom, decorated in shades of pink and cream, with a canopied, four-poster bed, a pink Princess telephone on the marble-topped table beside it. Impressionistic pastel drawings of ballerinas adorned the walls; the curtains, like the bedspread, were thickly flowered. There was a large, gilt-framed mirror on one wall, below it a dressing table, its glass surface covered with rows of tiny perfume bottles, each one different, more perfumes than she'd ever seen in one place outside a drugstore counter. She was briefly tempted to open and sample a few, but resisted the urge—that wasn't why she was here—and continued down the hall to check out the other rooms.

There was a room in yellow and white, with twin beds, white-painted wicker furniture and flower prints on the walls, and what appeared to be the master bedroom, full of dark, heavy furniture she assumed were antiques, with a connecting bathroom. There was also a sewing room and another bathroom. There was nothing that looked to her like a child's bedroom, nowhere she felt at home. For a few seconds, standing in the upstairs hall of a strange house, Agnes was scared, but then she felt the weight of Myles in her pocket, against her hip, and remembered she wasn't alone. She took him in her hand, and then she could move again.

Back along the hall to the white and yellow bedroom. If it didn't feel like hers, at least it didn't feel like it belonged to anybody else. She took off her sandals, pulled back the coverlet on one of the beds, and settled Myles onto the pillow. Then she lay down with her head beside him.

"Are you awake?"

Agnes surfaced groggily. She expected her mother, but when she opened her eyes she saw a strange lady, plump and blond, her painted face pushed far too close to her own.

She gave a yelp and wriggled to try to escape. Something knocked against her head: Myles. She grabbed him and held on tight to the one familiar thing in this terribly strange place.

"Do you know where you are, dear?" said the strange lady. Beyond her, Agnes saw another person, a black woman in a white uniform. "Can you tell me your name and where you live?"

Don't talk to strangers. That ritual admonition had been drilled into her so regularly that now it rose up and blotted out everything else. She shook her head. She had no idea where she was, or how she had come to be here, surrounded by strangers, but she knew that strangers were dangerous. She would never accept candy from them, get in their cars, or answer their questions.

The woman sighed. "Come on, sweetheart, you must know your

own name! You're a big girl.... How about your phone number, so I can call your mother and tell her where you are?"

When they tried to lure you into their cars, strangers might pretend they knew your mother. Agnes wouldn't let herself be fooled. She set her mouth firmly.

"I'm sure she doesn't live in any of the houses on our street—I've never seen her before, have you, Jewel?"

"No, Ma'am."

"Where do you live? Were your parents visiting someone nearby? Did you wander off and get lost?"

But Agnes wasn't talking, and after awhile the stranger gave up trying to win her trust. She sighed and stood up. They were still both on the bed, Agnes having refused to go anywhere with the strange woman. "I guess I'd better call the police. Jewel, please stay with her, all right?"

It had to be a trick. Agnes had learned in school that the police were there to help protect children against strangers. If a stranger bothered you, you could always go to the police for help.

Jewel sat down on a white wicker chair, looked at Agnes and shook her head. "You in trouble now," she said. "The police. Mmm, mmm, mmm. You don't tell them where you live, they put you in jail."

Although she was desperately thirsty, as well as hungry, Agnes refused all offers of food and drink. She asked to go to the bathroom and, when she was alone in the small room, drank water from the tap.

The police arrived, two men in uniform, and Agnes told them her name and address as soon as they asked, aware of the strange lady's exasperation.

"And how did you come to be in Mrs. Carter's house? Did somebody bring you here?"

"No, I walked."

"Did you knock at the door?"

She shook her head. "No. I just walked in. It wasn't locked."

"Had you been here before? Do your parents know Mrs. Carter?"

"No."

"Well, why did you go inside like that? Do you usually go into strange houses?"

"It didn't feel strange." She hesitated. She couldn't tell them about Myles; even if she did it wouldn't explain what she'd done. "I thought I knew it; I think I recognized it." That, at least, approached the truth of what she had felt.

One of the policemen said to the other, "There's a house on Pine Shadows looks sort of like this one." He looked at Agnes. "Maybe this house looked like one where your friends live?"

She nodded uncertainly.

"But why did you go to sleep?" asked Mrs. Carter.

"I was sleepy," she said simply, and was surprised when they all laughed.

Her parents concluded that she'd suffered from sunstroke. She lost her allowance for a week as punishment for crossing The Boulevard without permission, by herself, but the much greater sin, of going into a stranger's house, went unpunished. Probably because they couldn't understand why she would walk into a strange house and fall asleep, her parents interpreted her behavior as illness. She had stayed out in the hot sun too long, lost her way, and then, feeling dizzy, had entered a house that seemed familiar to ask for help. Inside, feeling worse, she had stretched out on a bed and fallen asleep.

Agnes knew that it hadn't happened like that, but she never contradicted her parents' story. She wasn't entirely sure herself why she had done it. She'd had some notion that in another place Myles would speak to her as he had spoken to Marjorie and to Leslie. Maybe she was trying to find a special place where magic could happen, or maybe she had thought that in a different house she would be a different person. She was home again now in the same house, still the same person, but what she had done had made a difference. Finally she had made contact with Myles, and she was certain he would speak to her.

But that night was the same as every other night, despite her certainty. Myles looked again like a lifeless doll, and he did not speak to her as she lay awake in bed while the house around them settled into silence as everyone else fell asleep. Finally she, too, drifted toward sleep, and as she drew closer to that far shore she thought she heard someone whispering.

Her eagerness to hear more woke her into an echoing silence. Only as she fell away again did she begin to hear the voice again. This time, she made some sense of what it was saying. But she could not be sure. The words, and the images that accompanied them, might just have been the beginning of a dream.

She was determined not to confuse dream with reality. From the beginning, before she'd ever set eyes on Myles, she had wanted him to be real. She wanted her dream to come true, she didn't just want to pretend, to have an imaginary pillow friend. The words had to come from Myles; she wanted to hear his true voice. It was so tempting, now that it seemed to have begun, to give in, to let herself believe that what she was hearing was not simply from inside her own head—but she fought against the easiness of it. Leslie had tricked herself, she'd decided. Myles had never spoken to her friend. Agnes wanted real magic; she wasn't going to settle for pretend.

Magic had rules, she knew that from her reading. Things didn't just happen because you wanted them; Myles was not a mechanical doll designed to speak to anybody; she would have to earn his companionship, learn the rules of his magic. She knew she had started on that path. Their relationship had changed on the day that Leslie had given him back to her. He had let her see him for the first time as he really was—as he *could* be. For the first time, when she looked at him, he had looked back. Now she had to find out how to make herself the kind of person he would talk to.

She couldn't simply go and live in another house, among other people: the police would bring her home again if she tried. She was stuck with her family and the name and address they had given her, so she would have to work on the things that were within her power to change. Parents and teachers would tell you what you were supposed to do to be a good girl and win their approval, but Myles was not so helpful. She had to guess what he wanted of her, but when she guessed right she was rewarded with another thrilling glimpse, another moment of contact with his real and living self.

Sometimes she went into other peoples' houses, but now she was careful not to get caught. She would eat something out of their refrigerators, or move small objects to different places. Some of the things she did were bold and daring, they required bravery and skill, while other actions were more like penances—having to eat six olives, or spending the whole night on the floor beside her bed. She didn't know where the ideas came from—they were dares, not commands, but they came into her head like suggestions from someone else rather than ideas of her own. She couldn't imagine why Myles should care what she ate or where she slept, why an old photograph from the family album had to be destroyed, or one of her sisters' lipsticks stolen, why certain trees had to be climbed or neighbors spied upon, but she did everything that came into her mind to do and was rewarded by the certainty of being on the right track, drawing ever closer to Myles.

She began to hear him speaking at last. It was always very late at night, just as she was on the verge of sleep, and it wasn't at all as she had imagined it would be. He didn't tell her stories; he didn't even sound as if he was talking to her. It was more as if she was catching fragments of a conversation he was having with someone else. She could only catch a few words at a time, and they didn't make much sense to her. She felt the temptation to try to make them make sense, to weave those few words and sentence fragments into a story, to create for herself what she had hoped he would tell her. But she resisted that urge, and concentrated on what he told her, trying to make sense of it by writing it down in a notebook she kept beside her bed.

Although she was glad to have been successful at last, the reality of her relationship with Myles was not as she had imagined it would be. It did not make her happy.

Summer ended and it was time to start school again. On the first day, Agnes abruptly made up her mind to go into second grade alone. She took Myles out of the pencil-box and put him back on her bed. She felt a little guilty about it, because he might not like being left behind, but there was also a great sense of relief as she ran down the stairs swinging her empty book-bag so it slapped against her bare legs. If Myles wasn't with her she wouldn't be tempted to do things that might get her into trouble. And if he punished her by keeping quiet at night—well, maybe that wasn't the worst thing that could happen.

As soon as Agnes got home she rushed straight upstairs to tell her doll about her day, and start winning his forgiveness. Her room was tidy, the clothes she'd left on the floor had been put away, her bed was made, and Myles was gone.

If her mother had taken him off the pillow when she made up the bed she might have put him on a shelf, or in the dollhouse, or on the table. He was in none of those places, nor was he even—and she emptied it completely to make sure—in the toy-basket.

"Mom! Mommy!" Shouting, she ran out into the hall and straight into Rosamund, who grabbed her and shook her slightly. "Stop that yelling! Mother's not feeling well, she's lying down in her room. Tell me what's wrong."

"I want my doll."

"You're big enough to fetch your own toys."

"He's gone! I left him on my bed and now he's gone!"

"Well, she must have moved him when she made your bed. If you'd make your own bed up you wouldn't have this problem. Come on, I'm sure we can find your doll without bothering Mother."

But no matter where Rosamund looked, Myles was not to be found.

"Are you sure you didn't take him to school? The way you were carrying him around all summer, I can't believe you left him at home."

"We don't take dolls to school in second grade," she muttered.

"Oh, we're all grown up now, huh? Look in your book-bag anyway."

Although she knew she hadn't taken Myles to school, her sister's question raised another possibility in her mind. What if Myles had been so annoyed by being left behind that he had tried to come after her, or hidden himself somewhere, to make her sorry?

Well, she was sorry, and she waited anxiously for bedtime, when she was sure he would return to punish her.

But Myles did not return, not that night, or the next, or the one after that. This was her punishment, she realized, not a temporary absence but total loss. She had been tested and found wanting.

She mourned him, she grieved, but her unhappiness was far from consuming. She was too young, their relationship had been too odd and difficult, there was too much else to think about, too many things to learn at school, new friends, a new teacher, books to be read, games to be played. Her days were very full; it was really only at bedtime that her thoughts turned, sadly, to her lost companion.

Sometimes she took up her bedside notebook to read and reread the words which were all that he'd left her, looking for an answer she never found.

a rose
never mind. Shrinking, and as my situation...
and I longed to

You would never
it was the promise of
unspeakable things
in the garden, moving swiftly across
neglected, in the shadows, waiting for
Indeed! Pray tell
a wind down the alley
the touch of your hand, or a breath
I should like to... I have never... when shall we ever
In the fire. Like something marvelous.
To recover what I had lost and quietly return
Again, but I must not repeat
resourceful
small and gleaming
there in the doorway
beneath the overhanging
trees, moving
invisible figures
when you finally understand what

They made no more sense on the tenth reading than they had the first. One day when she was bored she copied some of the lines onto another page and set herself the task of weaving them into a story. It was surely not the story that Myles had been telling to his invisible audience, but she found it strangely satisfying. There was something exciting about giving his words more meaning, and it was not long before writing in this way became her favorite bedtime activity, better even than reading.

That was the year she began to write, not just the private, bedtime stories, but poetry, in school, encouraged by her teacher. Some of her poems appeared in the school's mimeographed magazine, and one of them was singled out and won a prize.

That was the year she made friends with Nina Schumacher, who would gradually, over the next couple of years, replace Leslie as her best friend.

Second grade was also the year of air raid drills, and seeing a teacher cry; of the demonic Russians who wanted to destroy the world; of President Kennedy on television telling his fellow Americans that if the Russian ships did not turn back we might soon be at war. It was a particularly bad time for her mother, who often did not emerge from her darkened bedroom all day, leaving her family to cope as best they could.

By December the Cuban Missile Crisis was over and the world was not destroyed. Whether or not it was connected Agnes never knew, but the worst of Mary Grey's personal crisis had also passed. On December 15, she bought herself a new turquoise dress with matching shoes and put on her rarely worn mink stole to go out with her husband to celebrate their fourteenth wedding anniversary.

The twins were left in charge. Agnes had a bath and got into her nightie early, her agreement with her sisters being that she could stay up until they heard their parents' car on the drive—then she had to jump into bed and pretend she'd been asleep for hours.

Getting to stay up late always sounded like such a treat, but the twins would never play with her for very long and she didn't like watching television as they did, so she soon grew bored. She was tired of reading and didn't feel like writing. She was casting about for something else to do when she thought of her parents' closet and the Christmas presents which were sure to be hidden there.

That closet was strictly off-limits, and not just at Christmas time. It was full of her mother's clothes, many of them expensive designer dresses which had not been worn since before Agnes' birth. Before the twins were born Mary Grey had been a model ("mannequin," she said, which made Agnes imagine her frozen into a lifeless posture like the human-sized dolls in the windows of the big downtown stores) and had special discounts at Battlestein's and Neiman-Marcus. The old clothes were kept carefully stored in plastic wrap or garment bags. "They'll come back in fashion someday, and as long as I keep my figure I don't have to worry," said her mother. "So I want them kept nice. I don't want your grubby little paws all over them." Sometimes as a special treat she would give her daughters a fashion show, mincing along an imaginary catwalk in the living room. But it had been many months since she'd been in the mood to do that.

That night Agnes felt a wistful longing for her mother, as if she had been away for much longer than a few hours. She'd had so many headaches over the past few months, so many days when she was not to be disturbed, lying in her darkened bedroom, unhappy and as unreachable as if she were in another country. Although she'd been in a good mood all day, not enough time had passed for her family to relax and take her presence for granted again.

Agnes went into the master bedroom and closed the door quietly behind her. In the dark, she held her breath as she eased open the closet door and then took the big step over the threshold, from carpet onto bare wood and into the unmistakably charged atmosphere, cool and quiet and filled with the grown-up smells of cotton and silk and wool and leather, lavender, shoe polish, after-shave and her mother's perfume. In that rich air she entered an exalted state, an intense excitement that was also profoundly peaceful. Surrounded by her parents' clothing, their personal possessions, she felt a secret access to their lives; unseen by them she could draw near, becoming closer to them than was normally possible. If she ever dared to take one of her mother's precious old dresses from its protective wrap and put it on she would know the things her mother knew, would almost be her mother. That was why her mother forbade her to touch them, and that was why, someday, she would have to disobey. She reached out and felt for the light-cord, grasped it, pulled, and the light came on with a satisfying snick and golden glow.

Brightly wrapped presents glittered at her from the shelves above her head, but even more interesting were the various shapes, not square but rounded or bulging, more than half-hidden by brown or white paper bags, or rough cocoons of tissue paper. She sighed with pleasure but made no effort to reach or touch them. She preferred the anticipation to knowledge. It was more fun to glimpse the mystery and tantalize herself with guessing than to know for certain what she would find on Christmas Day.

She sat down and, as calmly as if this had been her own closet, these her own things, and hers the whole night to browse through them, picked up a shoe box and opened it. Ah, the red ones. She smiled as she stroked the smooth leather, then took them out and put them on the floor. She surveyed them, head cocked and forefinger laid along her cheek. "Well, I don't know. I like the color, but don't you have any with higher heels? What's in this box?"

These were black patent leather. She lifted them out and set them beside the red ones. "Hmmm, yes, they are higher, but I don't know.... What else do you have?"

She glanced around, hoping for a pair she hadn't tried before, shoes her mother had bought for some special occasion five or six years ago and kept unworn. There was one box half-hidden by others, pushed to the back. It looked promising, but when she took the lid off she was disappointed to see an old pair of brown moccasins—not her mother's usual style, although they looked well-worn. Then she noticed there was something else besides the shoes in the box, something wrapped in white silk. As soon as she picked it up, she knew.

It took some time to unwrap him, for beneath the white silk scarf he had been swathed tightly, obsessively, in strips of criss-crossing black silk. When she finally had him uncovered Myles seemed smaller than she remembered, his colors faded, older, less special. It was hard to believe how important this dull, dead thing had seemed to her during the past summer.

And yet he must be magic, he must be special: why else would her mother have stolen and hidden him away like this?

Something slithered across her bare legs and she yelped and flinched and clutched the doll close to her chest. It was only the strips of black silk which had bound him, sliding off her lap. But how could they move by themselves? Were they magic? They might have been meant to deprive him of his life, and they might have succeeded.

"Oh, Myles!" A wave of anguish, of love and regret, washed through her and she kissed his cold, hard face. Then up she scrambled and, never letting go of him, replaced the shoes and their boxes. Shuddering, she picked up each piece of silk between forefinger and thumb and dropped it into the shoe-box which had been his prison.

She went straight to her bed without bothering to check the time or tell her sisters. There, alone in the dark, with Myles on her pillow as of old, she could speak to him.

"I looked for you everywhere," she whispered. "Everywhere I could think of. I never thought my mom would have hidden you; I thought you must have run away yourself. I guess I'll have to hide you now, we'll have to be really careful. Will she know you're gone? Does she ever look in that box? Why did she take you?"

She wants me dead.

The sound of that voice, faint as a breath yet absolutely clear, set up a prickling shiver all over her skin. There could be no doubt that he had spoken. She had certainly not imagined it; she was nowhere near sleep. She could think of nothing to say.

That's why she bound me. To stop me growing. To stop me being. I was getting stronger when I was with you, but I'm so much weaker now.

"You're safe now," she whispered, then clenched her teeth to keep them from chattering.

No. Not safe here, not in this house. Never safe here. She'll find me.

"No, she doesn't know all my hiding places. I'll keep moving you, I'll keep you with me, you'll be safe with me."

I'm only safe away from here. Away from her.

"But—will you come back? Will I ever see you again?"

Away from her, I can grow. And when I've grown too big for her to hurt me, I'll come back for you.

She shivered, feeling a little sick. "Where will you go?"

You'll have to take me outside. Take me away from the house, put me somewhere safe.

Into her mind came the image of the huge old oak on the corner in front of Mr. and Mrs. Darwin's house. She remembered Leslie's dream of treasure and thought of the cubbyhole. Her mother would never look there, no adult ever would.

"I think I know somewhere you'd be safe."

Take me there.

She got up and went quietly down the stairs, barefoot and in her nightgown, with Myles clutched tightly in one hand. She could hear the television, and knew that her sisters would be too absorbed in some drama to wonder about her. The sound of the television would cover the sound of the carefully opened and closed door and, with a little bit of luck, she'd be able to get back inside just as safely.

This was like old times, like one of her dares, only this time she didn't have to wonder if Myles would approve; this time he'd told her precisely what he wanted.

The ice-cold pavement of the driveway burned her bare feet, but she was too excited by the promise of the dark and glittering night, by this dangerous and necessary adventure shared with Myles, to mind the cold. Her breath formed clouds before her face, and she pretended she was holding a cigarette, exhaling dramatically like Aunt Marjorie.

She broke into a run and that stopped her shivering. She ran in a broken, weaving pattern, hiding behind every bush or tree, to minimize her chances of being seen. But many of the windows she passed were dark, and those that were lighted had curtains pulled across to shut out the cold, dark night. Their neighbors who were still awake would have their attention turned inward, toward the television set or each other, without a thought to spare for whatever might be outside. She saw no one, not even a passing dog or wandering cat. She and Myles were the only living creatures out in the cold, streetlamp lit night. The front of Leslie's house was all dark, but she gave it a wave as she went galloping past.

She could see one light shining out from the side of the Darwins' house—she thought it was the bathroom—but had no fear of being observed. In her excitement, anyway, she was past such petty fears. She knew she would not be caught; Myles would protect her. She thought it possible that she might even be invisible while under his protection.

She paused at the foot of the oak tree just long enough to tuck her nightgown into her underpants and put Myles into the waistband. Then she raised her arms and gave a leap and swung up into the branches as nimbly as a monkey. She had never climbed a tree at night, but there was no problem; she could have climbed this tree with her eyes closed, she had done it so often. She settled herself into the familiar place, straddling the branch which faced the cubbyhole, and retrieved Myles from her waistband.

The night throbbed around her, alive with dangerous promise, as Myles, too, was alive. She looked at him and saw his eyes gleaming in the shadows, and brought him close to her face to kiss him. She held him to her cheek for a moment and felt his lips move as he kissed her in return.

A shiver rippled through her—cold or fear or excitement—so that she had to clutch the branch to stop herself falling, and nearly dropped the doll.

"Oh! Are you all right?"

He said nothing. As she looked at him, she saw that he had become just a doll again. But she knew that this was his disguise, his protection against the world; he had let her see what he really was, and she would never forget it.

"You'll be safe here," she said, pushing him into the cubbyhole, settling him safely out of sight. She wondered how long he would stay there, how soon he would move on, where he would go. "Don't forget to come back for me—don't forget me," she said, and then she clambered back to the ground.

Once there, she ran all the way home, ran so fast she didn't feel the cold, so fast she was nearly flying. She ran so fast and straight, so secure in her assumed invisibility, that she didn't even notice that her parents' car was on the drive and they were getting out, until it was too late, there was nowhere to hide, they had seen her.

She was grounded for a week. That meant she had to go straight to her room every day after school and stay there. She could come out to use the bathroom and to have dinner with the family, but that was all. She was in disgrace. The twins, who were in trouble, too, for not noticing she had gone out when they were supposed to be in charge, refused to talk to her. At least her parents, having imposed their restrictions, admitted she was still alive and their daughter. But for the duration of the week she wasn't allowed to go out, have visitors, or even phone calls. She couldn't check on Myles. She thought of asking Leslie, when she saw her at school, to look in the cubby and report back. But things were kind of strange with Leslie just then—she had her cousin Christie staying with her while Christie's parents were in Europe, and between Leslie and Mindy and Agnes and Nina there were a series of complicated negotiations evolving to determine who was best friends with whom. To bring up Myles with Leslie, excluding all the other girls, would mean complications she didn't want, so she told herself that it didn't matter. Myles would be fine; Leslie didn't have to know where he was.

When she complained about stomach pains her mother thought it was a bid for sympathy and said sternly, "No excuses, young lady. You're going to school whether you like it or not. And you'd better like it. Behave yourself, or you won't get any presents from Santa Claus this year!"

While she was at school her stomach pains got worse, so bad she began to cry. The school nurse called the doctor and her mother, and a few hours later Agnes was in the hospital with an appendectomy scheduled.

There followed a strange time in which dream and reality became inextricably confused. A leering red face on the wall terrified her and she didn't feel any better about it when a nurse told her it was Santa. She was alone in a strange room, or thought she was, but when she cried out for her mother, her mother appeared. Sometimes her mother was wearing the familiar, dark blue robe which she only ever wore around the house—she never went anywhere in it, she never wore it out of their own house, so were they at home? Why didn't she recognize the room as being part of their own house? When she asked her mother, her mother insisted that the room had not changed, it was the same one she'd always had. She couldn't understand why her mother was lying to her—or if her mother wasn't lying, why she remembered living somewhere else, somewhere so different from this small, hot room with white walls and linoleum floor, the high bed and so few toys. She was confused and frightened, and none of her questions brought the reassurances she wanted.

Something shone and glittered on the floor, moving like a strip of black silk. Yet when she begged the nurses to pick it up, they pretended they couldn't see it. She was afraid they planned to use it on her, or that her mother would bind her with it as she had bound Myles, and she would stop growing, lose the power of speech, die.

She heard Myles on her pillow, whispering an urgent warning, but when she turned her head to look for him he was gone, and she couldn't remember what he had said.

One evening Marjorie was there in a loose gray sweater and slacks, looking beautiful despite her untidy hair and a face without make-up. She'd brought a bag of peppermint candy, a jigsaw puzzle, and a book.

Agnes looked at the book, which was small, fat and red and had her own name on the spine. "What's this?"

"It's a novel. Probably still a bit too old for you, but don't worry about that, try it again in a year or two. You'll like it."

"Why does it have my name on it?"

Her aunt smiled mysteriously. "You'll have to read it to find out, won't you? She was quite a heroine, that Agnes Grey. Anyway, the reason I'm giving it to you now is because I'm going away. I don't know when I'll be back. I've had enough of Texas and small-town minds. Things are really happening in London now; I want to be there, too. I'll drop you a line, if I can. And I'll tell you all about it when I get back."

She couldn't bear it. "Can I come with you?"

"Silly! You have to stay here, get well, go to school.... Don't look like that! There'll be plenty of time for you to go places when you're older."

"I don't want to wait till I'm older; I want to go now."

"London will still be there when you grow up—"

"But I want to go with you!"

"Oh, I think your mother would have something to say about that."

"I don't care. Mother stole Myles."

"What?"

"The doll you gave me, the talking doll. You know. The pillow friend. She took him—she lied about it!—and she wrapped him up in strips of silk and put him in a box in her closet and she would have killed him dead if I hadn't found him in time, he said so. I saved him. I can't stay with her now, I can't. You have to take me with you."

Marjorie stared at her, her face gone as expressionless as that of her sister in one of her moods. Then she sighed and relaxed a little and shook her head. "I can't take you. I don't know the first thing about looking after children; there's no room in my life for—"

"I'll grow up," she said desperately.

"Well, I should hope so. And in your parents' house where you belong. I can't stay, I really shouldn't have come at all—there's a taxi waiting outside to take me to the airport. You be good, and get better. Don't forget me. I won't forget you, I promise."

Just like that, without even a kiss goodbye, she was gone. If it hadn't been for the evidence of the book Agnes might have thought she'd dreamed the whole visit.

A little later, after she had stopped crying, she opened *Agnes Grey* and tried to read it, but her head ached and the long, unfamiliar words blurred together. It was a grown-up book with no pictures. She could imagine her mother saying she was too young for it and taking it away, so she kept it hidden—first under her pillow, and later, at home, at the bottom of her toy-box—to keep it safe until she was ready for it.

She was allowed to go home on Christmas Eve. It was frustrating to be forced to spend so much time playing quietly or resting, forbidden to run or ride her bike or climb or do anything too active in case she pulled her stitches. But it wasn't all bad—to keep her happy, her sisters and her mother played board and card games with her, and her father read her stories and played her favorite records on the hi-fi. She could read as much as she liked, and during the school holidays Leslie came to visit every single day.

One day as they were playing together with the dollhouse Leslie asked her about Myles.

"Don't you like him anymore? Is that why you left him in the tree?"

It was like being slapped. "How'd you know I left him in the tree?"

"Cause I found him, of course. What did you think? Didn't your Mom tell you? I gave him to her to give you when you were in the hospital. I thought you must be missing him."

So Myles had not escaped. Her mother had him again, delivered back into her very hands by her best friend. She felt a thick, suffocating anger filling her, an anger which had no outlet. She couldn't blame Leslie, who had thought she was doing her a favor. Maybe, if she'd trusted her friend, Myles would be safe now. If she'd been more careful, if she'd thought things through— She had only herself to blame, and she knew that Myles would never forgive her. If he had survived.

"What's wrong, Ag? You don't look so hot. Aggie?"

She scrambled up and ran for the door, almost falling, screaming for her mother.

At first Mary Grey pretended not to understand but finally, out of concern for her daughter's health, she had to give in. "All right, settle down! You'll burst your stitches if you aren't careful, and you won't like it if I have to take you back to get the doctor to stitch you up again! Calm down! Yes, all right, all right, I'll get the doll, only be still!"

She stopped struggling and let herself be pushed onto the couch. Agnes and her mother glared at each other.

"Leslie, stay with her and don't let her move, got that? Agnes, I mean it."

"Just get him!"

She waited, clenching and unclenching her fists, trying not to think about how long her mother had had him, ignoring Leslie's puzzled noises.

There was her mother, with Myles in her hand. Agnes reached out, eagerly, and took him. As soon as she felt the stiff little body, even before she looked down at the still, painted face, she knew that this time she had been too late. Her mother had won. She had lost her pillow friend. Myles was just an old doll. He would never look back at her again.

PART TWO:

IN THE WOODS

I began with Things, which were the true confidants of my lonely childhood, and it was already a great achievement that, without any outside help, I managed to get as far as animals.

—Rainer Maria Rilke

Her parents had been arguing all week, quietly but ferociously, while she struggled to remain unconscious of the conflict, sinking ever deeper into her books. She read as a chain-smoker smokes; if she could she would have lived inside her books and never come out. When she had to do something that made reading impossible—walking, washing dishes, eating dinner with her parents—a voice inside her head described what she was doing, feeling or seeing. It became a necessary habit, a way of making her whole life as much like the experience of reading as possible.

No matter how she tried to remain unaware she knew she was the cause of her parents' argument.

Thirteen was old enough, according to her mother, to be trusted to look after herself alone during the day. When the twins were thirteen they'd been left to look after their younger sister, and she was no less mature now than they'd been then.

She was a good girl, and bright, and if there were any problems Jane-Ann was just down the road.

According to her father the point was not whether she was old enough to look after herself, but whether it was fair to make her. For a day or two, fine, but not for two weeks. It wasn't possible to get around Houston without a car. If Mary was gone, with Mike at work all day, poor Agnes would be confined to the house. With Leslie away at camp it wasn't fair to ask Jane-Ann to ferry her back and forth from the country club, let alone the library. What was the poor kid supposed to do all day?

"I don't know why Agnes couldn't go to camp, too," said her

mother. "I'm sure she'd be happier there, with other girls her own age, with plenty to do, than sitting indoors reading all the time. And then we wouldn't have this problem."

"We wouldn't have this problem if you just stayed home," said her father. His tone made Agnes feel chilly, although Mary didn't seem to notice how much less patience he had with her lately.

She overheard her mother on the phone that evening pleading with the twins to leave Austin and come home for just a couple of weeks, but it was a losing battle. Clarissa had already enrolled for both summer semesters and Roz had a job and a boyfriend she had no intention of being separated from. When the twins had been home at Christmas their father had baited them both about their taste in clothes and music and had been particularly merciless in his sarcastic attacks on Rozzy's long-haired "liberal" boyfriend. They didn't have to take it, and they didn't. Agnes envied them their extra years. When she was old enough to get away, she wouldn't come back either.

Her parents didn't ask Agnes what she wanted to do, and she didn't ask her mother where she wanted to go. She didn't want to hear another story about a bit part in a film which would end on the cutting-room floor. More than a year had passed since Mary Grey's last "trip to Hollywood." The twins had been living at home then, seniors in high school, willing to look after their younger sister and test their cooking skills, especially since their housekeeping duties included unquestioned right of access to their mother's car. She remembered that time, those two weeks, vividly because they had been so happy. Instead of working late and spending his weekends down at the bay, working on his boat as he did now, their father had started coming home earlier in the evenings, to take them out to dinner or, after a meal at home, out to a movie or to play miniature golf. One Sunday they all went sailing, and on the Saturdays, when her sisters were busy with their friends, he had taken Agnes to see the Battleship Texas and the San Jacinto Monument. He'd talked to her—mostly about Texas history, as she recalled, but the subject mattered less than the fact of his interested presence. She had wished it could always be like that with the four of them.

But Mary Grey came back from wherever she had been, the twins graduated and moved up to Austin, and Mike spent less and less time at home. The house which had once been so full of voices was now too quiet.

Things were getting worse, the way they always did before Mary went away. The long, tense silences between her parents would be punctuated by short, quiet arguments. There were many days when Agnes saw her father only for a few minutes in the morning in the kitchen before he left for work, and her mother only for a few minutes in the evening, in her darkened bedroom where she'd spent the day with one of her bad headaches.

Something had to happen; she couldn't understand why her father was being so difficult. He'd always let his wife go before, and things had always been better, at least for awhile, afterward. But now he was using her as an excuse to keep her mother home, and she couldn't even say anything because she wasn't supposed to know they were arguing.

It came as a complete surprise when her mother asked if she'd mind spending a couple of weeks with her Aunt Marjorie.

The name lifted her spirits like a promise of magic.

"Marjorie's coming to stay here?"

"No. You'd be going to stay with her, in East Texas. Where we grew up. Would that be all right with you? It might be kind of boring, I remember when I was a teenager I couldn't stand being stuck out in the woods like that, but you could take a suitcase full of books with you, and there's a pond where we used to swim, and..."

She had seen her aunt only three times in the last three years, but she often dreamed about her, and held imaginary conversations with her. To have her all to herself for two whole weeks was a dream come true. She threw her arms around her mother. "Oh, thank you!"

With a short, embarrassed laugh her mother pushed her away. "Oh, don't thank me. Thank Marjorie. And please remember, she's not used to having children around, and she'll have things she'll want to do, so... be as grown-up as you can. Don't make too many demands. Don't expect too much from her."

Agnes wasn't listening. She was already deep in imagining her perfect vacation with Marjorie.

Mary Grey left in a taxi on Friday afternoon. Agnes was to spend the weekend with her father before taking a Trailways bus to East Texas on Monday morning. She had been looking forward to that, imagining conversations and adventures, but her father was remote and uncommunicative. He avoided her—even when they were together he would not meet her eyes. When she asked him what he was thinking about he said "nothing" or "business." When she tried to share her pleasure at going to visit Marjorie he grew colder. He wouldn't even pronounce Marjorie's name, and his refusal acted like a spell that locked her tongue. She tried to draw him out, and felt like a fake and a fool, asking him questions about Texas history, as if she cared. Halfway through Saturday she gave up and escaped as usual into her books. But when the bus carried her away on Monday morning and, craning back, she discovered that her father was already lost to sight, her eyes filled with tears. She should have tried harder. She shouldn't have given up so easily. She ached with loss, feeling as if she was leaving her father for very much longer than two weeks.

She blew her nose and got her transistor radio out of her bag, settling the ear plug in her ear to listen to her favorite DJ and her favorite Top 40 station. She heard songs by all the best groups, The Lovin' Spoonful, Buffalo Springfield, The Turtles, The Beatles, The Young Rascals, and her mood improved with each hit. But then The Doors' "Light My Fire" began to fade out, and the Hollies singing "Carrie Ann" were even more wracked by static. The bus had carried her beyond the reach of the Houston station. For a time she station-hopped as best she could, but by the time she reached Camptown she wasn't receiving anything but country-western, and those twanging, nasal voices could not uplift her but only annoy.

Camptown was a settlement in the middle of the piney woods of East Texas, about a hundred and sixty miles northeast of Houston. There wasn't much to it: gazing out the window she saw a few houses, two churches, a short strip of storefronts and a filling station which served as the bus stop. Most of the people who lived there probably worked for the big sawmill whose whistle split the air twice a day. She was the only person who got off the bus, and there was only one person there to meet it. As always, the sight of her aunt gave her the strange frisson of seeing someone so much like yet unlike her mother. Mary would never have been seen in public unflatteringly dressed or without make-up; Marjorie, with her bare, lined face, frowzy hair, long cotton skirt and tie-dyed T-shirt, looked like a fading flower-child. In the past, she had seemed glamorous in her own arty, off-beat way; a beatnik. But beatniks had been replaced in the public eye by hippies, and this woman, she thought with a swirl of hot, disowning embarrassment, was too old to be a hippie.

Her aunt stepped forward and hugged her briefly and awkwardly. Agnes inhaled the mingled smells of stale cigarettes, sweat, and patchouli oil, and Marjorie withdrew.

"How was your journey?"

"Fine, thank you."

"Both of these bags yours?"

"I brought a lot of books. Mother said I should, in case..."

"That's right, you'll need them. I don't have television, and I won't have time to entertain you. You'll have lots of time for reading. Put them in there." She gestured at a little red wagon.

Agnes hesitated. "Where's your car?"

"That's it, princess. The baggage car."

"You don't have a car?" The idea was shocking. Until now, she had not met a single grown-up person without a car. "How do you—"

"I walk," said Marjorie shortly. "And so do you, unless you want to spend the night at the Camptown filling station." She grabbed the wagon-handle and marched away, pulling it behind her.

Agnes didn't move. She had a sudden vision of her mother on the telephone pleading, wheedling, blackmailing, and of Marjorie, unhappily, grudgingly, giving in.

It was hot and quiet and still, the air buzzing slightly with an insect noise, and no cars in sight. When she turned her head she could see the grimy windows of the service station office and, inside, a man in overalls sitting on a chair, his feet up on the desk, gazing at her with a bored lack of curiosity. Marjorie's figure grew smaller in the distance, walking back down the empty highway in the direction from which the bus had come, pulling the wagon with Agnes' luggage behind her. The sound of the wheels on the road grew fainter. She did not pause or look back. If she didn't move, nothing would change, nothing would get better, no one would come for her. At last she started to walk. Then, fearful of getting lost, she began to run.

She caught up as her aunt was leaving the highway for an unpaved road that wound into the forest. The air was still hot, despite the shade, and smelled of pine needles, resin and dust.

"Why don't you have a car?"

"Can't afford one."

"Oh." She had known that Mary and Marjorie had grown up "dirt-poor" in the backwoods of Texas, raised by their grandmother after their feckless teenaged mother took off for parts unknown. Mary had left Camptown the day after she graduated from high school and hitchhiked to Houston where she'd found a job as an assistant sales clerk and mannequin for Battlestein's. What Marjorie had done when her sister left, Agnes didn't know. She had assumed they'd left together, left their unhappy past behind forever, but here was her aunt, still poor, still living in the woods.

"Actually," said Marjorie. "That is not, strictly speaking, true."

"What?"

"Why I don't have a car. If I lived here all the time, I would. But I'd rather save my money for traveling, and in the cities where I like to be, New York or London or Paris, a car is a burden, not a necessity. When I'm out of the cities, when I come back here, I come to work, not to gad about. Being here is a sort of retreat, and I have to be very frugal. When the money runs out, back I go to the city to get a job."

"What work are you doing here?"

"I'm writing my autobiography. Here, we take the right fork, remember that and you won't get lost when you come by yourself. The left fork takes you to the pond."

"A pond? Can I go swimming?"

"Not by yourself."

"Will you take me?"

"I'll try to make time."

She had expected a Marjorie who was glad to see her, but this woman seemed as impatient and unforthcoming as her mother at her worst. In desperation she asked, "Are there any kids who live around here? Kids I could play with... maybe go swimming with... I mean."

"I'm sure there must be some children in Camptown. I haven't noticed."

"Your neighbors don't have any?"

"*These* are my neighbors." She gestured at the surrounding trees.

The forest was quiet except for the monotonous, low, locust-hum that seemed the voice of the heat. A jay screeched overhead and she could hear a fluttering in the branches. She felt tired and thirsty. "Is it much farther?"

"You're not tired already?"

She was, already terminally tired and bored. She imagined the next two weeks without company, with nothing to look forward to but the next book, and dull despair settled on her like a smothering blanket. She wished she'd never come. At home, at least, the boredom was familiar and known, and cool, unlike these dim, stifling woods.

"When we get in we can have a good old talk about what you've been up to since I last saw you." For the first time Marjorie's voice was kind. "Are you still mad about horses?"

"Horses?"

"That was all you could talk about the last time I saw you. Did I know how to ride, had I ever had a horse, could I talk your parents into buying *you* a horse..." She laughed warmly. "I understand completely—I went through a horse-mad phase myself, but we were so poor I never had a chance."

The closest Agnes had been to a horse was a ride on a weary Shetland pony tethered in a ring somewhere when she was about six. All she knew about horses had come out of books, and now she remembered that the last time she'd seen Marjorie she'd been in the midst of reading a series of books about a girl learning to ride and becoming a championship show jumper. It had been a brief, literary passion, and although she had occasional fantasies about owning a horse, she hadn't pursued it. If she'd really wanted it, her parents might have agreed to riding lessons. There was a stable with a riding school not far away—she knew a girl who went there. The truth was that she found this girl, like the specialized vocabulary surrounding riding, intimidating; the truth was, she was lazy. The fantasy of riding a horse like the wind, responsive to her every touch, was like the fantasy of being a brilliant dancer—they were what she imagined while riding her bicycle, or skipping around the living room to the strains of "Swan Lake." She had no wish to spoil the fantasy with the real, hard work of ballet classes or riding lessons.

But she didn't want to say any of that to Marjorie, who was sounding more like her usual, interested self, so she said, "Yeah, sure, I'd love to have a horse, but where would I keep it? They're expensive to stable, and the backyard isn't big enough, as my dad keeps telling me, so I don't guess I'll ever have one."

"Agnes. You can have whatever you want—have you forgotten that already?" Marjorie had stopped walking and now turned on her the full force of her brilliant blue gaze.

Agnes shrugged uneasily and continued walking.

"Hey, where are you going? We're home."

She had been aware of a building on their right but hadn't paid any attention to it because it was an old empty shack. Now she gave a little half-smile. "Oh, sure. Right."

"This is where I live."

"You're kidding!"

Marjorie frowned and shook her head. "What's the matter?" She hoisted the bags out of the wagon and said, "Well, you can stay outside if you want, but I need something to drink, myself."

She couldn't believe her eyes. An old, unpainted, weather-beaten wooden house with a tarpaper roof, it looked as if it would fall down in the next high wind. How could that be home? The high windows were screened and curtained, but there were no other signs of civilization: no neighboring houses, no driveway or paved road, not even a mailbox or a telephone pole. But Marjorie was going inside, so Agnes went up the steps after her.

Inside, though, it was different, obviously lived in. It was a real home, decently if sparsely furnished, clean and tidy, with pale painted walls and wooden floors that smelled of the polish her mother used at home. It was a square box partitioned into four rooms of roughly the same size, with no connecting passages. The living room opened onto a bedroom on one side and the kitchen on the other, and the second bedroom was entered from the kitchen.

The two bedrooms were linked by a narrow bathroom.

"I had the bathroom put in," said Marjorie. "When your mother and I were growing up the bedrooms were slightly larger, but we had to take our baths in the kitchen, and the toilet was in an outhouse."

"Gross."

"No. It was just the way things were. We might have been living in the last century, for all we knew. It wasn't really until we were in high school, taking the bus to Livingston, and meeting kids whose parents had cars, kids who lived in houses which had not only indoor plumbing but electricity and telephones, that we realized how much we were doing without."

"You didn't have electricity?" Her mother had never told her—her mother never talked about her childhood.

"Still don't," said Marjorie. "Don't look so horrified! This is an opportunity for you to find out first hand how people used to live. Aren't you interested in history?"

"What will we eat?" She spoke plaintively because she was hungry; it was past her usual lunchtime.

"People did manage to eat before the invention of electric stoves. What do they teach you at your school? Did you think that before this century people went around eating fruit off trees, chewing on raw potatoes and sucking raw eggs? Don't worry, I wouldn't let your mother down, I'll give you one cooked meal a day. I hope you won't squawk about cold cereal for breakfast and sandwiches or salads for lunch. I don't use the woodstove in the summer, it makes this place too hot. I've got a hibachi for grilling things outside, and if I want to boil water for coffee or something there's a little camping stove which uses bottled gas. Are you hungry now? A peanut butter sandwich suit you?"

She nodded.

"Tang or tea?" She gestured at the two jars on the counter.

"Tang, please. Is there any ice?"

"Afraid not. No freezer. I do have an icebox in the cellar, to keep things cool, but there's no way I can make ice for drinks." She turned away, taking a jar of peanut butter and a loaf of bread from a cupboard.

"You have a cellar?"

There was a tension in her aunt's posture which reminded her unhappily of her mother. "There is a cellar. You're not to play in it, understand me? It's out of bounds. You're not to go into the cellar unless I'm with you. Understand?"

"I was just asking."

"And I'm just telling. You must never go down there by yourself."

"Who said I wanted to? Don't worry, I won't. I'm not a baby."

"It's nothing to do with your age. It's just—I'm sorry, Agnes. I'm not used to having anyone else here. I live by myself, I do things a certain way—I guess I'm set in my ways."

It was true, she thought drearily. Marjorie hadn't wanted her here, not even for two weeks. Nobody wanted her.

"I'll try to keep out of your way."

Marjorie brought their drinks to the table. "I knew you would understand. We're going to get along just fine. And you're not going to have such a bad time, you know. In fact, I think you may find yourself feeling very, very glad you came." Marjorie leaned across the table toward her with a conspiratorial smile. "Let me tell you a secret about this place. This is a place where wishes come true. You can have whatever you want."

Agnes felt her stomach twist painfully as she remembered the last wish her aunt had granted, the doll she had convinced herself could talk. But she'd been a little kid then. Marjorie ought to know she'd grown up and no longer believed in magic. But when she opened her mouth it was only to take a sip of her lukewarm orange drink. Maybe she didn't believe in magic, but she would like to be proved wrong. She would just wait and see, and sneer out loud later, when nothing happened.

"And here is a candle to light you to bed," said Marjorie. It was a stubby white thing in a brown pottery holder. Although she wasn't usually afraid of the dark, Agnes found herself reluctant to go alone into her room with only this small light.

"Couldn't I have one of those lamps?" There were two hurricane lamps in the front room, one at each end of the desk. Marjorie shook her head.

"I'm afraid not. Reading and writing by candlelight sounds very romantic, but it's hell on the eyes. I'm going to stay up and work for awhile, so I'll need all the light I can get."

"So how am I supposed to read?"

"You'll just have to do the best you can. I'm sorry. Maybe you should go straight to sleep instead of trying to read—you look awfully tired. Tomorrow—I'll get another lamp for you, all right? So it's just this one night you have the candle. Don't wear such a long face. Pretend you're living a hundred years ago!"

"Playing old-fashioned" had been a favorite game of hers for years. But there was a difference between playing because you wanted to and being told to play. Anyway, she thought grimly as she washed herself in cold water by candlelight, a hundred years ago, even fifty years ago, this bathroom didn't exist.

She settled herself in the narrow, lumpy bed, and picked up *Agnes Grey*, her talismanic book. She had read it so often it shouldn't have mattered that she could not see the words on the page, and yet it did. It could not comfort her tonight. She set it on top of the bookcase beside the bed, next to the candle, and then took off her glasses and folded them carefully on top of the book. The strange shadows cast by the flickering candle combined with her near-sightedness to transform the room into a strange and threatening place, with weird figures crouching in every corner. She knew there was nothing there, but the half-glimpsed movements eroded her confidence. Darkness, without shadows, must be better. She turned her head and extinguished the candle with one puff of breath.

Darkness fell like a blow. She felt it rushing into her mouth, flowing up her nostrils. Closing her eyes made it no better; the darkness was still out there, smothering her. She fell onto her pillow and pressed her face into the itchy smell of old feathers. "I wish I hadn't blown it out," she whispered.

The feathers made her sneeze. She turned her face away and sneezed again and her eyes popped open briefly. She blinked again. She had seen something. And then her eyes opened wide and she could see the room perfectly well in shadow and in light—in candlelight. The fat little candle in its pottery holder was burning away as if it had never gone out.

"*This is a place where wishes come true*." Despite the heat, she held herself tightly, and wished she had something more than one thin sheet to hide beneath. She lay on her back, eyes wide and unblinking, while all around the shadows danced and sneered at her.

She wasn't aware of having closed her eyes, but she must have slept, for all at once she was awake, in darkness left by the burnt-down candle, straining to hear the sound that had woken her.

A murmuring voice from another room, and now a steady, rhythmic creaking—bedsprings? The murmuring stopped and started, but the creaking went on and on. She tried to imagine it: her aunt in the grip of a dream, tossing and turning, turning and tossing... She must have slept again, for the next thing she knew the room was light and it was morning.

They had bowls of cornflakes, slices of bread with apple-butter, and orange juice in the kitchen. Agnes was in her nightgown, but Marjorie was already dressed, in the same long skirt with a different top—a plain white one, and obviously no bra underneath. This morning her face looked fuller, with fewer lines, more relaxed. As soon as she had finished eating she lit a cigarette.

"What are your plans for the day?"

Agnes looked as blank as she felt.

"Have you made your wish yet?"

It was ridiculous, and yet—"Last night," she blurted. "I wished I hadn't blown out the candle, and I hadn't!"

"Don't worry about that. You can have more than one wish." She waved her hand with the cigarette and smiled.

"Oh, that's lucky," she said sarcastically. "So I don't have to be careful? I can make as many wishes as I want. Whoopee."

"You must be very careful. Because what you wish for, you get."

Agnes finished eating her piece of bread.

Was this for real? Did Marjorie still think she was a baby? She might have imagined about the candle, thought she'd blown it out when it was really just flickering and a breeze had brought it back to life... "So you're saying that I can have whatever I wish for. Like, if I wished for a horse I would get one? A real horse, that I could take back to Houston?"

"That's not up to me."

"Oh, no? Well, who is it up to?"

"You. Your parents. I don't imagine you could keep it in your backyard, so you'd have to find the money to pay for boarding it somewhere. You can have whatever you wish for, Agnes, but you also have to deal with the consequences of your wishes. It's not a game of make-believe. Something here, something about this place, makes wishes come true."

"For everybody? Anything?"

"I don't know what the limits are. I haven't found the limits."

Something in Marjorie's quiet voice made her skin prickle. They both sat, not looking at each other, and then, when her aunt stood up and began to clear the table, she went back to her bedroom and dressed quickly in shorts, shirt and rubber thong sandals. Then, out of a slightly bored curiosity, she wandered into the other bedroom. There was a heavy, sour smell hanging in the warm, still air, and the sack-cloth curtains at the windows kept the room dim and airless. Her skin crawled. She crossed the floor quickly and went through the other door.

By contrast, the front room was airy and light. A big, dark wooden desk dominated, seeming to take up twice as much space as it really did because of its reflection in the large, age-spotted mirror hanging on the opposite wall.

The wall behind the desk was the one which drew her attention. This was covered with unframed pictures of various sizes. Some had been clipped from glossy magazines, others from newspapers, still others were colored postcard reproductions of paintings. All were portraits, mostly of men, and although Marjorie said they were all famous, even "geniuses," most she had never heard of. There were exceptions: D.H. Lawrence, who had written a dirty book, and Robert Frost, whose poems she'd read in school.

One face in particular captured her attention, and her imagination. It was one of the smallest, just at her eye-level, a black-and-white newspaper photograph of a young man with large, dreamy eyes and shaggy, Beatles-style hair. He was young and "mod" looking, which set him apart from all the others on the wall. His presence seemed as much a mistake as if one of the Rolling Stones had been placed in a line-up of classical musicians. Yet beneath his picture were the words, *young poet.*

"Now, Agnes..."

"Do you have any of his poems? That I could read?"

"Whose?"

"This poet's."

"Ah, Graham Storey, the young English poet. He doesn't have a collection out yet. I do have a copy of the poem that was published in the *Times Literary Supplement* along with that photograph. It struck me particularly...."

"Could I read it?

"Yes, of course. I'll find it for you later. I don't have time to look for it now; I want to get down to work. So run along."

"Are you kicking me out?" She was joking; Marjorie wasn't.

"Look, I told you, I explained yesterday. This is my work-room; I can't work with someone else here. It's a small house. Of course I don't mind if you want to go into the kitchen for something, or if you have to come in to use the bathroom, but you can't just hang around in here. Go on, now. I'll see you later, lunchtime."

Agnes felt herself getting hotter and hotter. Her stomach churned. She felt like screaming: If you don't want me, I'll go! But where? Her parents had sent her here, to get her out of their house. She stomped out, slamming doors, raging. It wasn't fair, people were horrible and she had to take it, there was nothing she could do, because she was a child.

"I wish I was grown-up," she muttered as soon as she was alone outside. "I'd show her. If I could just stop being a kid, right now, and be a grown up..."

With a small pang of fear she realized she had just made a wish. The rage burned away and her head was clear. All at once, everything looked different: sharper and unnaturally bright, reminding her of how the world had changed appearance when she'd gotten her first pair of glasses.

She looked down at herself. She hadn't changed, from what she could see. Her chest was as flat as ever, her shorts and flip-flops still fit. She felt a little strange inside, but she could already guess that if she looked in a mirror, nothing would show. If her wish had worked and she had suddenly grown up, it could only be mentally, or spiritually, and she knew nobody else would believe it. And what was the point of being grown up if nobody else knew?

So this was a place where wishes came true?

Oh, yeah, sure. Marjorie would never have tried to convince a grown-up of such a thing.

But just in case—"I meant it," she said out loud. "I mean it. I wish I was really grown up, so Marjorie would have to see."

She didn't know if she felt more disappointed or relieved when nothing happened. Suddenly becoming a grown-up could have been a problem. How would she manage if her parents didn't recognize her when she went home?

But there was nothing to worry about, because there was no magic. She had just proved it. She wondered if Marjorie would admit she'd been lying—"teasing" was probably how she would put it—when she told her about the wish that had not come true. But then she realized what her aunt would say, what her excuse would be—she could almost hear her saying, with an almost-invisible smirk, "But you didn't really want that wish to come true, did you? You didn't want it enough." Or maybe she would say that maturity was a state of mind.

"All right, then," she said to herself. "I'll wish for something there can't be any arguing about, something that's either there or it's not." She began to walk, and as she walked she brooded on what she should wish for.

Marjorie had given her the idea, and it was not difficult to make herself want a horse; she'd had enough idle fantasies in the past, usually provoked by something she'd read, daydreams of galloping through forest and field, or along the beach, on the back of a noble, highly bred animal, her loyal companion, with a name like Star or Blaze or Shadow. The fantasy was about speed and effortless movement, as wonderful as flying; it was about being free from the boring restrictions of everyday life, of being somehow, through her connection with the horse, more than human, faster, more powerful, and completely confident in her own body.

She recalled these dreams as she walked through the forest. It was easy to imagine herself riding through these woods, this lonely wilderness where almost anything could happen.

"I wish I had a horse," she said fervently, clenching her hands into fists at her sides, and speaking to the rhythm of her rubber-sandaled feet as they came down, with a muffled, slapping sound, on the path. "I wish, I wish, I wish."

She had come as far as the path that led to the pond when she became aware of a flickering movement at the very edges of her vision, like distant flashes of light. She stopped and turned to look: slashes of white appeared, then disappeared again into the shadows. Against the tall dark trunks of the trees it was like something moving in a darkened cage, something like pale flesh. For one terrifying moment she thought a naked man was running toward her, and then she realized that of course it wasn't a person, but a large, white horse.

It was trotting, or cantering, or maybe loping—she knew the words, from books, but had no idea which one applied to this gait. The animal came out of the trees now, into the open, and stopped in front of her.

It was huge. She'd only encountered Shetland ponies in the flesh before and had not realized how large a horse would be. So big, and so spooky. There was something uncanny about its coloring, not only the ghostly white coat, but the big, rolling, blood-shot blue eyes. She had never imagined a blue-eyed horse; she thought all horses had brown eyes. But this one rolled an eye at her which was as blue as her mother's.

It stomped one enormous hoof and she jumped back. It snorted, contemptuous of her fear, the exhalation blowing out its lips and giving her a glimpse of huge, yellow teeth.

Horses did sometimes attack people. They could lash out, kick or bite if they were frightened, or mad. She had even read somewhere about a horse that fed on human flesh.

She backed away slowly, afraid to run, afraid to take her eyes off of the horse who followed her, reducing the distance between them with every step it took.

Advice from something else she'd read floated into her mind: *Don't let them see your fear*. It was so much bigger and stronger than she was that she hadn't a chance against it. The trees around here were nearly all pines, impossible to climb, and she couldn't outrun it, so her only option was to face it down.

She stopped retreating and the horse stopped, too.

"All right," she said sharply. "Just stay there a minute. Stand still. What do you want? If you really are my wish..."

It arched its great neck and inclined its head slightly toward her, offering itself to be ridden.

"How can I ride you?" she demanded, her voice rising in a whine. "You're too big; I can't even get on your back."

As soon as she spoke she remembered that they had just passed through an area of recent felling. There had been stumps there of different heights. The horse tossed his head and whickered and she knew he was thinking the same thing. It was like mind-reading, or talking, and it made a connection between them. All at once he was a little less scary.

They found a stump and the horse stood still beside it, as still as if made of stone, betraying no impatience. So, finally, after a little hesitation during which she realized she could not mount him as she would have liked—climbing on sideways—she flung herself at him, as if the horse were a tree she was accustomed to climbing, and then she slid into the rider's position. As soon as she was upright and wondering where to hold on, the horse began to move.

"Whoa!" she shouted, but he didn't. She grabbed handfuls of his mane and tugged. "Whoa!" Imagining that pulling a mane was like pulling someone's hair she bit back her squeamishness and tugged harder, as hard as she could. "Whoa, stop, stop!"

This had either no effect at all, or the opposite of what she intended. The horse had been walking, but now increased his gait to a jouncing trot. She was so bounced around that she worried about falling off. There was nothing but the rough, ropy strands of mane to hang on to, nowhere to put her feet, no way of feeling herself secure perched on top of this huge, strange animal without control.

But she didn't fall off. And after awhile she began to feel a little more confident. Instead of crouching fearfully over his neck, ready to grab on for dear life if she felt herself slipping, she straightened up.

She would have felt happier with reins in her hands and a horse who responded to her commands, but at least he hadn't thrown her. Would she really want to sit on the back of a horse who only walked, a plodding pony ride for children? Yet this jouncing trot which seemed to bounce her in and out of sunlight had been going on for too long. She was hot and sweaty and feeling queasy, with a strange, throbbing ache low in her stomach.

She imagined there might be relief for her discomfort if the horse began to run. She'd like to feel a breeze on her face which would dry her sweat and lift her hair, to be carried smoothly through the air, like flying in her dreams, not jounced along through dust and sun and shadow.

They came out of the woods then, into an open field. She realized she had no idea which way they had come, or where they were, or how they were going to get home again, and then, in the freedom of the open, the horse broke into a gallop.

The suddenness pitched her forward. The horse's neck was too big to get her arms around, but she clung on as best she could, sliding dangerously to one side. If—when—she fell, would she die? Would the horse trample her? One of her sandals fell off. She closed her eyes and pressed her face tight against the prickly hair, inhaling the dusty, salty, animal smell and sensing, through her terror, something else, something other, a fierce, mindless animal power, animal joy in movement.

After awhile they were back in the woods again and walking, the horse forced to a more careful pace by the many close-growing trees. She did not straighten up but remained slumped over his neck. She felt sick. Finally, as he began to trot, she couldn't hold it back any longer, and leaned out a little ways as if over the side of a ship and threw up. Her mother said that throwing up when you were sick made you feel better, but she felt worse. She began to shiver. She wanted so many things which were impossibly distant: ice water, a pillow, a bed, her mother. She felt pains now that made her think of a voodoo doll with pins stuck into its stomach.

The sound of a screen-door slamming made her open her eyes. She realized then that the horse was no longer moving.

"Agnes? I was expecting you back for lunch."

It was Marjorie, with the house looming behind her. Quickly, while she had the chance, she slid down the horse's side and landed on her feet.

"Oh my God. What's happened to you? Oh, sweetheart—"

Her bare legs were covered in sticky brownish-red, her shorts were soaking wet, and looking up she saw the horse's white back spotted with the same stuff: blood. The horse hadn't managed to throw her, but he had damaged her in some terrible way, had wounded her, perhaps fatally. She burst into tears.

Marjorie's arms were around her. "Agnes. Sweetheart. Try to tell me what happened. Did you fall? Did you cut yourself? Did someone... Where does it hurt? What happened?"

They worked it out eventually, through tears and fear and confusion. She was not hurt; the blood signified no injury but womanhood. Agnes had gotten both her wishes.

Although her aunt and her mother were identical twins, Agnes had never had any trouble telling them apart. Yet throughout this crisis, Marjorie seemed so much like her mother that it made her uneasy.

Even her face, and the way she moved, seemed to change.

She hoped she wasn't trying to be Mary to make her feel better, but that was not something she could say, and it came between them.

After she'd had a bath she got into bed. She'd been too squeamish to attempt to use a Tampax—Leslie claimed her cousin had lost her virginity that way—so she'd improvised a thick padding of tissues in her underpants.

She ached all over, and had no idea if that was from horseback riding or if it was another nasty side-effect of the curse. "The curse" was what Leslie and her other friends at school all called it, although Marjorie objected.

"Think of it as a blessing. Think positively and you won't have any problems. I know it seems strange to you now, but it's a part of life—it's a sign of life, proof that you're a woman."

So now she was a woman—not like her aunt or her mother, of course, but like Leslie with her Mary Quant make-up and her crushes on high school boys, and Janis Reed who was allowed to go on dates, and Mary Kilmartin who stuffed her bra with toilet paper and flirted with Mr. Jameson, because he *blushed*, and with the new Spanish teacher because he was cute, and with the fat old bus driver just for practice.

Like it or not—and she didn't—she had become part of that merry scene.

And to think she had actually wished for it —

But she couldn't blame a wish. This wasn't magic, it was just life.

"I'd better get up to the store before it closes, and buy you some sanitary napkins," said Marjorie. "If you'll be all right on your own?"

"Sure," she said, annoyed. What had happened to the Marjorie who used to talk to her as to another adult?

"Would you like anything else? What would you like for dinner?"

"I don't care. I'm not hungry." As resentful as if the changes in her body had been engineered by her aunt, she turned her face to the wall. "That's right, get some sleep. I'll make something light, and you can have it whenever you want. I'll get a few things. I'll be as quick as I can."

She did sleep, without intending to. She slept for hours, and woke when the room was gray with dusk, feeling ravenous. She still ached, and the tissues between her legs were blood-soaked pulp. But by then her aunt had come back with a big blue box of sanitary napkins and something like a garter-belt to keep them on. After she'd cleaned herself up she had a peanut butter sandwich and a glass of apple juice and sat in the kitchen with her aunt, who kept smiling at her, her face changing from familiar to unknown and back again in the shadowy room.

She was eager to escape, and soon went back to bed. Marjorie had bought her a flashlight which she used to read *Agnes Grey* for a couple of hours. It was a comforting read; there were no surprises in it anymore, and yet, strangely, this time as she read it she felt she was understanding it in a way or on a level which had not been available to her before. It was a love story, of course. Now that she was a woman, what about love?

She put the book away, turned off the flashlight and put it within easy reach beside her glasses. Then she lay in the dark and thought about the boys at school, who were all horrible, except for Devon Baker who was shy and kind of sweet—"queer," said Leslie—and about the high school boys who seemed remote and rather frightening. She thought about Mr. Jameson, and the way his blue eyes sparkled, and the funny feeling she'd had once when he smiled at her. She thought about Paul McCartney and George Harrison. That was more like it. She was certain she could love—did love—both—either of them, but so what? So did millions of other girls. They had the whole world to choose from. They were Beatles. Even if they came to do a concert in Houston, even if some fateful chance brought her into their presence, why should they notice her out of all the other adoring young fans? She thought about the young poet, Graham Storey. He was English, too, with a Beatle-style haircut, but he was not a Beatle. Some chance might bring him to Texas, she might meet him by another chance and then, if she was lucky, he might fall in love with her. She fell asleep thinking about being in love with Graham Storey.

There was a man standing in the doorway, a more solid darkness in the dark.

Her heart lurched and the breath caught in her throat. She was awake enough to remember that she'd had this nightmare before. She only had to perform some action—opening her eyes, or sitting up in bed—to make him vanish.

Her eyes seemed to be open already, so she rolled on to her side and propped herself up on one elbow. The man was still there, and now she remembered that the door had been closed when she went to bed. It had been the sound of the door opening which had woken her. It wasn't a dream. The man who watched her was real.

She felt choked and cold, despite the stifling heat of the night. She tried to scream, but, just as in a bad dream, nothing came out but a tiny mewling squeak.

The noise was too small to carry to another room, but the stranger heard it and he moved, taking a couple of slow, shambling steps into her room and toward her. He had his hands out, pawing the air, groping for her. In a few seconds he would have her. She was trapped in the worst dream she'd ever had, and the fear she felt was paralyzing.

But she wasn't paralyzed, and before he reached her she moved, scooting away, off the other side of the bed, snatching up the flashlight and brandishing it like a weapon. He was between her and both doors.

Unless she wanted to go out one of the windows—which meant opening the screen and then a nine-foot drop to the ground—she would have to pass him. Thinking of the window (the screen would just require a push) as her secret plan made her more brave. She would, she decided, dazzle him with the flash-light, and while he was blinded she would rush past, calling for Marjorie as she went.

She switched on the light and gave a rebel yell. But when she saw him, the yell turned into a scream, and she was frozen to the spot, unable to look away. He was completely naked. Apart from a few brief guilty glimpses of her father when she was younger—now imperfectly remembered—she had never seen a naked man before, not even in a picture. Some black and white photographs of classical sculpture in a book treasured by Leslie's cousin were her only preparation, and that was no preparation at all.

She screamed again, and suddenly Marjorie was there.

"What's going on? You! Get out of here! You're not supposed to be here—go on, get out!"

She spoke to him as if he were a dog and, like a dog, he obeyed, lowering his head and hunching his shoulders against an expected blow as he turned and slouched away. He went out of the room and, after a moment, the back door opened and slammed shut.

Marjorie reached out and took the flashlight. "What were you doing?" Her voice was accusatory.

"Me! I was sleeping—I wasn't doing anything! I was asleep, and then that man came in—I was trying to get away from him. I thought he was going to kill me!"

"Don't be ridiculous. I suppose you were dreaming."

She almost choked on the unfairness of it. "Dreaming? What are you talking about? That wasn't a dream. *You* saw him—you told him to get out! And you talked to him like—you must know who he is."

Marjorie switched off the light. "Of course I know who he is. He's mine, and you don't have any right to him. He shouldn't have been here with you."

In the darkness, her aunt was suddenly a stranger, the note of accusation in her voice weirdly menacing. It reminded Agnes unpleasantly of certain occasions with her mother, of being guilty of nameless, unspecified crimes.

"Well I didn't want him in here! He nearly scared me to death."

"You must have wanted him. He doesn't go where he isn't wanted. You were probably dreaming. He felt the pull of your desire, and he came to you."

"Could we have the light on?"

"Why? What do you want to see?"

"I just don't like being in the dark."

"Nobody does."

Her aunt was starting to frighten her more than the man. She backed away until she felt the edge of the bed and sat down.

"How could I dream about somebody I'd never even seen before, never even knew existed? How could I want somebody I don't know? Who is he, anyway? What's the deal with him?"

"I don't mean you wanted him, specifically. Just that you were dreaming of a lover. Well, it's natural. You're not a child anymore, you're a woman, and women have desires...."

"Stop it! What difference does it make what I was dreaming, if I was dreaming—*he's* not a dream. You can't say that, you saw him—"

"He's something like a dream. I don't expect you to understand right now, but someday you will. I call him my pillow friend. He's a wish—my wish. I told you that wishes come true here—I think you know that's true. He exists because I want him to; he exists to satisfy desire. And although he's mine, the presence in the house of another desirous woman... confused him. But now that I know I can be on guard against it. It won't happen again; I won't let him go to you."

"That's the most horrible thing I've ever heard! You're sick—you must be sick if you think I would want for some horrible naked old man to come crawling into my bed at night! I don't want a lover—I don't want sex—I'm not a woman, I'm just a kid!"

"My dear, you protest too much. He knows what you want—that's all he knows. He responds to desire—that's all he can do. And your body knows, too, even if you'd rather think otherwise. Your body's betrayed you."

"I need to go to the bathroom. Can I have my light back please?"

In silence, her aunt handed her the torch.

She didn't see the pillow friend again during her visit but she heard him at night with Marjorie. That was the meaning of the sounds she heard, the heavy breathing and soft moans, the rhythmic creaking of bedsprings: that was not her aunt dreaming, as she had first thought; that was Marjorie having sex. The thought made her unpleasantly excited, and although she didn't want to think about it she couldn't seem to help herself recalling the male nakedness she had seen, trying to figure out how something like that would fit together with her body, and why such a coupling would be pleasant.

Maybe the curse was a blessing, in some ways: at least Marjorie didn't force her out of the house every morning. She could lie in bed as long as she liked, read all day indoors if she wanted. By the third day she had read six of the twelve books she had brought with her and was feeling overstuffed with words and restless. She wasn't bleeding anymore and she wanted to move. She missed her bicycle and the company of other children. She began to think about the horse, her horse, in a different way.

Yes, she had been frightened, but there had also been something wonderful in the connection between them, the power that carried her along in response to her unspoken wishes. She found herself recreating the ride in her mind, changing it so that the fear and discomfort vanished and it became purely exciting, like something she'd read about. She became different, too, the skillful rider of the horse, someone brave and free. On the day that she finally went out to look for him she even had a name for the horse: Snowy Miles. It made her think of that poem by Robert Frost which she'd memorized a couple of years ago, "Stopping by Woods on a Snowy Evening." He was white, too, as white as the snow she'd seen only once in her life.

He was waiting for her, just where she'd known he would be, a little ways into the woods, beside a fallen log. He tossed his head at the sight of her and whickered.

"Hiya, Snowy. Good boy." She'd brought him an apple. She stroked his neck while he munched it. Then she used the log to mount him and they rode away.

The long, hot days passed in a dreamy haze. She rode him

barebacked and barefoot and was soon more comfortable than she could have dreamed perched up so high, controlling his movements with a nudge of her heels in his sides, or a slap on his flank or neck. He was immensely sensitive and responsive to her, despite his great size, and as she came to appreciate how careful he was of her, she no longer feared falling off. He would not let her fall.

As they explored the area, keeping well away from the highway and Camptown itself, they never met anyone. Sometimes they would catch sight of a logging truck or hear men's voices, but no one ever saw them. Sometimes she would take a packed lunch and have a picnic on the shores of the pond, where she would swim and float for a long time, washing away the accumulated dirt and sweat of the morning and enjoying the beautiful silence. She swam naked rather than risk raising her aunt's suspicions by taking her bathing suit—that was something she had never done before, and it added to the illicit delight. It didn't take long to dry off when she emerged in the heat of the day. It was always hot; it never rained.

Marjorie never asked what she did with herself all day and Agnes didn't tell her. Neither of them ever mentioned the horse or the pond. In the evenings, after dinner, they fell into a quiet routine. After the dishes were done they would sit out on the front porch with their books and a hurricane lamp to read by. Marjorie would have her glass of wine; Agnes drank warm Dr. Pepper or RC Cola. Sometimes Marjorie read aloud. It was always poetry. There were poems by T.S. Eliot, Emily Dickinson, Gerard Manly Hopkins, Wallace Stevens, D.H. Lawrence, Marianne Moore, W. B. Yeats. Often she did not understand what she was hearing, but still she was moved by the sound of the words. The horse and the pillow friend had come between them, but poetry drew them back together. Gazing at that familiar face in the lamplight while the magical words spiraled up and around them like scented smoke in the warm, dark air, she was possessed by longing, almost overwhelmed with love for this woman who was so close to her and so far away.

She wished that this was her life, that it would go on forever, but of course it was nearly over. On her last day she thought her heart would break when she said goodbye to Snowy. She had lain awake for hours the night before, fingers in her ears to block out the sounds from the next room, while she tried to think up a way around it. But even if she could make up some convincing story as to how she'd found him, even if she could convince her parents that he was her horse and talk them into financing his keep at a local stables—both tall orders—she couldn't believe it would work. She couldn't imagine Snowy with a saddle on his back, a bit in his mouth, the prosaic business of exercising him in some paddock or on a trail-ride through Memorial Park with a bunch of other kids and their ponies. They belonged to each other and always would, but he wouldn't fit into her real world of school and parents, carpools and scheduled visits. He belonged here in the country, in the shadowy woodlands where she could only be a temporary visitor. After their last ride together she tried to think of some way of explaining herself, realized that she couldn't and, praying that he would understand this as he had seemed to understand everything else about her, she kissed him, slapped him sharply on the flank, and then ran away. Head down, half-blinded by her tears, she ran until she collided finally with her aunt.

"There you are! I was beginning to think you might miss your bus. We have to walk into Camptown, you know. I've packed your things—what's wrong? Why are you crying?"

"Oh, please, I don't want to go. Please, won't you let me stay here? I won't get in your way, honestly I won't. I'll be out every day, just like before, and I'll help with the housework, I won't be any trouble, I could go in to school on the bus, just like you and Mother used to and—"

"Don't be ridiculous. Of course you can't stay here. You're going home where you belong. What's gotten into you?"

"Please. Just another week, then, let me stay another week—"

"Stop it. Just stop it. I don't have time for this. Run on in and wash your face and use the toilet if you have to and then we're off. You're not going to miss that bus. Not after what I promised your mother."

So she went back to Houston—what else could she do? It was just getting dark when she arrived, and at first when she stepped off the bus she could not see anyone she knew in the crowds. Then her father stepped forward and gave her a smile that looked like it had been borrowed from somebody else.

"Where's Mother?"

"What kind of greeting is that for your father? Don't I count?"

"Of course—I was just—"

"I thought I'd take you out to dinner. What would you like—barbecue or barbecue?"

Barbecue was always their special treat, just the girls and their father because their mother didn't like it. He took her to his favorite place, a few blocks from the bus station. The air was tangy, rich enough to eat, and the sliced beef sandwiches, the potato salad and pickles were as good as ever, but she didn't enjoy herself. It wasn't just that she was mourning the loss of Snowy Miles—and Marjorie, who had refused to make any promises or predictions about when she'd see her again—it was her father's attitude. He was unlike himself, remote and uncommunicative. He would reply if she asked him a direct question but otherwise he said nothing. She remembered how just before she had gone away he had seemed to avoid her, but this was worse. He didn't avoid her eyes now as he had then, but when her eyes met his there was no contact, no communication, nothing there.

Although she'd lost her appetite she wolfed the sandwich down and drained her glass of iced tea, eager to get home, back to her mother, to something like normality.

But her mother wasn't home when they got there.

"Where is she?"

"She's probably on her way." He sounded unconcerned.

"But where...?"

"Maybe you should ask her that." His voice was even, uninflected, unemotional as it had been all evening, yet she heard something horribly grim and final in it. She suddenly didn't want to ask him anything more, and escaped upstairs to her room. When she had unpacked and put everything away, she stretched out across her bed with a book and sometime while she was reading, half-listening for the sound of her mother's return, she must have fallen asleep.

When she awoke the next morning her mother was there but her father wasn't. There might not have been anything unusual about that—even though her mother spent the day in her room with the curtains drawn—except that he didn't come home that evening, or any other.

He had moved out, into an apartment he must have rented while she was gone. He had already taken all his clothes, his collection of Texana, his leather recliner and a few other things he cared about—if she hadn't gone straight up to her room she might have noticed the things that were missing earlier—but what difference would that have made? He hadn't even taken the opportunity of his time alone with her to explain what he was doing, or why; to assure her that he still loved her and wanted to spend time with her; he hadn't said, like the father in a book she'd recently read, that he wasn't leaving her but only his wife—no, he had left them both, and if there was an explanation for why he'd gone she never heard it.

In the midst of the nightmare, while her mother was still alternately hysterical or heavily tranquilized, either making frantic plans for her new life or lying weeping in bed for hours, school started, and Agnes found it a relief to get away. But there was no escape.

Everyone at school seemed to know something about it, or wanted to, and she wasn't sure whether the questions or the sympathy were more annoying. Then came something worse: Nina told her that she'd seen her father strolling along holding hands with some girl out at Northwest Mall. After that she didn't feel much like talking to Nina.

She wished she could just forget it. She wished it had never happened. But wishing changed nothing.

One morning, instead of getting on the school bus, she took the city bus instead, and went downtown to the bus station. She had most of her summer's allowance still unspent, as well as the twenty dollar bill her father had tucked into her book-bag some time before. It was far more than she needed for a one-way ticket to Camptown.

At the place in the woods where the dirt road split in two, one path leading to the house and one to the pond, the horse met her.

She felt fear at the sight of him, and then remorse. He'd gotten so thin! His ribs showed, his blood-shot blue eyes bulged from a long, bony skull, and his mane and tail were matted with burrs. He was the very picture of a neglected animal, and it was her fault, she knew, for abandoning him.

But that didn't make sense. Before, he had always looked well-groomed, well-fed—but *she* had not fed or groomed him—apart from picking occasional burrs out of his tail. She had given him apples and carrots to munch and once they had shared a box of vanilla wafers, but apart from that he must have survived on the grass and weeds he cropped everywhere they went. Not until now had she wondered where he went when he wasn't with her, where he sheltered at night. Not until now had it occurred to her that he might need food and shelter and that there was no one else to take responsibility for him but herself.

Easy tears sprang to her eyes. How could she have been so horrible?

People who abandoned their pets, the helpless animals dependent on them, were the blackest of villains. She had never imagined she could be one of them. She hadn't thought, and that was her crime. She had wished without thinking, without understanding or accepting the consequences.

Marjorie had warned her.

But she'd come back. This time she would not let him down.

"Oh, Snowy, I've missed you so much!" She threw her arms around his neck and inhaled the dusty, salty, horsy smell of him, felt the muscles trembling beneath the skin, heard him snort, and knew beyond a doubt that he had missed her, too. Maybe it wasn't a warm stable, a pile of hay and a curry-comb that he needed but only her presence to make him sleek and contented again. He was her wish... so what was she to him? Was she his creator, his god? It was a troubling thought, and rather than pursue it, she went with the horse to a nearby tree-stump where she could mount him.

Immediately he took off running, flinging her forward onto his neck. But although she clung to him, frightened, for a moment, she soon found her seat, and the glory of his speed, his power between her legs, lifted her out of fear and worry and everything else. There was nothing but this moment, the wind drying the sweat on her face, the sunlight hot on her bare arms, the dusty, resinous smell of the woods and the all-encompassing rhythm of his gallop bearing her along, taking her out of herself, melding them into one creature, at one with the natural world around them.

Although it seemed that he ran for a very long time, eventually they ended up, as they always did, at the edge of the pond. When he put his head down and began cropping the grass she slipped to the ground. She was hungry, too, but she had brought nothing to eat. She had expected to have lunch with Marjorie. Yet now when she thought of confronting her aunt her mouth went dry. Her aunt wasn't going to let her stay; the fact that her parents had split up might win her a little sympathy, but not enough. Marjorie didn't want the responsibility—she'd made that clear enough. She'd send her straight back to Houston.

She stripped off her clothes and walked down to the water's edge. It was deliciously cool as she waded in, especially where the bottom dropped away and she had to swim. For a little while she could enjoy herself in the water and not think, but eventually, as she lazily dog-paddled, her eyes fell on Snowy Miles and the anxious guilt returned.

She couldn't just leave him here a second time; she would not. He might die over the winter without her. She wondered how long it would take to ride him to Houston—a couple of days? Three? She wondered where they would stay at night, and how she would manage to find her way home through the strange, traffic-filled streets once she reached Houston city limits. And then what would her mother say when she turned up with a horse? She'd probably have a fit. She'd never let her keep him. But she had to. She had to make her mother understand....

She rolled onto her back and floated, staring up at the empty blue sky. She didn't want to think about all that, about how she was going to explain the inexplicable, how this horse might be incorporated into her new, fatherless life. If her parents really got divorced, they might be poor. There wouldn't be any money for extras like stabling a horse. How could she make her mother understand that Snowy wasn't an extra, wasn't a luxury, but a necessity, her responsibility? She wished she could just stay here. She didn't want to take Snowy into her own unhappy, complicated world, but to stay here with him in his. To extend those few summer weeks into a lifetime of riding through the woods in silent communion. Her idea of perfection.

So why shouldn't she wish for it? It was what she really wanted, more than anything else in the world, so it had to come true. At first her thoughts were chaotic, trying to marshal an argument, trying to think of all the little wishes she would have to make to build the edifice of the world she wanted, and then she decided not to bother. Snowy had come in answer to her wish without any logic to his appearance, so why shouldn't her life change just as simply?

"I wish I could be with Snowy forever," she said to the blue sky above. "I wish I never had to go back to Houston but could just stay in the woods with Snowy forever." It was so like a prayer she had to put her lips together quickly to keep from saying "Amen."

There was a muffled thudding sound. She performed a quick half-roll that brought her upright, treading water and facing the shore. The horse was no longer peacefully grazing. He was running straight at the pond, right for her.

She stared, mystified, half-expecting him to perform some trick for her. When he plunged into the water she still didn't understand—she remembered one especially hot day when she had tried to lure him in, using an apple as bait, and how he'd made it clear to her that he had no liking for bodies of water, no matter how shallow. It was only when he drew closer, and she could see from the way he strained to keep his head above water, from his rolling, bloodshot eyes, how much he disliked this, how much it went against his nature, that she glimpsed the truth. And when he still kept coming straight at her, making no attempt to turn aside, his powerful hooves lashing out directly at her, she knew that he was coming to kill her. Not because he was evil or hated her, but because it was her wish. He would kill her and die himself, and they would be together forever.

She tried to swim backward, tried to swim away, but fear and the water together strait-jacketed her. Or maybe it was her own wish which kept her bound and struggling before his approach.

"No," she screamed with all her might. "No! I wish *you* were gone, not me, not me!" And then, as he was nearly on top of her, she managed to plunge to one side and swim a little away from him.

She felt something, a heavy blow, a pain in her heart that took her breath away, but somehow managed to keep swimming, and she swam without looking back until her knees sank into the mud and she couldn't swim any farther, until she was crawling and stumbling ashore.

Only then, on dry land, did she risk pausing to cast a glance back over her shoulder. Then she turned around and stared.

The pond was empty. Empty and, on this hot, windless day, as still as if its waters had not been disturbed by anything for days. With its empty, quiet, glassy sheen it was a perfect mirror of the sky.

She began to cry. Only when her lungs ached as she struggled to draw breath did she become aware of another, worse, pain, and looking down at herself she saw the mark on her naked chest. It was on the left side, between shoulder and nipple, a reddish contusion, horse-shoe shaped.

PART THREE

IMAGINARY MEAT

"I go; but remember, I shall be with you on your wedding night."

—Mary Shelley

"*Jeder Engel ist schrecklich.*"

The words lifted her out of her seat; she quivered and was still, shocked awake and throbbing with attention.

The dull honors presentations, the students with their stumbling or fluent readings of English, French and Spanish texts, had nearly sent her to sleep. Roxanne, seated beside her in the warm, dark auditorium, had run out of caustic comments, and not even the faint hope of hearing her own name called for some unimagined achievement (most original book report? best poem to be rejected by the school magazine?) was enough to keep her focused in the present, until those words, the familiar, foreign words that opened Rilke's Second Elegy. She stared at the boy on the stage as if he were the poet reincarnate.

The boy's name was Alex Hill. He'd been in her social studies class last year, and he was assistant poetry editor—the position she had applied for, not realizing then that only students in the Special Progress English stream ever made the staff—on *Visions*, the school magazine. She had been aware of him without any particular feelings: he was just another "good" boy, tall and skinny and bespectacled (like herself), nonathletic, nonpolitical, studious.

And he liked Rilke. He'd actually chosen to translate one of the Elegies, and he'd won this year's German prize for it—he wasn't even a senior, just a junior like herself.

As she stared the stage lights combined with smears on her glasses to give him a halo. He looked as glorious and terrible to her as the poet's angel.

It had finally happened. One week shy of her seventeenth birthday, she had fallen in love.

She sought him out at lunchtime to tell him his translation had been brilliant and his prize well-deserved.

He looked apprehensive, as if he was waiting for the stinger to her compliment.

"I mean it," she said earnestly. "Believe me, I've read all the translations there are, and even tried to work out one of my own—hopeless, of course!—so I know what I'm saying."

"Well, thank you, uh—"

"Call me Grey. It's Agnes, actually, Agnes Grey."

"Sure, right, I remember. You were there that night we collated *Visions*. But you're not in my German class—you must be in Biedermann's?"

"I'm not taking German. I wish I was, now, but I've been doing Spanish since junior high and if I switch it'll just screw up the language credits I need. I'm not very good at learning languages, but I thought I might try German when I get to college."

Bushy eyebrows moved together above the horn-rims. "So if you're not taking German..."

"Oh, I read the Elegies on my own! In English, of course, but it was a dual-language version, and then I found another translation and, well, with the differences, I really wanted to read him in the original. He's such a *German* poet, don't you think? To try to understand him. So I got a German dictionary, and read everything I could find about Rilke and the poems, and—oh, I'm sorry, I'm keeping you from eating!"

"That's all right. I'd say sit down, but—" He gestured at the table she was leaning on, which was full. One of the other boys, a heavy-set blonde, had obviously been listening to their conversation, and his interested gaze made her abruptly self-conscious.

She straightened up. "Oh, that's all right. I haven't got my food yet, anyway. And my friend always saves me a seat. I just wanted to say congratulations you deserved it and I really loved your reading, and all that." She gave him a little wave and wandered off to get in the line for food even though, for once, she had no appetite.

The next time Alex saw her, passing her in the hall at the end of the day, he smiled and said her name.

She felt as if he'd blown up a balloon full of happiness and she'd swallowed it. She felt as if she could fly away, and even just the memory of his smile would keep her from coming back to earth for a long, long time.

Roxanne drove her home from school that day, as she often did, and noticed her friend's unusually buoyant mood, but was willing to accept that it was a natural reaction to the fact that her seventeenth birthday was on the immediate horizon, and after that, only a week of school stood between them and the freedom of summer vacation.

Agnes generally kept her friend well-informed about her emotional landscape, but she didn't feel like talking about Alex Hill just yet. She wanted to luxuriate in the experience of being in love by herself for just a little longer. She wasn't ready to hear why he wasn't good enough for her, or that he already had a girlfriend; she wasn't ready for plotting ways of "getting him." For the moment, anyway, the feeling was enough.

So she didn't invite Roxanne in to talk—they both had exams to study for—but waved goodbye to her in the parking lot, then walked around past the small, kidney-bean-shaped swimming pool and let herself in to the apartment she shared with her mother.

For the past three years, since her parents' divorce, this two-bedroom, two-story apartment in a small complex off Westheimer, near Post Oak, had been home. Although she didn't think her mother believed her, she really preferred it to their old house. She loved that her bedroom had a telephone jack and a balcony overlooking the swimming pool. She loved the swimming pool; she didn't miss the loss of their country club membership at all. And they were now within easy walking distance of a shopping center. It wasn't the mall where a lot of the kids she knew liked to hang out, but it had a drugstore with a soda fountain, a Mexican restaurant, and a record store, and she and Roxanne met there several times a week.

Really, she didn't miss anything about the old house, her old life, except her father. She missed him a lot; she always would. At least, she missed the person he had been.

The person he was now didn't seem to love her anymore.

Now that he had remarried and moved to Dallas she hadn't seen him for a whole year. She didn't know if he ever even thought about her now.

If her father had become a different person, so had her mother, but with her mother the change was for the better. Once she got over the initial trauma of it, her husband's desertion had galvanized her. There were no more days spent languishing in bed in a darkened room, no more blank, icy moods that lasted for days, no more fantasies about her great acting career. Instead, Mary Grey woke up and, with no one else to do it for her, took control of her own life. She got a sales job at Sakowitz, she made new friends, and she became much closer to her youngest daughter. The twins had their own lives up in Austin; it was just the two of them now.

But lately that closeness had started to itch. Maybe because she no longer had to fear her mother's icy withdrawals she dared to disagree with her. Maybe because as she was growing up she was discovering that her mother could be wrong about things, they argued all the time. They sniped at each other, and picked and criticized every trivial detail. Mary objected to her daughter's unkempt appearance, to her refusal to wear make-up, to the "Sisterhood is Powerful" button on the strap of her denim shoulder-bag.

"You'll never get a boyfriend if you carry on like that! You need to look softer, more feminine, you need to make a little effort. If you're determined to stick with those glasses, then at least you could do something about your hair." Mary's most recent attack had been only that morning, over breakfast.

There was no point in pretending she wasn't interested in a boyfriend; her mother knew better. "You're saying I should trick some boy into liking me? What's the point of that? I want somebody I can talk to, as an equal; I don't want a boyfriend who sees me as a sex object."

"*Sex object*? What kind of talk is that?"

"If you'd read some of those books I gave you—"

"No thank you. Feminism is for women who don't like men, or who can't attract them."

"Oh! That is so ridiculous!" She jumped up from the table and carried her half-full cereal bowl to the sink. "If you would just read what Simone de Beauvoir or Germaine Greer—God, you can't call Germaine Greer unattractive to men, you really can't!"

"Who?"

"I gave you her book. *The Female Eunuch*."

She sighed. "Agnes, I'm really not interested."

"I know you're not, but I don't understand why. You're a working woman, you must have faced discrimination, prejudice—don't you care?"

"We're not talking about me, we're talking about you and why you want a reputation as a man-hater when you're desperate for a boyfriend."

"I'm not desperate; there are guys I could go out with if I was desperate. If I was desperate, maybe I would paint myself up and pretend I was a pea-brain, but I'm not, so I don't." Her face felt very hot. "Anyway, if having a boyfriend is this big thing, where's yours?"

She saw the flicker—not as pronounced as a flinch, but it was there, a guilty flicker in her eyes—and then her mother got up from the table, smoothing her hair and her skirt, moving away, saying, "I'm going to be late if I don't get moving, and you—"

"Do you have a boyfriend?"

"I think that asking a forty-two-year-old woman about a boyfriend—"

"A lover, then. Do you have a lover?"

"That's enough."

"Are you seeing somebody? Are you dating? Don't I have a right to know?"

Her mother gave her what was meant to be, or to appear to be, a frank and open look. "If it affects you, then of course I'll tell you. I'm not going to check it out with you every time a man asks me out to dinner. Of course I'm dating. I'd be happier if you were, too. Now I really have to go."

As soon as her mother had left she'd gone straight to her bathroom, and there in the medicine cabinet was the evidence, the little gray rectangle bubble-pack of Norinyl, the pills as small as saccharine tablets, three gone. Her mother was on the Pill. Her mother either had a lover, or expected to have one.

She'd been almost desperate to share this shocking information with Roxanne, to explore her feelings about it, but there had been no time before school, and then the sight of Alex Hill limned in light, his soft, rather hesitant voice reading the Second Elegy, had simply knocked it all out of her head.

The memory of that morning's discovery was waiting for her when she got home, but its sharp colors had faded, it was something to do with her mother, not herself. She'd rather think about Alex than worry about her mother's sex life.

She got a Dr. Pepper from the refrigerator and took it up to her bedroom. There, she opened the doors to the balcony, put Leonard Cohen's "Songs from a Room" on her record-player, and stretched across her bed with *The Duino Elegies*. Between rereadings of the familiar lines she would sip her cold drink and gaze out through green leaves at the glittering blue water of the swimming pool, and every now and then the memory of Alex would make her shiver and smile. Oh Alex, Oh Angel.

He was her companion all that summer, her invisible friend. She shared the highs and lows of her life with him—another poem back with a form rejection slip from *The New Yorker*; her letter about women's liberation published in *The Houston Post*; another argument with her mother; her feelings on reading *The Magus* and the day she found, and bought, Graham Storey's first poetry collection, a narrow hardbacked volume with a dark green jacket called *The Memory of Trees*. This Alex in her mind received many of the same confidences as did Roxanne. He knew about Roxanne, but Roxanne still didn't know about him. But how could she tell her—what was there to tell? She knew perfectly well that her Alex was a fantasy, and as the weeks of summer wore on without so much as a glimpse of the real boy, the lover inside her head became ever more fabulous a creature, part Rilke, part Nicholas Urfe, part Graham Storey. The back-cover photograph of Graham Storey almost obliterated her memory of Alex's own face, and in her head he spoke with a slight but perceptible English accent.

It was a shock when September finally rolled around—still as hot as August—and school started, and she saw the real Alex Hill. She had known it would be a shock; what surprised her was that as she approached him in the hall on the first day of school he looked at her, saw her, smiled a bit tentatively, and said, in his soft, Texas voice, "Hello, Agnes."

Her heart lifted and swelled, the ground fell away beneath her feet, and she floated blissfully through the crowded, noisy hall, knowing that it was true, it was just like the songs and the poems had promised, she was really in love. He had remembered her name!

A little later her excitement increased when she discovered that he was in her English class. Or, it might have been more accurate to say, she was in his. He'd been in the Special Progress stream, like most of the other kids there; she'd only been transferred into Miss Beadle's class after a year of being at the top of Mrs. Parker's class—and bored out of her mind. No more sentence diagrams! No more reciting grammatical rules by rote! It would be literature all the way, and maybe a chance of getting something published in the school magazine, sponsored by Miss Beadle. Yet all of that sank into insignificance beside the sheer joy of being able to sit next to Alex Hill for fifty-five minutes every school day.

At first, just being in his presence was enough to make her happy. But love is demanding, and by the second week of school she was beginning to pine, yearning for more. She decided to confide in Roxanne.

Roxanne had been her friend for a little less than two years. Before that, she'd been aware of her as an exotic figure, a member of the drama club who dressed flamboyantly, wearing a black cape and black leather boots whenever the weather gave her the slightest opportunity. Agnes hadn't imagined they had anything in common until the day they met in the Paperback Exchange. She was in the science fiction section looking at a novel by Philip K. Dick, when she heard a voice cry, "Oh, *The Eye in the Sky*! I don't have that one—oh, you're not going to buy that one are you?"

Agnes had looked around and been astonished. A girl! Someone she recognized from school! "You read science fiction?"

"Well, of course I do! It's the most interesting stuff around! Have you read Delany? Ellison? You must have read *Dangerous Visions*?"

It was a revelation to Agnes, who had never met anyone who read science fiction, and only saw teenage boys buying it. Roxanne had been turned on to it, she said, by her boyfriend, a student at Rice University: "All the guys there read SF. So, who've you read? What do you like?"

They had started talking then and had scarcely stopped since.

Agnes had been bowled over by her, charmed by her, bewildered by her, and reminded a little of her Aunt Marjorie, someone she hadn't seen or heard from since the summer her father had left. On the day that she'd run away from Houston, she'd found the house in the woods locked and empty—even a new padlock on the cellar door. She hadn't dared try to break in, so she had hiked back to Camptown and then, when she found there wouldn't be another bus until the next day, called her mother. From that day on, Marjorie's name was not to be mentioned. She had tried writing to her aunt, care of the Camptown post office, but the letter came back: "NOT KNOWN."

She had told Roxanne about Marjorie in the first few days of their friendship. It was somehow very easy to tell Roxanne things she'd never told anyone before. Roxanne's parents were divorced—she lived with her father, her mother having gone to San Francisco to find herself—so she understood about losing a parent; and she believed in magic.

"There's someone I like," Agnes said solemnly that day after school as soon as they were in Roxanne's car and moving. "A boy."

Roxanne slammed on the brakes and gave a rebel yell.

Behind them, other people were trying to get out of the parking lot. A boy in a convertible honked his horn.

"So who is this paragon of animals?"

"Um... aren't you going to drive?"

"Not until I know his name! God, this is too exciting! How can I concentrate on driving when you hit me with something like that?"

"If you don't drive, those kids back there are going to lynch you. I'll tell you everything, just keep moving."

Roxanne's eyes were hidden by her sunglasses, but wickedness was evident in the set of her full lips. Agnes was afraid for a moment that she would simply, stubbornly refuse to drive on until she'd heard every detail, even if a full-scale riot was going on around her gold Camero. Then she took her foot off the brake and they shot forward out of the parking lot and into the moving stream of traffic on the street, miraculously without collision.

"We'll go to my place, yeah? Then you won't have to leave out any of the gory details just because your Mom comes in."

"There aren't any gory details. Nothing's happened yet."

"Only in your head."

"Well, there, yes. There."

Roxanne lived in a condo with her father. Agnes had never even heard of a condo before meeting her friend, and even now, after numerous visits, she didn't know what the word meant. It seemed to be a rich people's version of apartment, the way that "townhouse" was a fancy word for duplex. Anyway, Roxanne's condo was a big, six-room apartment in a high-rise on Woodway, with a view of the tops of a lot of pine trees. She had her own telephone, her own television and stereo system, and a fake tiger-skin rug thrown across the satin sheets of the four-poster bed where they now sprawled with their Dr. Peppers and a box of Mr. Salty pretzels. Joni Mitchell provided the background music.

Agnes felt exhausted. She had told everything, there was nothing left to tell, and now she began to feel anxious. Maybe she should have kept it to herself. She looked at her friend who was looking at the picture of Alex Hill in last year's Annual. It wasn't a flattering picture.

"Poetry editor of *Visions*. Figures. I mean, perfect for you. So does he write poetry, too?"

"I don't know. Oh, Roxanne, how can I make him like me?"

"You don't have to make him like you. You just have to make him notice you. He'll like you, I promise. How could he not like you?"

"So how do I make him notice me? I mean, there I am, I've noticed him, and I'm right there next to him in English class, I always sit next to him—it's not assigned seats but people tend to chose a seat at the beginning and stick with it—and I talk to him, he knows my name, he says hello, sometimes when he sees me in the hall or outside he smiles...." she sighed with longing.

"Ask him out."

"I couldn't!"

"And you call yourself a liberated woman."

"I do not. Liberation is a process, not an achievement, and no woman will be truly liberated—"

"—until the destruction of the patriarchal system which oppresses all our sisters. Yeah, yeah, I know all that, the point is revolution now and the personal is political, and why should you wait for him to make the first move?"

They had discussed it all in theory and were agreed that the old-fashioned dating system which prevailed at their school was unfair to both boys and girls. But it could be a long leap from theory to practice.

"I've asked guys out," said Roxanne.

"Not at our school."

"Only because I'm not interested in anybody there. You are, so why shouldn't you ask him out? Come on, Grey!"

"What if he doesn't like—what if he's old-fashioned?"

"Then you don't want him."

She felt a pain in her chest. "But I do. I do. I do want him."

They stared at each other in silence for awhile. "Poor baby," said Roxanne softly. Then, firmly, "But you're going to have to do it, you know. It's the only way."

"Just, like, 'Want to go see a movie on Friday night?' Like that? I couldn't."

"Why not? Boys do it all the time. You think they like risking being turned down?" Then Roxanne straightened up and pushed a curly mass of hair away from her face. Her dark eyes gleamed. "Sadie Hawkins. You can ask him to the Sadie Hawkins dance. Girls have to ask the boys to that, and it doesn't have to mean anything—perfect."

It was perfect. The annual Sadie Hawkins dance, named after the institution of Sadie Hawkins Day in the "L'il Abner" comic strip, was one of their high school's traditional events. It was held every October in the gym, and it was informal, based on the idea of a barn-dance or a hill-billy hoedown. Nobody dressed up; girls could wear either skirts or jeans.

"Perfect."

"Call him now. Use my phone."

"Oh, no, there's loads of time—"

"Yeah, loads of time for some other girl to get to him first. Let me find that directory...."

She had long ago memorized his telephone number, but she didn't say so. "Chicken," said Roxanne, thrusting the school directory at her.

She remembered phone calls made long ago to please her pillow friend. Numbers dialed at random. "*Do you know where your children are?*" then hanging up. She dialed his number.

"Alex?"

"Yeah."

"This is Agnes Grey, you know, from English class?" Immediately she felt stupid for identifying herself like that. She stared down at the orange and black of the bed to keep from meeting Roxanne's eye.

"Oh. Yeah. What do you want?"

I wanted you to love me, but obviously you don't. A line from Gerard Manly Hopkins came into her head, summing up her feelings. *No worst, there is none*. But it was too late to hang up now.

"Well, actually, I wanted to ask you to go to the Sadie Hawkins Dance." She closed her eyes.

"Oh. Oh, God, I'm sorry. I must have sounded so rude. I didn't mean to, it's just, it's a bad time, when the phone rang my Dad was just yelling—we were having a fight—but you don't want to hear about that, I'm sorry, that's all. I didn't mean to bark at you. Yes, thank you, I'd like to go to the dance with you."

It took her a little while, through the welter of "sorries," to understand that he had agreed. "He said yes." She fell back against the pillows after hanging up.

"Of course he did! I told you it'd be easy."

"Oh, Rox... " It struck her suddenly that this, her first victory, might be her last; certainly it was the only easy one. Now she had to go out with him, get to know him, let him get to know her, trying all the while to present to him the image, the persona, of someone he could like, someone he might love—it was impossibly daunting. "Remember you told me about a book you got in New Orleans, with love charms and a recipe for a love potion?"

Roxanne stared at her as if she'd said something genuinely crazy. "You don't need a love potion. You got a date with the guy; now just let things happen."

"But what if they don't happen? What if he doesn't like me?"

"Well, maybe you won't like him, either."

"I love him."

"No you don't. You don't even know him. You're attracted to him. You won't know what you really feel about him until you get to know him."

"Will you quit talking like somebody's mother? I know what I feel! I want him. And if he doesn't want me back, I don't know what I'll do."

"You've already done it. You've let him know you're interested. Now it's his move and believe me, Grey, he will make a move. I know you think he's hot stuff, but what are you, chopped liver? You're cute and funny and smart; he'd have to be crazy not to notice. Just let him make his move. If he's got anything on the ball he won't wait long."

Roxanne was right. The next day before English class, just after she said hello, he told her he had two tickets to the Rice football game on Saturday, and would she like to go with him?

"Would I?" She grinned hugely at her own words. "Would I! Do you know that joke?"

He shook his head, smiling slightly but looking worried.

"Well, there's this girl who has a harelip and she's terribly insecure about her looks, and she's never had a date. So one night she goes along to a dance by herself, and this guy starts talking to her. She thinks he's wonderfully good-looking and can't believe her luck. Now, as it happens, this guy actually has only one eye, and he's pretty poor so the best he could do for a replacement eye was to make one out of wood and paint it. But it looks pretty good, and this girl doesn't notice a thing, she thinks he has two beautiful sparkling blue eyes—but he's real self-conscious and can't believe she's not staring at it. But after awhile he thinks this girl—who is rather attractive except for her mouth, and who seems very nice—either hasn't noticed or genuinely doesn't care, so he asks her to dance. And she's so amazed that this handsome guy should want to dance with her, who's never had a boyfriend in her life, that all she can manage when he says, "Would you like to dance?" is to stammer gratefully, "Oh, would I! Would I!" So the guy hauls himself up, really affronted, and snaps back in her face: "Harelip! Harelip!"

Alex gave a snorting laugh, unexpectedly loud, and, gratified by her success, she laughed, too.

"How nice to hear you enjoying yourselves," said Miss Beadle from the front of the room. "Miss Grey. Mr. Hill. If you wouldn't mind giving me your attention now, we can begin today's class."

She had less than no interest in football but she was too pleased by the invitation to care where they were going. On Saturday morning, as she waited for him to arrive, she thought more about what they would do after the game, where they would go, what they would talk about. She wondered if he would kiss her, and then immediately tried not to think about it, crossing her fingers against the jinx. She had been kissed before, but had responded more from curiosity than desire. She had never wanted to kiss anyone the way she wanted to kiss Alex. All summer long she had dreamed about it. Her own desire frightened her a little, making her think about what Marjorie had said about wishes, and what she had learned about how they could backfire.

Her mother kept breaking in on her thoughts with unwelcome advice.

"I don't wear make-up. I'm not going to suddenly start now."

"Why don't you wear something a little more—"

"Nobody dresses up for a football game!"

"I wasn't going to suggest a formal. But that top you're wearing isn't the most flattering thing in the world. What about that little pink blouse?"

"I'm wearing this."

"You could do something different with your hair; do you want me to help you put it up?"

She had already rejected Roxanne's offer to help her with hair and make-up; this pressure now from her mother was intolerable.

"Just leave me alone, would you? I'm going like this. I don't need any help getting dressed, thank you."

"Are you going to wear one of your 'Equality NOW' buttons? Do you want him to think of you as just one of the boys? Is that what you want?"

"No I don't. I'm not a boy. But I'm not just a girl, either—I don't want him to see me as just a girl. I want him to see who I really am. I want him to know me, and not play silly games with make-up and high heels and acting helpless and flirting... pretending...."

"Then what are you doing going out on this date with him, pretending you have the slightest interest in football? Isn't that pretending?"

She felt hot and itchy, caught out, and hated having her own deep discomfort so quickly uncovered by her mother. "He's not exactly the world's biggest fan. It's just something to do, somewhere to go and sit outside and eat hot dogs. Look, it's my business, all right? Aren't you going somewhere? Don't you have shopping to do?"

"It'll wait," said her mother with a self-satisfied smile. "I want to meet your young man."

Agnes went and locked herself into her own bathroom. Then, because she couldn't bear to look at herself—her plain, round, bespectacled face, her plain straight brown hair—she sat down on the closed seat of the toilet and put her head in her hands, leaning over like someone afraid of fainting. She was doing this all wrong. She should have taken Roxanne's advice and her mother's, bought contact lenses and a new pants-suit, let her friend paint her face, learn to flirt—either go the whole way into it, or stick to her revulsion against dating and the high school social scene. Why had she let Roxanne talk her into this? Why had she asked Alex to the dance? She didn't want to date him. She didn't want that awkwardness between them. She wanted him, simply, in love with her. She wanted something dramatic to happen, the way it did on television, throwing them together.

Trapped in a basement while a hurricane roared outside, or taken hostage by gunmen, their bus hijacked—there could be other people around, that was all right, but in adversity they would find themselves drawn together. They would realize they loved each other, there would be no need for words. She'd imagined so many ways it might happen, but she hadn't had the patience to wait and let fate throw them together.

Her mother knocked at the door. "He's here."

Something like stage-fright made her stomach lurch. She got up like somebody else, without even thinking about what she would say, and went downstairs to greet Alex.

It all went smoothly enough. Her mother was friendly but not intrusively so, and said nothing embarrassing. Alex declined a soft drink, and they were outside in under five minutes.

He apologized for the car, a battered white station wagon which smelled ripely of dog.

"You have a lot of dogs?"

"They're my mother's—so's the car. She collects waifs and strays."

"Don't you like dogs?"

"Not really. They're so, so *doggy*, the way they stare at you with their big brown eyes, willing you to love them, and loving you no matter what you do."

She thought, sickly, of her own doggy eyes, always turned his way, trying to compel his love. "I would be your spaniel," she said sadly.

"What?"

"It's a line from a play. I think that's right. From *Women Beware Women*. I think. I didn't memorize it, it just came into my head. Doesn't it happen like that to you? You read something and then bits of it just stick and turn up in your head, not when they're useful, but like dog-hairs stuck to your clothes."

"I've always got dog-hairs on my clothes. You will, too, after riding in this car. I'm sorry."

"It's all right. I don't mind. They're just ordinary clothes." She looked out the window while he drove in silence. The route they were traveling was the same one she traveled most days to school, so nothing she saw surprised her. The only surprising thing was that she was in a car with Alex Hill. Maybe someday that would seem as ordinary as sitting beside Roxanne.

"So, you like football?"

"No," she said, without thinking, and then bit her lip. "I mean, well, I don't know, really. I don't care about it on television, I never watch it, and—well, actually, I've never been to a game. So I'm really looking forward to finding out. If I like it, I mean." She felt hot and sweaty with effort. "So, are you an Owls fan?"

"God, no. They're hopeless. I got the tickets 'cause my Dad teaches there."

"Oh, yeah? What subject?"

"Architecture."

"Will you go to Rice?"

He snorted. "Not even if they'd have me. I can't wait to leave home."

"Where're you going?"

"UT. How about you?"

If he became her boyfriend they wouldn't be separated after graduation. "Probably UT. My sisters went there—one of them still lives in Austin. Do you know what you want to major in?"

"I might go Pre-Law. I've got the grades for it. I don't know that I'd want to be a lawyer, but Pre-Law's a good start anyway. How about you?"

"Well, I've been thinking about anthropology, or maybe philosophy. Those are the things I'd really like to study. The thing is, I don't know what kind of job I could get afterward. The only thing I want to do is write, but you can't make a living out of poetry, so I thought maybe if I could get a job that had something to do with books, like maybe working for a publishing company, or as a librarian. Even working in a bookstore, but of course you don't exactly need a degree to do that. Anyway, I guess I'll worry about the job when the time comes, and enjoy my time in college. I'm really hoping I can manage to get something published before too long—so far, it's been nothing but rejection slips. I couldn't even make it into *Visions* last year! How about you? Do you send stuff out?"

"What?" He rolled his eyes, startled, in her direction.

"Poetry. I noticed you didn't have anything in *Visions* either. Kind of makes me wonder about the teachers who judged the entries, considering some of the stuff they..."

"What makes you think I write poetry?"

"Well—you're the poetry editor."

He snorted. "Not my choice. Miss Beadle makes the choices. I wanted to be Editor, actually, but Freer got that, of course, he's her bright-eyed boy. I don't know why she made me poetry editor. Not that it makes that much difference, you know the editors don't choose the material, we're just responsible for position and layout and making sure there aren't any typos."

"I know, but I guess I thought you must have a special interest—"

"I don't even like poetry. I don't understand it. Especially all this modern stuff, this free verse that doesn't even rhyme. I mean, what's the point? I think if you're going to have poetry, it should at least rhyme."

The football game itself turned out to be the best part of their date. There wasn't so much opportunity to talk, then, and what talking they did could easily be focused on the game they were watching. She asked questions and he explained what was going on. She enjoyed his nearness, the safe thrill of body heat as they sat thigh to thigh, his flesh separated from hers by only two layers of sturdy denim. Warmed by his body, aware of his every movement, she could for a little while simply enjoy her love.

Once the game was over, though, they were back in the difficult world of their differences, or of his differences from the romantic figure she'd created in her dreams. She struggled to build bridges, initiating conversations intended to bring them closer together, but she had an uncanny knack for saying the wrong things, hitting his sorest spots, drawing out of him always the things she didn't want to hear. Maybe it was because she was tossing the conversational ball to a man she couldn't see, to the figment she imagined in his place.

They went to a Burger King for hamburgers, and it was there, in that artificially cheery atmosphere, in a rare few moments of silence between them, while watching him eat, that she had a sudden, vivid memory of a childhood disappointment.

She'd had a dollhouse when she was small, before their family had broken apart, and in the kitchen of the dollhouse there were several tiny plates and bowls of artificial food. They were more real to her even now than whatever it was she'd had for dinner the night before, and she regretted now having let them go with the house, having agreed with her mother that, at thirteen, she was too big to play with dolls and dollhouses. And yet she knew that if she had them now, if she could put her hand into her purse this minute and pull out the tiny loaf of bread, the bowl of fruit, the beautiful brown roast chicken, they would not make her happy, they would still stir the same frustrated longing in her that they had then. They had always looked good enough to eat—they looked to her even better than the things she really had to eat—and yet they had been inedible. She knew that, she had always known it, and yet she had never, as a child, entirely believed it. There must be a way of approaching them, a special attitude or a particular time of day or night when they would be transformed into something delicious. Once, or maybe more than once, she had gone so far as to bite a tiny piece of the roast chicken. It tasted awful, like dust and old glue, and there had ever after been a notch in the breast where her tooth had chipped out a piece to spoil it and remind her of how silly she had been—and even then she couldn't quite shake off her belief that somehow, someday...

All of the food was realistic and identifiable, all except one, the most fascinating for its mystery, the plate of pink meat. She was sure it was meat, but what kind she could not imagine. It must have come from an animal she had never seen before. Her mother said it was ham, but it looked to her like no ham she'd ever seen. And why was it so big? On a plate the size of a quarter, it filled the whole space, there was no room left for the potato salad, or sweet potato pie, or succotash or green beans that normally accompanied slices of ham. The thought of the greedy carnivore who would devour a whole plate of strange meat was unsettling. She longed to taste this meat above anything else. It would be like nothing she had ever tasted before, and it would be better, she was sure, better and more satisfying than any meat had been.

She understood why Alex made her think of that imaginary meat. He wasn't the passionate, poetic, romantic boy she had imagined throughout the long, hot summer, but he still looked like someone that she loved, and not even a recognition of their incompatibility stopped her from wanting him. Surely there had to be a way for them to meet and understand each other? Surely the love she felt could not be wasted, meaningless?

Impulsively, she put down her hamburger untouched and tried again to reach him.

"Do you think people can want things that aren't right for them? Really want them, I mean; like, need them."

"Of course they can. All the time. Look at drug addicts. They 'need' something that's killing them. Or wasn't that what you meant?"

"Oh, well, I wasn't really thinking about addictions, things like drugs or cigarettes. I guess I meant more like, well, food, for example." She suddenly realized she could not use love as an example. If people never fell in love with the wrong person there'd be no broken hearts and no divorces.

"Food?" He looked baffled, and waved his burger. "We don't 'need' this stuff, that's for sure. If people only ate what they needed there wouldn't be so many fatsos in this country."

"I guess you're right," she said sadly. Wanting something fiercely was certainly no sign that it was good for you; maybe even love could be an addiction, a bad habit, like cigarettes or booze.

She didn't know why it should hurt so much. Alex Hill didn't love her, but he wasn't the man of her dreams. He was just a boy she wasn't getting along with very well. The person she had loved all summer wasn't real. She'd just have to reject her fantasies about that person in the same way that she'd refuse to swallow pills offered her by a sinister stranger. She didn't love Alex; she didn't love anyone. She didn't know why that should hurt so much. It shouldn't hurt at all, but it did.

It was barely seven o'clock when he took her home. They were both very polite when they said goodbye at her door, mouthing the little formula they'd been taught by their mothers to utter after every childhood party, visit or treat: "Thank you so much; I had a nice time."

She didn't invite him in, and he didn't try to kiss her.

Tears filled her eyes as soon as she was indoors; she shoved her hand in her mouth and bit down on it as she stared around her like a wounded beast.

Her mother had left a note where she always did, on the refrigerator door. It said she wouldn't be back until very late. There was chocolate chip ice cream, also cold cuts and chips, if she and Alex wanted a snack....

She took her fist out of her mouth and howled out loud. Then she staggered around the downstairs rooms, weeping and clutching at herself until she dropped to the floor, exhausted, and just lay there, snuffling and breathing raggedly. It was over. That was it. She got up and went into the kitchen where she splashed some water on her face and blew her nose on a paper napkin. Then, feeling hungry (she hadn't managed much after the first bite of hamburger) she put a couple of slices of pickle loaf on a plate with a pile of chips and a blob of mayonnaise, and took it upstairs with a glass of Dr. Pepper. She wasn't even thinking about her broken heart or Alex when she walked into her dark bedroom and, glancing through the glass of the balcony doors to the courtyard and swimming pool below, saw him.

Her heart leaped up. The figure was in shadow, standing away from the light, close to the ragged bamboo hedge which divided the courtyard from the parking lot, but she was absolutely certain it was Alex. She had watched him for so many devoted hours, memorizing his every movement and stance, that she could not be mistaken.

He hadn't gone. He must be feeling as miserable as she was at their failure to connect, at the stupid way their first date had ended. But he was afraid to knock at the door; he didn't know what to say to her.

She put down her plate and glass, turned and ran down the stairs and out of the apartment. She didn't know what to say, either, so she wouldn't say anything. That would be best; words had come between them before.

He must have started walking toward her as soon as he saw her come through the door. They collided by the side of the pool.

It was a curiously embarrassing shock to feel his body so close against hers, and she would have pulled away, apologized, if his arms hadn't gone around her at the moment of impact. Not a bump, then, but a hug. An embrace.

They just stood there holding each other for awhile. She moved a little, turning her head, looking up, wanting to see his face, but the harsh, bright poolside light was directly behind him, and she couldn't make out his features. The only thing she could see were the twin glittering circles of his glasses.

With a little shiver she recognized something creepy about this. He didn't try to stop her pulling away, which reassured her. When she put a hand out he took it. His fingers were warm.

"Let's go inside," she said.

By the warm glow of the corner lamp in the living room Alex looked wonderfully familiar, just wonderful. She was going to say something, she didn't know what, something to express her happiness, when he put a finger to her lips.

She smiled. He took his finger away and kissed her.

"Agnes? What are you doing down here? You weren't waiting up for me?"

She blinked up at her mother, disoriented. What was she doing here? Had she fallen asleep? Where was Alex? Her mother smelled of soap, like she'd just washed her face. Where were her glasses? "What time is it?"

Her mother laughed. "And what time do you call this, I'd like to know? No fair. I didn't give you a curfew, so don't try to pull that on me. It's after two. You weren't worried, I hope? I said I'd be late—didn't you get my note?"

"Yeah, yeah." She found her glasses on the coffee table and put them on. Alex's glasses, like Alex himself, were gone. She remembered, with a slippery, warm sensation low in her stomach, the tender practicality with which he had gently removed her glasses before taking off his own.

Her mother patted her shoulder. "I'm going up to bed, dear. I think you should too."

When her mother had gone she searched the room in case Alex had left her a note, but found no sign of him. But did she need a sign? Her lips were still swollen from his kisses; she had only to close her eyes to feel them again, the way, after a day at the beach, she would go on feeling the steady, insistent rhythm of the waves against her skin.

So, that was what kissing was about. She went up to bed happier than she'd ever been in her life.

Roxanne called her a little before noon the next day for the details.

"Well, the date was pretty much of a disaster, really."

"Oh, dear."

"I hate dating. It should never have been invented. I hate football. I hate trying to make conversation and all that getting-to-know-you garbage."

"Uh, was there anything about last night that you didn't entirely hate?"

"Yes."

"And what was that, Ms. Grey?"

"Kissing Alex."

"Kissing Alex."

"And being kissed by him, of course."

"Of course."

"It was like a dream—really, it was a nightmare at first. I was sure he hated me. I wanted to die."

"And then he kissed you goodnight?"

"No, no, no! We said goodnight at the door, I came in, burst into tears, blah blah blah, then I came up to my room and looked out the window and he was still down there. He was just standing there by the pool, like, he was just as miserable as me about the way things had gone—God, I can't tell you, we just disagreed about *everything*—but—well, when I saw him there, I went straight down to him and he just put his arms around me and that was it."

"So what did he say?"

"He didn't say anything. That's the point. He didn't have to. I didn't have to, either. We came inside and sat on the couch and, well, you know."

"You tell me."

"God, Roxanne. We kissed."

"And?"

"Kissed some more. That's all. Well, it's not all, it was more than enough. It was wonderful. We just kissed and kissed and—God, now I know what all those songs and poems are about!"

"Awwww. That's great, Grey, that really is wonderful. I'm so glad it worked out; I'm so happy for you. Want to go out and do something today, or are you going to be tied to the telephone all day, waiting for HIM to call?"

"I guess I should go out, or he'll think I don't have anything better to do than sit in all day waiting for HIM to call." She grinned as she spoke, so certain was she that there would be no need for games and strategies like that with Alex. In one enchanted evening they had leaped over all of that, into the sort of closeness she had dreamed of all summer. Maybe he would call and maybe he wouldn't; either would be fine, and they would see each other again tomorrow, at school, no longer just classmates, no longer unequal, but boyfriend and girlfriend.

From the moment she arrived at school on Monday morning she was one quivering, sensitive antenna attuned to his presence—but she didn't see him anywhere.

She loitered in the hall for awhile, hoping to catch him, but then she began to feel too nervous to pull off a casual act—and, anyway, she didn't want to act with him—so she went into the English classroom and took her usual seat.

Alex was not actually late, but the bell began ringing seconds after he slid his long legs beneath the desk beside hers. She noticed that his hair looked uncombed and his glasses were smudged, and he had a pimple on his neck. He felt her looking at him and turned to give her a smile that didn't quite reach his eyes.

She felt the radiance of her own smile die, felt it slip from her face to land rather heavily somewhere in her stomach.

The teacher had already started talking and there was no possibility of exchanging words with Alex. She had to get through the class, wait for the sound of the next bell, before she could say anything to him.

When the bell rang he began to gather his books together without even glancing at her; he seemed unaware of her presence.

She spoke despite the painful lump in her throat. "Want to eat lunch together?"

He rolled his eyes like a horse about to bolt. Maybe it was just surprise. "Uh, sure, if you like. I'll look for you."

"I usually eat with my friend Roxanne under one of the big trees out front—"

"Okay, I'll look for you. I'm sorry, I don't want to be rude, but I've got chemistry next, and I left my notes in my locker which is at the other end of the building, so I do have to run. But I'll see you at lunch."

She would see him at lunch. They could talk then. She held on to that promising thought to ward off the bleak memory of the way he had looked at her—and not looked at her. Not like her lover. Not like a lover at all.

It was raining at lunchtime. Usually when it was wet she and Roxanne ate their sandwiches beneath the overhang at the top of the front steps to the school, or in the foyer of the auditorium. But she hadn't made any contingency plans with Alex.

"Drag and a half," moaned Roxanne. "I can't stand the cafe; it'll be a zoo."

"Don't come, then."

"Are you kidding? I'm your chaperone, baby. I'm the only thing standing between you and complete moral ruin."

"Just you, the cafeteria staff, half the teachers and the entire student body."

"Can't be too careful when there're raging teenage hormones involved."

The cafeteria was worse than a zoo. At first she thought she wasn't going to be able to find him in the crowd. Then she caught sight of him, sandwiched between two members of the school debating team at a table without a single empty chair. She wasn't going to go over there and not get invited to sit down. And if somebody else made room for her, it would be worse than English class, having to sit next to him when he seemed so indifferent to her presence. In this public, crowded place, under the interested eyes of his friends, he would not hold her hand, would not touch her or kiss her or say anything she wanted to hear.

"This is awful," she said. "There's nowhere to sit. Let's try the auditorium. I'll find him after school. He'll call me tonight; I'm sure he'll call me."

But he didn't call, and she couldn't bring herself to call him. She could think of nothing else. Why had he been so cool to her? Did he regret what had happened between them on Saturday night? Or had he somehow misunderstood? When she fell asleep—was it possible he'd interpreted her utter relaxation with and faith in him as indifference or boredom? Oh, he had to call, he had to let her explain herself—he had to!

Just before she went to bed she walked out onto her balcony. She was thinking about Alex so hard, as she had been all day, that at first she didn't believe she was actually seeing him, that dark figure in the courtyard below, standing in the shadow of the bamboo hedge just where she had first seen him on Saturday night.

"Alex?"

It was only a whisper, but as if he had heard he stepped forward so that she could see him, and then, the next thing she knew, he was actually running toward her, and leaping up to scale the wall. Within seconds he was climbing over the railing and then—just as she was thinking her mother would have a fit if she knew how easily a man could break into her bedroom—he was beside her, and she was in his arms, warm and safe and loved again.

They went inside and lay down on her bed.

The idea of having sex with a man was frightening to her. No matter how it was dressed up with romance in books and movies, the mechanics of it (as far as she understood them) seemed to her peculiar, unpleasant and awkward if not actually brutal. Maybe someday she might be willing to have somebody's penis pushed inside her, but the change of attitude that would entail would have to be years in the future. In her summer fantasies about Alex she had sometimes waltzed up to the idea of sex, and then waltzed around it. They would kiss and hug and fondle, and he frequently brought her to orgasm, but if he ever tried to go further (because, people said, boys generally did) they would be interrupted.

She had no fear of Alex. She knew he would not try to take her further than she wanted to go; also, that he would go with her as far as she wanted. They loved each other in a gentle, unintrusive way for hours, without taking their pants off. She had several orgasms, but if he climaxed she didn't know it. His desire for her never pushed past the boundaries she set, so she never had to speak, never had to tell him no or stop him. She was blissfully unaware of the passage of time until her alarm clock woke her, and she found herself lying on top of her still made-up bed, half-dressed and alone at seven o'clock in the morning.

At school, in English class, Alex was again a stranger.

"Morning," he said, and yawned, turning away to page through his ring-binder.

"Tired?" He didn't seem to feel her stare, the anxious frustration that had her near to tears. He nodded and shrugged without looking at her.

"I guess you would be. I guess you didn't get much sleep last night, hmmm?"

He turned a startled face on her. "What do you mean?"

"You know what I mean."

"*Miss* Grey. *Mister* Hill. If you could manage to disengage your attention from your so-fascinating selves and give it to me, please?" She smiled when she saw that she had caught them, and nodded. "Thank you. So kind. As I was saying, if we consider the case of a writer still very much under the influence of Victorian morals and manners..."

As soon as the teacher began pacing and she felt herself unobserved Agnes looked at Alex. He had flushed a dark red and was staring fixedly at the front of the room. He did not look at her again.

"What's wrong with him?" she demanded of Roxanne at lunchtime, sitting in the shade of one of the big oaks on the school's front lawn. "He acts like we barely know each other."

"You do barely know each other."

"He doesn't talk, he hardly even looks at me—I look at him and he looks away, like he's scared."

Roxanne took a sandwich out of her lunch sack and began to unwrap it. "Well, maybe he is scared."

"Of me? Roxanne! Be serious!"

"I am. I don't mean scared of you, specifically, but of the situation. They'll never admit it, but boys are scared of sex, too. He doesn't know what's going to happen next but he knows it's up to him. Whoa! What's happening? Is he ready for this, does he really want a girlfriend? He probably just wants a little distance between you so he can think about things before he goes out with you again. Look at it from his point of view: you already wanted him, but he was fancy free, he'd never given you a second thought till you called him. So he goes out with this girl for the first time and boom! You get along like crazy, it's like magic, and—"

"But we didn't get along. Not when we were talking to each other. It was awful, really, every time I opened my mouth I either disagreed with him or said something he didn't like. It was only later, when we weren't talking, that things were better, perfect, really, when we started kissing. And when he—" She stopped suddenly, remembering that Roxanne knew only about the events of Saturday night. She hadn't told her about his visit last night.

"So now you expect him to want to talk to you? Give the guy a break! Look, I know it sounds like a cliché, and I know you don't like game-playing, but—he'll feel less threatened and be more interested if you play it cool. I promise you. Just lay back, give him some space, and wait for Saturday."

She had just opened her mouth to tell Roxanne about last night, about his visit, about the hours they'd spent in each other's arms on her bed, when she heard Alex call her name.

She looked around and saw him coming toward her across the grass, and at once she forgot everything except the intense pleasure of his presence.

"I remembered you'd said you usually had lunch under the trees. I wanted to ask—Hello."

"Hi. I'm Roxanne."

"Yeah, I know. I'm Alex...."

"I know. And you want to talk to Grey, so I'll take my sandwich and sneak away."

"No, no, don't do that. I don't want to chase you away—I can't stay, I have to go see the printer. Running errands for Miss Beadle, you know, the editor's primary task." He gave a crooked smile.

"That's for *Visions*, yeah? Well, Grey's on the staff, why don't you take her with you? I'm sure you could use an assistant, somebody to take notes while you talk to the printer."

"Oh, well..." the crooked smile vanished and he looked stiff and uncomfortable, shooting a little glance at Agnes but directing his reply to Roxanne. "It sure would be more fun with her along, but somehow I don't think Miss B. would see the necessity—I don't want to abuse the privilege. Maybe some other time... Anyway, Agnes, I wanted to ask you, about Saturday night—would you like to go out to dinner first? What do you think about The Red Lion?"

The Red Lion was considered romantic, a place for a special date, popular with teenage couples; very different from the bright, cheap fast-food restaurants everybody went to for refueling. "That would be wonderful." She felt like crying. His eyes still would not meet hers for more than half a second. It was hard to believe this was the boy who had been kissing her so passionately only a little more than twelve hours before. Still—The Red Lion was something, had to mean something.

"That's great. How about if I pick you up about six? Is that okay? Great. I have to move—I'll see you later, okay? Nice meeting you, Roxanne."

"Why didn't you say something?" Roxanne demanded. "Why didn't you go with him?"

"Because he didn't want me. You could see."

"That boy doesn't know what he wants. He needs somebody to tell him. You could have *made* him want you. Honestly, I don't understand you sometimes. If you want him, go get him!"

"I thought you told me to play it cool?"

She laughed and sighed, shook her head, then put an arm around her in a quick hug. "Maybe I was wrong. I don't know him. But—he's so uptight! But maybe that was my fault. Things might have been different if you were alone together."

"Things are fine when we're alone together. They are."

"Then there's nothing to worry about. That's all that matters."

She didn't expect to see him alone again until Saturday night. But on Friday night, bored, restless and lonely (her mother and Roxanne both were out on dates) she went out onto her balcony like Juliet and there he was in the courtyard below, her Romeo.

It was dark but still early, barely eight o'clock. They could have the whole, long night together in the privacy of her room. She thought, before he came up, that she would ask him about his behavior toward her at school, she would ask why he hadn't called her, at least. But when he was beside her, close enough to touch, that was all she wanted. Words were worse than unnecessary; like clothes, they got in the way. All that was necessary could be expressed without words, with hands and lips. It no longer mattered to her what had or hadn't happened at school, out there among other people; the only thing she cared about was him now, here, with her.

There was all the time in the world, and this, the two of them here together in this moment, was all that mattered. The feeling of his skin beneath her lips, the sound of his breath in her ear, the smell of him, the feelings he aroused in her. Gradually, eventually, they took their clothes off to embrace more fully and intimately. And finally, when all strangeness was gone, when she felt she knew his body better than her own, when there was no fear left in her but only desire, they did what had once, only days ago, been to her unimaginable. So this was sex! It astonished her. Not the intensity of pleasure—that she'd almost expected—but the strange familiarity of it. This was not a new exploration but a return—somehow, sometime, she had been here before. For a moment, looking at his face, she became disoriented, unclear whether she was looking down or up at it, and then it changed, his features altered, until she seemed to be looking into a mirror.

In that moment she could as easily have felt terror as joy—the whole range of possible emotions wavered before her, just there, she had only to reach out and pick the one she preferred. She could have whatever she wanted, be whoever she wanted—it was all so simple, it was all up to her.

And then, even as she understood that she and Alex were the same, that there was no meaningful difference between them, she felt understanding slipping away from her. It could not be held, only briefly apprehended, like this peak of pleasure, like this night of love, it was always in the process of ending.

She slept late on Saturday morning, and floated through the rest of the day, too happy to mind her mother's running commentary. This time her mother didn't object to her choice of clothes which were ethnic and romantic, a full skirt with a scoop-necked, embroidered Mexican blouse.

When Alex arrived her mother invited him in and offered refreshments, which he declined politely. "That's very kind of you, Mrs. Grey, but my friends are waiting for us in the car."

"Well, they're welcome to come in, too."

"We really can't stay—we have reservations for dinner, and they might not hold a table for us if we're late. It's a popular place."

"Oh, go on then. Have a nice time. And you don't have to worry about bringing Agnes home early—I'll be out late myself tonight."

"Friends?" she asked him as soon as they were outside, hoping he would laugh, and hug her, and say it was just an excuse to get away.

But he said, "Oh, yes, I hope you don't mind. My Mom's car is in the shop and my Dad wouldn't let me take his, so we're going with George and Lindy. You know George from English. He lives next door to me."

She knew George and Lindy; everybody did. George Sefton was a football player and also on the debate team, winning honor for the school in both areas. Lindy Silko was a cheerleader and a star of the Mixed Chorus, and a good bet for this year's Homecoming Queen.

The idea of going on a double date with their class' most admired and envied couple made her feel slightly stunned. It might have been somebody else's dream of the perfect date, the chance to be, or pretend to be, part of the "in crowd" for at least one evening. But what she wanted, time alone with Alex, was made impossible.

But she couldn't brood or mourn in the professionally friendly company of hearty George and sparkling Lindy. Dinner wasn't the romantic *tête à tête* she'd imagined, but it was fun, with everybody clowning and laughing a lot. Even the normally tense and serious Alex loosened up and visibly enjoyed himself. But he kept his distance: remove George from the picture, she thought, and an observer would not have been able to guess which girl was Alex's date.

At the dance, though, pairing off was required. At their school there was no tradition of cutting in or trading partners: you danced with the one who brought you. So she and Alex dutifully bopped around the floor together, performing the modified free-form versions of the twist, frug, shag and monkey which everybody attempted, with more energy than skill, but as soon as the band launched into a slow number, Alex headed back to their table to sit it out. The same thing happened with the second slow number, and she protested: "Oh, come on, you can't be that tired.... I love this song, let's dance."

He flopped onto a chair and said flatly, "I can't dance. I'm sorry, I should have warned you when you asked me out. I've got two left feet."

She didn't sit down but stood beside him, determined to get him back on the dance floor. "I don't mind."

"You would when I stepped on you."

"Oh, Alex, come on. I don't know how to dance either, not really. It doesn't matter. We'll just put our arms around each other and move to the music." She leaned over him, smiling, imploring him to remember.

His body strained away from hers and he wouldn't meet her eyes. It was such an alarming sensation—as if her own arm or leg had tried to escape—that she immediately pulled away and sat down with the width of the table between them.

"I'm sorry," he said weakly. "But I really can't. I think I must have been born without a sense of rhythm. It wouldn't be any fun, believe me."

She did not believe him. She remembered how easily and surely his body and hers had moved together on her bed. Why wouldn't he touch her now? Was he afraid that if he put his arms around her they'd lose all control and end up making love in front of everyone? She tried again to grapple with Roxanne's paradox: that he was afraid of what he most wanted.

"Alex, we have to talk."

"Yeah?"

"I mean, this is ridiculous, we never talk, and there are some things—"

"Hi, y'all, are these chairs taken?"

It was a relief to be interrupted. This wasn't the place or the time, especially with Alex being so unhelpful, keeping her at arm's length, looking at her as if last night had never happened—but the time would come. Tonight, she promised herself, they would talk about how they felt about each other before the kissing started. They would get some things clear and end this schizophrenic double life of strangers and lovers.

After the dance they all went for ice cream and coffee, and then George drove around River Oaks and Memorial, on the look-out for cars he recognized, evidence of an after-the-dance party they could crash. But they found nothing, and eventually, when the laughter was slower and interspersed with yawns, he drove back to her apartment building. Alex got out to walk her to her door.

"Take your time," said George. "But if you're not back in one hour I'm calling Alex's mother."

Finally they were alone in the courtyard where they had first embraced. It was darker now—the bright lights over the pool were timed to go off at eleven—but her mother had left their small entrance light burning.

The tension of being on show, in public, went out of her and another, more pleasurable, tension took hold. She began to breathe more quickly. Her skin tingled, anticipating his touch, and she moved a little closer to him. "Do you want to come inside?"

"I can't—they're waiting."

She almost laughed. "I don't think they'll miss you for ten minutes. They have each other."

"I'd better not."

"Well, I guess it's not worth it for ten minutes. We can wait." She swayed toward him, reached out and touched his arm. "Don't make me wait too long."

He didn't move or respond to her touch. She might have been stroking a tree. "What do you mean?"

She felt a chill. "I mean, hurry back."

He said nothing. She took her hand away from his unresponsive arm, feeling the deadness spread from it up her own arm, into her.

After a silence he said, "I'll see you on Monday, in class. It's been a really fun evening. Thank you for asking me."

She didn't say anything. She wished she had not spoken. They both stood motionless, close enough to touch, in silence until he said, prompting her, "I'll wait to make sure you get in all right."

As if her body was some large and unfamiliar machine she turned it around, fumbled the key out of her bag, opened the door and went in. When she turned in the doorway she saw that he was already walking away.

She was too deeply shocked for tears. Her movements mechanical, she locked the door, turned out the light, and went upstairs to her room. There she began to undress and put her clothes away until her half-naked reflection in the mirror on the back of the closet door arrested her. She looked at the pale flesh, the small, asymmetrical breasts, the mark on one of them like a horseshoe. It had been a horrible bruise once, and then it had faded, but it had never disappeared. What had happened to her, that strange magic, her wish, her near death, had marked her for life.

She got what she wanted. Her wishes came true. She was a witch, like Aunt Marjorie.

She began to tremble, such a violent muscular seizure that she couldn't move, could only clench her teeth and hunch over and wait for it to pass. When it did she felt wrung out. Moving cautiously, like an arthritic old woman, she pulled a robe off a hanger and wrapped it around herself. Then she went to the balcony door.

This time she didn't open it or go out. This time, for the first time, she was cautious, and only lifted an edge of the curtain to peek.

He was there, standing in the shadows, as he always was when she looked out, waiting upon her will.

She got the shakes again, dropped the curtain and fell to the floor, where she huddled and shuddered for a long time. She thought she would never feel warm or safe again.

But again the fit passed, and as she lay on the floor, weary and exhausted but miles from sleep, she knew that this night would pass, too.

It was the longest night of her life. She was awake through all of it. After awhile she got up and got into bed and lay there tensely, wishing for sleep. She heard her mother come home, come upstairs and go to bed. She heard a cat-fight outside, and every distant train that passed through town. Sometimes her eyes were open and sometimes they were closed. She thought as little as possible, reciting poems and nursery rhymes and riddles to keep her mind away from Alex and sex and Aunt Marjorie's pillow friend. When the first light appeared around the edges of the curtains she sat up, took a few deep breaths and then went to the window. There was no one in the courtyard. The bamboo leaves hung limply in the still air and the pool water glittered dully. Shaking with exhaustion and relief she went back to bed and fell almost immediately into a deep and dreamless sleep.

At school she kept herself remote from Alex, still saying hello, but never initiating conversations, never letting her eyes meet his, pretending to be absorbed in something else whenever he was near. She was careful, at home, to keep her curtains drawn after sundown and her balcony door shut and locked. She would not even look out into the courtyard after dark, and didn't go out unless someone was with her.

Roxanne thought she was suffering from a broken heart, or disappointed hopes, and Agnes didn't tell her the much stranger, more complicated truth. She told Roxanne she didn't want to talk about Alex anymore, and her friend accepted the ban with wholehearted, silent sympathy, and dragged her off to parties and after-school meetings to keep her spirits up and enlarge her circle of acquaintances.

Agnes thought this numb, frightened form of existence would continue forever, but everything happened fast that year. By Thanksgiving she'd met Larry Lang, a freshman at the University of Houston, a friend of a friend of Roxanne's. Larry had long hair, wore tie-dyed T-shirts and ragged jeans, liked comic books and William Burroughs and Thomas Pynchon, listened to heavy metal, smoked dope, and couldn't keep his hands off her. Her mother couldn't stand him. Life became tense and wonderful. They went all the way on New Year's Eve in the back of his car, and he wept against her hair and told her that he loved her. She forgot there was any reason for avoiding her balcony, and never saw anyone waiting for her in the bamboo shadows.

The real Alex didn't disappear, not from her life and not even from her heart. Deep emotions leave their mark, and she would always feel there was a connection between them.

Along with about a third of their graduating class, Alex and Agnes went to the University of Texas in Austin. He was in Pre-Law, she was in Media Studies, so their paths did not often cross. Yet every so often she would think of him and then suddenly see him on campus or in one of the local student hang-outs, eating a pizza at Conan's, waiting in line for a movie, or strolling toward her down the Drag.

In their final year, chance brought them together when they found themselves living in the same apartment complex on West 45th Street. He had changed a lot since high school—physical changes which made him more obviously and conventionally attractive. He had filled out and become more muscular, and now had a sexual confidence he had lacked before. His glasses had been replaced by contact lenses, and he had grown a thick mustache which somehow made his teeth seem larger and whiter—or maybe that was because he smiled more easily now. He always smiled at her when they met, and she couldn't help noticing that the smile always reached his eyes, but she was slow to realize what this meant.

When it came to Alex, in her own mind Agnes was the same awkward, unattractive girl she'd been in high school. She looked in the mirror and saw the same long, straight brown hair and big glasses.

Her figure had changed, and she was glad of that; she'd put on a few pounds to good effect, and her breasts were much bigger. Yet although she'd had several boyfriends, and generally found her interest in a man was reciprocated, she still thought of Alex as an unattainable idol.

They kept meeting by chance not only on the stairs of the apartment complex, but also in the laundromat, and the local shopping center. He had a car and she didn't. Seeing her waiting at the bus stop one morning he stopped and gave her a lift downtown, and this quickly evolved into a regular routine. Often when he was going out he would call her or stop by her apartment to ask if she wanted to go, too. He had a girlfriend and she had a boyfriend, so their relationship had to be platonic. They were just old friends from high school.

But one night during final exams week they shared a pizza and a bottle of Lambrusco alone in his apartment. They were giggling away at some silly joke, very close together on the floor cushions, when she saw his expression change. He looked at her with melting brown eyes and murmured, "God, how I want to make love to you."

The muscles of her legs tightened with lust at the same time as her mouth went dry. She was frightened, but the wine made her bold. She leaned forward—only a few inches separated them—and kissed him on the lips.

She was kissing a stranger. The feel of his lips, his tongue, the taste of him—it was all new, experienced for the first time. Startled, she pulled away just as he moved to put his arms around her and pull her closer.

"No, don't."

"Why not?" He looked astonished. "Am I such a terrible kisser?"

She laughed, weakly. "Of course not! Only, it's so strange, after..."

She saw by the change in his expression that he'd misunderstood; he thought she was feeling guilty, thinking of her boyfriend. He said swiftly, "It's just us, Agnes. It doesn't have to go further, it doesn't have to affect anything else. This is just for you and me, tonight."

"I was thinking about you in high school."

"Don't! Forget that dork!"

"I can't. I need to know—"

"I need to know what you taste like. I need to kiss you all over. May I? Please?"

She stopped talking and gave in happily; smiled and lay back on the cushions. What was the point of words when she could have his body?

But it was not the body she remembered, as she found later when they were naked together in his bed. And the differences could not be put down to just the passage of a few years. Whoever she'd taken into her bed as a teenager, it hadn't been Alex Hill.

She had, before that night, imagined the possibility of someday making love with Alex again. She had believed that if it happened it would be a life-changing experience, the ultimate, transforming sex she could lose herself in.

The reality was nothing like that. It wasn't wonderful or glorious or awful. It was, if sex could ever be described by such a word, curiously ordinary. It was good, but not extraordinarily so. Warm, sweaty, a little awkward, very pleasurable. And she knew, when it was over, that she was not in love with him.

"Whew," he said, as they rested. "If you knew how long I'd wanted to do that..."

"Not as long as I have."

He laughed. "Want to bet? That first day, when I gave you a lift to your bank, and then we went and got a coffee—"

"That wasn't the first day."

"What was for you?"

"The first time I *saw* you. '*Jeder Engel ist schrecklich*'."

"Every angel is... terrifying?"

"Don't you remember?"

Their faces were inches apart and his eyes were steadily on hers, but she had no idea what he saw, or thought, or felt.

"High school?"

"I was in love with you. Didn't you know?"

He smiled. "In love with me? In high school? How could you have been. I was horrible."

"I thought you were wonderful."

"You must have been the only person apart from my mother who did, and even she had her doubts."

He didn't seem to be taking her seriously, but she persisted. "You must have known. Why else would I ask you out?"

"God, who knows? It was a dance girls asked boys to, that's all. I don't think about high school very much."

"I asked you out because I wanted you to ask me out. Because I was crazy in love with you and you hardly knew I existed."

"Oh, I knew you existed."

"Then why didn't you ask me out?"

"I did."

"After. What did you think of me? Tell me the truth."

"It's ancient history. What does it matter? I'm not the person I was then, thank goodness."

"Alex, please, it's important. I want to know."

"You want to know why I shied away from you like the nervous little nerd I was?" He sighed. "If you really want to know, I'll tell you. I was scared of you."

"Why?"

"Um, every angel's terrifying? You were a teen angel." He sighed and shook his head when she didn't laugh. "Okay, dumb joke. I was scared of most girls then, but I was particularly shy of you because you were so smart."

"Oh, come on!"

"I mean it. I told you I was horrible. I was a complete male chauvinist pig, my only excuse is that we all were then, and I was uncomfortable around a girl who was smarter than me."

"But you were the honors student, you were in all the special progress classes—I was only in English! You were in the top percentile, you graduated cum laude, I didn't."

"I'm not talking about grades. Of course I got good grades. But you read books. Real books, not just for class. You not only read poetry, and quoted it, and understood it, you actually wrote it. It was a struggle just to keep up with you, and I felt I had to outdo you. That was my masculine role. I couldn't cope with someone like you; not then. Now, of course, although you're still smarter than me, and brighter, and more creative, and lots and lots prettier, I am a modern liberated man and I don't care." He drew her to him for a kiss. "In fact, I feel proud as hell to be able to attract someone as special as you. Now can we stop talking about how dumb I was in high school and do something a lot more fun?"

"Alex, wait." She held his head between her hands. "Tell me something. Did you—did we—" But it was impossible to ask. She'd never confessed those nighttime encounters to anyone, and she couldn't do it now, not to him. Yet she longed to know if he'd been aware, on any level, of what was happening. Perhaps he'd had dreams, maybe he'd remember something which would make her feel less alone, less strange. She temporized. "Did you want me? If you could have, if you hadn't been afraid of me... would you have made love to me?"

He sighed and closed his eyes. "Why...?"

"Please."

"Christ, of course I wanted you, I wanted every pretty girl I saw. I would have fucked anyone and anything then—if I'd dared. Only my fear was greater than my lust. I didn't have the first idea what to do. So I didn't lose my virginity until after I left home. It was true, what everybody said about those hippie chicks in Austin...."

He opened his eyes. "And now I have some idea of what to do. I don't think I'm as horrible as I used to be. And I'm not scared of you anymore. What do you think about me? On second thought—don't tell me unless it's good."

PART FOUR:

MAKING MAGIC

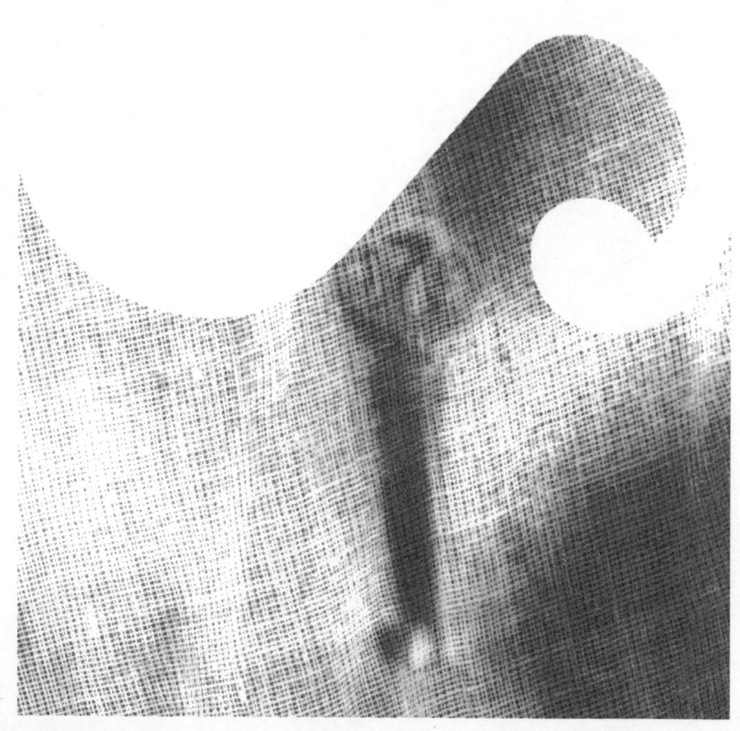

Do you exist?

Evidence:

These poems in which

I have been conjuring you,

This book which makes your absence palpable,

These longings printed black.

—Erica Jong, from "The Evidence"

After graduating from the University of Texas, Agnes stayed on in Austin with her boyfriend, guiltily allowing their affair to drag on instead of ending it, as she could have done by leaving town. Alex moved back to Houston, where there was a job waiting for him, and Roxanne went to Los Angeles in pursuit of the Hollywood dream. Although she liked to imagine herself leading a more cosmopolitan life in New York or San Francisco, London or Paris, Agnes found it difficult to leave Austin even after her boyfriend had become history.

Austin was a friendly, comfortable place where she felt at home. It had good bookstores, the university's libraries and film societies, and cafes where she could be confident of meeting someone to talk to if she was in the mood, or sit, reading or writing, with a cup of good coffee if she was not. She joined a local writers' circle and expanded her repertoire from poetry (which didn't pay) to short stories (which sometimes did). She had fantasies of a literary life like one she'd read about in books, set in London and New York, but how was she to afford it? She was too practical to want to starve and suffer while she wrote. In Austin she had a job she enjoyed, working for a small publishing company. This paid the bills, including her portion of the rent on an old house near the university, shared with a shifting population of graduate students, and also left her with a little spare time to write. She still felt that a fated existence waited for her somewhere else, out there in the future, but she was young and believed time and chance would draw her there eventually.

In between the boyfriends, who came and went, never affecting her very deeply, Agnes kept herself company with thoughts of Graham Storey. The crush she'd had on him as a child, seeing his shadowy, dreamy-eyed photograph on a scrap of newsprint, had become more sophisticated, but it was still a crush.

Reading the poems in his first collection, *The Memory of Trees*, as a high school student, she had decided he was an English Rilke. His poems had been as mysterious to her, and as moving. The poems in his second collection, which was published in America when she was in her final year of college, were less mystical. By then, her own tastes in poetry had changed, and she liked them even better. It seemed to her that she and Graham Storey had a similar outlook on life. He wrote the poems she wished she could write.

She had many favorite poets, others who moved her more profoundly, or seemed to speak to her more directly than he did—but they were all dead. Graham Storey was alive. Reading library copies of the *TLS*, *Stand*, the *The London Magazine* and other British periodicals, she often came upon not only his new poems, but also book reviews and letters, all of which she read greedily, combing them for clues to the person behind the poems. By chance, doing some research on W.H. Auden, she discovered that Graham Storey had been in correspondence with the older poet for a few years, and that Graham Storey's actual letters were a part of the Auden collection in the Humanities Research Center at the University of Texas.

As a student, she had access to them. She sat by herself in a small, cool, well-lighted room with a box-file open on the table and picked up the type-written pages in her hands, raised them to her face, inhaling with eyes closed. What might be left, besides the words, indentations and ink on paper, after so many years? Cell fragments from the skin of his hands, a hair, a trace of cigarette smoke...? She stared and stared at the signature in blue ink, the small, cramped hand. At first, the formality of his full name, but the last two letters were signed simply G.

How that initial reverberated, how personal it became, how it haunted her! The fact that it was one of her own initials did not detract but seemed to suggest a connection between them, proof they had something in common.

Just occasionally she would get carried away, caught up in a yearning so intense it was a physical pain and she was helpless before it. It frightened her a little, that she could be so overcome by emotion for someone she didn't even know, for a figure of her own creation. She had never felt such overwhelming love for a real person—only for the perfect lover she had once imagined Alex to be, and, as a child, for Myles.

But at least this time she knew her yearning could not be answered. She was perfectly aware that the real Graham Storey could not be the soul-mate she'd invented. That was why, although she had his address, she never wrote him a letter (or, at least, she never sent it), and although she was saving her money with the idea of making a trip to England, she did not fool herself by thinking that an English holiday would bring her any closer to the real man. She indulged in fantasies of meeting him by chance: she would be walking along the Drag one day, and there he'd be, walking toward her. She would recognize him from the picture on the back of his latest book. The English Department did sponsor a series of poetry readings; it was not impossible that they might invite Graham Storey. Or maybe she'd be visiting London, walking down Charing Cross Road, and see him inside a bookshop, signing books. She could walk in...

The truth was, she didn't really want to meet him. She didn't want to be forced to give up her fantasy. She could enjoy it for what it was, her own creation, and her idea of the poet could be an inspiration to her. But they would never meet.

Standing in Victoria Station, alone amid the alien crowd, unreal-feeling from jet-lag and lack of sleep, she stood and turned the tissue-thin pages of a telephone book. The sight of his name thrilled her, as always, like a familiar touch. All at once she felt more at home, able to deal with the problem of finding her way around this huge, unknown city.

The next day she set off for Harrow-on-the-Hill, which sounded to her as if it should be inhabited by hobbits, but was apparently no more than one of the far-flung tendrils of London's contemporary sprawl, easily accessible by the Metropolitan Line. His street she had located in her newly purchased *London A to Z* and she felt confident that she would find her way there from the station.

She had no plans for what she would say or do after she had made her way to his door. She was praying that magic would strike, that he would look at her and feel what she had felt when she'd first set eyes on his face.

It was a sunny day, but breezy and not very warm, even though it was June. She felt glad for her cotton jacket as she walked up the hill into the wind. Even before she saw the number and was sure, she had recognized his little white cottage with the honeysuckle twining around the green door. She knocked, and both her breath and her heart seemed to stop while she waited for a reply.

A woman opened the door. She was about thirty, attractive in a strong-featured, rather exotic way, with kohl-rimmed eyes and long, dark hair. "Yes?" She hadn't expected to encounter anyone else, and it took her a moment to find her tongue, and ask if this was indeed the poet's house.

The way the woman looked at her made her certain she would not be allowed in. To this woman, whatever her connection to the poet, she was just some person from Porlock. "Please, won't you tell him—

won't you ask him—but not if he's working, of course. Don't interrupt him. But if I could come back later, I wouldn't take up too much of his time...."

"You're American, aren't you?"

"Yes."

"Here on a visit?"

She nodded. "My first time."

"How do you know him?"

"I don't. Not personally. Just his work. I've admired it for so long...."

The woman suddenly smiled. "Oh, you're one of his readers! Well, he's not here right now, but would you like to come in anyway? I can show you round."

This was not at all as she had hoped it would be. "Maybe I could come back when he's in."

"Oh, he won't mind me showing you around. I'm sure he'd want me to. After you've come so far, I couldn't send you away with nothing. Please come in."

"Really, I'd rather meet him."

"Well, of course you would, and why shouldn't you? You can come back again in a few days—better ring first to make sure he's in. But as long as you're here now, come in for a cup of tea. Wouldn't you like to see where his wonderful poems get written?"

It would have been too awkward to refuse. Following her inside, she wondered about the woman who played at being keeper of the shrine. In her hippy, gypsyish clothes—cheesecloth blouse and long madras skirt, silver bangles on her arms and a ring on every finger—she was unlikely his housekeeper or secretary. She knew he wasn't married, but asked with false naiveté, "Are you Mrs....?"

The woman smiled. "I'm sorry, I should have introduced myself. I'm his girlfriend, Amy Carrick."

There was something in the woman's proud smile and the little toss of her head that made her suspect she wouldn't have made such a claim in the poet's presence.

"Where is he now? Will he be back soon?"

"He's gone away for a few days, walking in Scotland. He does that sometimes, when he needs to be alone for inspiration. That's how poets are. Wouldn't you like to see his study, where the magic happens? Just through here. This is his desk, this is his chair. He always writes long-hand, on a pad like this. There are his pencils, and a rubber, and a couple of biros, but he's taken his favorite pen away with him, of course." It was like being shown around a museum by a too-officious curator, facts forced upon one and never allowed a moment for thought or a meaningful private discovery. Although she knew she was being silly, she found herself disbelieving everything the woman said. No, this was not the room where he created his poems. Perhaps he wrote letters here, on that old manual typewriter shoved to the back of the desk, or typed out the final versions, but the poems had not been written at that desk, with the poet in that chair.

"Go on, I can see you're dying to try it. Go ahead, I won't tell him, sit down, see what it feels like to sit in the poet's chair!"

She backed away. "Could I use your bathroom, please?"

Amy led her to the other end of the small house, where the bathroom was beside the kitchen. "I'll make us a pot of tea while you're freshening up."

She ran the water to mask any sound, and had a look around the bathroom. There were no signs of a woman's occupancy, no make-up, moisturizer, or tampons, not even a toothbrush in the mug beside the sink. Only one person lived here, and he was away.

"Why don't you take a seat in the lounge, make yourself at home. I'll be in with the tea in a couple of minutes," called Amy as she passed. There was one armchair and a sofa in the room called the lounge, and by the evidence—a crumpled tissue and a paperback lying open on the seat—it was obvious that the other woman had been sitting in the armchair earlier. Perversely ("make yourself at home!"), she chose to sit on the chair, lifting the book (*A Bouquet of Barbed Wire* by Andrea Newman) and tissue and setting them on the nearest surface, then settling herself, wriggling her bottom deeper into the already flattened cushion. As she did so she felt something small and hard under her. Probably a button or a coin, she thought as she raised a buttock and slipped one hand beneath the cushion.

She had found a small gold key attached to a thin gold ring. The key seemed too small and delicate to be of any practical use, so perhaps it was the sort of charm that more usually would be worn as part of a bracelet or necklace. Without thinking, she slipped it onto her ring finger and it was a perfect fit. She turned it so that the key lay in the palm of her hand, and she closed her hand around it just as Amy came in with a tea-tray.

"Here we are! Milk or lemon?"

"Lemon, please."

"I thought so. I've noticed Americans don't often take milk in their tea. *He* never takes tea at all. He's a coffee drinker, but it has to be strong."

She craved all such details of his life out of habit, but resented this woman for being the source. Anyway, she might be lying. She certainly didn't live here with the poet as she had implied. "Have you been to America?"

"Me? Oh, no. I used to work in a cafe where we had a lot of American tourists coming in, that's where I noticed. My boyfriend says noticing little details like that is really important in a poet."

"Are you a poet, too?"

"I try," she said, casting her eyes down, more coy than modest. Then a thought alarmed her, and her eyes came up quick and fierce. "Are you?"

"Oh, goodness, no. I'm just a reader; I can't write." The lie soothed whatever dark suspicion had briefly disturbed Amy's complacency. She knew she'd been right in her reflexive, almost instinctive lie. She didn't want this woman knowing too much about her.

When she left—as soon as she had finished her tea—she was still wearing the key-ring. Distrusting the other woman as she did she couldn't bring herself to hand it over to her. She justified this with the thought that all the other rings on Amy's hands were silver, so this was unlikely to be hers. This might belong to the poet's real girlfriend, in which case it would be much better to give it to him when she came back another day. After all, it was his house she had found it in.

But as soon as she was outside on the street she was gripped by panic, realizing that however she justified it, she had just stolen a piece of jewelry. She should have shoved it back under the cushion again before she left—what had possessed her to put it on in the first place? The panic died away as she accepted the fact that it was too late now, and she'd just have to try to explain herself when she met the poet. Her hand made a fist around the fragile key as she walked away.

She fell asleep early and woke, disoriented but wide awake, just before dawn. It was too early to have breakfast or go anywhere, nothing would be open, and although she would have enjoyed just walking through the streets of London she was afraid it wouldn't be safe. With a sigh she reached for the book she had been reading the night before, but soon cast it aside. Her dreams lately had been more interesting, unusually vivid and strange. There had been one scene in particular....

Thinking about it, she remembered something she'd seen walking back from the poet's house in Harrow, and made a connection. Words hung in her mind, glittering slightly, suggesting new connections, conjunctions, interesting clashes. She scrabbled in her bag for her notebook and a pen.

By the time the maid knocked on her door several hours later she had completed a poem, and she had the thrilling feeling that it was the best she'd ever written.

During the next few days she saw the sights of London and she wrote. She wrote in the early mornings in her room, she wrote in cafes, tea-shops, and restaurants in the afternoons, and in pubs or her narrow little hotel room in the evenings. She had never known anything like this overpowering burst of creativity, and she'd seldom been so happy. Writing poetry had always been a struggle for her, and the results of that struggle usually mediocre. Now, everything was changed. The poems were not easy to write, they didn't spring into her head full-blown, she had to work at them, shaping and reshaping the initial idea, but it was like working in clear daylight after bumbling around in the dark for so long. She had something to say now, and the words to say it. The skill had come, perhaps, from all the years of practice, of looking and listening, reading and trying to write, but why here, why now?

She developed a superstition about the key-ring, which had not been off her finger since she found it, but it was not something she was able to put into words—it would have sounded too silly. Yet she had not gone back to Harrow-on-the-Hill, or even thought about it, during her week of writing, and now, as she began to think about the poet again, feeling that old familiar tug of longing, the thought of having to give the ring up, to give it back to him, was almost painful enough to make her abandon her original plan to meet him.

Finally she shut herself into a telephone box and dialed the number she knew by heart. A man's voice answered, repeating the last four digits she had dialed. Unable to think of any response, she hung up.

She put all her recent poems into a big brown envelope and set off for Harrow. She didn't know what she would say, but she would let him see that she wore the ring, let him read her poems, and then he would decide her fate. Standing before his green door, her hand poised to knock, something else seemed to take over and decide for her. Instead of knocking she bent down and leaned a little forward and pushed the envelope containing her poems through the letter-slot. Feeling as free, happy and satisfied as when she read through a poem she had just written and found it good, she walked away from his door.

Halfway down the hill on her way to the station she remembered her name was nowhere on any of the poems or the envelope. He would have no idea who had written them, or how to get in touch with her. But that didn't matter. She understood now that she had written them for him, and now he had them. She would get in touch with him after he'd had time to digest what she had written, and then they would meet as equals, two poets together at last.

She had grown tired of city life and the turmoil of London, so the next morning she packed her things and took the train down to Cornwall, dreaming of high white cliffs above the slate-blue sea, of quaint fishing villages, of ancient stone circles and wild moorland ponies. The weather was kind. She sat and wrote in the sun in the ruined castle of Tintagel, and in quayside cafes in half a dozen Cornish fishing villages. She lived each day—walking, looking, eating and writing—without thinking beyond the moment, and she was happy. When the weather turned and rain swept in from the sea, she got back on the train. She visited Exeter, Bristol, Bath and Brighton. And then one night, sitting in a pub in Brighton with a half-pint of bitter and her notebook and pen, she saw two lovers, a few feet away from her, holding hands and kissing. She felt a pang of loneliness as she remembered how she had loved the poet, yet never met him. She was scheduled to fly back to Texas in just over a week.

The next day saw her back in Harrow. She pushed her latest poems through his letter-slot, but then, instead of retreating to a hotel in London, she hauled her duffel bag farther up the hill where a pub called The King's Head had rooms for rent. She spent the rest of the day wandering around the hill, browsing in antique shops, gazing at the picturesque old buildings of Harrow School, and reading inscriptions on tombstones in the churchyard. She had dinner in the hotel restaurant, and afterward settled herself in a quiet corner of the lounge bar, having decided to spend the rest of the evening writing.

She hadn't been there long enough to set pen to paper when the poet walked in. He wore jeans, an open-necked white shirt, and a scruffy old tweed jacket going at the elbows. He looked around with a gaze as wide-open and innocently curious as a baby's and intercepted her stare. She was unable to look away. After a moment his eyes left hers and he turned to the bar. She shoved notebook and pen away in her bag. She was trembling. A few minutes later, as she had known he would, he carried his drink away from the bar, across the room, and joined her at her table.

It was an ordinary sort of pick-up, with nothing poetic about it. Probably, if she hadn't known who he was, she would have brushed him off—she had no liking for the sort of casual encounters that began in bars—but if she hadn't known who he was, she would never have stared at him in that way which encouraged, practically demanded, his attention.

When they got around to exchanging names, she did not reveal that she knew who he was. He touched her left hand very lightly. "Married?"

Her heart pounding very hard, she turned the ring on her hand so that the key was visible. "No. You?"

If he recognized the ring he gave no sign. "Never. Women never stay with me for very long. I can't blame them. I'm a selfish bastard, and my work comes before a relationship. No woman likes to feel she's second-best, not even those who seem the most sympathetic, even those originally drawn to me by the work." He hesitated, as if expecting her question, and then explained, "I'm a poet, you see, and one with a rather old-fashioned attitude toward the Muse. Oh, don't feel embarrassed because you haven't heard of me! I'm *quite* successful as a poet, but I know how little that means in this country today!"

When closing time was called, he gave her a look shifty and shy and invited her home with him.

This was the invitation she had longed for, the answer to her dreams, yet she hesitated at the intrusion of an unwelcome memory. "Do you have a girlfriend?"

He gazed at her with unbelievably guileless eyes. "Not yet. But I'd like to." He put out his hand and caught her fingers. "What do you say?"

She said yes. They were up most of the night, making love. She was ecstatic. They were so right together, their bodies a perfect fit, and they understood each other so well. He was the perfect lover she had always dreamed of.

In the morning they went back up to the King's Head to get her things, and she moved in with him. It was only supposed to be for a week, but when the time came for her to fly home, she forfeited her ticket and let the plane go without her.

Tears of joy shone in the poet's eyes as he pulled her back into his bed and made love to her again. But as they rested, still joined together, in the warm after-glow, he told her gently that she would have to find a place of her own. "I love you, but I can't live with you. How would I ever be able to work, knowing you were in the next room, knowing I could be making love to you? I need time to myself, to commune with the Muse. I can't live with anyone. Poets shouldn't."

She had never told him that she was a poet, too, although she continued to write, usually early in the morning while he slept, and was producing a complete poem nearly every day. Each one she left as a love-offering on his desk. Neither of them ever spoke of this.

She believed that she would be the exception, the one woman he could live with, but obviously it would take him some time to come around to this realization. In the meantime, she was determined not to be a drag on him in any way. It turned out to be surprisingly easy to tap into the black-market world of low-paying jobs, despite the soaring unemployment figures currently making headlines, and soon she was working as a cook-waitress at a cafe in South Harrow. She found a room to rent nearby, but spent little time in it. Now that she had a place of her own, the poet discovered that he wanted her as much as ever, and they spent every night together in his bed.

Two months passed, then three. She was still happy, although no longer writing. It might have been lack of time and energy—it was difficult, between her job and her lover, to ever get two consecutive hours to herself—but she felt the real reason lay deeper, that the well of creativity she had magically tapped into had run dry. Or maybe it was just that the need to write had gone. She didn't really regret it. Once she had wanted to be a great poet, but now she just wanted the poet to be her husband. She'd be legal then, she could give up the smell of stale fat frying that always clung to her clothes and hair and get a decent job, she could give up that poky furnished room in

South Harrow and live honestly with her husband, maybe they would have a baby....

One day after work as she let herself into his house she was aware of a charged atmosphere. The skin on her arms and back prickled. She thought she smelled something in the entrance hall, like a woman's perfume, but when she sniffed it was gone. She went to the kitchen to make herself a cup of tea and found the kettle still warm from recent use. Yet he never drank tea. The last of a pot of coffee, well-stewed by now, still simmered away on the hot-plate of his coffee-maker.

It was at that moment, sensing the recent presence of some possibly threatening stranger, that she realized the key-ring was gone.

She clutched her left hand in her right, tightly, as if she'd cut it and had to staunch the flow of blood. She couldn't remember the last time she'd noticed it, but surely it had been there this morning?

More than three months, almost more than four, now, since she'd first walked into this house, a stranger, and found the ring and put it on. She had never taken it off since, she was sure she hadn't taken it off, and it had always been a perfect fit, so how could she have lost it?

She began to search, frantically, crawling around on the kitchen floor, then rummaging through the cushions of the sofa and the easy chair in the lounge, aware even as she did so that she was more likely to have lost the ring at work. Maybe she had taken it off to wash her hands and left it beside the washroom sink.

She didn't find it, not that day and not ever, no matter where she searched. Her lover was no help. He said he hadn't noticed that she wore a ring. When, indignantly, she described it, he said yes, he remembered something like that, but she hadn't worn it for ages. He also denied that he'd had a visitor that day, gazing at her with his unbelievably guileless blue eyes, and she was afraid to insist. She had the sudden cold unwelcome thought, as he kissed her gently and told her not to worry, commented that she looked tired and perhaps should have an early night tonight, that he had fallen out of love with her.

She got up early the next morning and tried to write. It was the old, nearly forgotten struggle in the dark once again, and she knew, in the certainty of despair, that it would always be like this from now on, since she had lost the ring.

That evening he took her out to dinner at the Indian restaurant at the bottom of the hill. Over the nanns and the curry he told her he needed to go away for awhile, by himself. He thought he'd probably go to the Lake District, or to the Highlands of Scotland. He needed to do some walking and some thinking. The Muse hadn't been answering his call lately; he was in a rut. And while on the subject, he rather thought the two of them were in a rut as well; some of the magic had gone. A little time apart would be good for them. When he got back, they'd see how they felt. He'd phone her when he got back.

She clung to the fragile hope he offered, struggling to believe that when he got back all would be well, that all was not yet lost. He made love to her that night as one who performs a familiar task, his thoughts far away, yet she still tried to tell herself that it was as good between them as it had ever been.

The next morning she woke before he did, and wondered as she lay there beside him if there was any point in getting up and trying to write. She had just about decided there was not when she heard something fall through the letter-box. An image came into her mind as she heard the sound, of a large, brown envelope containing a sheaf of unsigned poems. It was hours still before the postman would come—this had to be a personal delivery, and the person who delivered it, she knew with absolute certainty, would be wearing a gold key-ring. Her name didn't matter, only her function as the poet's Muse.

PART FIVE:

MEETING THE MUSE

What is it in men do women require?
The Lineaments of Gratified Desire.
What is it in women to men require?
The Lineaments of Gratified Desire

—William Blake, "The Question Answer'd"

I must marry a poet. It's the only thing

—Elizabeth Smart

No, it didn't happen like that.

Agnes wrote a story, making use of her fantasies about Graham Storey, and she sold it to *The Magazine of Fantasy and Science Fiction*. When it appeared in print and she read it, nearly a year later, she realized that she felt differently about "her" poet now. Writing the story had cured her of her fantasies; she had moved on.

But she was still living in the same place, leading the same life, although the very comfortableness of it all was making her uncomfortable. She was twenty-eight, nearly twenty-nine, and she was still just playing at living. It was time to move on in reality, not just in her mind; time to make some commitments, time for marriage, or foreign travel, time for a more demanding job in one of those cities she had always dreamed of but never even visited—London or New York, Paris or San Francisco. Time to go out there and find her real life.

Walking up Guadalupe Street, "The Drag" directly opposite the University, she was scarcely conscious of her surroundings, the warmth of the spring evening, the storefronts and street vendors. Imagination put her in a cooler climate, strolling through the streets of Bloomsbury, searching for the British Museum. With part of her mind she considered her savings account: there was certainly enough to fund a vacation in England this year, but should she spend it on a two week vacation? Maybe she should pick up a copy of the *New York Times* in the University Co-Op and check out the jobs. If she found something and wanted to move, she'd need all her savings then. She'd nearly reached the Co-Op, moving easily, unseeing, through the crowds of students and street people, when one of the blur of faces suddenly burst upon her like a vision, with hallucinatory clarity.

It was impossible; he was, he must be, just some seedily handsome stranger, but he looked *astonishingly* like the author's photograph on the back cover of Graham Storey's latest collection of poems.

His eyes were large and blue, wide and wondering as a baby's behind round, wire-rimmed glasses. His hair, cut very short, was gray, and there were deep lines, like brackets, from his nose to the corners of his narrow mouth. He was a slightly built man who walked with a subtle stoop, like someone much taller.

As she stopped, staring at him with wonder close to fear, she heard a woman's voice speak her name.

There, standing beside her vision, right in front of her, was Lynne Haden, a local writer who had once been her creative writing teacher. "Just the person," said Lynne. "I know you'll be eager to meet our distinguished visiting poet. Agnes, meet Graham Storey. Graham, this is Agnes Grey."

"It *is* you! I thought I was dreaming!" With laughter, his face changed, became real, alive, more ordinary. His mouth was larger than it looked in repose, and his front teeth were slightly crooked, like her own.

If we ever have a child, she thought, it will have to wear braces.

"A pleasant one, I hope."

"Huh?"

He gave her a quizzical look. "Your dream."

"Agnes is always dreaming," said Lynne. "She's a writer, too."

"Only a children's book," she said, shaking her head frantically

"Only?"

She heard a mocking stress on the word and was seized by apprehension. What did he know? Had he read anything of hers? She felt herself blush. "Uhhh, and a few short stories, that's all, nothing very impressive."

"You don't find books for children impressive?"

Too late, she remembered he had written a children's book. "Some are, of course. Not mine. I loved *The Village of the Cats*."

"You've read it? It wasn't published over here; I couldn't sell it."

"I ordered a copy from England. I really did like it; it was so simple, but perfect, every word. Like a poem with pictures. The pictures were great, too. Was there ever a sequel?"

He gazed into her eyes. "There was supposed to be, but unfortunately the artist and I split up shortly after that book was published. She had been my girlfriend, and afterward it wasn't possible for us to work together. Not my wish, but she—"

"I hate to interrupt," said Lynne, "but there are other people waiting to meet you, Graham."

"I'm terribly sorry. But—would it be possible for Agnes to come along?"

Lynne shrugged, looking at her. "Sure. If you want. It's only drinks in the faculty lounge."

"I'd love to, thanks."

She floated along beside them, dazed by her magical good fortune. Not only to meet him, but to be allowed more time with him. "You're my favorite living poet, you know," she said.

He looked comically alarmed. "Thank you. You don't have to say things like that!"

"I'm only saying it because it's true. Well, it's between you and Adrienne Rich and Marilyn Hacker."

"The only Brit. I'm flattered."

"The only boy," Lynne pointed out. "Here we are. Brace yourself."

"Trial by sherry, I call these things," he muttered out of the side of his mouth to Agnes as they followed Lynne from the warmth of the street into air conditioning.

She had expected that he would be swept away from her by the others—mostly English Department faculty and graduate students—who had assembled here to meet him, and he was, periodically, but after every time he made his way back to her again, to turn the full, blue beam of his attention on her, flatteringly interested in whatever she had to say. After about an hour, when the party was visibly declining, he said, "It's a bit unfair of me to ask, but would you have dinner with me this evening?"

Some of the wine in her glass sloshed out. "I'd love to! Why is it unfair?"

"Because I'm about to lie, and make you party to the lie. Lynne's expecting to take me out to dinner, *tête à tête*, and the only way I can see of getting out of it is to plead jet-lag exhaustion and say I'm going straight back to my room, to bed, alone. She'll offer to drive me back."

"I have a car."

"Of course you do, bless you. I'm going to break the news to her. She won't be pleased, so put that glass down and get ready to scamper when I signal." As they left together she caught a look from Lynne which made her shiver and all at once feel more sober.

"Don't you like Lynne?" she asked when they were outside.

"She's all right. Just another lonely lady. Is she a particular friend of yours? I'm sorry. I shouldn't have involved you. I know it must have seemed particularly cruel, to dump her and go off so obviously with her younger friend, but I don't like predatory women, and I didn't fancy going to bed with her at all."

"Lynne's married."

"Of course she is, and intends staying that way. Which is why I'm the perfect lover: I come equipped with a comfortable hotel room and a guarantee that I won't be around long enough for things to get messy. I don't flatter myself that it's really me she's attracted to—I'm a poet, and even poets have their groupies."

She felt as if she'd swallowed something heavy. "Well, I'm glad I could help you escape. My car's just a couple of blocks away. What hotel are you staying at?"

"Oh, *don't*."

He stepped in front of her, forcing her to stop, and bent down anxiously, peering into her face in the gathering dark. "Why do women always think that everything a man says about another woman is meant to refer to them? You're about ninety-eight percent of the reason I wanted to get away from her. I'm not completely helpless; a firm no thank-you and a handshake at the door of my hotel would have saved my virtue. But I'm not actually interested in an early night alone. What I am interested in is you. I'd like to get to know you properly, have a conversation which isn't interrupted by someone else every three minutes. Please say you'll have dinner with me. If you don't find the prospect too revolting?"

She took him to her favorite Mexican restaurant and there, over the *sopa de elote* and fish cooked in banana leaves, they talked about themselves. Some of the things he told her about his life she already knew, or had guessed, from the poems and the research she had done—his affinity for the west of Scotland, the travels in India, his love of sailing—but she didn't let on. She soaked up every detail he let spill, as compelled and fascinated by this second-hand life as by some long-anticipated novel. When he asked, in turn, about her life, she was impatient, answered as briefly as possible, and pressed on with her questions. She wanted every crumb, every morsel about his childhood in Liverpool, the years of blue-collar jobs after leaving school at sixteen before going to teacher training college, and his life now, as a primary school teacher and a poet. She was fascinated by every detail, whether it was gossip about literary figures he had met, or the facts of his daily existence. She might never have such a chance again and couldn't bear to waste a minute of it by talking about herself.

"Now look here," he said sternly. "I've already been interviewed by someone from the *Austin American Flag Stateswoman Blatt* or whatever the thing is called, and there's a student reporter coming to grill me tomorrow morning—I'm sick and tired of talking about myself! I want to hear about *you*."

"My life is so boring compared to yours."

"Not to me."

"I could sum up my life history in about two minutes. I've never been abroad, I've only ever had the one job—well, apart from waitressing—you've just done so many more things, known so many more interesting people, been places... I've never even been out of Texas!"

"There's time," he said. "I must have at least nine or ten years on you."

"Eleven."

"There, you're not even thirty yet!"

"Twenty-nine in two weeks. But when you were twenty-nine—well, you'd had two collections of poetry published, and been to India."

"I was twenty-nine when I went to India. I thought I had to change my life. You know the poem by Rilke?"

She nodded, her heart pounding

"I had it by heart that year. I was—it was a strange time. Being thirty seems nothing now, but then... back then it was all 'never trust anybody over thirty,' and I'd spent most of my twenties absolutely certain I'd peg out before then, and there I was, twenty-nine and in rude good health, living in a squat, it's true, and smoking dope and conducting affairs with two women at the same time, but with my certification in hand, just about to get a proper job—the sort my parents would approve of—as a teacher, and—" he shrugged. "The women found out about each other and they both dumped me. I had a falling-out with someone who'd been very important to my career.... I thought there might never be a third book. Off I went to India, in search of my fate. I had to do something."

"I've been feeling like that. Feeling I need to make a move. But it's hard to know what to do."

"Don't go to India."

She smiled and shook her head

"Tell me about your writing. You've said hardly anything about it. What do you write? How did you begin?"

She shrugged dismissively, but gave him an honest answer. "I wanted to be a poet when I was very young, but I kind of gave that up in college—there was so much bad poetry being published in all the little magazines, and nobody really cared about it. I got depressed. I didn't even want to try to compete. I wrote prose instead. Stories. Little fairy tales, mostly. I sold one to a science fiction magazine the year I graduated, and a few others here and there over the years. And then one story just got longer and longer until it became a book—that was my children's book. Young Adult, really. It's a fantasy. I've written a second one but I'm still waiting to hear from my publisher about it—I think I'm going to want to rewrite parts of it no matter what she says. And I've got an idea for another one, but I'm not sure it would be suitable for children. It might just be a regular novel. Or an irregular novel." She laughed uneasily. Her voice suddenly sounded loud and blaring to herself, too loud, boastful. She hoped he didn't think she was egotistical, or trying to impress him. "There's not a lot to say about writing. I do it, it takes up a lot of my time—sometimes, it seems to be the most important, dominating fact of my life, but it's like a dream, it goes on mostly inside my head, it's very personal. I spend hours and hours dreaming these stories, but there isn't much I can say about the process."

"I know," he said, meeting her eyes. "I know. That's exactly how I feel. Exactly." They went on looking at each other for what might have been a very long time, or no time at all.

It was nearly midnight when she dropped him off in front of the Driskill Hotel.

"I'll see you tomorrow," he said, with a warm look, and got out of the car. She watched him walking away, waited until he was out of sight before she pulled away from the curb.

She had stopped drinking hours ago but was drunk with happiness, the sound of his voice still ringing in her ears. She could no longer remember if Graham Storey was as she had imagined him or not—he was real, now. But she didn't feel sad about leaving him because she still felt she was carrying his presence with her.

The rented house she shared with Melinda Akers was dark when she pulled into the driveway, and she felt a moment's disappointment that she wouldn't be able to tell her housemate about the evening's adventure. Not that Melinda would understand exactly what it had meant to her, but it would be nice just to say his name out loud to someone else.

As she let herself in and made her way through the dark, quiet house, she thought about calling Roxanne. She would understand, and it was earlier in California. She didn't turn on a light until she was inside her own bedroom with the door closed. When she did, she saw at once that there was someone in her bed.

The naked man sat up, pushing spiky black hair out of his eyes. "So whereya been?"

It was Jack, of course, Jack Laroche, drummer for the Dead Babies, proof-reader for the Texas State Legislature, and her boyfriend for the past six months. She liked him a lot, she even thought sometimes that she loved him, but for the whole of this evening in Graham Storey's company she had managed to forget his very existence.

Ashamed of herself, even a little shocked, she got mad. "I didn't know we had a date."

"Date?" He sat up. "God, I'm sorry. Was I supposed to meet you somewhere?"

"No. That's the point. We didn't have a date and I wasn't expecting you so I made other plans and—"

"Ahh, that's okay." He patted the blanket. "Come on to bed. I'm not mad at you, honest. You missed one helluva good dinner, cooked by yours truly, but that's okay, Melinda and her Big Guy were mighty appreciative. And if you're a good girl, I'll—"

"Why should you be mad at me? We didn't have a date, I didn't ask you to come over and cook for me. I can cook for myself."

"Opinions differ on that score. Anyway, it doesn't matter."

"It *does* matter. This is my room, in case you've forgotten. I live here; you don't. Who invited you into my bed?"

She knew as she saw his face tighten with hurt that she was being unfair.

"I didn't know I needed an invitation."

"Look, we're not living together, right? We're not married. You don't have this automatic claim on me whenever you feel like it. I don't like being taken for granted."

"I don't take you for granted."

"No? What's this, then. You come over, I'm out, so you invite yourself to spend the night."

"Why not? You never had any objections to sleeping with me before. I'm not going to force myself on you—we don't have to have sex just because I'm in your bed—even if we always have. If you want to stay up late I'm not going to complain."

"You're not getting it."

"What? You want us to go back in time? You want us to start *dating* again? I thought you hated dating."

She fidgeted uncomfortably. "It's just... what if I want to go do something by myself?"

"Go and do it."

"I don't mean *now*." She couldn't call Roxanne to tell her about Graham with Jack in the next room. "I mean, I don't think you should just assume that we're going to see each other, be together, sleep together, every night."

"I don't. I haven't been coming over here after my gigs, reeking of beer and cigarettes and trying to crawl into bed with you, have I?"

She felt suddenly very tired. She wanted to go to bed alone but she couldn't bring herself to throw him out. There hadn't been a car parked in front of the house, so he must have hitched or taken the bus. It would be a very long, dark walk home for him

"It's just—look, I'm exhausted, and I was expecting to crawl into bed and go straight to sleep."

"I ain't stopping you."

"I know." She didn't move. "Look—tomorrow night—I'm going to a poetry reading on campus."

"And you don't want me to come with you."

"You'd hate it, you know you would."

"Are you going with somebody else?"

"No."

"Well, what time is it over? We could do something after, go to a late movie at the Dobie or hit some of the clubs—"

"No. Just forget tomorrow night. I'm busy tomorrow night, that's all."

"And I've got a gig on Saturday. So do we see each other on Sunday? Can I have a date with you on Sunday?"

"Yeah, sure, why not." She began to undress

"I'll come over as soon as I get up, that'll be lunchtime. We can take a picnic to Zilker Park, maybe borrow somebody's dog and a frisbee and have an old-fashioned good time."

"Okay."

"I'm sorry I made you mad. I didn't mean to take you for granted. I'd never do that; I know I'm only here on sufferance."

"Oh, Jack, shut up." She tried not to look at him as she finished undressing; she didn't want to catch his eye. She pulled on her kimono and went down the hall to the bathroom, thinking about the man in her bed, comparing him to Graham. She liked Jack a lot, she found him irresistibly sexy, but there was no *magic*. And how could you have love without magic? She'd had sex with seven men and had applied the word "love" to three of them, although always uneasily. She knew, intellectually, that what she had felt for Alex Hill in high school had been only an adolescent crush, a fevered fantasy briefly made flesh, but it still seemed more real to her than anything that had happened since. Her reunion with him in college had ended up being little more than a one-night stand, and after graduation, although they had kept in touch with occasional phone calls, neither had made any effort to build or sustain a relationship. It made her sad sometimes, but she knew it was sensible to let go. The Alex Hill she'd been in love with had never really existed.

She was hoping Jack would be asleep when she got back, but although he was lying still with his eyes closed, she knew he was awake. The sight of his long, smooth back and the warmth of him as she slipped into bed aroused her. Her feelings had been at such a pitch all evening, she longed for physical consummation. But making love with Jack was out of the question; it wouldn't be fair to him.

Neither was it fair to him to go to sleep without a word, a kiss, a hug to let him know it wasn't his fault and she wasn't angry. They had never slept together without first making love, and it seemed wrong that the first time should be in the wake of a quarrel.

Just to let him know she wasn't angry, she moved closer, put her arms around him and kissed the knob at the base of his neck. She snuggled up against him and closed her eyes, meaning to sleep, but he felt so nice, she couldn't seem to stop herself rubbing against him and kissing his back and shoulders.

They ended up making love, of course, and she fell asleep blissful, mindless, satiated.

She bought a ticket and went into the auditorium like anyone else, like a stranger, and took a seat in the front row. When Graham Storey came on stage, wearing a white, open-necked shirt, dark blue corduroy trousers, and a dark blue jacket a little too small for him, he was a stranger until he looked at her. When their eyes met, a shiver went through her and she knew they would make love that night.

She felt embarrassed as soon as she had written it. Adolescent stuff, making magic, trying to anticipate and by anticipation control what would happen—let it be. She pressed the delete key and watched her words unbecome, swallowed by darkness. Then she turned her mind to what she was supposed to be writing: a piece on alternative medicines. Except that it wasn't, really; her brief was to praise physicians and to convince anyone who might be considering consulting a homeopath, *curandera* or other unlicensed practitioner to forget the idea. Lots of quotes from doctors and a few carefully worded descriptions of the loopier claims made by proponents of various methods. She had all the details, she knew what was wanted, she just couldn't bring herself to write it. Doctors traded on the faith of their clients just as much as the faith healers did. She thought that homeopathy sounded like a ridiculous pseudo-science, but if it worked for some people, then it worked. There was no sense in doubting that, or in chipping away at people's belief systems. You had to believe in something in order to get well, and if it worked, did it really matter whether it was pills you believed in, or God, or massive doses of vitamins, or the laying-on of hands? It mattered to doctors, of course, fearful of losing paying customers, but she was tired of being an apologist for doctors. This was one of those times when she was sick of her job. Often she enjoyed writing to order, thought of it as something like a crossword puzzle, satisfying but unimportant, but sometimes the spirit rebelled. She decided to take an early lunch break. Maybe if she rethought the piece she could come up with a way of writing something she wouldn't feel ashamed of which would still satisfy the people who funded the journal... or maybe she could just put it aside for a couple of months. In a couple of months she might be gone; she could have a different job in a different city, and this would be a problem for someone else.

On her way to lunch she stopped off in Scarborough's and bought herself a new perfume. She didn't wear make-up and felt embarrassed by overtly sexy clothes; scent was the only feminine magic she allowed herself. This one was called "Paris." There wasn't one called "London" or she would have bought that.

Graham wore the white, open-necked shirt she had imagined, but his aged corduroys were an unpleasant mustard color, a color she couldn't imagine anyone buying from choice. She wondered if he was completely indifferent, or color-blind, or if he had some superstitious investment in the suit, perhaps bought for him by someone else.

His shoulders were hunched when he came on stage and he looked around shiftily. Then he saw her. His posture immediately changed for the better, and as he caught her eye he winked.

She spent the next forty minutes in a haze of blissful, sexually charged hero-worship. Sometimes she closed her eyes, just letting his voice play on her nerves. In accent and cadence it reminded her of John Lennon. It was the voice of the Beatles, magic from her childhood, almost as familiar and loved as her father's voice had been, and just as long lost.

When she allowed the content of his words to register, that, too, moved her, because it was already, most of it, the well-known poetry she loved.

After the reading she felt shy, deeply moved by him, and she hung back, afraid to approach until, as the autograph seekers began to melt away, he beckoned her to him, and said to the small group of people who remained, "This is my friend Agnes Grey."

Lynne, the only other person she knew, did not look at her. She recognized another member of faculty, Dr. Jones, who smirked and said, "Ah, Miss Grey, the famous Miss Grey. You're a governess, I believe?"

"No, I'm a writer."

"I was thinking of your namesake."

His assumption of her ignorance irritated her. "I know that. She was a writer, too."

"A writer? Well, of her own tale. But chiefly a governess, I think."

"Jane Eyre was a governess. Agnes Grey only worked as one for a little while. She did other things to earn money, like writing for the penny dreadfuls, and of course she had all sorts of adventures."

He frowned over his smile. "I don't remember any of that. I always thought it was a dreary little book, myself."

"Dreary! It was my favorite book! I can still remember some of the scenes, especially the scary ones. And what about that feast scene, you must remember that, I'm sure it was an influence on Christina Rossetti when she wrote 'Goblin Market.' And of course it was a huge influence on Daphne Du Maurier. And I think even *Dracula* must have been partly inspired by the Prince, all the mystery about his background, and the suggestion that he might be a shape-changer."

"Prince? Are we talking about the same book?"

"The novel by Anne Brontë," she said impatiently. They had been walking as they talked, leaving the auditorium in a group. She looked around for Graham and saw him in conversation with a woman she didn't know.

"You've read it recently?"

"No. I read it a long time ago. But I read it probably five or six times when I was a kid. I've tried to find it—I don't know what happened to my copy—and do you know, it's not even in print?"

"It's not really a major work. But of course someone should reprint it."

"Grey!"

Hearing Lynne call her name she looked around. Then Graham's hand settled, marvelous rescue, on her shoulder. "Did you bring your car? Do you know how to find this restaurant? It's another Mexican one. Do Texans never eat anything else?"

"Of course, to all your questions. Let me just see what Lynne wants—"

"Me, I think." Leaving one hand on her shoulder he waved at Lynne with the other and called out, "Meet you there! I have my trusty native guide, no worries!"

"Gray for Graham, of course. I thought she was calling me." She smiled. "Could get confusing, both of us with the same name."

"Surely no one calls you by your surname." He sounded faintly disapproving.

"Well, yes, most of my friends do. I hate my name."

"Agnes is a lovely name."

"I don't think so. Although reading *Agnes Grey* did do something to reconcile me to it. I like the way it's pronounced in French, but try getting people around here to say 'Awn-yes'—affected? *Moi?*"

"In Scotland girls christened Agnes are usually called Nancy."

"Better than Nessie or Aggie. Ness is like mess, and Ag is like gag—oh, dear! You're not Scottish, are you?"

"By affinity only. My parents bought a second home in Argyllshire, before I was born. Have I told you about the bothy? It's in the middle of the most beautiful nowhere on earth, like going back to a better time. I've been going up there for holidays since I was tiny. After my mother died my father wanted to sell it, so my brothers and I bought it off him. If I could have afforded to, I would have bought it all myself. I don't like sharing it, and I'm the one who goes up there and cares for it the most. Someday, when I've had enough of the world and all its vain illusions, I'll become a hermit and retire there."

She thought of Aunt Marjorie's house in the piney woods of East Texas and felt an urge to tell him about it. But it was not the equivalent of his bothy, not really, and she'd only been there once. Before she could think of how to bring it up, or what she wanted to say, they'd reached her car and he'd changed the subject.

During dinner, separated by so many other people, they hardly spoke to each other, but she was happy just to watch him and sometimes hear his voice. After dinner he claimed tiredness when Lynne suggested continuing the evening at her house, but once he was alone with Agnes in her car he asked if they could go somewhere quiet to talk. "You seemed so far away at dinner. I've been missing you."

Her heart-beat sped up. She wished she could take him home, but Melinda was having her monthly poker night, and there would be no quiet or privacy for them there. So she took him to yet another Mexican restaurant, this one a *cantina* with a verandah built over a small creek where they could sit in candlelit semidark drinking iced coffee and talking.

"God, it's wonderful to be in a climate where you can sit outdoors at night!" He leaned toward her, his nostrils flaring slightly. "I like your scent. What's it called?"

"Paris." Feeling bold, she said, "I bought it today. If there'd been one called London I'd've bought that instead."

He laughed loudly. "London! What a name for a perfume. Who'd want to smell like London? Come to that, who'd want to smell like Paris? The fumes from a million cars, with a subtle hint of the *pissoir*, coffee, bread, and old *Gitanes*." He laughed again.

"I've never been to Paris. Or London. They're just ideas to me."

"Oh, you must, you must see Paris. Come visit me in London and I'll take you to Paris."

Her heart gave a leap and she almost stopped breathing. "Do you mean it?"

He looked startled and went very still. With a lurch of embarrassment she knew she should have accepted his offer as lightly as it had been made, not taken it seriously.

But his face relaxed, and he said, "Of course. It'll have to be in the school holidays, but not in August, when everyone in France takes a holiday, and unless I win the Pools you'd have to pay your own way, I'm afraid...."

"Of course. I'm used to that. Do you want another coffee? Something else?"

The moment passed, the conversation moved on. She loved the

way he talked to her, the interest he showed in whatever she had to say; most of the men she knew would have been dominating the conversation in some way, trying to impress her. It seemed to be part of the mating ritual, or maybe it was just the way men were. This approach, which she found far more seductive, seemed a more feminine style.

She also liked the ease with which he switched levels and topics, from emotional to intellectual, from witty to intimate. He quoted easily and often, without drawing attention to it. She noticed, because he seemed to have read the same books and memorized the same poems as she had herself. All her boyfriends read—it was an obvious connection, something they could always talk about—but no one she could remember talking to, male or female, had matched her so well.

She could happily have gone on talking to him all night, watching his face, listening to his voice, memorizing him, but when he yawned again she realized with a guilty start that they were the last customers left in the place.

"I'm sorry, you must be exhausted. Shall we get out before they throw us out?"

They were both silent, talked-out, as she drove through the streets of downtown, nighttime Austin. The radio was playing softly, songs from twenty or thirty years before. With a pang she heard "Johnny Angel," a song from her childhood about a girl waiting for that one, unattainable, perfect lover. Why not? There were pleasures to be found in unrequited love. She would never forget this evening, these past two evenings. She thought of Rilke extolling those who love without reward, and she thought, for perhaps the first time without a pang of longing, of Alex Hill.

"What are you thinking?"

Into her mind, as he asked, came the memory of herself at thirteen looking at a photograph of Graham Storey. "Of unrequited love. Of being thirteen and falling in love with someone I didn't know, someone I thought I'd never meet..."

"Who was it?"

She had thought she would tell him, but now she couldn't. She wanted him to know without being told. "A picture from a newspaper. A fantasy."

"How old were you when you first fell in love?"

"You mean... really? Really in love?"

He gave a short laugh. "What does that mean? Really? I mean in love, whatever that meant to you."

"I guess I was seventeen. Or just about to turn seventeen. He was a boy at school. I didn't know him at all, but I heard him recite some poetry and... got the wrong idea about him."

"As old as that? No one before?"

"Not really. Fantasies, like I told you. I guess I was a late developer. Why, how old were you the first time you fell in love?"

"Six. Six and three-quarters, actually."

"Oh, come on—"

"I'm serious. Other people might laugh, but I can still remember how it felt. I had the same emotions when I was six as I do now—don't you?"

"I don't know. I've never been sure about love."

"I was sure, absolutely. Susan Bishop. God, I can still remember things about her which I'm sure would embarrass her to hear."

He had mentioned other girlfriends during the course of the two evenings they had spent together, even a current girlfriend, Caroline, about whom he did not sound at all serious, and she had not felt a twinge of jealousy, until now, as her stomach twisted sickeningly. The grown women, his actual lovers, had not bothered her, but this little girl whose ghost made his voice go suddenly wistful, made her want to cry.

She pulled over to the curb.

"Why are we stopping?"

She switched off the ignition. "Your hotel is just around the corner and down a block. I won't be able to park in front."

"It doesn't seem to take very long to get anywhere in Austin. I still had things to say."

"Go ahead and say them, I'm not going to throw you out."

He looked at her and smiled and reached over to touch her cheek. "Why on earth do you put up with me?"

She felt tears spring to her eyes. "Because I like you."

"But you're so normal!"

"What?" She gave an uncertain laugh.

"Oh—I have a history of being attracted to women as neurotic as myself, so of course we always fall out, usually sooner rather than later. And on the occasions when I am drawn to a genuinely nice woman she usually has too much sense to get involved with me. I don't mean to say that you're involved with me—"

"I am involved with you. I've been involved with you since—before I met you!"

"And you haven't gone off me now you've met me?"

"You're better than I imagined!"

"God you are kind—or crazy. So I can see you again tomorrow? This doesn't have to be goodbye? Are you free at all? Could we have lunch?"

She was soaring. "Yes of course. We could—we could have breakfast."

"Breakfast?" He grinned, and she rushed on to say the obvious.

"I don't have to go home. I could stay the night."

He looked so astonished that she wished she could unsay her words.

"Or, I mean, of course I'll go home, we'll meet at some civilized hour in the morning, not too early—"

He caught her hand. "I'd love for you to stay. Only, you took me by surprise. I was just trying to think of a way of inducing you to come back to my room, and worrying that I might offend you, when you solved the problem. Very direct, you Texans."

She didn't believe him. She'd just proved herself to be one of the predatory women he so disliked, a poetry groupie only slightly more subtle than Lynne. He didn't want her, that was clear to her, but he would go through with it. Sexual etiquette, male pride, and the residue of his liking for her made anything else unthinkable.

As they got out and she locked the car, as they crossed the street and went into the hotel together, she kept wishing for time to roll back and deposit them in the car, her words still locked inside a fantasy. She felt nothing but dread and dismay as they went into his room. She struggled to come up with some last-minute, face-saving excuse, but her mind was empty.

He put his arms around her, tilted her face up to his, and thrust his tongue in her mouth.

She went rigid. She tried to pull away but he held her more firmly. Her petty resistance struck her as ludicrous—she'd asked for this, she'd dreamed of this, she'd wanted this—and she tried to relax, but she was as tense and unhappy and as utterly without desire as if she'd been in the dentist's chair. She tried thinking of how he'd winked at her from the stage, how he'd gazed at her across the table a few hours ago, but the man who was kissing her now, kneading her breasts through two layers of silk, was someone else, a stranger.

"We might be more comfortable on the bed," he murmured.

If only that might be true, she thought, letting him lead her there. They undressed, rather awkwardly, impeding more than helping each other. For a moment, when they were both naked, looking at each other rather shyly, not touching, she had the hope that everything would be all right after all. The hope flared in her almost as fiercely as desire, and she reached out to him, touched him, and began to kiss his face, his neck, his unfamiliar chest with its sparse, springy hair, his faintly freckled arms.

Then he pushed her onto her back, and she felt his erection against her thigh. She tensed, holding her legs closed, and he looked at her.

"Do we need to take precautions?"

"What?"

"Should I use something."

"I'm on the Pill."

"Good." She saw him smile as he leaned away from her and switched off the light.

"Oh—no—"

"It's better in the dark."

"But I like to look at you."

"I don't like being looked at. I want you to feel me." He put her hand on his penis. She gripped it uncertainly. "Put me inside you."

"I'm not ready."

"Then stroke me." As he spoke his fingers found her clitoris, and she flinched. "What's the matter?"

He sounded angry. She was alone and naked, utterly vulnerable in the dark with a stranger, here by an act of her own will, and it was far too late to tell him she'd made a mistake.

"I'm very sensitive there."

"Well, I should hope so."

"Please, be gentle. If you'd just—"

"I am always gentle!"

A silence. Neither of them moved. Then he said quietly, "I'm sorry. You seemed ready. Let's start again."

"Let's talk."

"No more talking."

He put his mouth on hers and then was still. They lay on their sides, facing each other, pressed close together but unmoving. The room was as dark as a grave, the only sound the faint, breathy whisper of the air conditioning. She couldn't tell what direction it was coming from and realized she had no idea where the window was, or the door. The room seemed to whirl around her, changing now that she could not see it, reminding her of childhood nightmares. She remembered how dark the room in Aunt Marjorie's house had been when the candle was out.

He began to rub himself against her, touching her breasts, pushing his penis between her legs. His breathing was harsh and hot against her ear, and she remembered the muffled noises she had heard from behind the wall, the bumps and the groans from Aunt Marjorie's room. This is sex, she thought, confused. This heavy, wordless thing. This is what grown-ups do in the dark.

As he pushed her onto her back, as he mounted her, she saw a faint light from the door, and the figure of a naked man standing outlined in the light, watching her. She was back in the house in the woods and the pillow friend had come for her. She cried out in fear, and his hand clamped down on her mouth. He thrust hard into her as she tried to move away, and she heard him groan.

She tried to say his name and tasted the familiar syllables flavored with his flesh and sweat. He took his hand away from her mouth, but she did not try to speak again.

She saw the lighter darkness that was the curtained windows, and the line of light beneath the door. The hotel room had come back. Graham rolled off her, muttering something about tissues, saying he was sorry.

She lay still. After awhile she heard his breathing change and knew that he had fallen asleep. If she slept, she didn't know it. Many thoughts chased through her head, and some might have been dreams. After a long time, the room began to grow light, she got up, carefully, and went to the bathroom. When she came out, he still appeared to be asleep, and he did not stir as she dressed herself in the clothes which lay scattered about on the beige carpet.

She wanted to go home and never see him again but she knew it could not be that simple. If she left without any explanation he would think she was angry, or that he had done something wrong. It was herself she was angry at, for imagining it was a simple thing to make a wish come true, but she couldn't explain that to him. He didn't know her and he never would. They were just two strangers who shouldn't have come together but had. Darting nervous glances at him, willing him not to wake, she found a piece of hotel stationary and scribbled a note with her phone number.

Didn't want to disturb your beauty sleep, but something I have to do at home. Give me a call if you have time before you go. She paused, chewed her lip, then signed it *Nancy*

One final look at him, lying on his back, a pale, funerary monument, and she was gone.

His telephone call woke her from a sound sleep a little before noon. Her heart jerked and jolted and began to race at the sound of his voice but she didn't know what she was feeling. He asked her to meet him for lunch, telling her nothing with his tone of voice.

They arranged to meet in a sandwich shop just around the corner from the Driskill Hotel. Walking along the street she glimpsed him through the plate-glass windows and could see, even from that distance, that he was practically quivering with a tightly controlled nervous excitement. Her stomach began to hurt. As she walked through the door and he saw her, he reached into his jacket and found a pack of cigarettes. By the time she reached his table he was lighting up.

"Um, I don't think you're allowed to smoke in here." They were not remotely any of the words she'd imagined greeting him with, but she'd seen the tight-lipped disapproval on the face of a waitress and had to warn him.

"Oh, *Christ.*" He held the cigarette away and looked around for somewhere to stub it out but there were no ash-trays, just "We ask customers to kindly refrain from smoking" cards on every table. He put the cigarette between his lips and stood up, rocking the fragile table. "We'll go somewhere else."

"I'm sorry," she said, stumbling after him, "I wouldn't have suggested it if I'd known, but—I never saw you smoke before."

"I meant to give it up. This trip seemed like a good opportunity, a natural break from all my old habits, but when I got up this morning, I really—where are we going? I wouldn't mind a stroll, usually, but it's raining."

She took him to the closest place she knew that served lunch, a cavernous bar in the next block which featured jazz bands in the evenings and creole specials for lunch. It was all but deserted this Saturday afternoon, and there were ashtrays on every one of the scarred, wooden tables. Graham stared at the chalkboard menu with a pained expression.

"The seafood gumbo is good," she said helpfully.

"All I want is something plain. All this spicy food is ruining my stomach. Don't you have ordinary cafes here? Does everything have to be ethnic?"

"We could go somewhere else."

"No, no, this is all right. I'll have a hamburger."

She had to translate his order for the uncomprehending waitress. "He wants a plain hamburger, nothing on it, just meat in a bun. No mustard or relish or anything like that, okay? Just a plain hamburger."

"He wants it dry?"

"Yeah."

Graham lit another cigarette and inhaled, his face closed and brooding. She sat and looked at him until he answered her gaze. He looked accusing. "Why did you leave me?"

"I left a note."

"Thank you very much for that. But it didn't explain anything."

She was aware of his pain, which itched and pricked as if it were something spiky she'd swallowed. "What was I supposed to explain? I had some stuff to do... I hadn't expected to be out all night. I didn't want to wake you. I left my number."

"So you wanted me to phone you?"

"Yes—well, only if you wanted to." She wasn't prepared for this conversation. Looking at the thin, tense, unhappy man across the table she could not believe she'd been to bed with him, nor did he at all resemble the poet she'd known so long in her head. He was a total stranger who pulled at her emotions as no stranger could; they didn't know each other, but there was a connection between them.

"Why shouldn't I want to?"

"I didn't want you to feel obligated. Look—there is no obligation. We're both grown-ups, you don't have to think—"

"Oh my dear, dear Nancy!"

The name jarred and yet her heart leaped, strangely. He reached across and grasped her hand. His was startlingly cold. "I'm not so casual about sex as you might think. I have very strong feelings, very strong, warm feelings for you. We hardly know each other, of course, but I want to know you better. Look, I have a week before I have to fly out of Houston, and the thing in the world that I'd most like to do with that time is to spend it with you. If you'll have me."

As he spoke those last words she was almost overwhelmed by an intensely physical memory of last night, and the urgent desire never to feel again that lonely, suffocating intimacy, that confusion in the dark. At the same time there was the habit of long desire: the poet she'd imagined had been so important to her for so long that she could not now easily walk away from the real man he had turned out to be. It would be a betrayal of herself to give him up so quickly. She had at least to try. Surely, she argued with herself, what had happened last night was a misunderstanding, some mistake which understanding and mutual good will could put right.

"I'd love that. But there's something we have to talk about."

Their meals arrived then, and he took his hand away and sat back in his chair and said nothing until the waitress had gone. Then he said, very gravely, fixing his eyes on hers, "Yes. You're right. I know what you mean."

The blissful sense of being understood, of knowing he was one with her, flowed through her and she relaxed and waited for him to explain everything.

"Of course I told you I had a girlfriend, and you must have been worrying about that, but Caroline is just someone I've been seeing, and there's nothing in that relationship for you to worry about. It's probably over by now—it's been on the rocks practically since it began. We have very little in common. It was a physical attraction, and once we got through that and got to know each other we discovered we didn't like each other very much. Really, I think she's only been hanging on to me until she finds a better prospect."

She felt disoriented by what seemed his change of subject; then, sadly, realized he had not known what she was thinking about. But how could he? She watched him cut up his hamburger with a knife and fork, and when he paused to fork a piece into his mouth she said, "That wasn't really what I meant when I said we had to talk. You did tell me about Caroline, but I honestly wasn't worrying about her. Although as long as we're confessing, I guess I should tell you I've been seeing someone, too."

He looked a little grim. "I thought there had to be someone."

"Yes, well... you only asked if I was married or living with someone, and I'm not. But we have been seeing each other for about six months."

"Is it serious?"

"Well—more for him than for me, I think. I never expected it to last forever." It seemed horribly unfair to Jack, defining the terms of their relationship like that behind his back, to a stranger, but she had to say something.

"Are we likely to run into him if we stay in Austin? Does he carry a gun?"

"Of course not! I mean, he's not violent, don't worry about that, but yes, we could easily run into him, especially if we stayed at my house. He doesn't always call first."

"Then we won't stay at your house. We won't stay in Austin. Where would you like to go? San Antonio? Dallas? Houston? Or shall we keep on the move, outlawed lovers on the run? I give myself up to your judgment. Are you with me?" She met his gaze and nodded, thinking how romantic this moment should be, but her stomach was twisted with dread.

They went back to her house where she packed a bag and called her boss at home. She was glad he wasn't in, because she was able to lie to his answering machine about a family emergency calling her away for the whole of the next week.

Then they drove to Salado, and checked in to the Stagecoach Inn. Salado was a quaint, pretty little town full of gift and antique shops, an easy drive from Austin, a popular place for a day out. Her mother had taken her there when she'd still been a student, and they'd had lunch where everybody did, in the huge dining room of the Stagecoach Inn.

Now, sitting at what might have been the very same table, over descendants of the same preliminary hushpuppies and clear soup she'd eaten with her mother, she could taste the bitterness of the betrayal she'd felt when her mother had told her she was getting married, and she wondered what had possessed her to return today. Was this where the inevitable, unpalatable words would have to be said?

"What's wrong?"

"I don't know."

"You look worried."

"I am."

"About what?"

"I don't know. About us. About what might happen." Then all in a rush she began to tell him about the last time she had been in this restaurant, how betrayed she'd felt when her mother told her she was getting married, about the earlier betrayal and desertion of her father. He listened quietly, asked questions occasionally, until she had talked her emotions out. Then they left the inn and went outside to walk through the streets of Salado and along the green banks of the river, holding hands.

That night in bed he held her for a little while but did not make love to her. When she tried to initiate a more intimate embrace he simply stopped her.

"Can we talk about it?" she asked in a whisper.

"No. It's better not. Trust me."

She was more relieved than disappointed.

The next morning, over breakfast, they discussed where to go next. She had no idea what he expected, what sort of places would appeal to someone from Europe.

"I'm not asking you to cater to my expectations, that's not what this is about. Most people in England think of *Dallas* when you mention Texas—or cowboys. I'm not that interested in the site of a soap opera or in dude ranches. It doesn't have to be touristy to interest me—better if it isn't. Can't we just sort of drive around and stop anywhere that looks interesting? Just explore... that's what I'd do if you were visiting me. And I'd show you my favorite places."

"Like the bothy?"

"Oh, definitely the bothy!"

"There's a place..." she stopped, uncertain.

"Go on."

"There's nothing to see, it's nowhere, really, just an old house in the middle of the piney woods. I went there the summer I was thirteen and... it was magic."

"Let's go there."

"It might not even be there anymore—the house I mean. It was pretty tumble-down. My aunt used to live there. I don't know what happened to her."

"Maybe she's still there."

"I guess.... I never went back to find out."

"Come on, let's go," he said, standing, tossing money for a tip onto the table.

At the car she tested his interest. "We could go to San Antonio, see the Alamo instead."

"Can't we do both?"

"Not in the same day."

"Getting cold feet?"

"I'm just afraid... it won't mean anything to you. It was important to me, but you might be disappointed."

"You mean you're afraid *you* might be."

The accuracy of this caught her in the throat, and tears welled in her eyes. His understanding made her love him.

"It doesn't really matter where we go," he said quietly. "We're just traveling to be together. Your whole country is strange and wonderful to me. Take me where you will."

Despite his attitude, she didn't think he had anticipated quite how long it would take to get there or how little of interest (in her opinion) there would be on the way. Traveling cross-country, they took a lot of back roads, and she got lost a few times. She only knew where Camptown was in relation to Houston; recalibrating from Salado was more difficult than she'd expected; all the roads seemed to take them in the wrong direction. But eventually, after a good lunch at a roadside barbecue stand, they reached Highway 59, and almost immediately after that there was a road sign for Camptown, and she caught sight of the turn-off to Aunt Marjorie's place, still a dirt road and still, after all these years, looking almost exactly as she remembered it.

The forest was different, thinner now; that was one obvious change. The last of the original, primeval forest had been cut down during her childhood, and new pines planted in straight lines.

She had remembered the dirt road as a long one, but distance that had taken so long to travel on foot flashed by beneath the wheels of even a slowly driven car. The last little stretch of their journey passed in silence. Her emotions were in turmoil; she was full of hope and fear. And suddenly there in the same clearing stood the old wooden house.

She braked and turned off the car, and listened to the silence of the forest on this hot, windless day.

"All it lacks is the chicken legs."

His bizarre comment caught her attention. "What?"

"Like Baba Yaga's house. So it could move to another part of the forest. Wrong country, I know."

Baba Yaga was the wicked old crone in Russian fairy tales. "You think it looks like a witch's house?"

He shrugged uneasily. "It's not the house, it's the forest. I've never liked these pine forests—birds don't like them, either, so there's something dead about them. All the trees the same, planted in regiments. They're destroying Scotland. The great Caledonian forest is gone, replaced by plantations of pine."

"Pines grow naturally here; there've always been pine forests in East Texas." She was near tears, feeling his rejection of this place as rejection of herself.

"Conifers are native to Scotland, too, but they don't grow in straight lines and too close together to give anything else a chance except when people plant them that way. I'm sorry." He touched her hand where it still rested on the steering wheel. "This is your special place; don't listen to me. Let's go in."

They got out of the car and approached the house. It became obvious as they climbed the steps to the front porch that the house was uninhabited. The screens on the windows were nearly rusted away where they were not caked with dirt, and the windows were smeared and webbed over. Peering in through the murk, though, she recognized her Aunt Marjorie's front room, the shape of the big desk against the wall spotted with postcard-sized shapes and curling, crumbling paper fragments.

Graham knocked on the door, and the blows resounded, startlingly loud in the stillness, and made her jump.

"I don't think there's anyone in," she said.

"Nor do I, but you have to make sure, observe the proprieties.... You want to try the door?"

She grasped the doorknob but it would not turn. "I always used the back door when I was here."

He nodded, and they went down the steps, around the house, passing the cellar door, which was padlocked. The back door was unlocked, and she walked in, feeling his presence at her back.

The kitchen smelled of dust and mold, the odor of unchallenged time. The floor was gritty underfoot, and everywhere she saw dead flies, cobwebs, mouse droppings and other dirt. No one had lived here for years.

Agnes walked through to the front of the house, feeling a pang of loss and anxious about Aunt Marjorie. What had happened to her that she had not come back here in so long, yet had never sold the house? Had she become so successful in recent years that she needed neither the house nor the money it might bring?

There was the portrait gallery of Marjorie's geniuses. Some had fallen off the wall as the tape that held them had perished, one was curled right up like a dry leaf. Her heart began to race as she searched with her eyes for Graham's photograph. She couldn't find it. She crouched and investigated the pieces of paper which had fallen to the floor. Marcel Proust gazed languidly up at her through a mottled, sepia background with nibbled edges. Next she picked up a piece of brittle, curling newsprint. Where the tape had been, something had eaten, and while she thought this was the picture of the young poet, most of his face was gone, and she could not be sure.

But it was silly to feel sad about the loss of a picture when she had the living subject right here. She straightened up and turned around, letting the meaningless scrap fall, and there he was. He had taken his glasses off as if expecting to have his photograph taken: this was one of his small and touching vanities. She was about to ask him why he'd done it when she was arrested by the expression on his face. He had never before looked at her with such profound tenderness, such unmistakable desire, and her body responded almost before she consciously understood. She took a step and went into his arms.

Very gently he removed her glasses and set them down on the desk. He looked seriously into her naked eyes as if reading what she wanted, and then he kissed her. Previously his kisses had seemed perfunctory, even impersonal, an empty form or a means to an end. This kiss, though, was an end in itself, gentle and lingering, a voyage of discovery.

She became hot and dizzy with desire. Her legs turned to water and she clung to him.

Their kissing became fiercer and more urgent and they ground their bodies together. A little time later, as they awkwardly attempted to shed their clothes while still holding each other, she half-pushed, half-led him into the next room. The bed, Marjorie's bed, smelled chokingly of mildew, but it was softer than the floor, and she thought as long as they stayed on top of the covers it wouldn't be too bad. She was beyond caring, anyway, all discomforts minor details easily ignored.

They got their clothes off as quickly as they could—Agnes almost wished hers would be torn as a lasting sign of the passion which had overwhelmed them. It was a quickly passing thought; all thoughts passed quickly, jumbled and overwhelmed by sensation. Everywhere his naked skin touched hers there was electricity. She was breathing hard and seeing flashes of light.

She lay back, and he began moving down her body, kissing lightly all the way. When he parted her legs she tensed, dreading a dutiful little licking session and hasty retreat, but this didn't happen. He licked and sucked at her as if he had no agenda, no aim beyond the moment, and soon she was lifted and carried away by waves of pleasure. The waves became choppy, closer and closer together, and she came suddenly, too quickly, a physical explosion before she was emotionally ready. She was disappointed and felt her body had let her down, but luckily he did not take her climax for any sign of ending but went on stroking and kissing until she was almost unbearably excited.

They changed positions, and the taste of herself on his lips and his cock stirred her arousal. When he finally slipped inside her it was with the most profound sense of homecoming, as if they had been separated long ago and had spent their lives yearning for each other. Now, with him anchored in her, she felt complete. She closed her eyes and held his warm, lightly sweating body as tightly as if by pressing close enough they could become one. For a long time they barely moved, breathing in rhythm. His warmth, the feel and smell of his body, made her happier than she had ever been.

Their first sexual encounter, in his hotel room, seemed no more now than a bad dream. Although she knew it had really happened, she understood that because it had happened too soon, in the wrong place, it had been a mistake. This was the reality. Then, they had been two strangers: he had done things to her which she had accepted or resisted. They were only really lovers now for the first time, understanding each other with their bodies, hearts and souls.

She moved her legs, and he began to thrust into her, in a steady, smooth, achingly sweet motion until she was crying out and clutching at him, begging him to stop and never to stop.

She had no idea of the time. They made love, and rested, and sometimes fell asleep still joined, and woke, and made more love, and slept again and dreamed of making love. She lost track of her orgasms, where she was on the ever-shifting plateau of arousal. It didn't matter; she was in that paradoxical state of bliss combining extreme sensitivity and arousal with a dreamlike remoteness from reality. They did everything together she had ever wanted to do with a lover.

Although on their first night together he had insisted on darkness, he had no objection now to being looked at for as long as it was light. When night fell, taking them by surprise, they coupled in darkness, half-asleep, and when dawn awakened them the grainy, gradual brightening of the room brought new discoveries.

They slept again and woke again to full daylight, and Agnes realized she was starving. She fended off his embrace, resisting her own desire with a great effort. "Come on, we've got to go get breakfast. If we don't, I'll end up eating you—and *don't* say you wouldn't mind!"

He laughed, kissed her, and let her go. She wrinkled her nose at the smell in the room—sex and mildew and dust—and went off to the bathroom for a cold water wash before dressing in the clothes she'd scattered about the bedroom the day before.

Breakfast was in the first roadside cafe they came to on the way to Houston. It was too soon to go to Houston, they agreed, but it was the simplest and most obvious route; she didn't feel up to tackling maps and back roads again so soon. Over their stacks of pancakes, with bacon and hashbrowns, grits and biscuits, they decided to drive straight through Houston and on down to Galveston. She'd gone to Galveston every summer as a child, but hadn't been back in years, and it seemed to her an appropriate place to take a visitor as well as being something they would both enjoy.

"There's lots of historical old buildings," she explained.

"My dear, I come from a land of old historical buildings—that's not what I look for in America."

"Well, it's pretty, anyway. And there's the beach, and lots of good sea-food." She met his eyes and had a *frisson* of sexual memory. "But it doesn't really matter where we go, does it?"

"Just what I've been telling you." He reached across the table to cover her hand with his.

"We could have stayed at Aunt Marjorie's." With her renewed desire for him she was on the verge of suggesting they turn around and drive back, but, with an unconvincing laugh, he wrinkled his nose and shook his head. His eyes were uneasy. "Hardly," he said. "It wasn't the most welcoming habitation."

She felt let-down by his response. It was honest, if you thought of the smell of mildew, the spiders in the corners, the lack of civilized comforts, but it was ungracious, considering what had happened to them there. She looked away, so he wouldn't see the hurt in her eyes, but he noticed, and gave her hand a squeeze.

"Come on," he said. "I know it was special to you—but it was *your* special place, not mine. I feel more comfortable—and much sexier—in a room with clean sheets and no insects."

She met his smile, and was going to remark that she didn't think her heart would stand any increased sexiness, but the waitress was there to refill their coffee cups, and the moment passed.

But that night in a Galveston motel room, although she embraced him with enthusiasm, he had become a stranger again, or she had, and they were clumsy and uncertain with each other. Her body still remembered the passionate intensity with which he'd explored and claimed her the previous night; she didn't know how to cope with his diffidence now. Had he, during that one long night of intimacy, exhausted all of his interest in her, or his tolerance? Did she smell bad, despite her shower? Did she have bad breath?

"It's not you, honestly. It's me. I've never really liked kissing; that's all."

"But—" She remembered the long, searching, knee- melting kisses of the day before. "So... you only do it to please me? Because you think I expect it? Or—"

"It generally is expected. Look, I'm not saying I hate it or we can never kiss. I'm only telling you, I'm not that comfortable with it unless I'm already aroused enough not to feel self-conscious."

Then what, she wanted to ask, had aroused him to such a pitch before she ever touched him at Aunt Marjorie's house? But before she could ask, he said, "Now, do you want to talk, or to make love?"

"Can't we do both?"

His sigh was answer enough; she shut up and began to touch and stroke him, trying to stir up an urgency she did not feel.

It was no good. The magical electricity which had sparked between them with every touch had gone, and she no longer found the texture and smell of his naked skin uniquely intoxicating—it was just skin. Ordinary skin against skin when they embraced; awkward, uncomfortable sex. She faked an orgasm—for the first time in her life—just to get it over with.

Never again, she thought. It doesn't work. What had happened between them in Aunt Marjorie's house should not have happened. Somehow, she had made it happen—unconscious wishcraft, witchcraft—she didn't know how, but it was beyond her conscious control, and it was dangerous. She had done it once before, in her teens, with Alex—and Alex had no memory of it. She wondered what Gray thought had happened, what he remembered, if he remembered anything. What had been a happy, glowing memory all day now frightened her. She didn't want to think about it. She closed her eyes and tried to wish herself to sleep.

There was a connection between them which was real, which she knew she was not imagining. They both felt it: the hot, itchy spark of sexual attraction, the warmer emotional pull of something that might be love. Intellectually, they were well-matched, and they spent hours, as they traveled together through Texas, talking about books, ideas, art and films.

She decided, after their first night in Galveston, that she would not have sex with him again. She had imagined having to refuse him, to resist his advances, and then to argue with him, but that did not happen. During the day, in public, he often embraced her, held her hand, stroked her hair or her back, and kissed her, chastely, but at night, lying naked beside her in their motel room bed, he didn't try to touch her.

Although they talked about so much else, they did not talk about sex. They didn't discuss their relationship, or try to define it.

Anyone seeing them sitting together in a restaurant, or walking hand-in-hand along the beach at any time during their travels from Galveston to Port Lavaca to Victoria to San Antonio and then back east to Houston, would have assumed they were lovers, perhaps a couple on their honeymoon. There was an electricity between them which made a simple friendship impossible. There could be no going backward. She had fallen in love with him in Aunt Marjorie's old house in the woods, but the man she had made love with there did not seem to exist outside, in the real world. Or, if he did, she could not seem to find her way back to him.

It had been her own decision not to make love with Graham again, but she was not happy about it. She enjoyed his company during the day, and their closeness built up a tension which was never released. She longed for something she could not have, for something which she knew to be impossible. She kept recalling her silly, childish desire to eat the dollhouse food, and one night, trying to laugh, she told him about it. She was grateful for the darkness which meant he could not see the tears in her eyes.

"*Tale of Two Bad Mice*," he said.

"What?"

"Beatrix Potter. Don't you know it? About the mice who break into a doll's house and try to eat the food. When they discover they can't, they try to destroy it—and then get even madder to discover that the fire in the grate won't burn!"

"I never tried to destroy it—I wouldn't do that," she said anxiously. "I just wanted to taste it—and knowing that I couldn't, that it wasn't what it looked like, didn't make me stop wanting. I couldn't stop wanting the impossible."

"That's why you write."

"Is it?" The comment startled her. In the darkness his voice was like an oracle; everything it said had the ring of inescapable truth. "So if I had everything I wanted I wouldn't write anymore?"

"No one ever has everything they want. Not while they're alive."

It was a confusing, emotionally draining week, and she was glad to arrive in Houston with the end in sight. But she realized as she was driving into the city that she didn't know where she was going.

She said so to Graham. "I don't know anything about the local hotels, I'm afraid. I always stay at my mother's."

"Don't you want me to meet your mother?"

His question took her completely by surprise. Before she could respond, he'd sensed something wrong. "Forget it. I'm sorry. I'd forgotten about him."

He meant her stepfather, Eddie Shawcross. But the idea of having a stepfather no longer outraged her as it had when she was nineteen. He wasn't the faceless stranger he'd been when her mother had informed her she was getting married—he was a pretty nice guy, actually.

"It's all right. You've just had my whole history dumped on you, but I don't dislike him at all. Really, there's no problem. We'll go there. I'll just get off this freeway and find a phone first, to warn her we're coming."

As she had expected, her mother sounded pleased to hear from her, was not startled to learn she had a boyfriend in tow, and invited them to come for dinner and spend the night. She didn't know why she should feel so dissatisfied as she put down the phone, why her stomach began to twist and turn with anxiety as she walked back to the car and Graham.

There was something wrong, something missing from her relationship with her mother and she didn't know what it was. Nothing she'd read in any book or heard from any other woman seemed similar to her own experience. She'd tried to explain it once, when she was part of a women's Consciousness Raising Group in college, but even in that small room vibrating with sympathy, even in the company of seven other women all willing themselves to understand, she had failed. She didn't have the vocabulary or the concepts, only the dim yet certain perception that something was wrong, something was missing, in her relationship with her mother. After her failed attempt to verbalize it, she had decided that the thing that was missing must be something in herself. It was her problem, not her mother's: her own failure.

That evening was like many others she'd spent with her mother and Eddie, perfectly pleasant, yet not what she hoped for.

"She's lovely, your mother," Graham murmured to her at one point. At another moment, when the two women were together in the kitchen, her mother said, "He seems very nice, this Graham Storey. You've always had a thing for poets, haven't you?"

Agnes stiffened at something unexpectedly knowing in her mother's voice. She was certain she'd never confided to her mother her fantasies about Graham Storey.

"Well, is this serious? Is he the one?"

"I only met him a week ago. How should I know?"

Her mother looked at her as if they'd never met and said, "If you don't know, I can't tell you."

Agnes didn't know what was missing in her relationship with her mother, but with Graham, she was sure sex was the missing element. They got along well on so many levels, and they connected, intellectually and emotionally. But they just weren't sexually compatible. She remembered something from a story by D.H. Lawrence, his description of an unhappy marriage as "a nervous attachment, rather than a sexual love," and for some reason the words, which had been written by another of Aunt Marjorie's idols, made her feel better. It wasn't the end of the world, and it had happened to other people before. There was no sense crying about it; the romance she had wished for simply hadn't come true.

As she lay in the guest room's double bed waiting for him to come out of the bathroom and join her, she remembered the flimsy, typewritten sheets she had read in the air-conditioned isolation of the Humanities Research Center, and wondered if his letters to her would look the same. Or would he write to her by hand, page after page in his tiny, neat script?

He came out of the bathroom naked and she felt embarrassed and turned her head away, thinking that she'd been silly to insist on this last night with him when she could have stayed in one of the other bedrooms just as easily. He turned out the light, got into bed, and began to caress her.

Startled, she drew away. She had not expected this in her mother's house, and she didn't want it. But although he was always so quick to sense her moods in daylight, now he seemed not to notice her unwillingness. Or, if he noticed, he took it as a challenge, for he became more ardent. Yet, while demanding, he was not crude. His hands upon her body were gentle. He was not the lover he had been in the house in the woods, his merest touch did not spark an immediate response in her, but he was patient, tender, slow and determined, and gradually she became aroused and began to respond. She realized then that his penis was flaccid; his persistence with her seemed prompted by something other than his own desire.

He stopped her from going down on him. "No, I don't want that. I'll bring you off with my hand."

He'd already started, and although she felt she would regret it later, she was too close to the edge to want to stop him. Her orgasm was the quick, rough untying of a knot; afterward she felt dirty and absurdly grateful. It was all too much; she'd been aroused and frustrated for so long, hopelessly wanting him, and it was all one-sided. He didn't want her. Embarrassed by herself, she began to cry.

"Shh, shh," he soothed her. "It's all right. It doesn't matter. Really, it's all right."

"But we have to talk—we've never even talked about it!"

"It's not something to talk about."

"I mean sex."

"So do I. It's better to let these things take their natural course. You mustn't take a little, er, hydraulic failure on my part as a slur on *you*. You're lovely. It's not your fault if I can't rise to the occasion."

Her face was burning hot, but at least her tears had dried up. She had never imagined that talking about sex with someone who was her lover could be so excruciatingly embarrassing. "I don't mean tonight. I meant sex in general, between us, how it's been... or not."

"Please don't let's get started on something that... you're tired and emotional. We both are."

"We haven't made love very often...."

"Did you think I hadn't noticed?" His voice, although low, was a howl of pain which caught in her throat. Tears flooded her eyes again, and she clutched at him. "Did you think I couldn't feel you willing me not to touch you whenever we were in bed?"

"Oh, Gray, oh, oh, darling, I did want you, I did, and I still do, only—" Sobs strangled her words.

"Hush, hush." He sounded weary. "Don't upset yourself. Don't try to say any more."

But there was one thing she was determined to ask him in the darkness, while they were still this close, one thing she had to know. She struggled to stop crying, to control her breathing. "The first time we made love wasn't the greatest—I thought it was a mistake, really, and that I'd kind of pushed you into it. That's why I left."

"Silly girl." He kissed the top of her head.

"But after that, the next time, when I took you to—when we made love, there, it was totally different. At least it was for me. Was it for you? Do you remember? Was it as good for you, that time?"

"Let's not dwell on the past."

"But I want to know. I need to know."

"Yes. Yes, it was good for me. And it will be again, even better. I promise you, it can be. I'm just sorry I couldn't prove it to you sooner." He sighed rather shakily, and then said firmly, "No more talk. We'll talk in the morning. Go to sleep now."

Relief flooded her. So he wasn't the same as Alex; he did remember, and he wasn't afraid of her. She realized how weary she was, and stopped fighting against sleep. Just as she was dropping off she thought she heard him say, "I love you."

Things were strange and strained between them the next day and it was hard to know how to fill the morning. They left the house after breakfast and she took him to the Galleria. It was either that or art galleries, and he hadn't been to a mall yet.

"Not that the Galleria is really typical of American malls. It's kind of more... well, ritzy and expensive. There's a Neiman-Marcus and a Saks."

"Hmmm, I don't know that my budget will run to souvenirs from Neiman-Marcus. I have scarcely any money left. Although there are a few people I really ought to bring presents back for, like the neighbor who's been watering my plants, and, um..."

"Caroline?" She heard the sharpness in her own voice.

"What are you implying?"

"Just that she might expect a present."

"Then if I don't bring her one that's another mark against me. And if I do, I'm trying to curry favor and we'll carry on—is that what you'd like? For me to continue with Caroline?"

He had told her too much about his problems with Caroline, although he probably thought he hadn't. She had been careful never to express anything but sympathy for him and had almost convinced herself that she was not jealous, yet knowing that he could be with the other woman tomorrow, she felt bitter. "I'm not telling you what to do. That's up to you."

"How about you? Will you be going back to your bloke once I'm gone?"

She shrugged uneasily. She'd had some painful moments of missing Jack, regrets about what she had done, but that was that. "We'll probably break up."

"Only probably?"

"I'll have to tell him the truth. He's an easy-going guy, but he's not a doormat. We'll break up."

"Will you be sorry? Have I just ruined your life?"

She was suddenly tired of all this emotion. She longed to be alone in her car, on the highway going home, three hours spent driving toward Austin without the sound of another voice except for that of the radio DJ calling out the hits. She thought she might wait a few days before seeing Jack. It would be good to have some time to herself. "Of course not. We were bound to break up eventually. Let's shop."

On the way to the airport, their final journey together, there were long stretches of silence. Anything said now had to be trivial or it took on an almost unbearable significance. Only a few more hours left to say everything there was to say. Agnes wished it over with.

She parked in the long-term parking lot and took him inside to check his suitcase and get his boarding pass. Then, with nearly two hours to kill before his flight was called, they looked for somewhere to sit down. She spotted an empty table in a cafeteria-style coffee shop and told Graham to claim it while she stood in line. "I'll get coffee and... do you want anything else? A sandwich? No? Sure? I'll get us both coffee, then."

She'd only been standing in line about a minute when she heard him behind her. "This is crazy," he said. "Come away from that queue. I was looking at you across the room and wondering what I was doing, letting you walk away from me. I don't care about coffee. I just want to be with you." She was shocked to see that he was crying.

"Oh, Gray!" She reached up to wipe the wetness from his cheeks. "Don't, please don't cry." Her own eyes filled sympathetically.

"I don't want to lose you. I can't bear it. I never expected this to happen, I never planned to fall in love with you, but I have. Oh, Nancy, please, please come with me. Come and live with me in England."

She stared at him in astonishment. It was like something she might have imagined long ago, but not now, not after what had not happened between them.

"I'm serious. I know I'm no great prize, I know I'm difficult to live with, I know my past history with women is—but I'm serious about you, I want something different with you, I want to change my life. Oh, God, I wasn't going to say it now, here, like this, but—I want to marry you. I want you to be my wife.

"No, don't answer me now, think about it, we can live together first and then decide if it really makes sense. I know life in England will be different for you, you might not like it, but please, won't you try it, for my sake? Give me a chance?"

She bit her lip. "I don't know what to say. I—this is a horrible place to talk about it, but... there is a problem, isn't there?"

"You mean the sex," he said readily. "I'm a disappointment to you."

"No! I didn't mean it like that!" She felt herself going red.

"This isn't the place to talk about it."

"I know, but—"

"But I'm pushing you. It's so unfair. Nancy, we hardly know each other, and that's the truth. But I do know I love you, and I *want* to know you. We can work things out. There's often trouble at the beginning, adjustments to be made. The sex will get better, I'm sure of it. All we have to do is want it to."

The sex could get better—it had been better, once. It had been the best ever. That memory would be with her always, the memory of their time in the little house in the woods, when he had been her perfect lover, better than she'd ever dreamed. If they'd had it once, why shouldn't they have it again?

"Yes," she said. No other decision was possible, this story had been written long ago. This was the life she'd been waiting to find, and he was offering it to her. To live with a poet—her poet—in England. It was the great wish of her life, and she had to accept it, whatever the consequences. She smiled, seeing he hadn't understood. "I do want to. I will try. I'll come to England."

"Oh, Nancy!" He threw his arms around her, squashed her to him. A button on his jacket pressed painfully into her breastbone. Just as quickly he let her go. "Come on, I'll buy you a ticket. I don't care what it costs if only there's a seat left on my flight!"

"Gray, I can't, not like that. I can't fly back with you now."

"Why not? You want to talk to your boyfriend first, decide if I'm really a better deal?"

"No, of course not, it's nothing to do with him."

"Get your roommate to pack your things and ship them to you, COD. You can write to your employers and your bank. What else... oh, your car. Surely you can leave your key here and call your mother, tell her to come and get it. She could keep it for you or sell it if you decide to stay. Come on, Nancy, if you love me, come with me now."

She was torn. Part of her resisted his urgency while another part responded to his desire with a reckless excitement of her own. How wonderful, to live life like an adventure, like a fairy tale, to run away with the handsome prince the moment he asked, to let the god in animal form bear her across the sea to Europe. He wasn't perfect, but he was the man of her dreams. Of course she could manage to work out all the boring details of quitting her job and selling her car through friends and the mail.

"Say yes," he urged.

She opened her mouth and winced as she remembered. "I can't. My passport's in Austin."

PART SIX:

THE POET'S WIFE

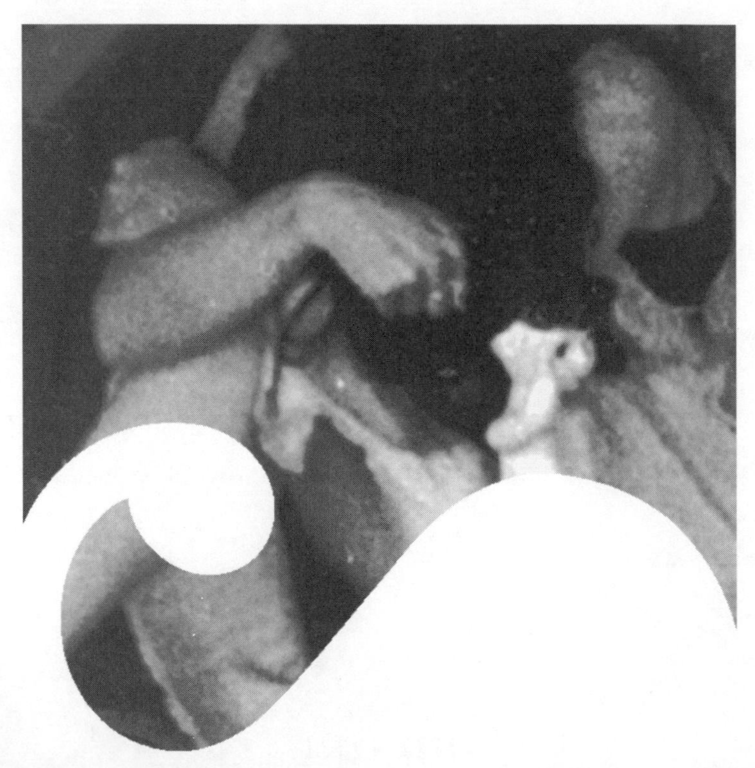

As dead-clammy meat turns to edible meat. As revulsion turns to appetite.

How is it possible you ask, the answer is it is possible.

The answer is it is.

—Joyce Carol Oates, "Thanksgiving"

She waited too long before she went to him.

Two months of preparations and conclusions, selling everything that wouldn't fit in two suitcases, giving farewell parties, rewriting her book, recreating Graham Storey inside her head until he became the man she loved, her future husband. She no longer doubted her desire to be with him.

The first thing he said when they met among the crowds at Gatwick, his voice a stark, accusing cry, was "You've cut your hair! Your beautiful hair—why?"

She'd worn her hair long and straight, a lazy fairy-tale princess, since she was sixteen. She'd cut it because she was grown up at long last, beginning her new life. She said, "Don't you like it?"

"It doesn't matter. I'm sorry. It's fine. Only—I did love your beautiful long hair."

"You should have said so." Regret seeped into her, a slow, distant pain. He looked more ordinary than she remembered, smaller and older. The lines that bracketed his mouth were deeper. Even the blue of his eyes had faded.

He smiled. It was a stiff, unconvincing grimace. "Never mind." He hugged her. "Welcome. I should have said that first. Nothing else matters. I'm glad you're here at last."

She knew, as she hugged him back, clinging too tightly and for too long, that she had made a mistake; they did not belong together. But she was not sorry she had come, because out there was London,

England, that real place she had visited so often in fantasy, had lived in for the duration of so many books throughout her life. Part of the lure of Graham had always been his Englishness, the promise she imagined of being able to slip into his life and know it from the inside.

He drove her away in his little black English car, up through South London into the center, pointing out the sights. Some she recognized from pictures or movies; others had previously been only words on paper. Now it was real. Traveling along the Embankment, gazing at ornate lampposts, pedestrians, the River Thames, her heart beat wildly, until she thought it would burst with joy. She was here. Her wish had come true.

Harrow was a disappointment. It was not the village she had supposed, but just another part of the suburban London sprawl, only redeemed by the picturesque hill with the old school on top. Graham's "cottage" was a tiny, cramped row house, and the front door opened directly onto a main road, without the buffer even of a small garden. The windows were grimy, and the sound of traffic was a constant, even late at night. Heavy goods vehicles rumbling past made the whole house shudder.

It was only two rooms up and two down (plus a poky bathroom just off the kitchen by the back door), and with the muffled sounds of their neighbors' lives a parenthesis about their own, it felt to her more like an apartment than a house. The rooms were poorly lit, the windows at the front shrouded in netting, and even now, in summer, with the back windows open, and flies coming in, it was cold. There was an omnipresent smell of damp paper, stale cigarettes and something else she couldn't identify. The furniture, inherited from his parents, was ugly and there was too much of it.

She could not imagine living in it. She felt certain, within hours if not minutes of being shown through her new home by Graham, that there could be no room for her own life in the little house so crowded with his furniture, memories and ghosts. She'd already heard from him that rental properties were scarce and expensive in London, but she didn't need a whole house. Surely she could find a room to rent for a few months. This idea went ticking through her head when he took her out for a walk up the hill and a pub lunch, but she didn't mention it to him. It would have been too rude to start talking about leaving when he had just finished showing her the preparations he'd made for her arrival: the table and chair he'd set up for her to work on in a corner of the bedroom; the space he'd cleared for her clothes in the huge mahogany wardrobe; the flowers, wine, and French cheeses he'd bought to welcome her.

But she was certain he felt just as she did: shocked and disappointed by the realization of the wish he'd made two months ago in the Houston airport.

That first day they made conversation like people on a first date. They were excessively polite and restrained, trying to avoid talking about anything with a potential for stirring up troublesome emotions. Agnes went to bed early that night, completely wiped out by jetlag, and didn't wake when Graham came to bed. In the morning she opened her eyes to find him gazing at her, his head close to hers on the pillow. When he saw she was awake, he kissed her.

Hope, like a flame, surged up inside, and she moved eagerly to embrace him. But the kiss had not been a prelude to intimacy; he pulled away. "Would you like a bath? The water will be hot; I put the immersion heater on last night."

"Why don't you have one with me?"

"I had one last night."

She heard the simple statement as a criticism—she hadn't bathed, she was dirty and smelled bad, how could she expect him to want to make love to her? She scrambled out of bed. "I'll go wash."

"The green towel on the rail behind the door is yours."

She bathed as quickly as she could, wishing for a shower, hoping he would still be waiting for her in bed when she emerged. But the smell of coffee drifted in to her as she was drying herself, and when she came out, she found him in the kitchen, fully dressed, slicing bread for toast.

The school summer holiday had started just before her arrival, which meant Graham would be home all day. But, as he told her over breakfast, he still had work to do. He was revising some poems, and had been sent a stack of books for review. Although he intended to spend a lot of time with her during the holidays, he said he would feel happier if he could clear away his work first. "Then I can concentrate on you," he said, looking anxious. "If you don't mind too much?"

"I don't mind at all," she said quickly. "I always meant to visit London on my own, anyway, before I met you. I can do all the touristy things by myself—I'll be perfectly happy. You don't have to worry about me; I speak the language!"

"I'm not so sure about that." He grinned, not wholly convincingly. "Well, if you wouldn't mind... there should be plenty to keep you happy in London for a few days. And then we can take some time off, to travel around the country together, the way we did in Texas."

Agnes wasn't sure she believed that the trip he spoke of would ever happen; or that it was desirable. She'd realized, since his good-morning kiss, that she still wanted Graham, and wanted him to want her. She wasn't as reconciled to the notion that their brief love affair had been a mistake which was now ended as she'd tried to make herself believe. She still wanted to have a future with Graham. But if it wasn't to be, she could still be happy. And she could still have London.

She said, "I don't want you to give up your writing for me. After all, it was your poetry which first attracted me to you. I don't need to be entertained all the time. Don't forget, I'm a writer, too."

"I know," he said. "I can't believe how lucky I am, to have found you. Oh, Nancy, I'm so glad you came!" He got up from the table and came to embrace her. She should have been glad, she thought, yet it seemed to her that the passion in his voice was there in an attempt to convince himself, as much as her, that he meant what he said, and there was something awkward, forced about his hug. She was sure that when she hugged him back he flinched away.

She went up to London on the train, and found it thrilling and awesome just to be there. She walked around, staring, until she practically reeled with sensory overload from trying to take it all in. She couldn't make up her mind which of the many starred attractions in her guide book to visit first, so, after stumbling through the streets of Bloomsbury and Soho and around Trafalgar Square until she was foot-sore, she bought a ticket to ride on the top of a special double-decker tour bus, and let the guide's amplified descriptions go in one ear and out the other while she stared and stared at the city from this new angle.

When she got back to Harrow in the evening and told Graham what she'd done he laughed disapprovingly and told her that tour buses were as naff as Madame Tussaud's.

"Naff?"

"Unbelievably."

She didn't know the word, but it was obviously undesirable to be naff. "So, no Madame Tussaud's tomorrow?"

"Certainly not. But you can go and see the Crown Jewels in the Tower of London with all the other Japanese and American tourists if you really want."

Once again she was pole-axed by jetlag and went to bed early. When she woke, Graham was already up. She could hear him talking, low-voiced, to someone in the next room.

He was just hanging up the telephone when she opened the door to his office. He turned and scowled at her. "What do you want?"

"I... just wondered where you were."

"In my office, working, as you can see."

"But it's so early."

"I'm not required by law to stay in bed until eight o'clock."

"I'm sorry." She backed away from his anger, but instantly his expression changed; he was contrite.

"No, *I'm* the one who's sorry—a sorry excuse for a human being!" He caught her in his arms. "Forgive me, Nancy, please. I'm an old curmudgeon. I'm so used to living by myself, having everything my own way—I'm not used to having to explain myself to anyone else."

"You don't have to explain yourself to me."

"No, but I want to."

She waited, hopefully, but that seemed to be the end of it. He let her go. "Bear with me, please," he said. "Give me a little more time. Don't give up on me."

"I won't."

And she hadn't given up hope, although she thought, as the days passed, that her expectations were unwise. They spent a lot of time apart, and when they were together they talked mostly about what they had done or thought or seen on their own. They talked about external, impersonal things, never about their relationship. Agnes didn't know what their relationship was. After a whole week together, they still had not made love, and they did not talk about the future, as if life would continue in this way forever. They were like strangers brought together in some dramatic way: survivors of a plane crash, the only two English-speakers in a hostile foreign place. They had shared something once, long ago, but it was hard now to remember exactly what it had been, or if it was still important, and undoubtedly they each remembered it differently. He stirred a complex of emotions in her which were powerful but not happy.

Traveling around the great foreign city where she knew no one, where no schedule or expectations bound her, Agnes was not exactly happy, either, but she was always interested. She felt sometimes as if her own identity had slipped away. She could be anyone—at least, until she opened her mouth and identified herself for anyone who could hear as another American tourist. But, as her second week in England began, she recognized that she was getting tired of being a tourist, spending her days in museums, galleries and bookshops. She needed to start getting on with her new life, she thought: have things out with Gray, find herself a place to live, get into a routine, start writing again.

On her seventh journey into London she wandered a bit farther afield than before, and it was getting late in the day when she came upon a neighborhood of quiet streets with names that sparked no literary associations. It was too quiet—looking down a curving lane of old, high buildings, which all seemed to be small businesses shut up for the day, she was suddenly aware that it was nearly six o'clock. She was foot-sore and hungry and thirsty, but although a "Coca-Cola" sign beckoned, it turned out to belong to a snack-bar as dark and closed as if it had never been open.

She had a *London A to Z* in her bag, but as she couldn't see any street-signs she chose a direction at random and set off walking. Navigating by map was difficult and time-consuming. The way the streets curved here and ran out and changed their names—and the way the street-names were often hidden away—confused her, but luckily it never took her very long to find an Underground station.

A porcelain doll, a stack of wooden boxes, a jumble of ornaments in a cluttered shop window caught her eye from across the road, and she walked across the silent, empty, narrow street (noting the cobbles underfoot) to have a better look. An antique shop, or a junk shop, she couldn't tell. Displayed in the window were lots of china ornaments, bric-a-brac, the doll, a somewhat moth-eaten old teddy bear. She put her hand against the glass and leaned close, peering into the darkened interior of the shop. That was an attractive old dresser, she thought. The top drawer had been pulled out halfway and was filled with stuffed animals and dolls, but her eyes scanned past them at first; she was more interested in the furniture.

Something familiar wrenched at her attention, and she looked again at the toys in the dresser drawer, her heart beating harder even before she understood what she was looking at.

There, wedged in between another moth-eaten teddy and a peculiar golliwog thing was a small, old-fashioned doll that she recognized as immediately as her own face in a mirror: it was Myles.

Her breath fogged the glass and she had to move, to look again. It was harder to make him out from this angle—if she moved too far one way he was blocked by the golliwog; from another direction he was lost in the shadows, a pale gleam, a slim, featureless toy.

For one moment she had been absolutely certain. Now, she was less so. There was only so much she could see from this distance. It might be another doll that looked like Myles. There must be some: other dolls made by the same doll-maker, in the same year. She'd always believed he was English.

But what if it was *her* doll? All at once it seemed absurd, impossible, that she didn't know, couldn't remember what had happened to Myles. He'd been so important to her once, and then—then she'd stopped believing he could talk. He'd no longer seemed alive, and the sight of him had been the memory of loss, so she'd lost sight of him. Probably her mother had taken him; maybe Marjorie had reclaimed him. And maybe Marjorie had come to London and, being hard-up, had sold him to an antiques dealer....

It stretched credibility. And yet... there was the doll. It might have been hers.

Impatiently, she moved away from the window and looked up and around. There wasn't a sign; the shop didn't seem to have a name, although there was the number 6 on the door. If she could find the street name she could come back in the morning, when the shop would be open.

As she entered the house she heard the tell-tale cut-off bell-sound that meant the telephone receiver had been replaced, and a few seconds later Graham came thudding down the stairs. He looked nervous. "Where've you been?"

"I'm sorry. I got lost, I lost track of time."

"Have you eaten?"

She shook her head. "It just took me a long time to get back out here."

"Let's go for a meal, then. I'm starved."

Over plates of pasta and a carafe of red wine he asked about her day, and she told him about finding Myles.

"But surely... it isn't likely it's the same doll? All the way from Texas?"

"Myles wasn't an ordinary doll. My mother said he was a valuable antique, but he was more than that. He was real. I mean, I thought he was alive, in a sort of way. He used to tell me stories." She felt her face getting hot, and was almost sorry she had told him even that much until she realized how his expression had changed. He was looking at her with open interest and excitement, as if he had just made a wonderful discovery. He had not looked at her like that since Texas.

"Go on. Please."

"My aunt Marjorie gave him to me, to be my pillow friend, when I was seven. He'd been hers. My mother didn't want me to have him, I never knew why. When she had the chance to steal him from me she did, and she tried to destroy him. I don't mean literally destroy him, I mean... she wrapped him up in these strips of black silk and somehow that would destroy the magic in him. Or at least, that's what I thought. God, I must sound crazy."

"Not at all. Not at all." He leaned over to refill her wine glass. "Things happen to us as children, we can see things in ways that are lost to us when we grow older. That doesn't mean they're not real. Far from it. It would be interesting to know what your mother thought she was doing."

"I think she thought she was protecting me." She surprised herself with that knowledge. "But I could never ask her. Even now. She'd look at me like I was making this crazy thing up. She wouldn't remember anything about it. But Myles was real. I mean, whatever he was, whether he was magic, or I only dreamed about him being alive, he did exist, and if I didn't find him again today it must have been another doll like him. God, I wish that shop had been open!" She ate some linguini.

"We'll go back tomorrow when it is open. You made a note of the address?"

"I tried to, but I couldn't find the street name. It was a really short street, kind of curved, and, oh, yeah, it was cobbled!"

He shrugged. "Did you notice the names of streets nearby?"

"Yes, definitely, there was one..." she frowned in annoyance. "Honestly, I kept saying it to myself until I had it memorized, and now I can't... it's just slipped my mind."

"Maybe it'll come back to you."

"It must. I can't believe I... it started with C, I think. I'm pretty sure."

"What part of London?"

"About a ten minute walk from Farringdon Station."

"In which direction?"

"God, I don't know. I have no sense of direction!"

"Never mind. We'll find it."

Her story had caught his attention. He was looking at her with a wondering warmth in his eyes, as if she had become someone new and very special. And as he looked at her in that way she felt a change in herself, a rekindling of her interest in him.

They became lovers that night, a new first time which almost wiped out their brief, shared past, offering them a chance of real intimacy.

The next morning as they were about to leave, the telephone rang and she stopped on her way to the door.

"What's the matter? Go on."

"I thought you'd want to answer the phone."

"No. We're going out." He spoke with some tension.

"We're not in any hurry. It might be important."

"It's not important. Nothing's as important as you—as us," he said fiercely.

She wondered if it was his old girlfriend on the phone and how he knew.

"Come on, we're going to find your doll," he said.

But although they spent a lot of time and effort searching, taking Farringdon Station as their center point and traveling out in different directions, they didn't find the shop again that day. Twice she thought she recognized the street, but both times she was wrong.

"I'm sorry," he said, finally, when they'd agreed to give up and go for a meal. "But maybe you walked farther than you thought; maybe you really weren't that close to Farringdon."

"Maybe the shop disappeared—it looked like the sort that might." They were holding hands now, strolling along Holborn Viaduct.

"Then maybe it'll turn up some other day somewhere else entirely, and you'll have another chance to find your heart's desire."

"Well, maybe. Only Myles isn't my heart's desire anymore."

"No?" He stopped and gave her hand a tug so that she faced him. "What is?"

She looked through two pairs of glasses into blue eyes nearly level with her own, at his face, luminous with interest and affection, no longer ordinary. He was the young poet and he loved her. This was the magic city. She felt like someone in a novel. Here was everything she'd wished for, a dream to be lived in. She had only to accept.

It was suddenly hard to speak. Her voice was hoarse and the words "You are" came out a question, not the statement it should have been, but he kissed her just as she'd wanted him to.

"And you're mine—oh, yes you are! I thought I'd lost you, I thought you'd never come back to me, but here you are."

They began to walk again, briskly now, his arm around her. "Let's run away together."

"What?"

"No, no, your line is, 'Yes, why not?' We've nearly a month before term starts; we're not tied down. We should get right away, while we can. Wouldn't you like to see a bit more of the country? We'll go up to Scotland; you'll see the bothy. We'll be together, no distractions, nobody else to get in the way, nothing to come between us."

It was a new start; that was what they had needed. Away from his house, things were easier between them. On the move, away from home, their personalities were less stable, they could be different people. There were fewer rules and fewer expectations, and they could enjoy what each day brought without worrying about whether it would last, or what the future would be.

He did all the driving and generally didn't even require her to navigate, so she could sit back, gaze at the scenery, and let her mind wander, or listen to the radio. She particularly loved the shipping forecasts, those mysterious chants, incomprehensible yet beautiful as they were read out in measured, dulcet tones. Fair Isle, Finisterre, Dogger, Rockall: forever after those names would have for her a romantic, melancholy magic.

Although they often stopped to sight-see or for meals or snacks, by the fourth morning they were crossing the border into Scotland.

She saw a sign with a place name she recalled from her reading. "Gretna. Is that like Gretna Green, where people used to go to get married?"

"People still do. Shall we?"

He had to be teasing. "Just like that?"

"You've changed your mind. You don't want me."

The misery in his voice was so stark she had to reassure him, without even thinking about what she wanted herself—if she knew. "Oh, Gray, of course I do! But it can't be that easy, that quick—what about blood tests?"

"Blood tests?" He laughed. "What the hell are blood tests? Is that something to do with AIDs? You don't think I—"

"It doesn't have anything to do with AIDs. People have to have blood tests before they get married."

"Maybe in Texas. Not here. Come on, let's go get married."

She didn't know him well enough to marry him. She wasn't sure she wanted to be married, to anyone. But she wanted to make him as happy as he'd made her these past few days. She went with him into the registry office in Gretna, where they found it wasn't quite so easy to get married. First they would have to have their names and intention to marry posted on the door of the registry office for fourteen days. Then, if no objection was raised, they could be married on whatever date they decided.

"Can't we have a special license? In England you pay a little more for a special license and you're married the next day."

"This isn't England," said the registrar, an attractive middle-aged woman whose attitude slipped now from friendly to formal.

"It's a ridiculously antiquated law—posting the banns! Two weeks, two days, two months, it wouldn't make any difference, nobody knows us here, nobody's going to raise any objection to us getting married—there aren't any objections to be raised!"

"I'm sorry, but that is the law. I didn't make the law and I cannot change it."

She could feel the irritation rising in him like water coming to the boil, and put a hand on his arm as if she could lower his temperature with the right touch. "We could come back here in two weeks, on our way home."

"I don't want to come back in two weeks; I want us to be married *now*." Then all at once the water stopped boiling and the steam vanished in a sound halfway to a laugh. "God, I'm being childish. How do you put up with me?" He squeezed her hand. His fingers were very cold. He spoke to the registrar. "You see, I'm afraid that if I give her two weeks to reconsider she'll recover her senses and head back to America without me! I'm sorry if I was rude; it's the excitement. I've never come this close to actually getting married before."

The registrar smiled. "That's all right."

"So, could we register our intention to marry, and have the first possible date?" He looked at her anxiously. "If you still want to?"

"Sure. If we can't wait two weeks, we probably shouldn't be getting married." She giggled nervously. "God, I sound like somebody's mother."

"Like everybody's mother. And like most motherly maxims it's sound advice. Two weeks won't make any difference to us."

Yet even as she smiled back at him, and gave the clerk the few necessary personal details required, she felt, disquietingly, that their moment had passed. Oh, they could still get married, but it would not be the same, would not be what it should have been. And that marriage which might have been would haunt them forever.

Scotland was utterly different from England. England had been fascinating, changing in character every few miles, yet all, somehow, of a piece, recognizable from books she had read, novels, poems and histories, or from paintings. England was known and knowable, cozy; Scotland, by comparison, was grandly beautiful, a bit intimidating. There was so much open space and, after the crowds of England, it felt underpopulated. She realized only after they were in the country that she had no specific expectations of Scotland, no clear mental images of it as she did of the smaller country to the south.

Instead of heading west immediately they went north to the highlands. Scotland's bloody history unrolled before her as they traveled, as she browsed in her guide books and Gray told her about famous battles and betrayals and the Clearances.

She felt an urge to see all of Scotland, to encompass it somehow. To satisfy her, he took them to Dunnet Head, the northernmost point of mainland Britain, and then drove across almost to Cape Wrath before heading south down the west coast. She enjoyed looking at the map and seeing all the ground they had covered, ticking off the villages they had passed through in her guide book. It gave her an obscure and, she knew, completely spurious, sense of achievement, as if, by merely covering ground in this way she were getting to know Scotland.

After more than a week they arrived at last in Knapdale, where Graham had spent all his childhood holidays. It was a windy, overcast, chilly day, more like autumn than late summer, but the beauty of the area was undeniable. The last five miles of their journey took them along a single-track road which followed the winding shoreline. Across an expanse of choppy, glittering silver-gray water, through the low cloud, she made out the heavy, uprising mass of mountainous islands, and the beauty of the sight was a pleasure almost sexual.

"What's that?"

"The Isle of Jura. The mountains are the Paps of Jura. It's even more beautiful when it's clear. You can't see much today."

"I thought the island was a cloud, at first. I'd like to go there. Could we?"

"Sure. There's a ferry the other side of Tarbert. We'll see about it."

They drove through forest and moorland, passed grazing sheep and a stag standing on a rocky uplift as if posing for his portrait. Then the road descended and twisted inland for a little way, and they passed through a tiny village.

"The nearest petrol pump," Graham explained. "The nearest post office. Nearest place to buy milk, biscuits and a newspaper. It's walkable."

According to him, the name of the settlement, Clachan, was the generic name for village in Scotland, a Gaelic word which meant "a place of stones"—or anywhere with buildings.

After it left Clachan the road sought the shore again, and soon brought them to the small, plain white house that was Graham's bothy. She was thrilled that the house faced Jura; that would be the view from the front windows, the view she already felt was the most beautiful she'd ever seen.

The front door was so low they had to duck their heads to enter. It led directly into the main living area. She saw a fireplace, bookshelves, a few pieces of unremarkable furniture, a curtain. Behind the curtain there was a poky scullery. A door at the far end of the living room revealed a narrow, winding staircase—"I never saw stairs in a closet before!"—which led to the bedrooms. Upstairs had presumably been one big room later divided into two small rooms now almost completely filled with beds and books. She went immediately to one of the windows to look out at her favorite view, and sighed with happiness. She turned around to smile at him. "Thank you for bringing me here."

"You like it?"

"I love it. I don't understand why you don't live here instead of in Harrow."

"Nor do I." He wriggled his shoulders and rubbed his hands together. "I'm going to chop wood. You can start getting yourself settled in while I see to the fire. Maybe you could make us some coffee? There's a jar of instant in the survival kit."

"Okay. Oh—where's the bathroom?"

"Isn't one. We wash in the kitchen sink—or in the loch if you're feeling really hardy!"

"We don't have to pee in the sink, do we?"

"Oh, it's a toilet you want, not a bath—why didn't you say so? That's outside. I'll show you."

She feared the worst, but there was a flush toilet in a stone-built outhouse only a short distance from the back door—it was oddly cozy. She didn't mind the spiders in the corners, being a life-long fan of *Charlotte's Web*. She could hear Gray somewhere nearby chopping wood.

When she came back in again she walked around the main room, liking it more and more. The house was probably about the same size as the one in Harrow and might have been the same age, but the two places could hardly be more different. It was quiet here, and airy, and simple. She had felt oppressed and excluded by the memories that clung to everything in the house in Harrow, and this house, too, contained memories that did not include her, but it was different. The memories here were holiday memories of long summer days and peace and quiet. The ghosts who inhabited these walls were kindly, and they would make room for her.

In the cupboard under the stairs she found a small electric heater and plugged it in before she went out to the car for their luggage. She took the provisions into the kitchen, filled the inevitable electric kettle at the sink, and plugged it in.

Graham came in with a basket of split logs and kindling.

"Coffee's just—"

He frowned fiercely. "What the hell is that?"

"What?"

"That—electric heater."

"It's—an electric heater."

"What's it doing on?"

"I turned it on."

"Why? I told you we're going to have a fire—I went out to chop wood for a fire." He glared at her and she looked blankly back, nervous but baffled by his anger.

"Well, fine, we'll have a fire, that's great. But in the meantime, I was chilly and—"

"Oh, well, if you were chilly, then of course you had to get the whole place warm immediately. You couldn't put on a jumper, of course you couldn't."

"Are you worried about the electricity bill or what? I found the heater, so I put it on. In Harrow you've got electric heaters in every room and you've never said—"

"We're not in Harrow. This is not England, this is not America. When I said I was going to lay a fire I thought you would understand that things are different here. We do things differently." His voice was still angry, yet the look he gave her was more pleading than anything. He was begging her to understand.

And suddenly she did. This was his special place, the magical home of his childhood, a place out of time, where nothing changed and things were always done in a certain, traditional way, to preserve the magic. She thought of Aunt Marjorie's house and wondered if it had really been poverty which had made her live without electricity. She went and unplugged the heater, asking as she went, "Is it all right to use the electric kettle?"

"Of course. How else are we going to have coffee?"

"Mmmm, I don't know, I guess when you get the fire going we could boil a pot of water on it somehow."

"If you want to try, I won't stop you. But I'd like my coffee before I die of thirst."

"Sure. But—what did you do when you were a kid? Before this place had electricity?"

He stared at her. "I didn't drink coffee then." Then he smiled, grudgingly admitting complicity. "We had a camping stove. The electricity came in—well, actually it came in all along this road in the 1960s, so it was available then, but we didn't bother to get it. My father didn't think it was worth it, for the little time we spent here. It was my brother, when he married, when his daughter was born—I think his wife and daughter wouldn't have come up if there wasn't electricity, so..." he shrugged. "The new order. However, part of the deal was that the others pay the electricity bills, so I use it as little as possible. I still wish we were without... it makes this place too much like anywhere else. I can hardly conceive of it, but James brings a television up here." He knelt before the clean hearth and began to ball up pages from a pile of newspapers.

"Well, I guess when you have children you have to..."

"Don't you believe it! The telly's for him. And then he complains about the reception. God knows I watch too much junk; it's a relief to go somewhere I can't give in to the craving. If my brother ever leaves a television set here it goes straight into the loch."

She heard the kettle come to the boil and switch itself off, and went to make the coffee. When Gray got the fire going they sat before it drinking instant coffee and eating chocolate digestive biscuits, speaking very little. She felt happy and at peace, as glad to be here as she knew he must be, and believed they were in harmony, both enjoying the stillness and warmth after so many hours in the car.

Then he set down his empty cup on one of the stone flags of the hearth and stood up.

"I'm going to go stretch my legs."

"I'll come too."

"No, I want to be alone." He made a face. "Please don't take it personally. I need some time to myself, that's all. And it's something I've always done when I first get here, I have a wee stroll to check things out. By myself. Of course, I'm usually here on my own, so—

it's going to take me a while to get used to the new order. I hope you don't mind."

"Of course. I'll see you later." She did mind, she minded terribly. Not just that he didn't want her with him, but the way he'd confined her to quarters. She felt like a walk, too, after so long in the car, and would have enjoyed exploring the area, but if she went out now he would think she was following him.

Luckily she liked this house and didn't feel trapped here. There were plenty of books and she always enjoyed browsing. After she'd rinsed out their cups and left them beside the sink she began to prowl among the bookshelves. Except for a few old hardbacks about nature and the history of Scotland, most were paperbacks, chiefly fiction. Many were by authors whose work she knew—Iris Murdoch, John Fowles, Dorothy Dunnett—but there were others she'd never heard of, and a lot of green-spined Penguin mysteries which made her tingle with anticipation. In one Penguin, *The Private Wound* by Nicholas Blake, a photograph had been used as a book-mark. She took it out to look at it, and her stomach clenched with shock. She was looking at a picture of herself.

It was an old snapshot, taken when she was about seventeen. She was not aware of having seen it before, but she knew herself. Even in profile, her face slightly blurred, partially obscured by a strand of long, brown hair, she recognized her younger self. That was her smile and the slightly too-round curve of her cheek, those were her old glasses, and she even remembered the orange shirt, bought on an expedition with Roxanne to an import shop which had smelled of joss-sticks.

But what was it doing here? For a moment her sense of place deserted her, and she looked around wildly, half-expecting to find herself back in Austin, the past weeks with Gray nothing more than an especially involved daydream. But the fire still burned in the hearth behind her, there was the smell of woodsmoke in the air, and the peace of the countryside surrounded it all. She relaxed, secure again, and looked back at the picture, feeling small prickles of excitement.

How had Graham come by it? Was it possible that he had met her aunt in London, that she had given him a photograph of her niece, that he had been attracted, and dreamed over it, even as she had fantasized about his picture in Marjorie's house?

She asked him about the picture as soon as he came in, too excited to wait and pick a better moment.

He frowned and almost snatched it away. "What are you doing with this? Where did you find it? Have you been going through my personal things?"

"It was in a book, on the bookshelf."

He was still frowning, not seeing her. "Was it? Oh. I'm sorry I snapped at you. It was a shock—I'm not sure why. After so many years it shouldn't matter. It's not as if I ever really knew her."

"That's me. That's a picture of me."

Now he looked at her. There was no liking in his eyes. "Don't be ridiculous."

"I'm not. That's a picture of me."

"It doesn't look anything like you."

"When I was seventeen. Those are my glasses, that's my face, I had long hair—look, I know it's me!"

"I didn't know you when you were seventeen, and I'm the one who took the picture."

She wavered a little, but it was hard to give up something she'd felt so sure about. "Who is it, then?"

"Just someone I met, a long time ago. A girl I met in India. It never came to anything. I thought it might, for a time, but—nothing really happened. I never really knew her. I don't know why I kept her picture for so long." He hesitated, and then he crumpled it in his hand.

She gave a little cry.

He scowled at her. "What's the matter? You should be pleased. I'm through with my past, with all my old girlfriends. You're the only one I want now; you're all I need."

She had hoped, indeed she had almost come to believe, that some magic would be worked in the bothy, that they would come together in some final, irrefutable way and she would know, once and for all, that this was the man she had been waiting for, that they would make each other happy.

But real life was not so obligingly certain as her daydreams. They did grow closer during the next nine days as they talked a lot, more frankly than ever before, and they made love more often, with more tenderness and more abandon.

"You see," he said one night as they lay together in bed, relaxed and sweating with pleasurable exertion, "You see, it does get better when you know each other. It'll keep on getting better."

"It will?"

"Of course it will, as long as we want it to. As long as we try. We just have to decide we're going to be happy together, and we will be."

It was what she wanted to hear, wanted to believe. It was time to stop waiting for magic, and to accept what she had. Her wish had come true. She would accept the consequences.

On their way to Gretna they detoured to Stirling to check out a second-hand bookshop Graham had heard about. They were always happy in bookshops; before they'd met it had been a solitary pleasure, but now it was something they could share.

This time he made one purchase she didn't know about until after they were back in the car.

"Here you are," he said. "Here's a wedding present for you."

It was a copy of *Agnes Grey*, the first copy she had seen since she'd lost her own. It moved and excited her beyond words. More than that, it seemed to her an omen, a final and compelling reason to marry this man.

"Oh, Gray, oh my goodness—thank you! If you knew how much this means—"

"I think I do, actually."

"I didn't get anything for you, I don't have a present for you."

"The only present I want is you as my wife."

And so, a few hours later, with the reckless, terrified excitement with which someone might leap off a cliff in the expectation of being rescued by angels, she formally agreed in front of witnesses and became the wife of Graham Martin Storey.

On their wedding night, in a dingy hotel room in Carlisle, with her husband on the bed beside her reading the second volume of James Morris' *The Pax Britannica Trilogy*, she began to read *Agnes Grey*. The first page was so unexpected that it made her dizzy. She read it again, her disorientation increasing:

"*All true histories contain instruction; though, in some, the treasure may be hard to find, and when found, so trivial in quantity that the dry, shriveled kernel scarcely compensates for the trouble of cracking the nut. Whether this be the case with my history or not, I am hardly competent to judge; I sometimes think it might prove useful to some, and entertaining to others, but the world may judge for itself: shielded by my own obscurity, and by the lapse of years, and a few fictitious names, I do not fear to venture, and will candidly lay before the public what I would not disclose to the most intimate friend.*"

She turned the pages, reading snatches at random, searching for something she remembered, anything she remembered, without success. Each new thing she read, every familiar name she failed to find, increased her disturbance. It was hard to catch her breath and there was an odd smell coming from the pages of the book which made her feel a little sick.

"What's wrong?"

She waved the book at him. "This—this isn't the book I read, I don't know it at all!"

"That often happens. The books we particularly loved as children—"

"No, it's not the same book, I'm sure of it. I've never read this before. Could there be—there must be—another book with the same title?"

"Not by Anne Brontë."

"Maybe it wasn't by Anne Brontë, I don't know, I can't remember noticing the author's name on the copy my aunt gave me."

He raised his eyebrows and shrugged. "Well, I'm sorry. That's the only *Agnes Grey* I know of. Why don't you read it, maybe it'll come back to you. Probably your memory edited out the dull bits."

She could see he wanted to get back to his own book; he couldn't understand her distress. Anyway, she couldn't think of anything better than his suggestion, and so she again began to read it, for the first time.

The book she remembered was a tumultuous romance with fantastical elements, full of suspense, passion and melodramatic situations. This book, which Gray had given her, was completely different, a prim, dry tale about the daily life and misfortunes of a governess in nineteenth century England. There were no pirates, no wild horseback rides, no fairies, no scenes of low life in London. The only thing her remembered book had in common with this one was its title, the name of the heroine.

By the time she had forced her way to the modestly happy ending, Gray had put his book aside and fallen asleep. Nothing was as she had thought it would be: England, Graham Storey, *Agnes Grey*, true love, her wedding night. And what about marriage? She turned out the light and lay awake in the dark for a long time, listening to her husband sleep and wondering what she had done.

They had been back in Harrow for about two weeks when the phone call came. It was evening, and they had just finished dinner. He leapt up at the first ring and galloped upstairs to his study to answer it.

She imagined him returning immediately, saying it had been a wrong number. When he didn't, she took the dishes to the sink and began to wash up, feeling lonely.

She had finished the dishes when Graham came in, looking like a ghost. He came to her and clutched her hands, seeming not to notice that they were wet.

"What is it?"

"You won't leave me, will you?"

"Sweetie! Of course not! What's wrong?"

He threw his arms around her and held her tight. She could feel him quivering. Then he drew a deep breath and let go. "You'll be sorry you married me."

"No. Why? What's happened?"

He was looking at her through narrowed eyes, as if trying to assess what danger she might be to him, and she wondered who he was really seeing. He drew a little way back from her and said, almost coldly, "That was Caroline. She says she's pregnant."

"What's that got to do with you?"

He widened his eyes at her innocence. She tried taking a breath but couldn't draw it deep enough. "How pregnant?"

"Six to eight weeks, she says."

It would be six weeks tomorrow since she'd arrived in England; she had noticed that while making this morning's diary entry; now the knowledge made her choke with rage. "How could you?"

"Oh, God, don't you start! I need your support, not more—"

"Six weeks ago I was on my way to you, and you were screwing her. No wonder you weren't interested in going to bed with me the next day."

"Don't be ridiculous. I'd broken things off with her long before then."

"Long before? Then what's your worry? It must be somebody else's ba—fault."

He sighed and his shoulders slumped. "I wish. I made out I believed it was. But she says she hasn't been with anyone since me, and I believe her. This—well, it can't be six weeks, I promise you. Not if it's mine, absolutely not."

"Eight weeks?"

"Or nine or ten. She was never very good at keeping track of her periods."

"You said you were going to break things off with her as soon as you got home."

"I did try. It wasn't that easy. I told her there was no hope, we had no future—I told her about you and it still didn't make any difference. I've never understood her motives."

The unknown Caroline's motives were perfectly obvious; his weren't. "Why didn't you tell me? You told her about me."

"Because I couldn't. I didn't want to lose you!"

"Then why did you go on sleeping with her? Why, if you didn't care about her and you cared about me, why, when you knew I was coming over here to live with you?"

He backed against the wall, as far from her as he could get without leaving the room, and glared, trapped, frightened and furious. "But I didn't know, did I? I'd asked you, yes, but you kept putting me off. Maybe you would and maybe you wouldn't. Maybe this month, maybe next, maybe not this year at all. I didn't know what you were getting up to in Texas, with your old boyfriend, or maybe somebody new. I wanted you, but did you want me? I knew she wanted me, on any terms at all. I was lonely and vulnerable, and she knew what to do. I never could resist her, sexually. If you'd only come right away, when I asked you to, this would never have happened."

His eyes were wide, his mouth hung slightly open. She could feel his misery; her heart ached with it. Years of imagining Graham Storey into existence made it all too easy for her to identify with him, to accept his version of the truth and take the guilt onto herself. Anyway, she was his wife now. His interests were hers.

She took a painfully deep breath, struggling to fill her constricted lungs. "All right," she said, sounding calm. "It's happened. Now, what are we going to do about it?"

The facts were these: Caroline had phoned in a state of extreme anxiety to tell him she'd just learned she was pregnant. She didn't want an abortion, she wanted the baby, and the baby's father. She had asked him to come and see her, to reconsider their relationship. When he told her he was now married, she had become hysterical and hung up.

He was sure she would ring back as soon as she'd had a chance to calm down a little, but the evening wore on and the phone did not ring again.

"Maybe you should call her?"

"Absolutely not! If I did, she'd think I was hooked, that she had a chance to get me back. You don't want that, do you?"

"No. Of course not. But if you got her pregnant, don't you think—"

"I'll pay for the abortion. I'll do more than that. I'll pay for her to have a holiday afterward, to recover. But I don't owe her any more than that. She has no right to make me a father."

They stayed up late, talking. They were a couple, united against this threat from outside. Trying to understand what Caroline might do, what she might be feeling now, Agnes asked questions about the other woman, and Graham obliged with all sorts of intimate details from their relationship. She knew, even as she urged him on, greedy for more, that she would regret furnishing her imagination in this way, but at the moment this knowledge seemed a necessary thing.

At only one question did he balk: that was when she asked for Caroline's last name.

"What do you want to know that for?"

"I'm just curious. You said she's an actress. I wondered if I might have seen her in anything."

"You wouldn't know her by name, and I'm sure you've never seen her. She's only been on British television, and provincial rep. I've only seen her once, in a rather bad comedy series. It's not on anymore."

"Tell me her name anyway."

He leaned forward suddenly and grasped her hands and gazed intently into her eyes. "You mustn't think of getting in touch with her yourself, you really mustn't. I need you with me, supporting me, not trying to do a deal with her behind my back."

"Of course I wouldn't!"

"And don't imagine you can talk logic to her, or call on some sisterly solidarity. She's not like that. She's not reasonable. She's not like you at all. I know her, I know what she's like. Leave her to me."

Two days later Caroline phoned again, late, as they were getting ready for bed. Gray was on the phone with her for over half an hour; he came back into the bedroom looking sick and angry.

"What happened?" She was in bed, a volume of Leon Edel's *Life of Henry James* in her hands just as if she'd been able to read or think about anything else.

"Bitch." His hands were shaking as he fumbled out a cigarette from the pack in his jacket pocket. Usually, out of deference to her, he didn't smoke in the bedroom—which doubled as her office—but she said nothing as he struggled to light it, and waited for the answer which came after his first drag. "She says she can't decide what to do. I gave her the hard line: I'd pay for the abortion in a private clinic and a holiday after. If she wouldn't take that, she wouldn't get anything: I wouldn't acknowledge responsibility, I'd have nothing to do with her ever again."

"She won't have an abortion?"

"She won't say. She says she can't decide what to do until she's seen me again. She wants me to meet her and talk about it."

They had agreed that they were united on this, acting as one, that they would never allow Caroline to drive a wedge between them. But although she knew her interests were the same as Graham's, her imagination was traitorous. She couldn't help putting herself mentally into the other woman's position, imagining how hurt and furious—and terrified—she would have been had Graham left her pregnant in Texas and then gone off and married someone else. It could have happened; it was a scenario frighteningly easy to imagine. It had happened, only not to her.

"Well, maybe you should," she said. She didn't dare admit her treacherous sympathy, but what Caroline was asking seemed little enough.

He gaped at her. "Are you serious? You want me to go and see her? You'd like that?"

"I didn't say I'd like it, I just said maybe you should. If that's all she's asking... You're not getting anywhere over the phone. Maybe you could convince her in person."

"Meeting her 'one last time, just to talk,' during those weeks before you arrived was the last mistake I made with her."

"That was then, when you were lonely. Are you saying I couldn't trust you with her even now?"

"It's her I don't trust. You don't know her. I never really loved her, but there was something... irresistible about her. Even now, I'm still not sure, if she threw herself at me, that I could resist."

She was naked, only the width of the bed away from him, and he was looking straight at her, but she had a horrible, shrinking sensation, as if she had become invisible, or a child again. If even his memory of the beautiful, sexy Caroline could reduce her to this, she knew she would never survive a meeting with the real woman.

Gray shook his head and began to undress. "I'm not saying that if I went and met her in a pub that I'd be trying to get her clothes off. But I'm vulnerable, and she knows it. I do owe her something, if it's mine; I can't deny that. I can keep her at a distance over the phone, but if she got me to herself for a couple of hours she'd get to work on my guilt, and God knows what she'd have me agreeing to. I'd change my mind later, of course, but by then it might be too late. If she has the abortion soon it's a simple procedure, but if she leaves it much later—well, then it gets more complicated. But I've told her that. If all I've said doesn't make her see reason—"

"Maybe we should go and see her together."

"Are you mad?"

"I thought—"

"Don't. Don't think about it anymore." He turned away to find somewhere to stub out his cigarette. "I don't want you involved in this craziness."

"But I am involved; I'm your wife."

"Then leave it to me, all right? Give me your support; trust me to sort things out. You don't know Caroline, and I don't want you to. I think she'll see reason soon enough, when she realizes there's nothing she can do to get me back. She'll have an abortion, I'll pay the bills, and then we can forget about her. And if she doesn't—then we still forget about her. We have to. If she wants to ruin her own life, that's her decision; I'm not letting her ruin ours. We forget about her. Whatever happens. Now let's stop talking about it."

They stopped talking about Caroline, but the shadow of her unresolved pregnancy continued to hang over them. She phoned twice more in the next week: once to say she would have an abortion, once to say she would not. They heard nothing more.

Agnes didn't know how often Graham thought about his former girlfriend and she didn't want to ask. She herself thought about the other woman almost constantly, obsessively. She bought a book about pregnancy and childbirth and kept it hidden in a drawer beneath her sweaters. She didn't want Gray to see it, certain that if he did he would realize that instead of spending her days writing her next book she was studying the details of each stage of pregnancy, learning them by heart, as if in this way she could somehow get to know, and help, the woman he had said they were to forget. Sometimes she almost thought she was Caroline, that the other woman was her other self, existing out there somewhere, apart from Graham.

In November, Graham took her to her first publishing party, and Agnes felt that the life she'd always imagined she'd find in London, full of parties and literary types, was about to begin.

The party, to launch another poet's first novel, was held in an upstairs room of a club in Soho, with free wine and trays of dubious looking canapés. There was an animated hum of voices in the air, and it didn't matter that she was a stranger, she knew she would enjoy herself. Graham introduced her to a couple of people, including his editor, but soon left her to look after herself.

"Hi," said an American voice. "I don't think we've met. I'm Alice Keremos, publicity director." A tall thin woman with dark-rimmed eyes and a shock of hennaed hair, in the sort of skin-tight black dress Agnes would never dare wear, stood in front of her, holding a glass of white wine.

"I'm Agnes Grey."

"Heyyyy, I've heard of you. Didn't you do some work for the Brontës at one time?"

"No, that was my duller, primmer sister."

"So whom do you work for?"

"Nobody—yet."

"You're looking for a job in publishing?"

"Maybe. I don't know. In Texas I was an editor, but it was pretty small potatoes. Nothing like book publishing. And I'm a writer. I've been published in America, but I haven't managed to sell either of my books over here yet."

"I hate to ask the obvious question, but what brought you to England, since it wasn't fame or a job?"

"Oh... love."

"And?"

She drew a deep breath. "'Reader, I married him.'"

A huge smile stretched the other woman's face, and she reached out and lightly caressed Agnes' arm. "I'm a sucker for a good love story. Let's go scout out some more wine, and then I want you to tell me absolutely everything about the romantic Mr. Grey, especially whether he's got any unmarried brothers."

"What were you talking about for so long with that dreadful woman?" Graham asked as they emerged from the noise and heat of the party to the cold, rainy street.

"You can't mean Alice, she's my best friend!"

"You're drunk." He gripped her coated arm and steered her along. "Watch out, there's sick on the pavement."

She tottered a little in her heels and was grateful for his support. "Of course I'm drunk. People kept filling my glass. Aren't you?"

"I would hardly be proposing to drive us home if I were."

"Well, it was your idea to drive. We could have taken the tube." Her drunkenness—which was not as extreme as his distaste implied—had the blessed side-effect of insulating her from his disapproval.

"So what were you talking about? You were with her all evening."

"Mmm. Just stuff. What two American women in London would

talk about—Fairy Liquid, parades of shops, roundabouts, free houses..." She started laughing.

"Don't take the piss. I have a reason for asking."

"I'm serious! That's what we talked about. The stately disappointments of England. It all sounds so wonderful and exotic in books and then you come over here and—the language is full of traps. Imagine calling a dishwashing detergent 'Fairy Liquid'! It sounds like something that would give you eternal life. And parades of shops sounds so gay—like roundabouts—and really they're about the grimmest things imaginable, both of them. And there's nothing free in free houses, and oh, 'Take Courage'—I love that one, that one ought to be imported to America."

"It's just an advertising slogan," he said wearily. "I seem to recall quite a few of those in America."

"And the signs you see—Refuse Tip. No Football Coaches! I'm not complaining, really. I think it's sweet. I know people say that English and American are two different languages, but you can't really appreciate how true that is until you live here. Alice was saying—"

"Spare me, please. I don't want a blow by blow account of your conversation."

"Oh, I thought you did. Why did you park so far away? I'm getting soaked."

"Well, walk faster. I parked as near as I could."

"I can't walk faster, not in these shoes."

"Why do women wear such ridiculous shoes?"

"These aren't ridiculous!"

"Then you must be extremely drunk, because you can hardly walk. I hope to Christ you didn't tell that woman anything."

"Tell her what? State secrets? I don't know any, honest!"

"You don't seem to understand. I do actually have a reputation. And I would like to be known for my work, not my private life, which I like to keep private."

She spoke very solemnly. "I'm afraid she knows you're married. I did tell her that private detail."

"She works for my publisher. She would have known you were my wife as soon as she saw us walk in together."

She glimpsed a possible explanation for his annoyance. "Is she an old girlfriend?"

"I know you're jealous, but that is ridiculous. It may seem to you that I've slept with every woman in Greater London, but, I assure you, I have not. And Alice Keremos is exactly the kind of pushy, neurotic American woman I can't stand. Her idea of small-talk is to tell you just how awful various boyfriends of hers were in the sack, or how many orgasms she is capable of, and then she wants your vital statistics in return. I shudder to think what you might have said to her about me in your drunken state."

"We hardly talked about you at all. And she didn't regale me with details of her sex life, either." His cruel assessment of her new friend made her angry.

"So what did you talk about with her for so long?"

She remembered a lot of laughter, and touching. Alice was a toucher. Agnes had not been touched, except by Gray, since she had left America, and she had not realized how much she missed the easy, undemanding way her female friends embraced or touched her when they were together. She had no friends here. Alice's fingers on her arm, her arm around her shoulder, her breath on the side of her face when she whispered something confidential, had stirred her longing and also made her feel that their closeness was already a fact, their intimacy long-established. "Oh, we talked about all sorts of things. Did I know anybody from Providence or Boston, did she know anybody in Austin or Houston. Finding out what we had in common."

"Not much, I'll bet."

"Quite a lot, actually. She writes, too, you know."

"Oh yes?"

"She's had two poems published in *The London Magazine*."

"Really."

"And she's nice, Gray, really. If you—"

"She's not 'nice' at all. I'll tell you what she is, she's a vulgar, ambitious star-fucker. There was a big poetry promotion last year, a dozen poets, I was one of them, sent around the country to do readings in schools, libraries, village halls, other venues. She was along, supposed to make sure all went smoothly, and what she did was, she made a dead-set at—" he named a poet slightly better known than himself—"married bloke, I might add. All right, he wasn't blameless, but she was the one who did the running, and he was vulnerable, lonely, away from home, drinking.... After the tour she kept after him, and eventually his wife left him, poor bugger, and then she dropped him." He paused long enough to draw breath and then he went on. "And do you know what she has hanging over her bed? A self-portrait, full-frontal nude. Such bad taste: 'Here I am, boys.' Unbelievable."

"How do you know what she has over her bed?"

"It was nothing like that," he said irritably. "She's my publicity lady—she had a drinks party at her flat—there were lots of people there, it was utterly innocent. I had to use the loo. You had to go through the bedroom to get to it—typical, that."

She couldn't tell if he meant it was a typical floor-plan for a London flat, or if he was implying Alice had designed her living quarters to ensure that all male visitors would have to pass through her bedroom, where she hung the bad-taste portrait as a lure or, perhaps, as warning. She had been feeling angry, but the idiocy of this made her burst out laughing. They had finally reached the car; with relief she let go his supporting arm and fell against the side of the car, howling with laughter.

"You don't believe me," he said bitterly. "Well, I have no reason to lie. And I'll tell you another thing, although you obviously don't want to hear it. Alice Keremos is no friend of yours. She never will be. She was making up to you at that party as a way of getting closer to me." He had unlocked her door and now he went around to the other side to let himself in. "Will you get in the car? It's pissing down."

Alice Keremos was her friend. If there was at first a certain restraint on her part because of Gray's disapproval, it was neither strong nor disagreeable enough to inhibit Alice who, at their first lunchtime meeting, handed over a piece of paper with a name and telephone number on it, and told her to call about a job.

It was only a temporary position, covering for someone on maternity leave, but it meant six months paid experience working for a trendy newish publishing company in London: a business, a city, a field she knew nothing about.

"Why on earth did they hire me?" she demanded of Alice in the wine bar where they met to celebrate. As soon as the initial exhilaration subsided she realized she was terrified.

"They liked you; you impressed them; they thought you were the best person for the job. Fran liked you. That's important. She obviously felt she could work with you. And she will. Don't start thinking you're going to get dumped in it to sink or swim—if I know Fran (and I ought to; we shared a flat for six months) she'll be calling you from the delivery room to check on whether you fixed up an interview with *Time Out*. And... don't forget, it's only for six months."

"You mean even I can't screw things up beyond repair in only six months?"

"I mean," said Alice, taking her hand across the little *faux*-marble-topped table and squeezing her fingers, "How many people with experience, who are any good, are actually going to be going after a measly maternity leave cover-job? It's a good start for you, a way of getting experience for your next, real, job. You'll learn what you need to in no time, don't worry about it. And if you ever have a question, and you can't get Frannie on the phone, you can always call me."

Another squeeze of the hand. The public hand-holding embarrassed her, but she didn't like to show it. Having so miraculously stumbled on the two things she most wanted so quickly she was determined to do nothing to risk either the job or the friendship.

Gray didn't really approve of her job, she knew, because of his complex, chip-on-the-shoulder attitude toward publishing. He was not one of those poets who had found themselves a comfortable position in either publishing or academia, and his attitude toward those who had was made up of derision, dislike, and jealousy. But at least she wasn't working for *his* publisher, and her job was to promote books, not decide which ones should be published. And anything that made her happy, he said, made him happy. He even, after the friendship appeared to be established, was willing to admit he might have been wrong about Alice Keremos, might have misjudged her, and allowed his wife to invite her to dinner one night. The evening was a success. Gray declared Alice to be, behind her mannerisms, "really rather sweet," and Agnes glowed with the professional matchmaker's pride.

Time passed quickly now, the days full, tumbling over one another. A life was taking shape around her, very different from her life in Austin, yet just as authentically hers. Occupied, she was happy, with no time for brooding about Caroline. She did not forget her, but was no longer haunted by the other woman and her phantom pregnancy. There were other things to think about. She was meeting people and learning things; weekdays were for working, weekends she had Graham.

One day shortly before Christmas she arrived home from work and sensed someone else in the house. She didn't know how she knew—was it a scent? had she glimpsed some movement through the net curtains at the front window?—but she felt it was someone familiar.

"Graham?" she called, going through to the lounge, then the kitchen. Both rooms were empty, although the cooker was on and she could smell potatoes baking. She went back to the hall and mounted the stairs, not calling his name this time, a little nervous.

There was no one in his office, or their bedroom, yet the feeling persisted: she was not alone.

She heard Graham's key in the lock downstairs just as she saw what was on the bed.

Strips of silk. Long silk scarves. Four black, one white.

"Nancy?" He came bounding up the stairs. "I thought that was you! I was in the off-license when you walked past."

"Was there somebody here?"

He looked puzzled. "Who? When?"

"I don't know. Just now. Before I got home."

"I was here until ten minutes ago. I just nipped out to get some fags. No, there's been no one. Why, did you see someone? We haven't had a burglar?"

"No, nothing like that." She fought her inclination to turn around and stare at the scarves on the bed. She wanted to see his response. "It wasn't that sort of feeling—it was a good feeling I had when I came in, like somebody I knew was here, somebody I'd be really happy to see."

He made a face. "Not someone like me?" He gave her a quick kiss. "Sorry I wasn't here. I've got to go check the spuds. Come with me."

That night when she went up to bed he was ahead of her, wearing nothing but a wicked smile. The room was dimly lit; a diaphanous cloth had been draped over the bedside light—she recognized the white silk scarf. The black silks were in a cool heap on the sheet beside him.

"Well, what shall we do with these, you naughty girl?"

She had wondered what it would be like to be tied to a bed with silken cords, to have her hands bound—at her own request—while someone made love to her. She had imagined she would enjoy it, in a scary kind of way, but in fact she didn't like it at all. She was uncomfortable the whole time. She hated not being able to move her arms or legs; the fact that she could not, physically, stop him touching her wherever, however he liked frightened her as much as if he'd been a total stranger. Perhaps he handled her gently, but it seemed brutality to her. She could not relax.

He took no notice when she asked him to untie her.

"Graham, please. I mean it."

He grinned, running his hands up and down her naked body, pausing briefly to cup her breasts and lightly pinch the nipples.

"Look, I don't like it. Let me go."

"Maybe I should have used that other scarf to tie your mouth, so you wouldn't keep telling me what to do, hmmm?" His fingers moved teasingly between the legs she could not close.

"Don't!" Couldn't he see that she meant what she said? Unable to stop him any other way, she burst into tears.

At once his grin vanished. He looked baffled at first, then angry. "Jesus, Nancy. What's with you? First you complain I'm inhibited; now, when I try to do something to please you—oh, stop crying, would you? I haven't done anything. I'm letting you go, if I can only get this damn knot...."

As soon as she was free, he switched off the light and turned away from her.

"I'm sorry," she said.

"Yeah."

"I mean it. Please don't be mad at me—I was scared, that's all."

She turned to embrace him but his back was to her, hunched and unforgiving. "I don't blame you."

"I should bloody well hope not! I was only doing that because I thought *you'd* like it."

"Yeah, well, I thought I would... but I didn't. I didn't like being tied down. I really hated it. And when you didn't seem to believe me, and I thought you weren't going to let me go, I..."

"Well, of course I was going to let you go! Who do you think I am? Don't you know me at all?"

"I'm sorry," she said again, hopelessly, knowing that words would never bring them closer. She wanted him to read her heart. She wished she could read his. An impossible thing to ask, except that lovers down the centuries, all over the world, did manage it, according to what she'd read.

"Just forget it," he said. "Least said... let's get some sleep."

She lay awake and listened to his breathing change and thought about the huge gulf between fantasy and reality. She thought of how the house had felt to her when she'd come in this evening—how it still felt, that familiar, charged atmosphere. And the silk scarves on the bed. She'd been so sure there was someone she knew in the house. Who had she been thinking of? Someone from her past. Marjorie? Her father?

And then suddenly she knew.

Myles. He was here, alive again.

She wanted to jump up and look for him, but she made herself lie still and think it through. Gray must have found the junk shop; he'd found Myles and bought him for her. All she had to do was wait until Christmas Day and he would be hers again. And then—she knew, because the whole atmosphere in the house told her, despite this night's sexual failure—the magic would happen again.

They had their first major row on Christmas Day.

It was her disappointment which started it, a disappointment which, because it could not be admitted, had become anger. Gray's gifts to her were a necklace, a book and a box of chocolates; no doll. Now her former certainty of Myles' return seemed crazy. Midnight madness. The longing for something which could not be. And what had she been expecting—the return of an object, or of magic? Magic was dangerous. She should know better by now than to wish for it.

She lashed out at Graham because he was there and Myles was not. He responded in kind, his own previously unspoken disappointments and dissatisfactions roiling up and spilling out. There were tears and shouting and unforgivable remarks, cold statements of dislike which seemed utterly final. Although they apologized to each other before bedtime, bad feeling still filled the little house like a poison gas, and they were estranged from each other for most of the week.

On New Year's Eve she couldn't stand it any longer. They had plans to go out in the evening, but it was still afternoon, and he'd been in his room for the past couple of hours, "tidying away a few things before the year ends," and she'd been seated at her own desk in the bedroom as if with the same intention, yet in fact unable to do anything but brood about the state of their marriage. "Gray, we have to talk."

He scarcely looked up from his notebook. "What about?"

"Us."

"What do you mean?" He closed his notebook and put it away in the top drawer, not looking at her.

"You know what I mean. We can't go on like this. We have to do something, or—do you know, we haven't been married long enough to get a divorce?"

"What are you talking about? We're not getting a divorce. If you try to leave me, I'll lock you up." He rose from his chair and put his arms around her. "Dear heart, what's wrong?"

His sympathy brought tears to her eyes. “I don’t know. Things aren’t working between us.”

“Aren’t they? In what way?”

“Oh, Gray, you know perfectly well. The things you said—”

He let go of her and stepped back. “That’s not fair. We agreed to forgive and forget. If you’re going to keep throwing things I said in the heat of the moment back at me—you said some pretty harsh things, too.”

“Things haven’t been right since.”

“Because you haven’t let them be. Because you’re still brooding about it—you, not me. And it was you who started it in the first place. If you think there’s a problem—”

“We never make love.”

“Oh, and that’s my fault? That’s totally up to me?”

“I want to. You don’t.” She forced herself to go on, determined to have it all out. “You’re not really that attracted to me, are you?”

“Not when you’re like this, no. Not when you’re picking fights and blaming me for your own bad moods. If you want me to feel sexy, you have to give me some encouragement. I didn’t get any the last time I tried. You may recall.”

“That was a mistake. I’m sorry.”

“All right, all right. You’ve said so. Let’s forget it. Come on, let’s go downstairs, have some coffee.” He sighed. “Then we can talk, since you’re so determined we should.”

They spent hours talking that afternoon and evening, managing to get past the danger of a row and the idea of assigning blame or accepting guilt, to talk about shared goals, fears and desires; the future of their marriage.

They went out to dinner, with champagne to celebrate a new beginning, and afterward carried on drinking brandies in the restaurant, and then more in the local pub. Making their way home they paused often on the short journey to kiss.

Agnes glowed with hope. Graham was teasing and amorous as they went to bed, and she touched his erect penis, happy that he desired her.

But he stopped her hand. "No."

"What do you mean, no?" She giggled. "Your lips say no, no, but your cock says yes yes!"

"I'm drunk."

"Me too. I'm drunk and horny, and so are you."

"That's right. No, don't, Nancy, I'm serious. It's no good." He caught her wrists and held tightly. "I want a fuck, that's all. And that's no good. It's not fair to you. We're going to have a new beginning as we promised each other. The real you, the real me. The way I feel now, I could fuck anyone, you could be anyone."

"I don't mind. I know who I am." His explanation baffled more than irritated her. A stiff cock, she'd heard it said, had no morals. His, however, seemed to have more moral arguments for restraint than a Jesuit.

"Well, I mind. And you should. I'm sorry, I shouldn't say that when I've just agreed not to write your rules for you. But if you knew how I actually felt, you wouldn't want me fucking you. It would be degrading. You deserve better. You deserve to be made love to properly, and I'm too drunk for that."

He kissed her, then said, "Good night," very firmly, and turned his back to her.

She was astonished and angry but also quite drunk. She fell asleep quickly, but not for long. She woke suddenly, uncomfortably dry-mouthed, sensing another presence in the room.

The yellow haze of the streetlights came in through gaps in the curtains, providing enough illumination to show there was no one else in the room. She rolled over on her side to face Graham and he was facing her, watching her through narrowly opened eyes.

She touched his face. She lightly kissed his lips. He did not move at all, but he said her name. Not Nancy, not Agnes, her true name.

A shiver passed through her, for Graham certainly didn't know that name.

"Myles?"

"You called me back."

"Are you going to stay this time?"

A sigh ghosted through Graham's lips. "I'm here whenever you want me."

There were too many things to say, too many questions to ask him, to settle on just one. But she also realized it didn't matter what she asked. All she wanted was connection. What she had wanted most when she was seven she wanted still, nearly twenty-three years later.

"Tell me a story."

In the morning she knew it had been a dream, but also that it was more. It was an opening into another world, and she understood that if she wished she could go through and continue the relationship with Myles.

She chose not to.

Despite the many subtle disappointments of her marriage, this was her real life, one that many people would envy, and she would make the best of it.

It was easier to keep to her decision when she was happy, when she'd had a good day at work, and she and Graham were in harmony. When she wasn't happy, when some petty disagreement or misunderstanding put them at odds with each other, she sometimes lay awake and watched her husband sleeping, and had to grit her teeth against the desire to make him speak to her, to make him, temporarily, someone else.

And, although she had not consciously thought about it for some time, she had not forgotten that Caroline's baby—if it still existed—

was due near the end of April. So it was that one rainy evening in April, when her job had less than six weeks to run, as she and Graham sat down at the kitchen table to the meal he had just cooked of pork chops, fried potatoes and cabbage, she spoke the forbidden name out loud, asking, "Do you ever hear from Caroline?"

For a moment he looked as if he didn't know who she meant. Then: "God, no. What do you—that was over ages ago. Why should I? What made you think of her?"

"I just wondered if she'd phoned you."

"I would have told you if she had." He looked down at his plate and began to eat.

"I just thought—well, I can't help wondering—I mean, if you never heard from her again—"

"Of course I didn't. What is this—jealousy? Of her? After all this time?" He cocked his head, a wondering expression on his face. He made it sound, she thought, as if they had been together for many years.

"After all this time she might have had a baby."

"Oh—that. I shouldn't think so."

"Did you pay for her abortion?"

Wide eyes, partly opened mouth, a face of wounded innocence. "Hey, what is this? What have I done? I would have told you if I heard from her again."

"Then—"

"I don't suppose she was ever really pregnant."

"What?"

He ate something. "She was lying. I should have realized at the time, but she could be very convincing. Well, it's her job. She's an actress. And, of course, I had reason to feel guilty."

"But... why would she lie about a thing like that?"

"You don't play poker, do you."

"You know I don't."

"It was a last, desperate bid to get me back. As long as I was single she could fool herself into believing she had a chance, but once I got married the stakes were so much higher. What could beat a wife? Possibly, just possibly, a baby. It was the only possible claim she had on me. If she'd talked me into meeting her, she'd have tried her best to seduce me. She always thought that because I fancied her I must love her, or that she could make me love her, through sex. But there's more to love than that." He put down his knife and fork and reached across the table for her hand. "You're the one I love; you're the one I married. You're my wife. You must see you've nothing to fear from anyone else. The other women are all in the past. You're all I want."

"Yes… I know…" She felt trapped by his hand on hers; almost claustrophobic, as if the kitchen had suddenly become too small. "I'm not jealous, Gray. I'm trying to be… practical. Because if there is a baby, your baby—"

"There isn't."

"How can you be sure?"

He sighed. "I can't believe you're so upset. Have you been worrying about it all this time in silence? Look, I knew Caroline; I knew her for a liar. She was always telling me lies, things to make herself seem more important—it was pathetic, really, and I didn't think it mattered, because she never mattered that much to me; it was just the way she operated. They were only little lies, before, but the principle was the same. Anyway, if she ever was pregnant, by me or anyone else, she's certainly not pregnant now, because she's still working. Or she was a few weeks ago. I saw her play reviewed in *Time Out*."

"What play?"

"God, I don't remember the title. It sounded dreadful."

"Why didn't you tell me?"

He took his hand away from hers, made a face and spoke in a funny voice, "Oh, look, darling, one of my ex-girlfriends has just been called 'competent' by a reviewer in *Time Out*."

"You might have said something. It was an awful experience—did you think I'd just forget it?"

"You never said anything."

"You asked me not to talk about it; you didn't want to hear her name again!"

He looked baffled. "Well, no, of course I didn't want to keep talking about something that was upsetting you so. I was trying to make life easier for you, for us, just then, not laying down the law forever and ever, amen. How can I know what you're worrying about if you don't tell me? I can't answer questions you don't ask."

She wanted to press him for more details about the play, when it had been reviewed, Caroline's last name—but she knew it wouldn't get her anywhere she wanted to go. "I'm sorry."

"Poor darling. If I'd known you were worried, of course I would have said something. I thought you'd put it out of your mind. When I didn't hear from her again, after I'd twigged she'd made the whole thing up, I forgot it."

She thought he was going to take her hand again, but he picked up his knife and fork. "Eat your dinner, darling. Don't let it go cold."

The horse's head had been severed and nailed above an archway. The blood dripped down, splashing the white paving stones. Obviously, freshly slaughtered; obviously dead, yet as she stared at it, full of grief and rage that her faithful friend had been killed, the eyes opened and looked down at her and she heard a voice say a single word.

As she woke she tried, desperately, to hang on to the dream, to understand it. But she was awake, and even the sound of the voice had vanished, leaving behind only one word, bereft of meaning. Falada. She knew it meant something, but although it seemed vitally important, she could not remember what.

The dream stayed with her throughout her day at work, hovering behind everything she looked at, but it was not until very late in the evening that she finally remembered the fairy tale from which the image, and the name Falada, had come, and understood what it meant.

That night, her sister called long distance with the news. Their mother was dead.

PART SEVEN:

THE PILLOW FRIEND

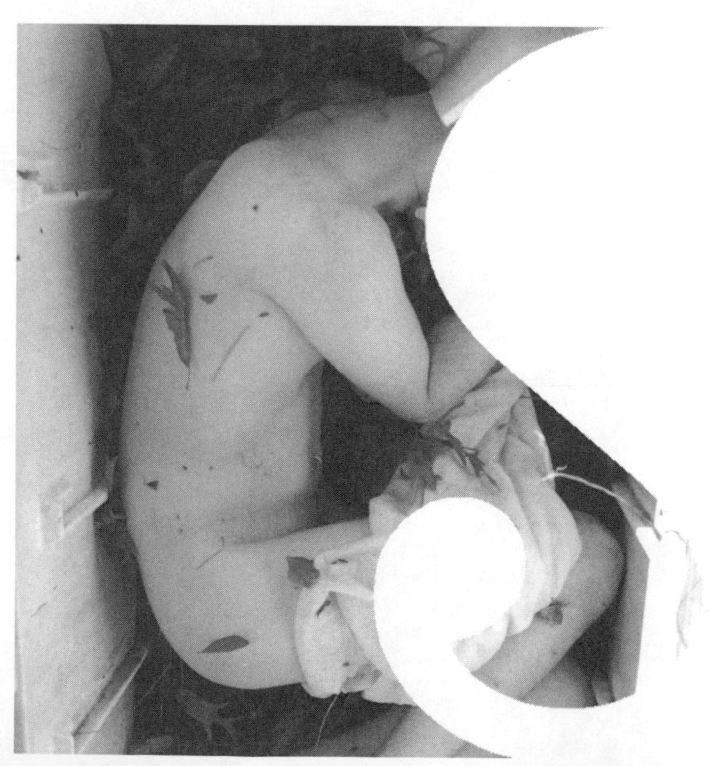

...in all childhoods and in all the lives that follow them, the mother represents madness. Our mothers always remain the strangest, craziest people we've ever met.

—Marguerite Duras

After the funeral close friends and family went back to the Shawcross home in River Oaks. Agnes had never seen the large house filled to capacity before, and she was surprised at all the people she didn't know. Among this crowd of strangers she was baffled by an absence: where was Marjorie?

On the other side of the room Eddie Shawcross was going over the details of his wife's death again for her sister and brother-in-law. He felt guilty because he'd argued with her about her leaving. If they hadn't argued she would have left earlier and never met the drunk driver who had ended her life in a smash-up on Highway 59.

She had heard it all last night when she arrived, but she edged closer to hear it again.

"Where was she going?" asked Ros. "Why didn't you want her to go?"

"She said she just wanted some time to herself, time to think. She wouldn't say where she was going. It's not that I would have tried to forbid her going somewhere, but I didn't think she knew where she was going. I didn't like the sound of it. If she wanted a short vacation from me, fine, but she didn't even have a destination in mind, it was obvious."

"Of course she did," Agnes interrupted. "She was going to Marjorie's. Why else would she take 59?"

Ros nodded. "You were right to try to stop her."

"Who's Marjorie?"

"Her sister," said Agnes.

He frowned. "A sister? Mary didn't have a sister."

"Her twin sister." She looked at Ros for confirmation, but Ros was looking elsewhere, summoning the support of her own twin. It was a familiar look, and she found herself remembering the time the twins decided she was old enough to know the truth about Santa Claus. "I don't know why she's not here. Did anyone tell her about the funeral? If you didn't know her, then of course—Ros? Has anyone been in touch with Marjorie?"

"Agnes—really." The big-sisterly tone stirred up a desperate, childish rage. Tears pricked her eyes, the first since she'd left England.

"What's that supposed to mean? I'm asking a simple question. Was Marjorie invited to the funeral."

"I don't think she knows," said Clarissa.

"Well where is she? Can't anyone find her?"

"Marjorie doesn't exist," said Ros. "She was one of Mother's fantasies, like her acting career."

"We thought you knew."

"But—No. She couldn't be! I stayed with her one summer. For weeks!"

"That's why we thought you knew."

She was hot with shame. They must think she was an idiot, and they were right. How could anyone not know her own mother? Then she felt furious at her mother, for tricking her. Then she remembered her mother was dead, which meant Marjorie was, too.

She looked around and saw that everyone was paired—even the widower was being comforted by his grown daughter, the child of his first marriage. She was the only person in the room who was alone. She hated herself for crying, because she knew it was only self-pity, but even so she couldn't stop.

The next day she rented a car and drove out of Houston on Highway 59, drove without stopping all the way back to Marjorie's house.

As soon as she entered the kitchen through the unlocked back door she was aware of the difference. Although it was still uninhabited, it was obvious someone had been here since her last visit, probably within the past month. The floor and other surfaces had been recently washed; the litter of dead insects and the other dirt she remembered had been cleaned away. She opened a cupboard and found a couple of cans and an unopened box of Ritz Crackers still far from its sell-by date. She closed the cupboard and went through to the living room.

She smelled fresh paint. The wall behind the big desk was cream-colored and entirely blank, showing no evidence of any of the portraits which had once been taped there.

Despite Eddie's ignorance, his wife must have come here at least once in the months before her death, and probably more often. It wouldn't have been difficult to pretend she was going shopping, drive out here first thing in the morning, do some cleaning or painting, and get home in time to cook dinner—but why do it? Why keep it a secret? Had Marjorie been planning her return?

She still couldn't entirely accept that Marjorie was not real. She had known her. And her memories of Marjorie were of an individual quite distinct from Mary Grey. She began to go through the desk, looking for evidence.

In the bottom right-hand drawer she found a pink folder with "Poems" written across the front, another labeled "Notes," and an old blue paper box which contained a book-length manuscript titled "The Heart's Journey." Flipping through it she encountered pornographic descriptions on every other page. She set it aside, embarrassed and edgy.

Other drawers held a jumble of things, mostly paper: newspaper clippings, pages from magazines, handwritten sheets ripped from spiral-bound notebooks, envelopes, writing paper, postcards, half-used notebooks, paperclips, ancient rubber bands, pencils, long-expired coupons, corroded batteries, and then, at the very bottom, something which had been hers: the small red leather-bound book titled *Agnes Grey*.

It was so obvious, as soon as she picked it up, that it was homemade that she could not understand how she had been fooled. Even as a child she must have recognized that it was not typeset but merely typed, on ordinary typing paper cut down to size and bound together. It wasn't a real book.

Sitting on the rough, bare wooden floor beside the desk she opened the little book and began to read. Reading it was like falling back into the past, into one of her childhood fantasies. Only now she noticed, with her critical adult eye, that the writing was florid and graceless, a crazy quilt of clichés lifted from the most easy and undemanding of generic romantic novels. Yet the story still seemed to her wonderful, even though she recognized sources for some of the scenes—this from Rebecca, that from Jane Eyre, something else from Frankenstein, bits and pieces from all her favorites, which had also been her mother's favorites: E. Nesbit, Mrs. Molesworth, Louisa May Alcott, Robert Louis Stevenson, Hans Christian Andersen and the Brothers Grimm.

She read feverishly, as she had read as a child, taken out of herself, utterly involved, herself a part of the story. She got through it in less than an hour. It was less like reading than like remembering a particularly vivid daydream, a sexual fantasy from the days before she knew what sex was.

She got to her feet, clutching the book like a talisman, dazed and thirsty. Only the shallow middle drawer of the desk remained unexplored, and now she pulled it open. Pens, pencils, more paperclips, old stamps, gnawed erasers, and a small, polished wooden box, surprisingly beautiful, out of place in that anonymous mess of office-ware. Inside the box there was a braided silver ring and a key. The ring fit her middle finger perfectly. She wore it and clicked it against her plain silver wedding band: "Sterling from Stirling," Graham had said.

It was the first time she had thought of him all day, and she realized with a guilty start that she had not phoned him, as she had promised him she would, to tell him her plans, post-funeral. On such short notice, she had bought an open ticket between London and Houston, good for six months, and had made no definite plans for when she would return. She still didn't know what she was going to do, but she ought to talk to him.

She would drive into Camptown, she decided; get herself some lunch, and call Graham. She hoped there would be somewhere to eat other than the Dairy Art. If not, there was another town only a few miles further up the highway; she could drive on, or head back toward Houston.

As she was turning to go the key she'd found in the box with the ring caught her eye. She wondered if it fit the padlock on the cellar door. She was curious about the cellar, which had been out-of-bounds in her youth, and wondered what Marjorie had kept there. Good French wines had been a favorite luxury. Or, this being a dry county, perhaps a still?

The key fit. She pulled the door open and then, because it threatened to swing shut, found a chunk of wood to wedge it open. But even with the door firmly open she did not go in. All at once she was afraid. Why was it forbidden territory? Why had Marjorie warned her away so vehemently? It was too dark under the house; daylight penetrated only a very little way inside. She wouldn't be able to see much if she went in. After a moment's indecision she went up into the house to look for a flashlight. She found one in the kitchen, in roughly the same place where they'd always kept one at home, but the batteries inside were horribly corroded. She took a white candle and a box of matches from the same shelf. The matches chattered like teeth in her hand. She concentrated on her breathing and tried to empty her mind. This was no time for fantasies. There would be nothing that could harm her in the cellar with the possible exception of a few scorpions, and she was wearing shoes.

She lit the candle, tucked the box of matches into her pocket, and went down into the dark. Shadows stretched, lunged and wobbled. The enclosed space was warm and humid and smelled of earth and dust and very faintly of something unpleasant: shit, she thought, and rotting meat. She heard scrabbling sounds as small creatures fled from her or hid themselves, but they didn't frighten her. It was the unknown, some mystery, the large dark shapes looming in the shadows, the cardboard boxes and shrouded furniture rotting away on the floor which made her muscles tense and her heart beat harder. There was something down here which her mother had hidden from her.

Her leg grazed a cardboard box and she crouched cautiously to open it. The cardboard, in the process of disintegration, felt like a cold flap of skin. It was a box full of bottles—she extracted one, holding it to the light—a case of French wine—twenty-year-old Bordeaux! She gave a little groan of rueful amazement and wished she had someone with her to share the treasure.

Encouraged by this discovery, she became bolder, examining everything around her with increased interest. Wooden chairs, a table with a chipped, laminated top, rusting oil cans and bedsprings, an old, foot-operated sewing machine. Other boxes contained clothes, curtains, bed-linens, all reeking of mold and mildew; stacks of twenty or thirty-year-old magazines with titles like Gent and Dude; coffee cans full of nails, screws and pieces of wire; old shoes; cheap crockery—all the household detritus you might find in any cellar or attic; stuff that should have been thrown away, kept until whatever minimal usefulness it had once possessed had been eroded by time, insects or water. She grew bored. Her fear was forgotten. She straightened up, holding the candle at arm's length, and saw an old white chest-freezer against the far wall. She wondered what would be in it: boxes of Fudgicles and Dreamsicles quiescently frozen twenty years before? Steaks and hamburgers rotting away since the early sixties? Her amusement vanished as she remembered: there was no electricity in this house and never had been. So why a freezer? All at once it stopped being a familiar and mildly amusing household object and became weirdly menacing. She didn't want to look, but had to know what was inside.

By wavering candlelight she picked her way around boxes of junk and made her way to the far wall of the cellar. She wasn't sure she would be able to lift the lid one-handed, but it came up easily and she leaned over it with her candle, breathing through her mouth, braced for the stench of something rotten.

She saw the body of a man, naked, lying on his side with his knees drawn up.

She sucked in air hard but did not pull back. Her grip tightened on her candle and she quickly measured its remaining length with her eyes. She didn't want to be stranded in the dark. In a minute she would run like hell, drive away from this place forever, but now curiosity held her. She wanted to understand what she had found.

Was it a dead body? She had seen only one dead body in her life—her mother's. She still didn't know how dead bodies looked. Whether it was the transformative power of death itself, or the embalming and cosmetic attempts to conceal injuries received, the body of the woman in the funeral parlor looked like nothing which had ever lived.

This thing in the freezer—was it a lifelike, life-sized sculpture, or a corpse? She leaned in over the edge, relaxed her breathing, inhaled.

There was no stink, no hint of rot, not inside the freezer. What she inhaled carried the smell of live male flesh, a whiff of perspiration, the tang of salt and yeast. The unexpected, terrible, familiar intimacy of it made her shiver. In her hand the candle dipped and dripped. One drop of hot wax fell on the pale flesh below, and she saw the body flinch and quiver.

She felt as if the air had been vacuumed out of her lungs. Alive! Yet though she watched and waited for it, gripped by fear and fascination, there was no further movement. It did not turn or sit up. The eyes did not open.

"Come out of there," she said in a voice that scarcely carried. "I know you're alive. Get up."

The effect of her words was like a current run through the body. She could see all the muscles becoming galvanized, like a flickering beneath the skin. Or was that the wavering of the candle? Before she could doubt her eyes, he sat up.

She stepped back, out of reach, and watched the naked man clamber out of the freezer. She gazed at his body, particularly at the genitals which were alternately displayed and concealed by shadows and movement, with as hungry a fascination as if she had never seen a naked man before. And maybe she hadn't. This creature coming toward her now was a wholly new thing, something dreamed of and desired, yet never before known. She was afraid, yes, but not of him. And the fear she felt was insignificant compared to her curiosity, and her unexpected desire.

He stopped a few feet in front of her, as if she had told him to. She held up the candle and had a good look. She didn't have to say anything: whether he read her mind or the faint motions of her head and hand, he seemed to know what she wanted and moved, posing himself, to give her the best views. She found it most difficult to look at his face. At first because she expected his eyes to open—and hated the thought that he could look back at her while she was looking at him—but then, as she accepted the idea that his eyes would stay closed (or at least until she wished them open), she still did not like to look at his face. Although she had not recognized his features (and could not even call them to mind while staring at his hairless chest or the rounded cheeks of his buttocks) she was apprehensive that she might, if she looked more closely or stared for a longer time, see someone she knew.

Breathing shallowly, she looked around for somewhere to set the candle. She wanted to see, but didn't want to risk setting the place on fire. She looked at the freezer. With the lid closed, she had a flat surface at a reasonable height. She dripped a little wax from the burning candle onto it, and then set the candle on top. She did not realize that the naked man had followed her until she turned around and bumped into him.

She gasped and caught hold of his arms to steady herself. As soon as she touched him, she wanted more. She needed to feel—she began to touch him everywhere with her hands, grabbing at his flesh, kneading it. It was so soft and resilient, so warm, firm, yet giving—it was as if she had never felt another person's flesh. It soon wasn't enough just to touch. She began to tear at her clothes, clumsy in her desperate need. His eyes were still closed; he couldn't see what she did; she could do anything. She pushed and pulled him to the ground. She hugged him and he hugged back. She could do whatever she wanted, and he always responded, he always did just what she most wished him to do, without a word spoken.

The candle had burned down long ago. Her eyes had adjusted to the darkness, she could see as much as she wanted to see, but now the daylight that sifted through the open door was thinner, paler, and the shadows of the cellar grew thicker, darker. She felt the beginning of a kind of panic; she could not bear to be here after dark; she must get out before night.

She struggled to disentangle herself from him, to get to her feet. He meanwhile made no move to help or hinder but lay there as if dead. On her way toward the lighter region of the door, stumbling around picking up her clothes and dressing as best she could, she bumped into the case of wine, recognizing it by touch. She abstracted one bottle and carried it, along with her underwear, out of the cellar and into the house.

There were no clocks in the house, and she didn't know where her watch was. There was probably a clock in the rental car, but it didn't seem worth the bother of going out again to look. She guessed from the angle of light that it was after five, maybe as late as six. A reasonable time to have a drink. She found a corkscrew in the kitchen, and a wineglass she was sure she remembered seeing Marjorie use. She opened the wine and poured out a glass, then held it up to the kitchen window to admire the dark red gleam before raising it to her lips.

It was an exceptionally good wine. She was no oenologist, but one sip was enough to inform her that this was a very much better wine than she was used to. Awed by her luck, she carried glass and bottle into the living room and settled herself in the only comfortable chair.

Occasionally a purely sensual memory passed through her body like a shudder, but she kept her mind as blank as she could, determinedly neither remembering nor planning, justifying nor questioning, just living in the moment, putting back the wine and watching the familiar room grow crepuscular. She felt the wine wrapping itself around her in a warm, comfortable haze, and reached out for the bottle to refill her glass.

The second glass was not as good as the first had been, and by the time she reached the third she had the definite impression that her once-fine wine was turning to vinegar in the glass. She drank it down grimly, anyway, and then, fearing that she was about to pass out, staggered off first to the bathroom and then to bed in what had been Marjorie's bedroom. The bed-linen smelled powerfully of mildew, but fortunately it was warm enough to sleep without covers, and she used a couple of her own T-shirts rolled up as a substitute for a pillow. She thought for a minute that she would be sick, but before she could try to do anything about it she was asleep.

She woke up ravenous, dry-mouthed and with a pounding headache sometime the next day. In the kitchen she drank two glasses of water and swallowed a couple of aspirins she found in her purse, then made a breakfast from the Ritz crackers and a can of barbecued beans. She'd always preferred them unheated. She longed for a cup of tea or coffee, but there was none, so she went to take a shower. There wasn't any hot water and she didn't enjoy it, but afterward she felt better. The aspirin had started to work.

She dressed in a clean T-shirt, a cotton skirt and sandals and stuffed yesterday's clothes into her suitcase without examination, half holding her breath. She had the idea that they smelled, and she didn't want to think about why or of what. Along with the few things she had to repack she added the notes and manuscripts she had found in Marjorie's desk and the copy of *Agnes Grey*. She wondered if there was anything else she was forgetting, and noticed the ring on her middle finger.

By association she thought of the key she had found with the ring, and her skin crawled. She had managed to keep the memories at bay, to convince herself that it had been a dream, and yet—now she doubted. It could not all have been a dream; she must have been down to the cellar to get the wine, and besides that, where was the key now?

She wandered around the house rather aimlessly looking for it, although she suspected that if she had not dropped it in the cellar she would find it still inserted in the padlock outside, hanging on the propped-open door. Her heart was beating like something trapped, she couldn't catch her breath, and she was sweating. She didn't want to go down there again; she wouldn't even let herself think why. What a pathetic attempt she had made to forget, to fool herself with the notion that it was only a boozy dream—there was something down there, something horrible waiting for her in the cellar, so horrible that she was incapable of letting herself remember the details. Around and around she went, kitchen, bedroom, bathroom, bedroom, living room, kitchen, bedroom, around and around like a mouse in a cage, and she knew that the cellar door was open. There was no safety in this house. But to go out, when the cellar door was open—

Around and around.

Finally she broke and made for the door. Outside on the porch it was as hot as inside, not a breath of wind stirred the needles of the surrounding pines, but at least she could look down and see the rented car parked only a few feet from the front steps. Her breath came more easily, with escape in view. She wouldn't even have to go past the cellar door. And yet, now she knew she didn't have to, she decided that she would go and lock it. Unable to remember what she was afraid of, she chose just then to believe that it was nothing. There could be nothing real in the cellar to threaten her; only ancient, childish terrors. "A dagger of the mind." She would go down now and lock the cellar door.

But there was no key in the padlock. She must have taken it into the cellar and lost it; probably she had dropped it on the floor. She took just one step across the threshold, hesitating, remembering she had brought no light, starting to turn back before she'd truly entered; just one step, and she was lost.

The cellar smelled like him. That one step took her into his embrace; she inhaled and was enfolded. She stepped forward, blindly, reaching out, and met his outstretched arms. She began to gasp with desire now, not fear, as the memories she had earlier refused came flooding back. She fell against him and he caught her; she fell back into the dream.

It was nearly dark when she emerged from the cellar. She went straight to the kitchen and gobbled down the remainder of the Ritz crackers and drank glass after glass of water. The other can in the cupboard was a small one of sliced peaches. She opened it and ate them, and was still hungry, but also trembling with exhaustion. She made her way back to the bedroom and fell into bed without even noticing the smell of the bedclothes.

When she woke the room was full of daylight, and her husband lay sleeping beside her on the bed. She stared at him in bewildered joy, wondering how he had managed to find her, grateful for this miracle. It was only as, his eyes still closed, he began to make love to her, that she knew it wasn't really Gray. But it didn't matter who he was, because he was everything she had ever wanted. She would probably never see Gray again; she might never leave this house.

He had brought the wine up from the cellar, and from time to time they paused in their sexual activities to open another bottle and drink it. It had to be drunk quickly, for the years below the house, largely unprotected from the violent temperature shifts of the Texas climate, had taken their toll. As soon as the bottle was open, oxidation began, and a fine wine began to turn to vinegar.

Another night, another day. She could not keep track of time. She left the bed only for brief visits to the bathroom. After she had discovered the roll of Polo mints in her purse there was nothing more to eat. Sex had been a distraction, but now hunger dominated everything. Life had been reduced to the simply physical, and she had become simple, too, more helpless than a child in her inability to see any way out. Her thoughts could not penetrate the walls that held her. She was hungry but there was no food.

She wept at her own helplessness. "What am I going to do?" she demanded.

Her lover said nothing.

She stared at his naked body, as familiar now as her own and yet mysteriously still desirable. Unable to help herself, wallowing in her own helpless, mindless lust, she gave him a little push so he was flat on his back, and mounted him. He was always ready for her, always erect, he never came, he never spoke, he never imposed his own desires—the only desires he had were hers. She stared down at his blank sleeping face and felt hate rise in her, hot as passion. "What am I going to do, damn you?"

He still said nothing. She squeezed his cock inside her and clenched fists that wanted to squeeze his neck. "Look at me!"

His eyelids fluttered and, for the first time, rose. The eyes that looked up at her out of her husband's face were not blue. They were muddy gray flecked with hazel; not his eyes but her own.

She had a moment of absolute terror. She couldn't move; she was joined to him irrevocably, he was a part of herself she could never escape. And then she accepted it. The fear passed. And she was still hungry.

"I'm starving," she whined. "I need to eat. If I don't eat, I'll die."

In answer, he lifted his arm toward her face. She looked at it: solid, meaty. He raised it a little more and she felt it brush her lips. She opened her lips, touched his flesh, as so often before, with her tongue. Then, when he did not draw it away, she let him feel her teeth. When he still did not move, she bit him. That first, tentative, lover's bite did nothing, so she bit him again, and this time tore away a chunk of his flesh in her jaws.

There was no blood. His flesh was dry and chewy, the texture that of a dumpling or a half-cooked roll, and it tasted a little like salty bread.

She swallowed the first mouthful and was instantly ravenous for more. She looked at him, still offering her his arm, and saw herself looking back. She flinched at that, but then saw it as validation of what she was about to do. If he was her, then he was hers, to do with as she wanted. Obviously he was feeling no pain. More than that: he was enjoying it. He was smiling slightly, she recognized the voluptuous pleasure relaxing his features, and she could feel him still erect inside her.

She leaned down and took a large, deliberate bite out of his shoulder. It was delicious. It tasted like nothing she knew, and yet she had the sense that she had always been longing for it. Even before she'd swallowed her mouth was watering for more. The more she ate of him the more the craving grew. As she consumed his arms and chest she was soon no longer starving, but as her actual need decreased her appetite became even stronger. She wanted to eat every bit of him.

Eating his head was the strangest, scariest, most difficult part. She felt like a monster: that she wanted to do what she was doing was the hardest to accept, as hard as seeing her own eyes in Gray's familiar face staring knowingly back at her. She closed her eyes and growled as she tore his ear off.

And then he was gone from the waist up. But she could still feel his penis inside her. Suddenly she couldn't bear it any longer; the situation was too horrible. For a while she'd been able to imagine they were sharing in her cannibalistic feasting, as if eating was just another type of sex. But not now that his head was gone, and he had no face. She felt neither sexy nor hungry. She was beginning to feel afraid. She moved to disengage and found she could not; his penis seemed to be stuck inside her. Horrible stories heard in adolescence, images she'd believed long forgotten, flared in her brain. Although she was in no pain a panicky fear made her jerk and fight, and in a moment she was free, crouching beside the legs and lower torso. Before she could even begin an approach to calm she had seen that the torso had testicles but no penis. It had broken off inside her.

She opened her mouth, feeling a scream building, and then she forced her head down to his weirdly empty groin and made herself eat. She had to finish what she had begun; there was no other way. It made no difference that she no longer wanted him: he was hers, and she had to take him all inside.

Her jaws ached from chewing and her throat from swallowing. She was so full she could not imagine containing any more, but she knew she must. The taste of his flesh, once so compelling, now was sickening. Mouthful after mouthful she forced down, hardly chewing, holding her breath sometimes, keeping her mind a blank. If she thought about what she was doing, what she had done, she would be sick, and it was too soon for that. If she was sick, here and now, she'd only have to eat him all over again. She didn't question her knowledge; there were rules which had to be obeyed.

She made herself keep eating until there was nothing left to eat, and then she fell asleep.

She had no idea when she woke what time it was or what day. She felt bloated and unhappy, unrested, but she made herself get up. Getting to her feet she had the faintly uncomfortable sensation of wearing a tampon which had shifted from its usual position and needed to be removed, but when she checked with her finger there was nothing there.

Although she felt an urgency to get out of the house, she nevertheless took a shower—cold, of course. It was easier to do that than spend the rest of the day worrying what she smelled like, or what strange substances might have spotted her skin. Then she dressed quickly in clean clothes, stuffed everything else back into her suitcase, and left.

Two hours later she was entering Houston in rush hour. Creeping along the jammed freeway, she realized she would have to make a decision soon, or the prevailing currents of traffic would carry her off to Sugarland or worse. She'd had no destination in mind beyond Houston. She could go stay with her sister, as she had done before the funeral, but she didn't want to. She tried to remember which of her high school friends were still around.

The exit sign for West University Place caught her eye and she moved, managing, through a combination of luck and determination, to get into the exit lane before it was too late. She made her way to the village shopping center where long ago she'd hung out with Roxanne. As she'd remembered, there was a pay phone on the corner by the Mexican restaurant. She thought about calling Leslie's mother, who had been so kind at the funeral.

But as soon as she picked up the phone she knew she had to call Gray first. Making arrangements for where to spend the night was not as urgent as her need to speak to him, to hear his voice. She needed to be reminded of their life together, to be pulled back into the real world. All at once, in the familiar, hot, humid Houston evening, she missed the cool, damp little house in Harrow quite desperately. The sound of the abrupt purring ring of their telephone in her ear—so different from the American ringing tone that the first time she'd heard it she'd thought it was a busy signal and hung up—made her stomach tense with anticipation. In a moment she would hear his voice.

But the phone went on ringing, unanswered, until the operator said, "I'm sorry, there's no reply."

"Thank you. I'll try again later." But it was already later—it would be after midnight there. He should have been in bed. Maybe he was in the bathroom? She marched up and down the block until she'd convinced herself of this, then went back to the phone to try again.

Still no reply, although she asked the operator to let it ring a little longer "in case he's asleep." But she knew perfectly well that Gray could never sleep through the ringing of a telephone. If he wasn't answering the phone he must be out.

"Um, Agnes?"

The soft, familiar voice caught at her heart. She turned around, astonished.

Alex Hill smiled at her. "I thought it was you. I saw you go past the window when I was in the restaurant, and then when I came out, you were on the phone. It's really nice to see you. Are you going to be in town long? Oh—" He stopped smiling as he remembered. "I heard about your mother. I'm really sorry."

She started to say thank you and then stopped. Surely that wasn't right. What did you say when someone offered commiserations? How did you accept? She hadn't figured it out at the funeral and it was even harder to know what to say now. But she had to say something, if only that it was nice to see him, too. He was still waiting for her response. She opened her mouth. "I," she said helplessly. "It's..." She began to cry.

He put his arms around her and held her. He said nothing at all, just let her cry. Occasionally he patted her on the back.

"I'm sorry," she said when at last she was able to stop. She pulled away from him although what she wanted most was to go on resting against his chest, feeling protected.

"Don't apologize. You have a good reason for crying. I wish—are you here by yourself? Were you going somewhere?"

"I was just trying to call my husband. There's no answer; I want to try again."

"Come home with me. You can call him from there."

"It's long distance."

"I know. I'll send you a bill. We don't take as big a rake-off as some hotels.... Where are you staying?"

"I don't know. I just got back—I need to call somebody, find a place to stay."

"Look no further. Where's your car? You can leave it there. Get your things. I'll bring you back in the morning, drop you off on my way to work. My office is just up the street."

She made no protest because this was just what she wanted. It was such a relief to be taken care of, to have decisions made for her, and it was all the better that the white knight of her fantasies should be the first boy she'd ever loved.

Sitting beside him in his car, being driven home, she felt entirely comfortable for what seemed the first time in years. She paid no attention to where they were going. She listened to the tapes he played: Bonnie Raitt, Pat Benatar. She wished the journey could last forever.

His house was a new, narrow townhouse that looked like all its neighbors, sand-colored brick and pale wood. Inside there was an impression of bare, sparse modernity: a large, open-plan space with white walls and minimal furniture of chrome, glass and black leather. Black and white photographs adorned the walls. She saw a stack of *Vogue* magazines on the chrome and glass table, but no books. It seemed a little bleak to her, and impressively clean.

"Nice place," she said.

"It's all right. Do you want something to drink? Have you eaten? There's stuff to eat."

"I could eat something." She followed him into the kitchen, a narrow, beige and white area separated from the dining area by a long counter.

"I still can't cook—I can only offer you a sandwich, or something from Lean Cuisine." He gestured at the freezer.

"A sandwich would be fine."

"Peanut butter and jelly?"

"Great. Do you know what jelly means in England?"

He shook his head, getting out the bread.

"Jello."

"So the idea of a peanut butter and jelly sandwich..."

"Exactly." She sighed happily, crossed her arms and leaned on the counter, watching him as he moved. He had put on weight since college and the buttons of his blue shirt strained slightly across his stomach. There was the softness she had felt when she had rested in his arms, and it was something he probably looked at and pinched with dismay after every shower, promising himself to do something about it. Lean cuisine, she thought, and remembered how he had liked to eat, how they had all liked to eat, and drink, during their last semester together in Austin. Remembering how they had eventually ended up in bed together she wondered why they hadn't done so sooner, or why that once had not developed into the affair she had always wanted. They'd had other involvements, their lives had progressed in different ways. She wished it otherwise. She could almost believe it was, at that moment in his kitchen, the two of them bound in wordless intimacy as she watched him make her sandwich. It was wonderful to watch; he took such care. First he buttered both slices of bread, then spread Skippy peanut butter on one and Welch's grape jelly on the other. After he pasted the bread together, he cut the crusts off before cutting the sandwich in half slant-wise. It was exactly the way she'd liked it as a child, and she hadn't had a peanut butter sandwich made for her with such care and delicate attention to detail since then, when her mother had made them for her. He invited her to sit at the dining table and served it to her just as her mother would have done, on a small plate, with a glass of milk.

"This is wonderful," she said after swallowing the first bite. "This is great. Delicious."

"Oh, hey, come on. It's a peanut butter sandwich!"

"But beautifully prepared. Perfectly made. Really, I haven't had such a perfect peanut butter sandwich since I was a kid."

He shook his head. "Well, I guess I can keep you happy as long as your needs don't get any more complicated."

His eyes sparkled down at her and she smiled back. "Oh, my needs are very simple."

He turned away from her, toward the fridge. "I think I'll have a beer. Want to join me?"

She looked at her untouched glass of milk. "Mmmm, maybe later. This really calls for milk, not beer. I don't want to spoil the peanut butter experience."

"Certainly not! You don't want to spoil that dinner it took me so long to make. Maybe when Mon gets home. She should be back in half an hour or so. She never wants to eat in the evenings, but she sometimes likes a drink."

Her shoulders, which had felt so relaxed, were suddenly tight again, as if she were still driving. "Who's Mon?"

"Didn't I say? She's my wife."

Despite his liberal use of "we" and "us" when he spoke, he hadn't mentioned a woman, and she hadn't thought of one. Absurdly (she now realized) she'd imagined the plural pronoun referred to a housemate or, at worst, a girlfriend living safely far away. She'd imagined herself in the midst of a gentle seduction.

"Mon," she repeated vaguely and took a bite of sandwich to give herself time to adjust to the idea.

"Short for Monica. Married nearly two years now. She was—you might have known her. Monica Willies. She went to our school. Of course, she was two years below us."

"Oh, Alex. You married a sophomore?"

While he laughed she ate the sandwich he had made for her. But as she tore out a bit of the sweet, chewy stuff it seemed to her that the texture was all wrong for a sandwich. And as she chewed it turned to flesh in her mouth, raw and indigestible. She chewed and chewed and chewed until her jaws ached. As she tried to swallow some of the pulpy mass, her throat closed with revulsion.

Pushing back the chair she struggled to her feet.

"Are you all right?"

"Bathroom," she muttered thickly.

"Through there—by the front door—to your right."

She made it just in time to throw up into the toilet. Oddly, although she heaved and retched until she was exhausted, apart from the small amount of undigested sandwich, only a little, greenish liquid came up. It seemed that her stomach was completely empty.

She lay in bed in the guest room with the light on, a glass of ice water and an empty bowl close at hand. The guest room was also Mon's sewing room, and she stared at the sewing machine and dressmaker's dummy in the far corner until she fell asleep.

As soon as she woke up she knew by the fact that the room was now dark that someone had come in. They might have just turned out the light and gone away again, but she sensed a presence. She lay perfectly still, moving only her eyes, until she saw the figure lurking in the dark.

"Alex?"

There was no reply, but she thought she saw the figure move slightly. In a normal voice she said, "Alex, I can see you."

Still he said nothing, but in a flash she had a vision of Alex standing there in the doorway with his eyes closed and arms outstretched, shamblingly seeking her out like the pillow friend, and she screamed.

"Agnes, hey, it's all right, you were dreaming, that's all." She felt his hands, his arms around her, his bare chest and she whimpered and went limp. When she opened her eyes the room was glaringly alight. Alex looked back at her, his eyes fully open and enlarged by a pair of thick, black-rimmed glasses. His hair was tousled and he wore a pair of baggy shorts. "You were having a nightmare," he said.

"I thought... someone was in the room." Now she could see that the door was not where she had believed it to be, and she could see the dressmaker's dummy in its place. Alex pointed at it and she nodded. "I'm sorry."

"Don't apologize. Everybody has nightmares sometimes." He was still holding her, sitting comfortably close on the bed. She could smell the soap and salt on his body and feel the warmth of his bare skin. She felt like stripping off her T-shirt and rubbing her nipples against his.

"Are you all right now?"

"Stay with me a little longer." She rested the palm of one hand lightly on his chest, to feel the spring of his hair.

"Mon probably hasn't even noticed I'm gone. She kind of stirred and muttered when you started screaming, but I think she didn't really wake up. I guess, if we ever have babies, I know who's going to have to do the three a.m. feedings."

She slipped her hand down his chest and into the waistband of his shorts. He caught his breath but made no attempt to stop her. He was already erect as she fondled him. His penis strained and butted her hand like a happy pet.

After a little while she withdrew her hand to strip off her T-shirt. He stared as if he'd never seen a naked woman before; as if he couldn't believe his luck. His excitement thrilled her; she felt eager to increase his pleasure, to show him how generous she could be.

As she pulled him down to her she felt him resisting what they both wanted, and saw him starting to frame his excuses. She didn't want to hear his wife's name again; she didn't want any more words to come between them. She put a finger to his lips and then, sitting up to face him, her breasts pushing against his chest, she whispered very low into his ear, "Quickly. No noise. Just do it."

He tugged down his shorts and she lay back and opened her legs. He positioned himself between her legs and then—she couldn't understand what was happening—tried and failed to enter her. She was eager; she wanted him as much as she'd ever wanted any man; he was evidently fully erect. She tried to guide him in with her hands, thinking that excitement had made him clumsy, but that wasn't it. He was in the right place. The head of his penis butted, again and again, against the lips of her vagina, finding something blocking his entrance. She was beginning to feel sore and he was beginning to droop when he abruptly got up and pulled his shorts back on.

"Not a good idea," he whispered. "Obviously." He flashed her a strained, chagrined smile. She bit her lips and held her hands out to him, knowing as she did so that there was nothing she could do to hold him now, no reason he should stay.

She lay on the bed with her knees up and legs parted after he had left her, horribly aware of the broken-off cock inside her that remained as a barrier to any other lover.

PART EIGHT:

THE QUESTION ANSWER'D

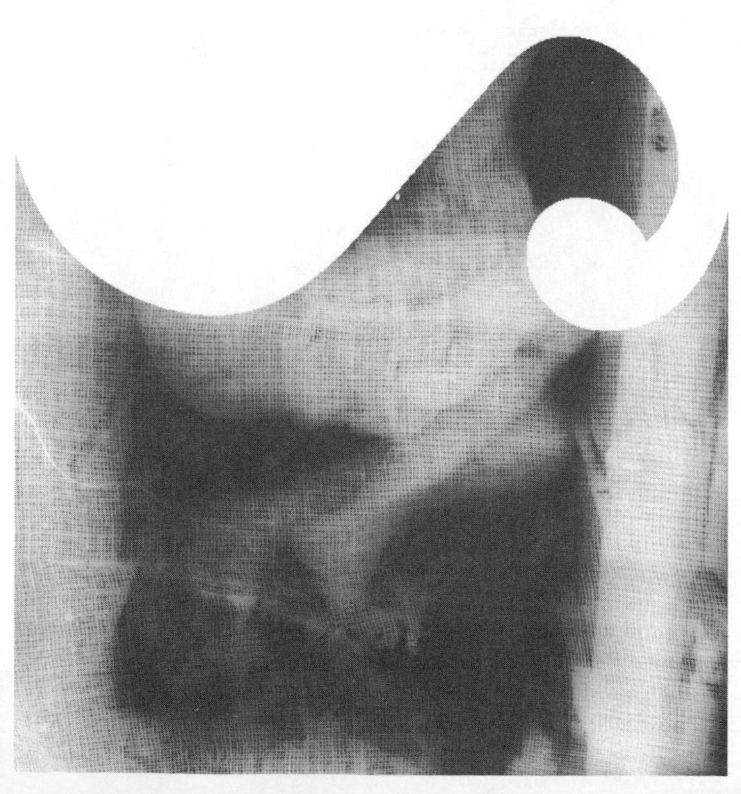

When one has stopped loving somebody, one feels that he has become someone else, even though he is still the same person.

—Sei Shonagon

London looked old and gray and unwelcoming. After Houston it felt cold, but no less humid. She took the train from Gatwick to Victoria, and then, unwilling to struggle home on the underground with her suitcase, took a cab. During the long, slow journey out to Harrow she tried to cheer herself with the London views and oddities glimpsed through the window. But she found no pleasure today in pub signs, Victorian architecture, eccentrically dressed pedestrians, or advertisements exhorting her to "Try a saucy faggot!" Those were a tourist's pleasures, and what she wanted more than anything now was simply to feel at home.

Leaving Alex's yesterday morning she'd gone straight out to the airport with the intention of simply staying there until she could get a seat on a flight to London. There had been one available that very evening, and she had taken it.

At the airport, she'd bought a small mirror, and had spent several long sessions locked inside a toilet cubicle examining her vagina. She couldn't see anything unusual, and her own fingers encountered no obstruction, but she was still uncomfortable. She had a slight sensation of heaviness, a faint genital irritation, a little like having a constantly full bladder, yet without the urge to urinate.

Gray didn't know she was coming; she hadn't been able to reach him. She hoped he didn't have plans for tonight and would be coming straight home after school. She had been attacked by a kind of waking nightmare while trying, unsuccessfully, to sleep on the plane, and she couldn't quite get it out of her head. In the nightmare she came back to discover that Gray did not exist, had never existed outside her own mind. Her marriage to him had been a fantasy, like her mother's acting career, like Marjorie.

The little house had never looked better to her. The honeysuckle around the front door was in bloom: even in a city the English spring made itself felt. Indoors it smelled, as always, of damp paper and stale smoke, only now that smell made her heart beat faster, and she was possessed by a yearning nostalgia for her early days of living here, as if she had been happy then.

Now she was home, and could relax. She made herself a cup of tea and sat down to look through the small stack of mail and magazines Gray had left for her, but halfway through she felt impelled to rush to the bathroom and check her vagina again, this time with the aid of a larger, magnifying mirror, and a small flashlight. When she had assured herself there was nothing there, she had a bath and washed her hair. The water was only lukewarm, because she hadn't left the heater on for long enough, but she felt compelled to have a thorough wash, in case any trace of either the pillow friend, or Alex, had survived the shower she'd had before leaving his house. Nothing that she had done in Texas could be allowed to contaminate her life here, or her marriage. She was convinced her only safety lay in forgetting. It had been a time of madness, but it was over now. Graham must never know, never suspect.

After she had changed into a clean, if slightly musty-smelling, sweat-suit she found in the bedroom wardrobe, she unpacked her suitcase. Everything in it would have to be washed, and she noticed that the laundry basket was full. A trip to the launderette at the bottom of the road was obviously called for. She didn't really feel like leaving the familiar safety of their house until she'd seen her husband, but it would be hours before he got home, and those hours had to be filled somehow. Gray would be pleased she'd done his washing, she thought; he hated the launderette more than she did.

She was exhausted and finding it impossible to concentrate by the time she got back. Some of the images which came into her head unexpectedly were as vivid as flashbacks, and frightened her badly. She made herself a cup of coffee and tried to eat some bread and cheese, but when she dozed off with her mouth full of bread she decided to stop fighting it. She put away the clean clothes, stripped off her own, and crawled into bed. She was asleep in seconds.

A high, shrill scream of terror sliced into her sleep.

"What is it?" She sat up, heart pounding, and felt around on the bedside table for her glasses. Without them she could only see Graham—even in dim and fuzzy outline she knew him—standing stock still in the middle of the floor.

She got her glasses and focused on his face. "What's wrong? Did you scream?"

"Jesus Christ! You might have told me—I wasn't expecting —I thought the house was empty, I thought I was alone, and then I see someone in the bed—Jesus!" He seemed to be trembling, patting at himself; not until he located the pack of cigarettes did she recognize the familiar gesture.

"I tried to call you, but..."

"You couldn't have tried very hard."

Guilt settled like a heavy quilt around her shoulders. "I'm sorry. I was staying—out in the country. My aunt's old place, you remember. And there's no phone. I did try to call as soon as I got back to Houston, but there was no answer."

"You should have tried again."

"I know. I'm sorry. I thought I'd wait until I knew what plane I was going to be on, but by then you were out. I didn't want to wait; I got the first plane I could." There was a burning sensation in her throat; she wished he would smile at her, put his arms around her, hug her, tell her he was glad to see her. The words came out in spite of herself. "Aren't you glad to see me?"

He looked at her. "Of course I am. Just a bit—shaken. You don't know how I—how *worried* I was, not hearing from you, especially after I called your sister and she didn't know where you were. She said you'd vanished. Where were you?"

"I told you. I went to East Texas. My, my aunt's house. Where my mother was headed when she died. I didn't realize—I didn't mean to be gone long; time just kind of..." She trailed off, realizing, as she spoke, that she still didn't know how long she had been away, how many days she had spent in the old house in the woods. She was reluctant to ask, to be precise about her sins and remind him of her guilt; later she could find a newspaper, discover today's date, get out her desk diary to find out when she had left, and reconstruct her time away for herself.

"You've lost weight."

She remembered she was naked and pulled the sheet up over her breasts. "I'm sorry."

Finally he smiled. "Well, don't apologize! It looks good. You were just a little bit plump, before. I have missed you, you know. And I was worried. But now you're here and everything is all right again. Come on, get dressed and I'll take you out to dinner."

It turned out to be her birthday. Graham thought it was funny she'd forgotten. "It's supposed to be the husband who forgets things like that, not the wife—not her own birthday!"

He had no presents for her: he hadn't expected her back. He promised to take her out shopping on Saturday, to find something she liked, but in the meantime they would celebrate with a meal out. He suggested that, as it was a pleasant evening, they walk to a nearby restaurant. Everything looked strange to her, hyper-real and glowing from an invisible source of light, like an air-brushed painting. She couldn't get a fix on what time it was: he had just come home from school, and the angle of light seemed that of late afternoon, yet they were going out to dinner.

"It's summertime," he said patiently. "It'll be light until nearly eight. Even later next week. Don't you remember from last summer?"

"It's too cold to be summer." She had put on a dress in deference to his idea of celebration, but then had to go back for a sweater.

"Not for an English summer. You're still on Texas time, that's all."

She was hungry, but when she looked at the menu in the restaurant she saw nothing she wanted to eat. It was all meat, it seemed to her, all the unequivocal meat and potato dishes he liked. She wished she had thought to suggest the Italian or the Chinese restaurant; she could just about manage a plate of noodles. But now that they were here she couldn't say anything. This was his special treat for her and she mustn't spoil it.

"Why don't you have a steak and a glass of wine?"

"Oh, I don't really feel like a steak... my stomach's a little... I want something a little less..."

"Well, I'm going to have the gammon steak. With the fried mushrooms to start. Will you have a starter?"

She went for the leek and potato soup, to be followed by fillet of plaice.

Her soup was very salty, but she managed to get it all down, not wanting to make a fuss. She could feel him willing this evening, their reunion, to go well. She wouldn't let herself think about what it would mean if things did not go well.

When the main course arrived she could hardly believe her eyes. Set on the table before Graham was a real-life, grown-up sized version of the doll-house meal she'd found so compelling as a child. There was the mysterious pink meat, filling almost the whole plate. It also had the strange round circle on top; a circle she could now positively identify as a ring of pineapple, fresh from the can.

"What *is* it?"

"Gammon. What does it look like?"

She told him, eager to share, but she could see that he did not understand.

"I always wanted to know what it tasted like, I always wanted to be able to eat it, and I couldn't. It was like fairy food, and now I see it's something real...." As she bumbled on, elaborating, trying to make him see, she found it becoming less clear even to herself. Wanting to eat a doll's food? What kind of nonsense was that? Yet as she watched him carve out a piece with knife and fork and lift it to his mouth she was almost overwhelmed with envy. That he should be able to eat it when she had never managed to, when it didn't even *matter* to him—

"Please, could I have a bite?"

She had known he would look like that. He couldn't stand sharing a plate or a glass, would never offer or accept "a bite"—it was one of his "things." He had told her that in Texas, instructing her in his idiosyncrasies, and had reminded her very firmly on the occasions when she'd slipped up and offered him a bite of her sandwich or asked for a taste of his ice cream.

"If you wanted gammon you should have ordered it. I said you could have whatever you wanted."

"But I didn't know gammon was what I wanted! I don't even know what gammon *is*! Oh, please, Gray, I just want to taste it—I wouldn't ask if—please, it's really important to me."

"And my feelings aren't. How can you do this when I've told you, when you know how I feel—here, take the bloody thing." He lifted up his plate and thrust it at her across the table.

She moved her own plate of fish, untouched, to one side, and put the plate of gammon in its place. His anger had already settled as an indigestible lump in her stomach but not even that could overwhelm her curiosity, her long-standing desire to taste this impossible food. Trembling, she ate.

"It's ham!"

He shrugged.

"You said gammon."

"Gammon *is* ham. That's a gammon steak. It's the cut, I suppose, or maybe the fact that it's cured. I don't know why it's called that. Don't you like it?"

"Well—it's ham, that's all." She felt a great, sad disappointment. "I'm sorry, I—"

"I don't want it back. I've told you before. It's yours now."

"Well—we can trade. Is the fish all right for you? I haven't touched it."

"It'll have to be, won't it? If I want any dinner at all."

She passed her plate across to him, pleading with her eyes. "I'm sorry, Gray."

"Sure you are."

"I *am*! I didn't want to spoil your dinner."

"But you did, didn't you? Who made you, then? If you didn't want to, why do it?"

"I told you—I tried to explain—when I was a kid I used to have these fantasies about what that meat was and how it would taste—I thought it was an imaginary food, not something I'd ever get to see in real life. And there it was—I had to try it, I had to taste it—don't you see? Can't you see that?"

"I could if you were seven years old. But you're not a child. You're supposed to be grown up. You're thirty years old."

Before she went to bed she locked herself in the bathroom to examine her vagina once again. Having annoyed Graham, she knew he would not be interested in her sexually tonight, but she was still wary. As before, she could see nothing and feel nothing with her fingers. She thought that even the faint sensation of blockage was gone, although after so much poking and prodding and worrying it was hard to remember what "normal" felt like.

By the next morning, she had convinced herself that everything was back to normal. The last physical trace of the pillow friend had vanished, dissolved inside her, she supposed, and all she had to concern herself with was forgetting.

She called Alice, hoping they could meet for lunch or for drinks after work. Gray would be home late—after school he was going into the West End to have dinner with his agent. He'd apologized: he'd made the appointment thinking she'd still be away, when he was looking for alternatives to another lonely night in. Agnes didn't fancy a long day on her own, but Alice was rather abrupt on the phone, saying she was very busy, finally agreeing to lunch on Wednesday.

Hanging up, Agnes wished she could think of someone else to call, but she hadn't made any other friends in England. She imagined that the people she had worked with so briefly in her publicity job would already have forgotten her; she couldn't think of any real reason for trying to arrange to meet any of them.

She went into the bedroom and sat down at her desk. The sooner she got back to her work, the better. But although she tried to start writing something, anything, even to answer a letter, the bed loomed at her back like a ghostly presence—she kept imagining that someone was in it, and had to turn around to look. If she didn't turn around to look the feeling got worse. Concentration was impossible.

She went out, finally. She took the Piccadilly Line to Leicester Square and found a newsstand where she could buy *The Bookseller* and *Publishing News*, and then she browsed in the bookshops on Charing Cross Road. Cappuccino and gooey chocolate cake in Soho, a visit to the British Museum, and the day was nearly gone. She thought about going to a movie or maybe even to the theatre. Touts were selling cut-price tickets to *Les Miserables* in Cambridge Circus as she hurried past. She'd skipped breakfast and forgotten about lunch. She was hungry. In the streets around her the posher restaurants were opening for the evening; others had never closed. Fast-food or slow, she ignored them all, drawn by the memory of one not far away, on Tottenham Court Road. It was inexpensive and served hamburgers and pasta dishes, and featured a huge salad bar where you could eat all you wanted for a set price. Gray had taken her there a couple of times—good times, she remembered, because she had enjoyed it and he had been so pleased with himself for discovering this "American-style" restaurant. The waiters barely spoke English and it was full of tourists, singly and in groups. It was a place she knew she would feel comfortable eating alone, an easy, anonymous place.

Arriving, she paused before the restaurant's big, plate-glass front to check the availability of tables. And she saw them, a few yards away on the other side of the glass, a man and a woman, her husband and his wife, Graham and herself.

Her eyes slid away in denial—couldn't be, impossible—and fastened on the undeniable, on the man whose face and body she knew better than her own. It was unquestionably Gray, those long fingers resting on one side of the angular face, the deep lines around his mouth, the eyes slightly hooded and intent upon the woman he was with. And then, as he moved, leaning back in his chair as his hands began to grope for a cigarette, his gaze also shifted slightly and he saw her, his other wife, the one outside staring at him through glass.

There was no denying the shock on his face, the shock of someone who has seen the impossible, a ghost, a *doppelganger*. It was like seeing her own shocked face looking back at her. Before that could happen (she would not survive it) she turned and ran away.

On the train going home she came to terms with what she had seen, and what it meant. She knew she wasn't a ghost, so if Gray was going out with somebody who looked exactly like her it had to be—it could only be—his pillow friend.

"We have to talk," said Graham.

Terror and exhilaration. All along he was the one she had wanted to talk to, but the subject had been impossible to raise. It was no longer impossible; she was no longer alone.

They sat together in the poky little lounge in their usual places: she on the couch, he on a chair nearby.

"This is so difficult," he said. "I don't know how to start. You saw us; you must have some idea—but probably not the right one. I don't know; I don't want to hurt you; this is so difficult to explain."

Sympathy leaped up to meet the agony on his face. She wanted to take the pain away.

"You don't have to explain. When I saw you this evening I knew—you have a pillow friend, too."

She could tell, as soon as she spoke, that he wouldn't have used the term "pillow friend." But it didn't matter, because he'd understood.

"You, too?"

She could feel the dizzying heat of a blush but made herself sit still and look at him and say, "Yes. In Texas. It was such a strange thing, I didn't know how I could ever tell anyone, especially you, but when I saw you there at that table with me, I knew the same thing somehow must have happened to you."

There was such a strange look on his face: bewildered pleasure, triumph. He was happy, she realized; she had made him happy; she had finally done something right.

"You screwed somebody in Texas?"

"Well—not *some*body—it was —"

"She was right. I'm astonished. Alice said you would. She said it always happens at funerals, that it's some kind of hormonal imperative. She said I should have gone with you, and since I didn't it was my fault, I couldn't blame you for having it off with whoever happened to be available. I said you weren't like that; she said everybody was like that under the same circumstances."

"Alice? When did you talk to Alice?"

"It was because I was feeling guilty. I thought she was just trying to make me feel better."

"You called Alice?"

"Only because I was thinking of you; only because I was worried out of my mind and your sister didn't know where you were. I thought you might have said something to Alice, maybe she would know the name of somebody you might be staying with."

"You called Alice?" There was something there, something horrible which she sensed but could not yet see.

"I told you why; it's the honest truth. I had nothing else in mind. She suggested we meet for a drink; well, why not? We were both at a loose end, a bit lonely. A friendly drink. I wasn't looking for anything more and neither was she. It just happened."

"What did?"

"You know how it is when you look at someone, and your eyes meet, and suddenly for the first time you really see each other? That's how it was: we saw each other. After that—well, I suppose if I'd had you waiting at home for me I would have gone home and tried to forget it. But there was nobody waiting at home for me, or for her. Maybe, if Alice wasn't such a—a direct person I could have—"

"Alice? Alice Keremos was with you in that restaurant tonight?"

He frowned. "You saw her. You saw us together."

"No. I saw—I didn't recognize her."

She saw him realize that he could have avoided this confrontation; could have lied his way out of it. Before he could make some disastrous attempt to recant she asked the most painful question: "Are you in love with her?"

"God, no! Don't even think it. Not like I love you. This is nothing at all like that, and it doesn't affect my feelings for you, it honestly doesn't. You're my wife. I don't want that ever to change. This is something different. It's—" His eyes met hers with a gaze she could only think of as completely candid, and he said in a rush, his voice slightly lowered, "I don't know what it is, only I can't control it, and I can't walk away from it. Not yet. Please—" He put out his hand and she caught it and held it tightly.

Lunch with Alice cast her into misery. She had expected to meet her friend, not her husband's lover—or, rather, she had not considered that the first might be subsumed by the second. But Alice, withdrawn and nervous, chain-smoking, told her that she didn't feel comfortable discussing her relationship with Graham. Agnes could think of nothing else she wanted to talk about. Her own relationship with Graham perhaps, perhaps the pillow friend—but not with someone who'd demarked her own emotions with a No Trespassing sign.

Publishing gossip kept them going throughout part of the meal, who was thinking of changing jobs, who was in love, who was getting divorced, or sacked, or promoted. She hoped Alice might help her find a new job, but she said she knew of nothing going. Alice asked about the funeral and her family, expressing concern, and although she had meant to keep as aloof as Alice, after a couple of glasses of wine the need to tell someone was too much for her, and the story of her mother's double life came spilling out. Alice responded with as much sympathy as anyone could have hoped for, but much later, at home, Agnes began to cry, overwhelmed by the feeling that she had betrayed not only herself but her mother.

Gray had told her that he was not ready to give Alice up; the implication was that someday he would be, but only if their affair was allowed to run its course. He didn't elaborate and he didn't press her at first, but one night he said he'd like to spend an evening with Alice.

She had been expecting it and had planned her words and her manner. But now her mind was as blank with terror as if he had trained a gun on her.

"Oh! Sure. What night? Will you be coming home?"

"Yes, of course! I thought Friday, unless you'd rather it was another night?"

"Friday would be fine. I might go out myself."

"Well, of course, you must do what you like—oh, my love, don't look so miserable! You mustn't worry. There's nothing to worry about, I promise you."

That night they made love for the first time since her return.

She had been thinking about it before they went to bed. She had been thinking that it had been a long time—too long—and that if they left it any longer they might get completely out of the habit of making love. She had been thinking that she might feel less abandoned, and less jealous of Alice, if Gray made love to her first. She took a bath in scented oil and got into bed naked, feeling embarrassed, certain he would comment, but he only looked up from his book to ask, "Aren't you going to read?"

"Not tonight. You won't read long?"

He sighed. "No."

He kissed her when he turned out the light, but chastely, and did not respond to her tentative advances. She wasn't feeling sexy anyway—her wish for him had been more preventative than passionate—so she did not persist, and soon fell asleep.

She was awakened some time later by the pleasant sensation of having her breasts gently fondled and kissed. For a brief, dream-fuddled time she thought she was back in Texas, in bed with the pillow friend, but as he parted her legs and moved on top of her she recognized her husband's body, and the different darkness of their bedroom. He slipped inside her slowly and easily, finding no obstruction. He lay heavily on top of her and, once inside, scarcely moved. It was not his usual mode of love-making, but she enjoyed the sensation until she began to wonder if he had fallen asleep. She began to thrust upward with her pelvis, and after a little while she felt him respond, and a sluggish, sexy rhythm developed. As she became aware of the changes in his breathing and muscular tension which foretold the approach of his climax she realized her own was upon her. For the first time in their marriage they came together.

Lying there afterward with his weight on top of her, holding him in her arms, she felt very close to him, sure that everything would be all right.

It was harder to hang on to that thought when he was out with Alice and she was home alone, but she tried. Over the next few weeks she often called on her fading memory of that close, warm feeling for reassurance.

She started writing a new book, a fantasy about two American children sent to stay with an aunt in London and having magical adventures, and although it felt rather forced and schematic to her, it helped to fill her days. She also applied for jobs she saw advertised in *The Bookseller* and *The Guardian*, but received no positive responses. The days grew longer and the weather more reliably warm. Soon school would break up for the summer holidays. She didn't know what would happen then. Would Gray continue to divide his spare time between his two women, or would Agnes and Gray go away together to Scotland, as they'd planned last year?

One evening, out of the blue, he said something about her mother's schizophrenia. They were in the lounge, the television on but disregarded, the remains of a take-away Chinese dinner scattered around.

"What?"

"Isn't that the term for someone with a split personality? Or—no, I'm sorry, I'm behind the times. It's not split personality anymore, is it. It's Multiple Personality Disorder. Did she have more than two?" He looked at her, waiting for an answer.

Her mouth was very dry. "I don't know. I never thought about her like that. I never even knew, until after the funeral."

"Why didn't you tell me?"

"Didn't I?"

"You told Alice."

"Alice told you?" She'd imagined that Alice's niceness about

Graham—her refusal to discuss her lover with her lover's wife—would extend to a refusal to discuss her lover's wife with him.

"She mentioned it. She assumed I knew, of course."

"You mean you talk about me? You and Alice?"

"What do you think we do, jump on each other and fuck like bunnies every time we meet? Of course we talk."

"About me."

"Not particularly about you." He got up and switched off the television. "It just came up. We were talking about her nervous breakdown, in fact, and the fact that *her* mother was always considered unstable; we were talking about mental conditions being passed down in families. That's not important. I'm just curious why you felt able to pass this information along to her but not to me."

It hurt, the image of them discussing her, the thought of Alice telling him everything she'd ever said to her. On some level she'd still believed that Alice was her friend and that they'd get back together again once this business between her and Gray had played itself out.

"Why couldn't you tell me?"

She glared. "You didn't ask!"

"Oh, I see, it's my fault for not being sensitive enough."

"I didn't have a chance to tell you. It wasn't easy, I was still trying to come to terms with it myself when all of a sudden I'm landed in the middle of this thing about you and Alice, and after that, that's all we ever talked about. Our marriage. Your feelings. Her feelings. Our future. There was never any space to talk about my mother."

"Keep your voice down. I don't want the neighbors knowing our business."

"If you'd cared—" She couldn't go on. There were tears in her eyes and tears in her throat, choking her.

He looked disgusted. "It's impossible to have a rational conversation with you when you're like this."

"Like what? What do you mean?" She was sobbing, but got the words out.

He began to gather up the plates and cartons from their dinner, taking himself away from her. "When you're irrational. Not like yourself. When you cry. Premenstrual, I suppose."

His parting shot stunned her. She didn't go after him; their argument shrank into insignificance as she realized she hadn't had a period since she came home.

She'd been on the Pill ever since her first pregnancy scare in college, more than ten years. Much too long, probably. But she hadn't taken one since she'd been in Texas. She'd forgotten all about it during that timeless time in the woods, and when she remembered again, back at home, she didn't know where she was in her cycle. It had been too long, she would have to wait until she got her next period, and that hadn't happened.

In the morning she walked down to the chemist's and bought herself a home pregnancy testing kit. It was expensive, but simpler and quicker to use than she'd imagined. Within an hour she was staring at the pink circle that confirmed her pregnancy.

She went for a walk that afternoon, needing to get out of the house and do something with the excitement churning inside her. It was an excitement that was at least three-quarters fear. She knew Gray would react by seeing her pregnancy as her way of pressuring him, her way of pulling him back from his adventures with Alice. It seemed odd to her now, but they had never discussed having children.

She had walked up Harrow hill, past the school and through the churchyard to come down the other side, thinking vaguely of catching the train and riding out to walk in the countryside she thought existed at the end of the Metropolitan line. It was a warm, close day, intermittently sunny, and she was sweating slightly from exertion. She was aware of her own faint, familiar body odor, of traffic fumes, dog turds and an indefinite moist green smell. As she came over the brow of the hill and started down, a cloud passed and the sun blazed out. She raised her head and saw, beside the path that wound down before her, a tree. She had to stop and look.

It was a horse chestnut tree, one of four she walked past every time she came this way to the station. In the autumn the path was littered with conkers, and with children gathering them or throwing them at each other. Just now the tree was in full leaf, dark green and spreading a canopy of shade all around it. It was magnificent. She felt as if she had never seen it before, as if she had never really seen a tree before, how alive it was, how beautiful and mysterious. She was aware of a connection between herself and this tree, a connection among all living things. All at once she understood something about life. And then, as suddenly as it had come, it vanished. Something remained—an awareness of having touched something—but the understanding itself could not be grasped. When she tried, later, to write it down she could only produce rather obvious metaphors about blooming and bearing fruit, the sort of clichés she felt embarrassed reading, let alone writing.

But the memory of the tree stayed with her. She knew at that moment that she wanted the baby. She wanted it more than she'd ever wanted anything.

She said nothing about her baby to Gray. It was so fragile now, only a cluster of cells, it might so easily be lost, she couldn't risk his anger. Time was on her side; the longer the pregnancy, the more inevitable the baby. And she found she liked having a secret from him; it was some compensation for Alice.

He spent more days and nights away from home once his summer holiday began, but she minded less than she'd expected. She had something else to think about. One rainy night, rereading the pregnancy book she'd bought so long ago for Caroline's pregnancy, she realized she'd made a mistake in thinking she was just now six weeks pregnant. Medically, pregnancy was not reckoned from conception (the date of which might not be known) but from the first day of the last period, and she didn't know when that had been. The last one she'd marked in her diary had been April 27, which was the day she'd left London for Houston. She remembered that it had been a few days early, and found herself recalling the drip, drip, drip of blood from the horse's severed head in her dream. She remembered the embarrassment of asking for the ladies' room at the funeral home. And after that? She leafed through the pages of her diary. Between the 28th of April and the 23rd of May was a stretch of unmarked pages. Looking at them—so many of them!—made her feel frightened. It was hard to believe she had been away as long as that, and that most of that time, nearly three weeks, had been spent in Marjorie's—in her mother's—house in east Texas, without electricity, without human contacts, without food. With a box of crackers, a crate of wine, and the pillow friend. But she must have had another period somewhere among those blank pages, in that house among the pine trees, although she could not now recall it. She must have. Otherwise, she was eleven weeks pregnant, and Graham could not possibly be the father.

On Saturday they went to a friend's barbecue. It had rained off and on for most of the week, but that day the weather was kind. People sat in the long, narrow strip of back garden on folding chairs or rugs, getting sunburned despite straw hats and sunglasses, drinking beer or a triple-X fruit punch. Even Gray was drinking, although, for the sake of the baby, Agnes stuck to fruit juice and soda. She didn't realize quite how much he'd had to drink until they were walking home from the station in the soft, light, late evening and he reached over to fondle her bottom.

She stiffened, startled, and he put his arm around her and pulled her close. She made herself relax against him. He hadn't touched her sexually in weeks—not at all except for that one, middle-of-the-night encounter, since before she'd gone to Texas.

At home, he detained her in the hall, a hand on her breast, and kissed her. This was not one of his usual dry, tentative-seeming kisses, but a real down-the-throat job. He kissed her like a desperately lustful stranger, without finesse, kneading her breast with a clumsiness that was almost painful. He tasted of cigarettes and beer and he felt like a stranger. She didn't understand where this sudden, transforming lust had come from. All she could feel in herself was discomfort and embarrassment for him.

All at once he broke off the kiss and pushed her away. He made a strange sound. It took her a moment to realize, in the darkness of the hall, that he was crying.

"Gray, what's wrong?"

"Don't touch me, oh, God, don't touch me!" He drew a deep, sobbing breath and then exhaled. She waited until his breathing sounded calmer and then said uncertainly, "Should we talk?"

"Yes." He sighed. "Oh, yes. Yes, we must talk."

She followed him into the lounge. "Do you want some coffee? Shall I make coffee?"

"Yes, please. It was that punch of Roy's. It doesn't taste as alcoholic as it is; it tastes quite nice, actually, so you have a second glass, and then another, and before you know it you're pissed as a newt." He was seeming more like himself again. He went off to the bathroom while she went to the kitchen to put the kettle on for instant coffee. When they met up in the lounge to take their usual positions, he had a well-scrubbed look about him. He was wearing a clean shirt and his hair was damp.

"We have to be honest with each other," he said. "Utterly honest; ruthlessly. There's no other way."

Her stomach clenched, anticipating pain, and she watched him roll a cigarette. She picked up her cup but the coffee was too hot to drink so she set it down again.

"You must realize it's over."

Her heart lifted. "You and Alice?"

He blinked and gave his head a shake; lit up, took a drag. "Didn't you feel it then, in the hall? I know you did. Nothing. Worse than nothing. It felt wrong."

She said cautiously, "I haven't really been feeling very interested in sex lately; it's not you—"

"But it is you. It's you with me, me with you. Don't take that the wrong way. I don't mean it's your fault. I mean whatever it is that draws people together, whatever physical, chemical, hormonal thing makes sex possible, is no longer there between us. Our bodies—don't fit."

"Alice turns you on and I don't."

"No. No. No. Well, yes. But that's not it. Forget Alice." He leaned forward and took her hand; his fingers were very cold. "I still love you; I'll always love you, but I no longer feel sexual toward you. I don't know why it is, and I hate it, but when I think of making love to you I feel sexually dead. I tried to force myself tonight, but it was no good. It's been like that since you came back from Texas. I know you didn't change, but to me it felt as if you had. Physically, chemically changed. So that we can't fit together anymore."

She knew the truth of what he was saying and it made her sick. He'd smelled the pillow friend on her; she'd had the creature's penis inside her and now she was carrying its child. She fought against her own despair.

"But we did—we did make love—"

"Yes, of course. It was fine, it was all right. It was never the major thing in our relationship, but we were fine together. Christ, do you think I would have married you if we hadn't been? Would you have married me? It was all right once upon a time, but then something happened."

"Yeah, you fell in love with Alice."

He let go her hand, throwing himself back in his seat. "Alice is nothing to do with it! Alice was coincidence. Look, this isn't one-sided.... Our sexual relationship is dead, and you know it as well as I do."

She shrugged helplessly. She didn't know what he felt when he touched her; she'd never known. "Just then in the hall it wasn't right, but that's—there are reasons—" She paused to take a sip of her coffee and then shuddered at the sour taste. She kept forgetting there were things she no longer liked. "It's like this coffee...."

"What?"

Of course what she was saying made no sense to him; he didn't know she was pregnant. She wished she had told him sooner. Now, in the middle of what seemed to be a memorial service for their marriage, was not the time she would have chosen, but it was now or never.

"The last time we made love it was all right, wasn't it? Really, better than just all right."

He was giving her a look that might have been sympathetic or pitying. "Probably... I'm sorry, I don't remember. But that was then, before you went away, before Alice—all right, I'll admit that—"

"It was only a few weeks ago."

"No."

"June the fourth."

"I don't remember the date, but we haven't had sex since you came back."

She leaned forward, fists clenched, quivering. "I can't believe you're saying that! I can't believe you don't remember—you woke me up! It was the middle of the night. I'd been hoping we would make love when we went to bed, because we hadn't done it since I'd gotten back, but you didn't seem interested, and I went to sleep and the next thing I knew you were kissing my breasts."

"You were dreaming."

"I was not dreaming. You fucked me. We both came. I didn't dream that; I didn't dream the smell of your sperm on me the next morning."

"Keep your voice down!"

"I'm not shouting. I'm just saying the truth."

"There is no truth in it. We have not made love since April. It's not something I'm likely to be mistaken about."

"Or me. It happened; I know it happened; I have proof." She stopped herself. "Maybe you were dreaming, and that's why you don't remember. I thought it wasn't your usual style. You weren't very energetic. Maybe you were asleep, maybe you were dreaming I was Alice."

"If I had to be asleep and dreaming you were Alice in order to fuck you that's a pretty grim comment on our sexual relationship. I don't know why you'd want to believe something like that."

"It's not something I want to believe. It happened; we had sex that night. I don't know why you don't remember."

"Well, I don't. What does it matter, anyway, whether we had one final meaningless sexual encounter last month."

"Not meaningless." She held herself where she thought the baby was.

The corners of his mouth turned down and he shook his head very slightly at her. "I'm sorry."

"I'm pregnant."

"Don't give me that."

"It's true. I should have told you earlier, but I was afraid, and I wanted to be sure."

"I'd thought better of you."

"For Christ's sake, Gray, you know I'm not a liar! I may misunderstand or get things wrong, but I don't lie. And it would be a pretty stupid lie to tell somebody who has no intention of ever sleeping with me again!"

She had reached him; she felt as if he was really seeing her for the first time that day. "What makes you think you're pregnant?"

"I did one of those home pregnancy tests."

"Oh, those bloody things. They can be wrong."

"They can be wrong on the negatives, not on the positive."

"You haven't been to the quack?"

"Not yet."

"So you're not sure."

"I *am* sure. I was going to call for an appointment next week. I know I'm pregnant, I can feel it. Things taste different, I get tired more easily, my libido is completely flat, and of course I haven't had a period...."

"When was your last period?" His gaze sharpened. "You haven't had one since you've been back. When—wait, I remember. You'd just come on before you left. I remember we stopped at the chemist's so you could get a box of Tampax. So that was..."

With a feeling of dread she watched him making the same calculations she'd made earlier. He came to the same conclusion.

"So you should have come on again the week you got back, or a few days later. And you didn't. Which means you were pregnant when you got back, but not when you went away." His eyes were very very cold. "And there you sit, trying to convince me that I've fucked you when I haven't. And no wonder I haven't wanted to, no wonder you seem so strange. There you sit, in my house, with another man's sprog in your belly, and you have the nerve to complain about *me*!"

It was the end of their marriage. Gray announced that he was going up to Scotland for a week of solitude and writing, and then he was going to Greece with Alice. He'd be away for just over three weeks, which should be time enough for her to get herself sorted, he said. He gave her £500, enough to cover the costs of an abortion and her return to Houston, although he didn't say that was what it was for. He didn't have to.

If it was the pillow friend's penis she carried, she didn't know what might happen, but was certain that the outcome would be horrific. It might grow larger and larger until it split her open, or maybe it would never come out at all, but grow into her, transforming her into something else. Or she might give birth to a shapeless mass of flesh, or to him, the pillow friend, an anonymous male creature.

But maybe Graham was wrong and it was his child. She'd read that former Pill users didn't always have regular cycles—it could take months for the body to recover and resume its natural functions. What if her first ovulation had been on or around the fourth of June? Maybe it was Graham's child, a normal baby, that she carried. She had to find out before she could decide what to do.

She made an appointment with Graham's GP, whom she'd never met. To her surprise, he did not examine her—he scarcely looked at her, preferring to refer to his calendar-blotter to count the weeks before telling her that he would refer her to the ante-natal clinic at the nearest hospital—unless she had some other preference?—and they'd soon be in touch with her.

Now sixteen weeks from her LMP, as the medical records put it, she sat in the hospital's ante-natal clinic, waiting to be summoned to meet the consultant. She'd already had her history taken by a midwife, been weighed, her blood pressure taken, and delivered a urine sample. It was becoming more real by the minute. Before she left the hospital today they would want to make a tentative booking for a bed to be reserved for her at the time of her expected delivery.

Her name was called and she went into a small office where a good-looking, youngish man behind a desk looked up long enough to give her a quick smile before turning his attention to her file on the desk before him. He asked her a few questions, the same ones she'd had from the GP and the midwife, responding to her answers in a tone at once distracted and cheery, "Fine, fine!"

After less than five minutes he stood up to say goodbye. "Nurse will take you—"

"Aren't you going to examine me?"

"Why? Is there some problem?" He began to look at her file again, as if the answer would be found there.

She had grown up seeing films and reading and hearing about women who went to their doctors in all innocence, sometimes thinking they were ill, and emerged from their offices glowing upon hearing the magic words, "You're going to have a baby!" She said slowly, "I guess I just wanted to hear somebody tell me that I really am pregnant, some proof that I am going to have a baby. And—well, that it's all right. I'm not really sure about the date of conception, you see. I was on the Pill, and then I stopped taking it, and—"

"You're down for an ultra-sound scan today," he said. "We usually do one at about sixteen weeks. We'll be able to tell how developed the fetus is and have a better idea of when conception was, and also make sure that all the bits and pieces are there, developing normally. You'll be able to see for yourself."

She would be able to see the baby. She hadn't thought of that, hadn't realized that scans were routine. She'd imagined the horror reflected on the face of someone else, a doctor or nurse, as they discovered the shapeless mass growing inside her—but she would see it for herself.

The nurse led her through corridors, took her up in a lift, and through more corridors to some distant part of the hospital. It was much quieter there, practically deserted.

"I think they're having a tea break; they'll be back soon," said the nurse. "You sit here and I'll bring you some water."

Agnes sat down on a straight-backed chair. On the opposite wall, next to a closed brown door, was a small black and white sign that read ULTRA SOUND B303. Next to it a hand-written notice was taped to the wall: DO NOT ENTER UNTIL YOUR NAME IS CALLED.

The nurse came back with a large plastic jug of water and a small glass. "Here."

"Oh, thank you, I am a bit thirsty."

"Never mind that. You drink it all. It's to fill your bladder, so they can get a good picture. You must drink it all."

It was something to do. When the nurse had gone away she set about drinking. She wondered what was growing inside her, and if she really wanted strangers to see it. She could get up now and walk out, keep her secret to herself—and keep it from herself.

It was better to find out what she carried now, while it was still possible to stop it being born. If it was so horrible they would surely recommend, probably even insist upon, a termination. She drank another glass of water and then another. She remembered a line from a poem by James Fenton—"Every fear is a desire"—and she drank another glass of water.

Thinking about the scan, she had imagined a room like a high-tech operating theatre, full of people, most of them men, in white gowns. But there were only two women in a darkened room crowded with furniture and machines. One of them, the doctor, was about her own age and spoke with a soft Scottish accent. The other woman, an Asian, looked even younger and almost painfully sympathetic.

"Should I undress?"

"No, no, just lie down on the table and pull your trousers down to—that's fine. Now, we're going to spread some jelly—it's warm, Ayesha, isn't it?—on your tummy—terrible stuff when it's cold, a real shock, but I think it feels rather nice like this, no?"

"Mmmm."

"Your bladder's nice and full?"

"Feels like it's about to burst."

"Ach, well, I hope we'll be through before that can happen."

"How good will the picture be? I mean, what will you be able to tell about the baby?"

"Oh, we should be able to tell what size it is, and if it's got all its bits and pieces—but you'll see for yourself, on that screen there—Ayesha?"

She turned her head and saw a television screen. "Never thought I'd be having a broadcast from my womb."

"Oh, we've seen them all," said the doctor. "It's not the womb so much as who's inside." She was rolling the transducer over her greased belly now, pressing gradually harder than was comfortable. Agnes said nothing, gazing at the screen, looking for her baby. She felt neither fear nor excitement now, only acceptance and a sort of muffled curiosity. But she could see nothing. The screen, to her, appeared completely blank. She'd read, in her pregnancy book, that the video picture would be very blurry and would have to be interpreted for her by someone skilled. Yet she saw nothing which seemed to offer any scope for interpretation, and as neither the doctor nor the technician spoke and the silence, with the transducer being rolled back and forth and around her middle, over and over again, stretched on and on, she felt the faint prickings of alarm.

"I can't make anything out," she said. "Where's the baby?"

"Just what I was wondering," said the doctor in an odd voice. "That is, there doesn't seem to be a baby. There is no baby. You're not pregnant."

It should have been a relief, although not untinged with sadness, but she couldn't believe there was no baby, despite the evidence. She still *felt* pregnant.

She went back to Gray's little house and packed a few things: only the most necessary clothes and books, her Walkman and a few tapes, her notebooks. Everything else she left behind, including tapes she knew he would never listen to and dresses he would certainly never wear.

She was free, whether she believed it or not; she could go anywhere. She had been thinking about the bothy during the past few weeks, and the yearning to be there, to see Knapdale again, had been growing stronger. She had resisted her desire, imagining

Graham's anger at the thought of someone else living in his special place, but now she thought: So what? So what if he was angry? She couldn't disappear, cease to be, just to make his life easier, and she needed a place to live. He must be in Greece now, and the bothy would otherwise be empty at least until the spring. Why shouldn't she live there until they worked things out and got officially divorced?

Money would not be a problem. Besides his £500, she also had $7,000, inherited from her mother. She was sure she could live frugally enough in Scotland to eke that out for more than a year.

She arrived in Glasgow by train early the next morning, and caught the morning Campbeltown bus from Buchanan Street station. It took her as far as Lochgilphead, where she had an early lunch. She was asking in the hotel bar about the local taxi service when a woman's voice behind her said, "I can take you. It's on my way."

She turned and saw a solidly built woman in her thirties, wearing a blue dress that looked like a uniform, and low-heeled shoes. She had curly light brown hair, lively dark eyes and an attractively friendly round face.

"Is it really? I didn't think Clachan was on the way to anywhere!"

"Depends on how you define 'anywhere.' I have a patient to visit, beyond Clachan, at Kilrue, so you're right on my way. I'm Nancy Gates."

"Agnes Grey. You said patient—are you a nurse or a doctor?"

"Midwife. Where is it in Clachan you're staying?"

"Not actually in Clachan. The house is a little farther along the road, about a mile, I guess. I've only been there once before. It's only small, a bothy, they call it. It belongs to my husband's family."

"Which I suppose answers my question as to how an American comes to be in these parts. Your husband's a Scot?"

"English."

"Well, we won't hold that against you. Are you ready to go now, or did you want a drink or something first?"

"No, I've had lunch. I'm ready whenever you are. These are my bags."

"They'll fit in the boot with the messages." She picked one up, ignoring her protests, and led the way outside. "You'll be here for a long stay, then?"

"I think so, I'm not really sure. I'd been thinking about staying until the spring, but I might change my mind. It just depends...." She trailed off, unable to say what her plans might depend on, and the other woman did not press her.

It was a warm, clear day, much better weather than she'd had for her first visit, and she enjoyed the drive and the beauty of the scenery too much to do more than give brief, distracted answers to the various conversational openings which Nancy offered. When Jura first came into view, dark brown and purple against the blue sky and silvery sea, her heart lifted with a joyful sense of homecoming, and she cried out, "Oh, it's good to be back!"

But when they reached the bothy she discovered that both doors were locked, and, of course, she didn't have a key.

"Oh, this is so stupid, I should have thought..."

"Shall we try and force a window?"

Agnes looked at her in amazement. "You're very trusting!"

"How do you mean?"

"You don't know me or anything about me, I say I have a right to be here, but I don't have a key—"

"Ach, I'm always forgetting my own. Which is why I usually don't bother to lock anything, and leave the keys in the car."

Then she remembered. "There's a woman in the village, Mrs. Macsomething, who has a spare key. She runs the village shop."

"I'll run you back there."

"I'm sorry, I'm taking up so much of your time."

"It's no bother, honestly."

"I should have thought of it before we came this far." She worried that Mrs. Mac-something might be less trusting than Nancy, but the shopkeeper recognized her as soon as she spoke, remembering their single meeting of a year ago, and got the key for her without seeming to find it odd that she had come so far without her own.

"And will you not be wanting a few things, milk, bread, tea?"

"Oh! Yes, I'd better get some things—I wasn't thinking. There probably isn't very much in the kitchen." She surveyed the shelves, trying to anticipate her needs for the next few days, and then broke off to say to Nancy, "It was very nice of you to drive me, but you don't have to stick around—I can walk back."

"With all your bags? Honestly, I'm in no hurry, and I'm quite happy to drive you the last mile, whenever you're ready."

She became a little suspicious of the existence of this supposed patient in Kilrue when the midwife accepted her rather perfunctory offer to come in for a cup of tea. As if reading her mind Nancy said, "There's always time for a cup of tea, and there's no rush to see Mairi, I only told her I'd look in sometime before five. One of my great sins is nosiness. I never could resist an invitation into a house I've never been in. All the times I've driven along this road, passing this wee house..."

"So you've never met my husband, or his brothers?"

"Not to my knowledge. The only thing I know about this place is that it's owned by some folks down in England, and it stays empty most of the year. There are plenty of other houses the same around here."

She had expected the house to be cold, remembering her last arrival, but the sun had been streaming in the front windows for at least half the day, and of course it had been occupied only last week. It felt warm and cheerful. She put the kettle on to boil while she inspected the cupboards and put away her recent purchases. There were a certain amount of emergency supplies as she had expected: tins of soup, fruit, and baked beans, condensed milk, sealed jars of oats, rice and sugar.

"Is Nancy a nickname for Agnes?" she asked, handing her guest a cup of tea.

"I was christened Agnes Isobel Gates, but no one at any time has ever called me anything but Nancy—and my mother and her mother the same! You'd think that by the time I came along they'd have dropped the Agnes, which no one ever uses, and just christened me Nancy, wouldn't you? I can tell you, if I ever have a daughter, her name won't be Agnes or Nancy. Are you always called Agnes?"

"The only person who ever called me Nancy was my husband. But—Nancy never really felt like me." She drew a deep breath, coming to a decision. "Actually, we've separated, my husband and I. That's why I'm here. I mean, I had to go somewhere, and London's so expensive, and I didn't want to go back to America—or not yet, anyway."

Nancy nodded. "Well, I hope you'll feel it was the right decision. Of course, I think Argyll is the most wonderful place on God's earth, and it's been my choice to live here, but—aren't you going to miss your friends? You might feel cut-off, and when a marriage has just ended, that can be a time when you need friends the most."

"All my friends are far away, they were far away already. There's really nowhere else I could go." She looked up and out the window, to the sea and the sight of mountainous Jura on the horizon and felt again that lifting of the heart, that sense of being at home, and said with deep conviction, "And there's nowhere else I'd rather be."

She was happy in a way she had not expected, and had perhaps never been before; happy when she woke in the morning to the sight of the sea and the sky and the islands, or even to the clouds and rain. She went for long walks, regardless of the weather. She read in the devouring, eclectic fashion she'd had as a child, picking up whatever came to hand, whether it was a mystery, a Victorian novel, or a natural history guide, and reading until she felt like trying something different. She kept a journal, and for the first time in her life it was not about her feelings or her fears or her experiences with other people. Instead, she made notes about things she was reading and things she saw, listed plant names, kept track of the changing weather, described the scenery, again and again, struggling for accuracy. And she was writing poetry, for the first time since high school.

Most of the time the solitude she had chosen suited her, but at the beginning of her second week, just as she was starting to feel lonely and wondering if she'd done the right thing, Nancy turned up.

"I hope you don't mind unannounced visitors," she said. "But as you don't have a telephone I didn't know how else to ask if you'd care for a lift into Lochgilphead for your shopping. 'Getting the messages,' we call it here."

It became a regular thing after that, the visits from Nancy and the shopping trips. She enjoyed the other woman's company, although she felt guilty that Nancy was doing all the giving and she the taking. Nancy, she suspected, was someone who adopted waifs and strays, and she didn't like to think of herself as fitting into that category. But the truth was she needed help and friendship and could not afford a standoffish pride.

Then one chilly, late autumn day as the early evening was drawing in and they were sitting together in front of the fire, Nancy said in a quiet, conversational tone, "You know, whatever you intend to do, and wherever you intend to go later, you're not doing yourself any favors by staying away from the local doctor now. Why don't I—"

Agnes turned to look at her in astonishment. "I don't need to see a doctor."

"Why don't I come by and pick you up tomorrow morning and take you in to the surgery in Lochgilphead. The consultant from Glasgow will be—"

"I don't need to see a doctor! What makes you think I do?"

"Agnes, I'm a midwife. I'm not blind."

"And I'm not pregnant."

"You mean you wish you weren't."

"I mean I know I'm not." She stood up and moved away from the fire. "I'm not some silly little—"

"Not so little, no."

Agnes looked down at her belly. She smoothed the wool of her sweater as gently as if it covered a precious child. "I know what it looks like. I know what it feels like. For sixteen weeks I was sure I was pregnant, even though my husband said it was impossible. And then I went for an ultra-sound scan and—there's no baby in there. There's nothing. The doctor said so."

"I can't believe that."

"Neither could I." She laughed a little, sounding surprised. "Neither *can* I. They told me I wasn't pregnant, they showed me the screen with nothing on it, nothing inside my womb, and I thought: right, that's the end of that—but it wasn't. I put the money Gray'd given me for an abortion into an account, and I came up here to decide what to do with my life now that my marriage was over and I wasn't really pregnant, and I kept on feeling pregnant and I kept on getting bigger. I don't know how it will end."

"It will end with a birth," said Nancy. "You must see a doctor. Who were these people who told you you weren't—"

"They were doctors and technicians at Northwick Park Hospital, Harrow. They weren't cranks, Nancy, they weren't fakes. I can give you names and a phone number. They offered counseling. They wanted me to see a shrink. Well, I didn't want to do that. I didn't see the point. I thought an hysterical pregnancy must be like a balloon, one prick from reality and it'd deflate. I guess I was wrong.

I guess there's still a part of me that believes there's going to be a baby."

"Why did your husband want you to have an abortion?"

"Because it's not his. This baby doesn't have a father. It's just mine."

She never knew if Nancy checked up on her story. She made a point of giving her the name of the consultant and the GP in Harrow, but never asked her afterward if she'd used them. It wasn't necessary. The midwife clearly had accepted Agnes' truth: she was pregnant, but not with a material child.

Agnes had to accept the contradictory, impossible truth, because it was hers. That Nancy did so was an act of genuine friendship. She was grateful, in more need of a friend now than perhaps at any other time in her life. She didn't know what would happen when the expected delivery date of January 30th arrived, but she was glad she wouldn't have to go through it alone.

She had never spent so much time alone; she had never felt less lonely. A certain satisfaction had entered her soul from the moment she realized she was pregnant, and it had never, despite what had happened since, entirely dissipated. But no matter how happy she was walking through the woods, gazing out to sea, sitting beside her fire with a book or lying in bed imagining her baby, there were times she wanted companionship. Sometimes she walked into the village and chatted with Mrs. MacPhee and whoever else came into the shop, gradually making the acquaintance of people who lived in the area. And every few days Nancy called by on her way home from work, and once a week took her to get the messages in Lochgilphead.

For Christmas, she went with Nancy to her parents' home in Ayrshire. She was uneasy about the prospect of spending the holidays among strangers, but the Gates' made her feel welcome immediately. They had a large, comfortable house, and there were lots of visitors coming and going. She was away more than a week, from Christmas Eve right through New Year's Day, and although she was exhausted by the end from the unaccustomed strain of associating with so many different people, she did not regret it.

She was even more pleased she had gone away with Nancy when she got home and discovered that someone else had been in the bothy while she was away.

They had been very neat, and the evidence they had left of their presence was not enough to tell her who they had been. Gray and Alice? His older brother and his family? His younger brother with friends? She wondered if the visitors, whoever they had been, had been able to translate the signs she'd left, and for the first time since she had left Harrow worried about her husband. What was he doing? Was he thinking of her? Was he still with Alice? Did he want to get in touch? Until now, he would have had no way of doing so. But if he'd spent Christmas in the bothy, if he'd noticed, and recognized, the clothes and other personal possessions she'd left behind, he would know.

For the next week she worried and watched for the postman, but no letter came for her. No one knew she was here; her secret was still safe.

She knew she would have to get in touch with Graham eventually. Things would have to be settled between them, formally ended; there would have to be a divorce. But not until her pregnancy was over. She felt she was under a spell, wrapped in some charm—for good or evil was impossible to say—until the thirtieth of January.

Nancy, who made daily visits now, warned against fixing all her expectations on that one day. "Babies get born early and late. And two weeks before or two weeks after the expected delivery date isn't even considered early or late. You might still be pregnant come Valentine's Day."

"Oh, I don't think so," said Agnes serenely. "This is no ordinary baby, after all. Nobody got me pregnant. I wished it. It won't give me any trouble."

"Oh no? Your wishes have never given you any trouble before?"

The other woman's words, and voice, implied a knowledge which frightened her. She'd never told anyone about the pillow friend. "What do you mean?"

Nancy cocked her head, puzzled at the tremor in her voice. "You must know that saying, 'Be careful what you wish for. You might get it.'"

"Oh. That. Oh."

"Oh, dear," said Nancy, and came to sit beside Agnes on the couch and put an arm around her. "I shouldn't have said anything. I didn't mean to worry you—there's nothing to worry about! But all the same, I wish you'd get a telephone."

"I can't. It's not my house. Graham would—well, he'd hate it."

"Then move in with me, just for these last few weeks. Or with *someone*. Get a room in the Argyll Arms. I bet I could get the landlord to do you a deal, January is such a dead time. Or I could ask one of my friends who does bed and breakfast...."

"I want to stay here. I want to have the baby here. Or I would if there was a baby. But there's not, so there's nothing to worry about."

Nancy took her arm away and studied her face. "There's you, big as a cow, saying there's no baby."

"Do you think there is? You've examined me. You couldn't hear a heartbeat, or anything."

"I don't know what to think. But I don't like taking chances, and leaving a pregnant woman on her own, without a phone or a car or even a next-door neighbor goes against everything I know." She sighed heavily. "How about this. You stay here in your own cozy nest—but I move in with you, just until we see what's what."

She didn't want anyone else living with her, but there was a certain steely glint in Nancy's eye which made her give in. If Nancy was here, to help her with the birth, she wouldn't have to go into hospital. That was what she dreaded most. Although she had read in her pregnancy book that women in this country had the right to choose where to give birth, she suspected that if a midwife and a doctor believed she was willfully endangering the life of her unborn child she might find herself under restraint. She had gained twenty-three pounds and her breasts were huge. She looked and felt pregnant; no one would believe she was not. They'd have to get her into a hospital to scan her belly and learn the truth, and then, well, might not an hysterical pregnancy be considered a sign of insanity? What if the doctors decided among themselves to keep her locked up and under observation. Frightened by this imagined scenario, she meekly agreed.

"Thank you. That's very kind of you. I know it won't be as comfortable for you as your own home...."

"It'll be more comfortable for you," said Nancy, relaxed into graciousness. "That's the important thing."

Contractions began on the evening of the twenty-third of January, as they were listening to "Kaleidoscope" on the wireless. She'd been feeling a sensation which Nancy had told her were Braxton Hicks contractions—tightening sensations getting her womb ready for the real thing—for several weeks, and now they were stronger and more frequent. After about an hour she realized they were much stronger, and heaved herself off the couch in some excitement to look for her watch.

"What's up?"

"Contractions," she said importantly. "It's started!"

Nancy didn't move. "How frequent?"

"That's why I'm looking for my watch—where is the thing?"

"You usually leave it next the sink."

Now that she was paying attention, getting ready to count, she felt nothing. She slumped down on the couch and chewed her lip impatiently. She waved her hand in the direction of the radio. "Oh, turn that thing off, would you? It's too distracting."

"You'll be wanting some distraction soon."

"Well, I can't stand that man's voice, and I'm not interested in modern art anyway, especially on the radio. There's one!"

Nancy glanced at her wristwatch, then gazed at the ceiling. Agnes kept her own gaze fixed on the watch in her hand. Time crept past with agonizing slowness until at last she felt another. "There! Eight minutes!"

"And another."

This one came seven minutes later, which she thought a promising sign, but the one after that took almost nine.

"We've got a long wait," said Nancy. "It won't be tonight. This might even be a false start—contractions can start and stop and start again for days before you're really in labor."

"I'm in labor now!"

The midwife shook her head. "They'll have to get a lot stronger—"

"How do you know how strong they are?"

"—and a lot closer together. Until they're less than three minutes apart there's no point in even thinking about it. You need something to take your mind off it. Want to come over to my house, watch a video?"

But she wasn't going to risk going anywhere now. She was staying where she was. So they played Scrabble, and then cards. Nancy taught her how to play poker. All the while the contractions continued, but although they remained regular and got stronger, they were no closer together than they had been when they started by the time Nancy began to yawn and said she was going to bed.

"But what about me?"

Nancy looked as if she was trying to keep from laughing. "You go to bed, too. You'll need all the rest you can get, because once you're really laboring you won't be able to sleep."

"I can't sleep now!"

"Try. Remember those relaxation exercises I taught you? This is a good time for them. Lie down in bed, in the dark, and just relax as much as you can. It'll be a long time until morning if you don't."

It was a long time until morning. She spent a dutiful seven hours in bed, in the dark, trying to sleep and failing. The contractions weren't painful, but they were too strong to ignore; rippling, internal sensations which reminded her, every few minutes, that she had embarked irrevocably on a process which she could neither stop nor control, and which would end in nothing she could predict. It was like being strapped onto a powerful horse taking her to an unknown destination. But it was excitement she felt, not fear; excitement which kept her from sleeping and resisted the relaxation exercises. It was too late now to worry about what sort of monster she might be carrying. She felt it was herself that was about to be born.

When day brightened the windows she got up and went downstairs to make tea and toast. Nancy joined her a few minutes later, grumbling, "I don't know what I'm doing up so early; nothing's going to happen for hours, maybe for days, yet. This has all the marks of a very long labor."

"And nothing to show at the end of it," said Agnes. But she hugged her huge, hard belly, not believing her own cynical words. There would be something, although she didn't know what.

As it was a dry day, they went for a walk after breakfast, but the weather was so cold that they cut it short and hurried back inside to build up the fire. To pass the time they played cards, told each other jokes and stories, and listened to music. "I should have brought the video," Nancy said.

By late evening the contractions were only two minutes apart, and so strong that she could concentrate on nothing else. All earlier distractions failed. She could only try to rest in between.

"Am I nearly there? When do I start to push?"

"Let me take a look at you. Lie down."

"Can you see anything? Can you see the baby?"

"My dear, you're barely dilated."

"How long...?"

"Hours yet. Tomorrow, maybe late tomorrow."

She began to cry. "I can't. Not that long. I can't bear it."

"My dear, you have to. There's no other way. Unless you want me to phone for an ambulance."

"No! I'm staying here."

Her breathing exercises did nothing for the pain, but they did give her something to focus on, something else besides the pain. When the contraction ended the pain vanished utterly, but she couldn't use the time, the minute or so in between the pain, for anything. She felt exhausted, desperate, with no resources to call on. Her mind wandered back to childhood, and she remembered the dream. It was the dream which had started it all, the dream which had implanted the desire in her which had led finally to this labor, this struggle which she began to believe would never end.

Yet for just a moment, remembering the dream, she seemed to reenter it, and was lifted above the pain as she felt again that miraculous, thrilling closeness, the happiness that the doll-baby had inspired.

Other memories from childhood came flooding in, and she lost track of time and place, speaking to figures from her past as if they were still with her. It occurred to her that this birth she was struggling through was in fact her own—she was being reborn, and had to live through her own life again before she could move on to something new. Then she forgot that, and thought that Nancy was Leslie. Later, she was sure Roxanne was in the room. Then she realized it wasn't Roxanne. Someone else, another woman, was in the house with them.

"Who's here?" she asked.

"It's me," said Nancy, at her side, wiping her face with a cool cloth.

"No, someone else—who is it?" She peered across the room, but her vision was blurred. "What happened to my glasses?"

"Do you want them? You asked me to take them off a little while ago."

"I want to see who it is."

"It's me, Nancy."

"Not you, the other one." She saw the figure of a woman approaching her, and for a moment thought she knew who it was. "But my mother's dead! I'm hallucinating."

"It's all right," said Nancy. "It happens; don't worry about it."

"It's me," said Marjorie. "Don't you know your own..."

"I thought you were dead! I thought you were my mother."

"I'm not your mother. It's me." And she held out her hand to be gripped just as another contraction made her cry out with pain.

She hadn't thought it possible for the pain to get worse, but it did. "Go ahead and scream," said someone, she wasn't sure if it was Marjorie or Nancy. "There's no one here to mind. Make a noise, let it out. Push it out."

"Go on, push," said Nancy. She was on one side of her, Marjorie on the other, and they were lifting her up. "It's time now, it's coming. Bear down, hard as you can, push!"

She bore down so hard she knew she must be bursting veins, so hard so felt she would turn herself inside-out, void her womb and everything else. Then, out of the hot, splitting pain, there was a cool, slippery sensation, and the pain and effort were abruptly over.

She lay still, her eyes closed, panting, relieved. It would be so easy to fall asleep just now, but something, an inner alarm, warned her not to rest, not yet. There was something wrong. The room was much too quiet.

She opened her eyes and saw Nancy. Without her glasses she could tell that Nancy was holding something, but not what it was. It seemed too small to be a baby, and it was dark, perhaps with blood.

"The baby," she said. "Where is it? Let me see the baby."

"There's no baby."

"Then what are you holding? Come here, closer, where I can see—let me see—where are my glasses? What is that?"

"It's not a baby, it's a doll. A little, old-fashioned, porcelain doll. Not a baby, a man."

"A doll?" Her heart leaped. "Myles? Bring it here, bring him here!"

Nancy came up beside her and handed her her glasses. "I'll make you a cup of tea."

"No, wait—Myles, what happened to Myles?"

Nancy's face was sad and tired and puzzled. "Who?"

"The doll. You said—oh, just give him to me!"

"Agnes, you're hallucinating. You haven't had any sleep for days. You must rest. Lie down."

"But the baby!"

"There is no baby. That may be hard to accept after what you've been through, but you've known it all along. You were the one who told me there would be no baby."

"Maybe not a baby, but there was something, I pushed something out, and I saw you holding it."

"There's nothing," said Nancy, showing her empty hands.

"You have blood all over you."

"Yes. You voided quite a lot of blood. Old menstrual blood, that's all you've been carrying. I'm going to get you a cup of tea and clean myself up and clean you up and then if you'd like something to help you sleep? Or maybe," she said as Agnes sank back down, closing her eyes, "Maybe you won't need anything."

She struggled not to cry as Nancy walked away. It must be hormones making her feel so empty and bereft. She hadn't lost a child, she had lost nothing, there had never been a baby. She had known that all along, just as she'd known she didn't need or want a baby and all the responsibilities and problems it would bring with life as a single mother. But, still, she wanted something after all that, some resolution, her unspoken wish finally granted. What had she been struggling for these past two days, what had she been carrying inside her, besides the blood, these past nine months?

Sleep was pulling her down, unconsciousness waiting to claim her, when she was startled awake by a voice close to her ear saying her name.

She opened her eyes and saw Marjorie clearly for the first time. She was not her mother, she was herself, and she was holding a baby, small and naked and alive, its sex unclear.

She reached up to take it, and heard Marjorie say, "You know this baby is no more real than I am."

"That's all right," she said. She knew she must be dreaming, yet she felt it solid and warm and real in her hands. Why did people speak so dismissively of dreams, as if they were unimportant? She had been trying to find her way back to this dream for all of her waking life. "It's what I want. It's mine."

The baby opened dark blue eyes and gazed with a sort of knowing wonder into her eyes. She felt a profound shock at the depth of their instant connection. And then the baby smiled at her, opening its mouth as if about to speak, and she knew she had everything she wanted.